POINTER'S WAR

BY ROBERT L. WHITTLE

For my girls: Anne, Lucy, Lindsay and Jane

And for my great friend, G. Moffett Cochran V

This is the Happy Warrior; this is he

That every man in arms should wish to be.

--William Wordsworth

PART ONE

THE SAUCE

PRELUDE

Mexico

1917

Lieutenant George S. Patton calmly sighted down the barrel of his big Colt Peacemaker, deciding in an instant to take out the horse first; the rider would be next. He squeezed the trigger, the big white horse crumpled to its knees and Pancho Villa's man somersaulted over the steed's head into a heap in the dust. Patton, along with five of his troopers, proceeded to fill the man with lead until he lay dead on the Sonoran desert floor.

The second Villista likewise met his fate, leaving only Julio Cardenas, commander of Villa's personal bodyguard, alive. Patton spotted him running about 200 yards from the hacienda.

"Halt or we'll shoot, detener!" someone shouted. The "General"

Cardenas paused—fatally, as it turned out, as the troopers inflicted multiple wounds, the coup de grace *delivered by an ex-Villista named E.L. Holmdahl, now working for the Americans. In less than five minutes George Patton's first combat experience was concluded.*

Like so many of his exploits, Patton's raid into Sonora represented a first in military history. In 1916 General John J. Pershing was ordered to lead a punitive expedition against the forces of Pancho Villa, who, on a raid into New Mexico, had killed several Americans. Pershing had been impressed by young Patton's enthusiasm for the mission and had named him his personal aide. Patton had volunteered to take three Dodge Brothers touring cars into enemy territory to forage for maize for the Cavalry horses, but had taken this little side trip to hunt for banditos.

Chapter One

Patton

NORTH AFRICA—II CORPS HEADQUARTERS

March 1943

"We began to absquatulate across the border with three banditos tied to the hood of the car! And don't you know, my friends, that was the first-ever motorized assault by U.S. troops. By the way, when the newspapers got hold of the story, Dodge sales shot through the roof! I got a telegram from the Dodge brothers heartily thanking me. Goddam if they shouldn't"! General Patton enthused.

"Old Black Jack Pershing called me *bandito* from then on—KkkkHAH!" he guffawed in his Pattonesque way.

The occasion was a dinner at II Corps HQ with Patton hosting his general staff plus invited guests. The General wasn't boasting about his exploits. As the host, he felt it was his duty to entertain his guests, and any story related to military feats—from the Trojans to Genghis Khan to Dwight- by- God- Eisenhower—was in play.

His headquarters were housed in a building designed in the French Colonial style. There was a cupola atop the building with three imitation minarets. Inside, Patton had imported mahogany paneling for his study and the dining room, not to mention many furnishings to his personal taste. It was the rainy season in Algeria so there was a crackling fire in the oversized hearth and candelabra were putting out a festive glow all over the reception and dining rooms.

"Now, tell me how the men are reacting to the new regs," he asked the table with no one in particular singled out.

Patton had taken command of II Corps, relieving Major General Lloyd Fredendall, a few weeks before. II Corps was based in lovely downtown

Djebel Kouif, Algeria. Try saying that five times fast. One of his first orders was that the men had to shave daily, the officers were to wear ties and everyone had to wear the unpopular lace-up canvas leggings which prevented scorpions, spiders and rats from climbing up a soldier's trousers.

"Goddamn scorpions'll bite you right in the balls!" he'd said when issuing the order to the Corporal who'd taken dictation.

"Well, sir, the men are grumbling as we knew they would, but we haven't had to levy any fines yet," ventured a lieutenant.

"Fine then," growled Patton.

The General himself cultivated a certain *je ne sais quoi* when it came to his appearance. It was...distinctive. On his head was a finely polished helmet. On his hips were khaki riding pants as well as ivory-handled pistols, a Colt Single Action Army .45 Peacemaker and, later, a S&W Model 27 .357. His shining boots were of the high cavalry style. His vehicles carried over-sized rank insignia and sirens. Major General George Smith Patton was not a subtle man.

The dining salon was befitting the man and the occasion. The officers were banked around a polished Chippendale mahogany table, shipped in from London. Likewise from London were the two candelabra, candles ablaze, illuminating the ancient tapestries on the wall, which the General himself never failed to illuminate by explaining all of the historic scenes that they depicted. Underfoot was an Oriental rug worth five times a commissioned officer's annual salary. The *piece de resistance* of the room was an ancient Moorish mosaic which appeared to show God feeding the masses.

Typically, his entry into North Africa had been spectacular. Patton and his staff had arrived in Morocco aboard the heavy cruiser USS *Augusta* which came under fire from the Vichy French battleship *Jean Bart* while entering the harbor of Casablanca.

"Goddammit! The fighting's ashore! Not out here in this rust bucket," he shouted at his staff as bombs exploded right, left and overhead.

After two days of fighting, Casablanca fell. Patton's reputation, as ever, had preceded him and, despite largely participating as an impatient bystander, he was presented by the Sultan of Morocco with the special Order of Ouissam Alaouite, with the citation, *"Les lions dans leurs tanieres tremblent en le voyant approcher."* (The lions in their dens tremble at his approach).

"Goddam finest award I ever received," he muttered to the Sultan as he handed the award to an aide, saluted smartly and bowed his way out.

Dinner that evening was a turtle soup, followed by roasted lamb and a *crème broulee* for dessert, accompanied by several fine wines from the General's cellar. The conversation moved from Patton war stories to the morale of the men and, inevitably, to the readiness of the troops for battle.

I was an invitee and it was my first up close exposure to the great man. I liked him immediately. I knew that he was a genius, versed not only in the history of warfare, but also in the Classics, the Arts, and sports. He had, after all, competed in the Pentathlon in the 1912 Olympics in Stockholm—and had performed quite well.

I studied the General out of the corner of my eye as I sipped turtle soup with a dash of Sherry. He had a high patrician forehead, thin lips drawn in a half dinner-party-type smile and piercing eyes under bushy white eyebrows. When he spoke, his voice was a bit high pitched, a little reedy. His posture: as erect as on a parade ground.

I served as an Office of Strategic Services (OSS) officer assigned to II Corps with a special liaison assignment to U.S. Navy Intelligence. My special skills, which had seemed attractive to the spy agency, consisted of my facility with language. I spoke French, German and Italian and was fluent in Sicilian dialects. I was pretty sure that the

Director, Wild Bill Donovan, and his gang didn't want me for my partying skills which had been on gaudy display for four undergrad years at Washington and Lee University. Maybe Patton had gotten the Order of the Ouissam Alaouite, but I had an easy chair at the Phi Kap House named for me.

I am a strapping fellow, 6' 2", 195 pounds. I have sandy, wavy hair, dimples (yes, dimples; didn't seem to hurt with the ladies) and a nose that had been broken twice, once on the football field and once in a nasty scrape in a bar on a visit to DC in my senior year. So, I am a combination of cute and pugnacious looking.

The dinner guests ranged from assorted Colonels, Lieutenants, *aides de camp,* a Red Cross matron and the Mayor of this fine Algerian outpost and his wife. The Mayor was attired in traditional garb, which featured flowing white robes, a blood-red sash, a scimitar which clanked against him as he walked, and Arab headdress. He spoke broken English but was fluent in French, so I was able to converse with him. He was a big, roly-poly chap and was very proud of his town. The Americans were just the latest in a long line of foreign interlopers stretching back to the Phoenicians and most recently the French. His conversation centered around the rain, the town fund for the ancient mosque which was the center of his and his wife's life, and how long it would take the General to blow the Nazis out of North Africa.

I was sipping my after dinner Port when I heard my name. "Pointer, how are things back in the States?" It was the General. Somehow I didn't think that that's what he really wanted to know.

But I replied, "Fine, sir. Folks are really supportive of what we're doing over here."

"And what's that old sumbitch Wild Bill doing sending one of his boys over here to my end of the world? Thinks I need some kind of goddam babysitter?"

"Well, to tell the truth, sir, I really don't know yet. Colonel Donovan tends to, uh, compartmentalize information. All I know is that it's to do with Sicily," I answered mostly truthfully. I wasn't going to tell everything I knew in front of all these people. Especially about the real reason I was in-country, which concerned a certain famous Mafiosi.

"Sicily! We haven't crushed the Krauts here yet. Matter of time, of course. But what the hell is Wild Bill thinking about goddam Sicily for?"

I took a chance. "Maybe I will end up being your Casanova, sir."

"Ah, Giacomo Casanova. A great spy for the Venetian Inquisition-- 18th Century. Do you likewise have an eye for the ladies, Mr. Pointer?" There was mischief in his eyes.

But now I was on my turf. "Sir, the ladies represent my greatest weakness. I fell in love 14 times in school, and that was just undergrad."

The General studied me. The party was silent. His laugh started as a low growl and escalated into his "KkkkkkHAH!" With a palpable sense of relief, the rest of the guests joined in, most laughing a little too hard.

Chapter Two

Pointer

Everyone calls me Pointer. I am from small-town Virginia. My sister and I grew up under the steady influence of two unusually prescient parents. More than anything, they valued education— and not just the kind found in books. They wanted us to have what Mother called life experiences. To that end, by the time I went away to college, I had been to Europe three times, Africa once, the Far East once plus one trip to Argentina. It's where I picked up my language skills. I was also tutored by my Great Uncle James Pointer, or Unc, as we all called him. Unc was a teacher of German at Episcopal High School in Virginia, and drilled me on the fine art of conjugation and other niceties of language study.

My other facility with language was poetry. If I liked a line—and I liked many—I had the ability to memorize it almost immediately. I drove my family and friends nuts by my declamations whenever I found myself in a situation that demanded a quote from one of the Masters. Usually I did this with a finger pointed into the air in mock solemnity.

Father was the major influence in my life. He was admired by everyone in our town. He had written two books on the history of the South, the first on the Revolution and the second on the lead- up to the Civil War. He detested bigotry of any kind and was known to be stern with rascals and kind to orphans and small animals. His law practice afforded us a middle class existence with enough money left over for our travels. His one hobby was sailing, and he took us on voyages on the Chesapeake Bay every fall, when the wind was reliable there.

As for me, I tried to live up to his legacy. Notice I didn't say his expectations because he made it clear to my sister and me that his and Mother's job was to make sure we got an education and had a good example of how to live a good life. But the rest was up to us. That created some pressure, and as a youth, I didn't always measure up. I went through a hell raiser phase when I went away to school—and while I managed to graduate from the University and law school, I haven't quite graduated from the hell-raiser phase to this day. I like the girls; I like to have a good time, but it's nothing I won't grow out of— eventually. People say that I have a sweet nature, and I suppose that's true. But I also have a temper, and my crooked nose is a testament to the occasional scrap or barroom brawl.

I was a serial dater back in the States and *did* fall in love a lot, but never all that seriously. So, at the age of 29, when I was recruited by the OSS, I was footloose and fancy-free, as they say. Like most of my countrymen, I was outraged by Pearl Harbor, by Hitler, by Mussolini, and was thrilled when FDR was pushed into war. I signed up for the Marines as soon as I could. A year later, Wild Bill came calling. Now, as corny as it may sound, I was ready to lay down my life for my country. But as long as I was breathing, I thought it was also my duty to also have a fine time.

As Mother had put it, "Robert, you're not especially mature for your age." And I suppose she had a point. Here I was in North Africa dining with General Patton and getting ready for God-knew-what kind of undercover mission in Sicily, and I was still the good old worry-free Pointer. Should I adopt more of an air of self-importance? Lord knows, there was plenty of that around II Corps. Officers bustling here and there with furrowed brows as though the fate of the war were their sole responsibility. It's not that I didn't have a serious side; maybe it was I didn't know what I didn't know—and I understood that cosmic fact.

I knew the only reason Wild Bill Donovan had assigned me to this job was that I had come away with some surprising results in my first assignment, which was to interview a world-famous mobster who was in prison in New York State. I fully expected Donovan to yank the rest of the assignment from me at any moment in favor of a more experienced agent. But until then, I figured I wouldn't be any better off by putting on airs. I was self-aware enough—and maybe a little cocky—to believe I could pull off anything they threw at me.

As for "keeping it in my pants" as my old drill sergeant termed it, I had no intention of doing so if I could help it. So far, the only females I'd seen were goats and camels. That is, until this morning. Walking to mess, I'd spotted the most gorgeous creature I'd ever encountered. She had been coming my way along the walkway, and it gave me a few seconds to think of something to say.

When we reached each other, I said, "Hi". How smooth was that? She gave me a little smile and continued on her way. Who *was* that? I wondered, and I was determined to find out.

In the meantime, I had an appointment with my opposite number in the British military. I did not know then that my experience with him would become central to my life as long as I was on God's green earth.

Chapter Three

Binky

What I knew about my assignment in North Africa was that I was to establish working relationships with key contacts in both the American and British armies and that I was to be a conduit for strategic information about Sicily. Much of the stateside origin of that strategic information was a mystery to people outside the OSS and Naval Intelligence. But fate had put me squarely in the middle of the info, its origins and, now, the implementation of the plan that sprung from the intel.

There was the distinct possibility that I would be sent to Sicily well before Allied troops would arrive. That was exciting, but there were about 300,000 hostiles over there, and it would be me, my British counterpart and a few grunts against the Hun.

Patton was right, though. The Allies had not finished the job in Africa. The Brits had been fighting there for nearly three years. Their principal opponent had been the brilliant Nazi Field Marshall Erwin Rommell aka "The Desert Fox" and his *Afrika Korps*. I thought about nicknames of famous Generals. Many were grunts-only monikers; that is, the press never found out about them because they were only whispered among the troops. Examples were "Old Dog Farmer" and "Stinky". No one wants to be General Stinky.

But then there was "The Desert Fox" and Patton's "Old Blood and Guts". I had heard that the grunts' take on that was "our blood and his guts". But it was said with a certain resigned affection.

My first stop that morning was a call on one Leftenant Edmund Randolph Symington Binkford aka "Binky" who was stationed with Bernard Montgomery's command. The dossier that my superiors had provided me was extensive and, one might say, a tad lurid. Binky, it seems, was from the upper crust. His family home was in St. James Place in London. There, they had a full complement of Downstairs hired help, ranging from Chief Butler to Cook to Head Housekeeper to Valets and Chauffeurs. The family had occupied the residence continuously since the 18th Century. Evidently, the only acceptable family job was attending the King or being a soldier. Binkford had been in North Africa since late 1940 and had apparently seen action on more than one occasion—both at Tobruk and at Kasserine Pass. According to my intel, he had comported himself well, if not with distinction.

The lurid part of the report was that Binky was a homosexual. He was not open about it; in fact, he kept quiet about it. He was, after all, in the military. But the spies left no doubt as to his orientation. The part that puzzled me was that if my spies knew about it, *their* spies knew about it. My theory was that they did know, but because of Leftenant Binkford's position in society and, who knew, maybe he was an extraordinary agent, they looked the other way.

When I arrived at British HQ, I presented my papers and was asked to wait in an anteroom by the desk Sergeant. This was a rather grand room off to the side with grand furnishings and portraits of Montgomery and the King. There were a couple of discreetly arranged sofas and chairs for private conversations as well as a table and chairs. Since I knew that the Brits could not do business without the benefit of tea, I was not surprised when an Indian servant inquired about refreshments. Being an amiable chap, I agreed that tea would suit quite well, thankyouverymuch.

In a moment, in strode Leftenant Binkford, who favored me with a smile, stuck out his hand like he meant it, and shook mine with enthusiasm.

"Ah, Lieutenant Pointer, so pleased to finally meet you. Did you have a pleasant voyage? And how have you found Africa?"

"Well, the ship captain actually found it; I was just along for the ride." I didn't really say that. Shouldn't hit them with

your "A" Material on your first
meeting.

"Fine, Leftenant. I really haven't had
much time to look around, but things
seem fine enough," I answered.

"Binky! Please call me Binky. Everyone
does."

"Alright, Binky. Everyone calls me
Pointer."

"Pointer and Binky it is, then", he said.
"Tea?"

The servant had set down an elegant
silver service. At my nod, he poured
both of us a cup. Or cuppa as they say.

I studied Binky while the servant
prepared refreshments. He was a large
man with an inordinately large head.
He had a shock of blonde hair with
some untrained strands sticking
straight in the air. There was a solemn
and studied air about him as though
the talents of the servant's tea pouring
were of national importance. Was his

thick waist padded with fat or was that muscle?

"I was thinking, Binky, that a good start would be to compare our respective orders and start to get a feel of how we should work together," I ventured.

"Agreed," Binky nodded.

"Alright then. As you may know, I came here almost directly from the prison in upstate New York where I met with, uh, 'Husky' over the course of a couple of days. I brought with me certain correspondence and other proof of his endorsement of our plan."

"Yes, I am aware of Husky," Binky said.

"I've also been supplied with the usual maps of the regions of Sicily into which we will infiltrate. Only these maps are as much about mafia territorial domains as they are about geography."

"Most helpful." I was beginning to feel that, like the servant, I was under Binky's scrutiny. And, of course, I was.

"Likewise," he said, "my intelligence is all about mafia territories, primarily on the east coast of the island. The initial plan is for Monty to move up the eastern coast and for Patton to go up the center and to meet in Messina in the north. Drive the Krauts right across the Straits of Messina into Italy. Does that match your understanding, Pointer?"

"Perfectly," I said. "The feeling from Colonel Donovan is that we can save a lot of time and lives if we can neutralize the mafia, or, better yet, turn them into allies. They have certain ways to make supplies and men, er, disappear. My orders are to make sure it's German supplies and men going missing, not Allied supplies."

"Precisely," agreed Binky. "I also understand that the Mafia have acute sniper skills. Tell me, Pointer, how reliable do you believe is your intelligence from Husky?"

"That is a capital question, old boy." I thought speaking the British version of our language might loosen old Binky up a bit. "Like the Sicilians we'll be dealing with, the first thing you have to do is figure out where his self-interest lies and then study what he says through that filter."

"Let me take a guess," said Binky. "Husky wants out of prison first and foremost and will say anything to achieve that end."

"Well, yes, of course. But he's a very complex fellow. There *is* his self-interest and we'd do well to never forget that, but there are other big emotions that sway him. One is extreme patriotism—of both the U.S. *and* Sicily. And the other is that the guy has to win—at everything. He is, you know, an organizational genius. So, even if you were skeptical of the intel he gave us, his thoughts on organizing the mission are pretty damned good."

"Organizational genius?"

"Absolutely. Husky took the five mafia families of New York, added those from Chicago, Detroit, LA , among other cities—and formed a governing body of all of these disparate gangs. A ruling Commission that sets rules, dictates territories, settles disputes— that sort of thing. Anyone who can organize a bunch of hoodlums and train them like so many dogs has my admiration."

"Impressive," agreed my new friend.

"Right. But instead of bylaws and courts, he uses garrotes and .38 Specials to make the rules stick."

"But now that he's in prison?"

"Doesn't matter. He rules from his suite of rooms there in Albany. They already moved him from a dungeon in upstate to better quarters for the help he gave Naval Intelligence on the New York docks problem."

"More tea, Pointer?"

"No thanks. Gotta get moving. Just found out my boss is coming to town and I'm on for dinner tonight."

"That would be your Wild Bill?" Binky arched an eyebrow.

"The same. Patton is throwing a dinner party for him at HQ. Seems that Old Blood and Guts likes an audience when he dines."

"Oh dear," Binky sighed.

As Binky was seeing me to the door, he stepped out onto the portico with me so that we were out of earshot of the two sentries posted there.

He tapped me on the shoulder and said, "You will know, Pointer, that I am a homosexual", he said matter-of-factly. "We are likely to be in dicey situations over there." He nodded vaguely in the direction of the North African coast. "We—and by we I mean those of my sexual proclivities—have a reputation for being...timid. I want to assure you that such is not the case with me."

I had never knowingly known a homosexual—or queer, as they were commonly known in my hometown in

Virginia (as well as in college and law school). Yes, I had the same conceptions as virtually all of my contemporaries—they were pansies, sissies...queer. But here was someone in the flesh who was on the "dark side". He seemed perfectly normal; he wasn't wearing a dress; he didn't seem effeminate. So, I was flustered to be confronted directly.

Sensing my confusion, Binky continued, "It's actually made me a bit tougher than I would be otherwise. Something to prove and all that bit."

Then he said something I'll not soon forget. "Pointer, old boy, I'm queer and I'm here." He smiled wickedly, turned on his heel and strode back through the door.

March 13, 1943
Lieutenant Robert Pointer, APO II Corps
Algiers, North Africa

My Dearest Robert,

Your mother joins me in wishing you felicitations and Godspeed on your endeavors in Africa. She is, naturally, terribly worried and, it must be said, so am I. You will take good care, won't you, son? I sometimes fear that you are a bit brash in your actions. Ready- Fire- Aim. Promise us you will think before you act, please.

Things in South Hill are quiet. There's the Emergency Preparedness (EP) Committee, which I agreed to head, that meets every Thursday at the barber shop. Your mother drives to Weldon three times a week to wrap bandages for the Red Cross. Beyond that, all is quiet. I cannot think of a single young man still here who is under 30. Strike that. There's the poor Johnson boy who's soft in the head, and I am now handling the cases of two young men who are suing the

Draft Board for being rejected. One has a suspect ear drum and the other has a high school football injury to his knee. I try to counsel them to be careful what they wish for.

Do you remember the Gaskins boy whose father used to deliver firewood to us? Jimmy Gaskins? Things may be about to go from quiet here to quite raucous. Jimmy came to see me the other day to talk about his enlistment options in the Army. As you know, most of the military choices for Negroes are for non-combat positions like cooks, medical aides, general laborers, runners and the like, at least in certain states. It seems that young Jimmy would like to fight for his country in the infantry like his white counterparts. I know a myriad of cases where the plaintiff has sued to get out of serving in the Army—conscientious objectors and the like. But I know of no precedent for bringing suit to get into a war in a combat position.

What about segregation? How would a Negro dine or sleep or fight side by side with a white man? They cannot enter our hotels and restaurants here; would we have separate-but equal-mess halls, barracks...latrines?

But those are simply smoke screens for the real issues. You well know my stance on race relations. I have always believed that Men are created equal in the eyes of God. Jefferson and Lincoln, in their turns, both put the great stamp of the United States Government on that concept. But the good folks of South Hill and the rest of Virginia, indeed, the rest of the South, do not see it that way. It is a fine concept, but not one that governments have seen fit to put into practice. Folks are afraid that if they give a Negro a gun and teach him how to use it that someday they will find themselves on the business end of said weapon. Moreover, dear son, my white friends do not believe that the black man has the mental capacity to participate in combat.

I am not yet sure how to handle the desires of young Gaskins. But you will agree that his is an interesting dilemma. Shall I sue for the right of a citizen to be equal even when it comes to killing his fellow man? We shall see.

There is a development in Alabama that is bubbling up that I intend to keep my eye on. It seems that a group of Negroes in Tuskegee who have learned to fly are hell-bent on getting into the War and seem to be well on their way into a combat role. Perhaps that will serve as a precedent for my young friend Gaskins.

You know that Lincoln had a great facility with words. He called the Civil War The Great Trouble (of course, it is known in South Hill as the War of Northern Aggression). You, my son, are in the midst of our current Great Trouble. I pray that you return to us safely and in a single piece.

I remain,

Your Loving Father,

Robert Pointer

Chapter Four

Lucky

GREAT MEADOW CORRECTIONAL FACILITY

ALBANY, NEW YORK

May 1942

Charles "Lucky" Luciano, the first true *capo de tutti capi*-head of all heads- of the American Mafia, was ready for the second course of his evening meal. The spaghetti with clam sauce, Lucky's favorite, was being prepared by his chef and fellow inmate Dave Betillo who was always careful not to boil the linguine too long.

Ever since Lucky had been approached by the Navy to help with certain troubles on the New York docks in 1941, life in prison had gotten a lot more relaxed. Tom Dewey, the prosecutor who had put him away, be damned! The intelligence groups had dubbed him Husky.

"When is Meyer coming?" Luciano asked Betillo for the fourth time that day. He was referring to his longtime friend and partner, Meyer Lansky.

"I told you, boss. He's spending the night in town and will be here right after breakfast. Now, eat your noodles, please, don't let 'em get cold. Here's your bread," said Betillo, setting down a wicker basket of Italian garlic bread with a red and white checked cloth keeping the heat in. "Y'know, boss, them secret agent guys are coming to the meet too." As if his boss would forget that.

The first words Luciano had ever uttered to Lansky when they were both 14 years old in the Lower East Side of Manhattan were: "Listen you little kike. You pay me or I'll beat the snot out of you. You don't pay me, me *and* the micks'll beat the snot out of you. You *do* pay me and nobody's gonna touch you or your friends. *Capiche*?"

And thus was born the greatest criminal empire of the 20th Century. At one nickel per week, they were Lucky's first ill- gotten gains, and millions upon millions of nickels, sawbucks and other forms of *lucre* later, the money was still pouring in. Loan sharking. Prostitution. Narcotics. Gambling. Extortion. And outright theft. All protected by a force of button men armed to the teeth and more than happy to employ those arms to enforce their bosses' wills. All *organized* under Lucky's grand plan so that one boss's scheme did not interfere with that of his neighboring boss.

The one will that mattered more than anyone else's belonged to Lucky Luciano. And his will was implacable. He had personally killed, maimed and tortured many of his enemies. But he had ordered the deaths of many more. It did not matter that he was imprisoned. One word to a *capo* like Lansky or his other *major domo* Frank Costello was all that was required to bring mayhem and ruin into peoples' lives. No one was feared like Lucky Luciano was feared. Not only in New York, but also in Detroit, Chicago, Buffalo, LA, and Cleveland. And not

only in the United States, but in Italy
and Sicily as well.

Lucky ran an international operation.
He imported opium from the Far East
and prescription drugs from Central
and South America. During Prohibition,
he had brought liquor in from Canada
and the Caribbean. In doing that global
business, Lucky and his boys had
developed loyal followers, especially in
the Old Country. He had friends, family
and workers throughout Sicily and
southern Italy. When a guy got
deported back to Sicily, which
happened frequently, Lucky would set
him up with one of the families there.
If he was skilled in, say, street sales,
well, so much the better. He'd teach
the Sicilians the latest techniques in
street sales. Likewise, if he was good
with a gun or a knife or a garrote, well,
there wasn't that much he could teach
the Sicilians on that score.

When a guy emigrated to the United
States, if he was part of a family, his
first stop after Ellis Island was Lucky's
place where he would find gainful

employment. He could start by running numbers on the street. He could pimp for Lucky's prostitutes, either on the streets or in one of the many houses Lucky's minions ran. Or, if circumstances dictated, he could be a look-out in a truck heist, or a driver or a cook or a messenger—or any one of a hundred jobs that needed doing. Don't speak English so good? No worries. Neither did half of the other members of the family. This was just like being home, except, *mama mia,* business was booming! And the girls! The girls loved the lifestyle. Wads of cash being thrown around. The clubs. The whores! *Dio Mio!*

Just do what the bosses said. Don't cheat them. Don't slap your wife around in public. Be kind to your *madre.* Go to Mass once in a while— hey, it won't kill you—especially if it's St. Peters which some of the bosses favored—doesn't hurt to be seen doing the right thing every now and then. And never, ever, screw the wife of a fellow Mafiosi. *Capiche?*

It had not been easy for Luciano to rise to the top of the heap. It took a lifetime of conniving, double dealing, double crossing and brutalization. At age 14, he had won $244 at a craps game and, with his new fortune in hand, promptly dropped out of school. It was 1910 and the Lucianos had emigrated from Sicily three years previously. Charlie (he had not yet acquired his moniker) spent his teenage years running Italian gangs on Manhattan's Lower East Side. From the start, Charlie had ecumenical practices—he welcomed Lansky and other Jews as well as Irish into his circle. This practice was antithetical to the "Mustache Petes", the older mobsters who refused to deal with anyone who wasn't of Italian or Sicilian heritage. This democratic working style was one of the things Charlie did that attracted the notice of the established Mafiosi.

On January 17, 1919, the Eighteenth Amendment to the U.S. Constitution was ratified, and the biggest business opportunity that any of the New York mobsters ever had or would ever encounter began. It was called Prohibition. Turned out that masses' thirst for alcohol did not disappear with the passing of a Constitutional Amendment.

Charlie joined the gang of Joe Masseria, one of the Mustache Petes, in 1921. Masseria was old school— uneducated and crude. Lansky introduced his friend to the gambler Arnold "the Brain" Rothstein and, at his first opportunity, Charlie jumped at the chance to leave the gang and join his new acquaintance. There was good reason for Rothstein's nickname—he was smart and he knew how to make money. His methods were those of a well-run business, and he taught Charlie the finer points of running bootleg alcohol and how to generate big bucks in the bargain.

Rothstein understood that there was force and that there was the *threat* of force. And he taught Charlie that the one was nearly as powerful as the other. Appearances matter, Rothstein believed. If he lost at the tables, his demeanor was no different than when he won. If he planned to kill you within a matter of hours, his mien was the same as if he planned to buy a shipment of booze from you in the next five minutes. His attire of three-piece custom made suits and camel hair overcoats and handmade shoes was not lost on his young protégé.

In 1923, Charlie and Lansky arranged to buy $10,000 worth of heroin from an "importer" whom they had befriended at the docks. They saw an opportunity for a quick profit by cutting it four or five ways and selling it off in increments to bosses around the city. The two friends figured—wrongly as it turned out—that they could put together half of the cash necessary to make the buy, and pay the balance from proceeds from the sale. Word of the score began to circulate around town as people watched with interest how the young Mafiosi would comport himself.

On the appointed night, Charlie met with the dealer. When he handed him the five large, the dealer said, "What's this Charlie? Where's the rest of the money?" Charlie explained his financing plan whereupon the dealer laughed in his face. "*Paisan*, I ain't a bank and you ain't a little old lady with a trust fund. You gotta be fucking kidding me! Get the fuck outa here and don't come back!"

Charlie was stricken. He knew that his loss of face and the episode would be all over the five boroughs by the next morning. And he was right about that.

He went to see Rothstein the next day who, of course, had already heard about the botched deal. "Kid, your name is mud today with the people who matter," Rothstein said, confirming Luciano's worst fears.

Charlie was disconsolate. "What can I do?" he almost pleaded.

"The Brain" thought about it for a minute. "Tell you what. You got five grand? Fine. Go buy 200 of the best seats to the Dempsey-Firpo fight and spread the tickets around to the bosses, capos, cops and politicians. And, kid….save some money for some goddamn new clothes. You and me are going on a shopping spree to Wanamakers."

And that's exactly what Luciano did. With his new threads, his best looking girl on his arm, and 200 new best friends in the Bronx arena, Charlie strode in like he owned the place. He took his seat ringside next to Rothstein. His mentor leaned over and murmured, "You did it, kid. Remember: appearances, Charles. Appearances."

By 1925, Charlie's end of Rothstein's gang was grossing $12 million per year, mostly from liquor, but also from gambling. The costs of running the operation were substantial, though, especially bribing cops and politicians. As a result, his net was $4 million. More importantly, the importation involved international trade. Scotch whisky from Scotland, rum from the Caribbean and whisky from Canada.

Charlie learned to think and act big. He also learned to bide his time. He always knew that he'd be the Big Boss when he was ready and when the opportunity was there.

On November 2, 1928, a bookie shot and killed Rothstein over a gambling debt. Charlie did not hesitate. He quickly declared himself Masseria's man, and eschewed the entreaties of Salvatore Maranzano, his new boss' chief rival. Like Masseria, Maranzano began his criminal career in the Old Country and felt bound by a peculiar code of honor, tradition, respect and dignity. But he was as crude and ignorant as Masseria.

The Mustache Petes stood in contrast to the Young Turks who, like Luciano, had begun their careers in the U.S. From time immemorial, there had been a battle of old versus young; tradition versus the new ways. And so gangsters like Luciano, his friend Frank Costello, Joe Bonanno, Vito Genovese, Carlo Gambino and Tommy Lucchese, not to mention Jews like Lansky and

Bugsy Siegel, viewed old schoolers Masseria and Maranzano with a jaundiced eye. Meanwhile, there was a war. Maranzano had come from Sicily to run the Castellammarese clan. His clumsy management helped escalate hostilities between gangs into a full scale underworld war which raged from 1928 to 1931. Sixty mobsters would die in the Castellammarese War.

In October 1929, Luciano was introduced to the New York press, who, in turn, elevated his profile with the public. Abducted at gunpoint by three men, he was beaten, stabbed and left to die on a beach in Staten Island. Someone called the cops. After ascertaining that he would live, the cops were unable to wrench any information out of Charlie. He claimed he did not know his attackers. But he certainly suspected Maranzano. He was forever marked with a scar and a droopy eye. But he was lucky to have survived, and so he was Lucky.

Lucky realized that Maranzano's attempt on his life was just business.

His incredible sense of which way the winds were blowing in the world of organized crime led him to secretly ally himself with the man who, just two years previously, had tried to murder him. Lucky and Maranzano plotted to kill Joe Masseria, Lucky's boss. On April 15, 1931, Luciano invited Masseria and two associates to lunch in a Coney Island restaurant. After a cordial meal, it was suggested that the mobsters play cards. Lucky excused himself to go to the men's room and four gunmen, including Bugsy Siegel, moved in and slaughtered Masseria and his two men. Lucky seized control of Masseria's gang and became Maranzano's top lieutenant.

Lucky's pal Tommy Lucchese soon got wind of a plan by Maranzano to get rid of Luciano permanently. Luciano was accumulating too much power. Mad Dog Coll, an Irish gangster, was recruited to murder Lucky. On September 10, Maranzano ordered Luciano to come to his office at 230 Park Avenue. Lucky decided to act first. He sent five Jewish gangsters posing as government agents to Maranzano's office. The Jews made a particularly gruesome mess of Maranzano. They stabbed him multiple times before riddling his body with bullets. Lucky's message: "There's only room for one Boss of Bosses and his name is Lucky Luciano."

Lucky wasted no time consolidating his power. He became the dominant organized crime boss in the U.S. He elevated his most trusted Italian colleagues to his highest level advisors. Although he could not give his Jewish friends official titles, both Lansky and Siegel became trusted advisors as well.

It was during this era that Luciano organized the Commission, which set rules and settled disputes, not only for the five families of New York, but also for the families in Philly, Buffalo, Chicago, LA, Detroit and Kansas City. Even Al Capone submitted to Commission power.

And like the arrest and conviction of Capone on tax evasion, U.S. Attorney Thomas Dewey found his path to a conviction of Lucky through Luciano's relatively minor crime of prostitution. From 1916 to 1936, Luciano had been arrested 25 times on a variety of charges, but had never spent any time in jail. On June 7, 1936, Luciano was convicted on 62 counts of compulsory prostitution and was sentenced to 30 to 50 years in state prison.

And that's where I met Lucky. I had only been with the OSS for a couple of months, and this was my second visit to see the great Lucky Luciano. Wild Bill had originally chosen me for the assignment precisely because no one ever thought anything would come of it. I may have been green, but I thoroughly understood my place in the chain of command—very near the bottom. However, Lucky's intel had proven correct already once and had been deemed helpful to the war effort. Shortly after Pearl Harbor, the then-largest ship in the world, *The Normandie,* had blown up at the New York docks. And after that, German U Boats began sinking freighters bound from New York to Europe carrying vital war materiel. Naval Intelligence knew that Luciano's gang controlled the docks so they had arranged, through Lansky, to come see the gangster in his upstate confines.

Not only did the mob root out German spies from the docks, but the sinking of freighters ceased. And Luciano got a lot of the credit. Hence his move to this country club from Dannemora and hence his unrestricted visitors and hence as much linguine and Chianti as he could consume.

"Lucky," I said, after we had shook hands all around, "FDR and the nation are grateful to you for your contributions." I had decided early-on to call him Lucky. He wasn't used to it, but I figured he was in jail and I wasn't, so he would have to deal with it. Not exactly like poking a stick at an animal, but close.

"That's just the start," Lansky said. "Mr. Luciano wants to take a more active role."

"Such as?" I inquired.

Lucky decided to speak for himself. "I figure the reason you're here is that the road to Germany leads through Italy, and the road to Italy leads through Sicily. And no one knows Sicily like I know Sicily. Am I right?"

"Well, you're at least correct about the geography," I said.

What a negotiator I am. Didn't want him getting too cocky too early. But he was right about why I was there.

"So the smart thing to do is to put me on a plane, teach me to parachute and drop me in on the *paisans* and let me clear the way for the army. I know all the bosses over there, they'll do exactly what I tell 'em. Swear me in or whatever they do, and I'll be in the army."

I looked at Lansky to see if this was a joke. "He is deadly serious, Pointer", Lansky said. "Mr. Luciano rarely jokes—about anything."

"Well, Lucky, I gotta tell you that's not what Colonel Donovan has in mind. For one thing, you're-what-45 years old. For another you've got about 30 more years to serve."

"Listen, kid," Lansky said. "The way we figure it is that no one needs to know where Mr. Luciano is and what he's doing. Secret agent shit, you know? With this plan, your invasion is a success and you've effectively deported Mr. Luciano. *Capiche?*"

The over/under on someone's saying *capiche* around here was five minutes.

"My superiors want to know, first, if you really do have any valuable information about Sicily and, second, if you will share it with us," I tried to be stern.

"You go back and tell your Colonel that this is the way it's gotta be. Send me over with a couple of my boys and we'll clean everything up for the troops. It'll be like a USO party when they get there. We'll hold a dance for them at City Hall in Palermo." Lucky said.

I said, "I'll convey your wishes, Lucky, but you shouldn't hold your breath. The plan is for you to give us the lay of the land, tell us who hates who and who controls who and let us deal with them."

"Yeah? What's in it for me? And don't say the love and respect of FDR." Lucky's eye began to droop more than usual.

"Well, one thing I am authorized to tell you is that if you cooperate, we will keep Mr. Dewey out of it". We knew that if the prosecutor had anything to say about it, he might let Lucky jump out of a plane, but it would be *sans* parachute.

Lansky and Lucky exchanged looks. They knew this was meaningful.

"Tell you what, Lucky," I said. "I'll report our conversation to Colonel Donovan and I'll come back and see you again tomorrow morning. The Colonel wants to get this wrapped up now."

"You do that, kid. Just remember, nobody knows the Old Country and their ways like I do. If I am there personally I will guarantee success. If you send a bunch of spies, it'll be child's play for the bosses over there. *Capiche?*"

They always *capiched* you when they really wanted to make a point.

"Maybe I'll come back tonight instead. What's for dinner, Lucky?"

The one eye continued to droop, but in the other was murder.

I went back to the FBI field office in Albany and wrote up my report. I left out the part about coming to dinner, but included everything else. The report was cabled to Washington. An hour later, the response came back. "Negative on Husky personally attending. Stay with Plan." No surprise there.

I returned to the Country Club the next morning. Lansky and Luciano were just finishing Western omlettes, courtesy of

Chef Betillo. After the dishes were cleared away and cigars lit, we were ready for Round Two.

"As I suspected, the government wants no part of you playing soldier over there, Lucky. If you have useful information, we'd like to have it," I began.

"Yeah, we figured that's what you would say," said Lansky. "So, what guarantees do we have that Dewey will be *butt-outski?*"

I pulled a letter out of my tunic and handed it over to Lansky. The letter was from the Under Secretary of the Navy and indicated that if Luciano cooperated fully on the matter of Sicily, then the second letter that was attached would be forwarded to Luciano's attorney. It made no overt promises about parole, but it transferred jurisdiction over the case from Dewey's office to the Navy's. It would become a military matter.

Lansky and Lucky again exchanged glances. I wondered how many times over the years they had done that and how many crimes had been committed from these two old friends' virtual telepathy. They knew that this was not a great deal for them, but they also knew when not to keep selling beyond the close.

"When the attorney receives this letter," Lansky said, "we'll talk about Sicily."

"He should have received a copy about an hour ago," I said. "It remains conditional on Lucky holding nothing back. And the sole judge of that is one Robert Pointer, Jr.," I added proudly. "So, it's time to open up the kimono, Lucky."

More murder in the eye.

Chapter Five

Elizabeth

II CORPS HEADQUARTERS

NORTH AFRICA

March 1943

Guests began assembling for General Patton's dinner party in honor OSS Chief Wild Bill Donovan. I had business to conduct with my Colonel if he wished to talk business. If not, we had a meeting scheduled for the next day. Leftenant Binkford was invited as were other ranking officers in Patton's and Montgomery's army.

Wild Bill and Patton were old friends. They had first met on the Mexican border when both had been assigned to chase Pancho Villa around the Southwest. Donovan was a staunch Republican, and he and Patton tended to see eye to eye politically. He had attended Columbia University with FDR, and while the two were political opposites, Roosevelt had nonetheless

appointed Donovan to be the first
Chief Intelligence Officer.

Paralleling Lucky Luciano's
Commission, which regulated disparate
factions of mobsters, Donovan's OSS
centralized all of the military
intelligence services. The one notable
hold out in consolidating intelligence
was J. Edgar Hoover who insisted on
hanging on to intelligence oversight of
South America. Hoover hated
Donovan, but that was hardly news
worthy. Hoover hated everyone whom
he perceived as a threat to his own
personal power.

Heretofore, each branch of the military
had, to one degree or another, spies.
There was little to no sharing of
information among services. In fact,
the military and political elite of the
U.S. considered spying ungentlemanly.
It was fine for certain nations whose
sense of honor and fair play was
skewed, but not for Western powers.
The U.S. government often relied on
wealthy businessmen like Donovan and
Joe Kennedy whose travels took them

to foreign countries where these men often extended their business trips to meet with Ambassadors and heads of state abroad. As a public service, when they returned, they often gave reports of their impressions and findings to a grateful State Department or White House. That all changed, of course, with the rise of Hitler and the Empire of Japan.

A bluff Irishman from Buffalo, Bill Donovan had won the Medal of Honor in France during World War I and had returned home to a lucrative career as a Wall Street lawyer. FDR had come to trust his reports from his travels in England, France and Germany. Donovan had given early warnings of Germany's and Hitler's ambitions in Europe, and FDR, looking for reasons to help out Churchill and other allies, had embraced Donovan's views.

Donovan was now in North Africa. To meet with yours truly. I thought about that. Was he here to thank me for making a deal with Luciano and gathering intelligence on Sicily and then decide to dismiss me so that a more senior officer could take over? Was he here to chastise me for ever putting any stock in Lucky's ramblings about the structure of the Sicilian Mafia and how it could help with the Allied invasion? Or was he here to give me further orders on Operation Husky? Would Binky and I lead an advance party or parties into Sicily to clear a path for Patton and Monty? I supposed that I would find out tonight or, at the latest, by tomorrow morning.

"Wild Bill, you old sumbitch!" Patton bellowed. Colonel Donovan had arrived in the foyer of HQ. Patton gave him a quick salute, and then a bear hug, lifting the hefty OSS Chief off the floor. "How the hell are you, man?"

"Fine, General, fine. Thank you for having me. I've had a steady diet of Army hash for over a week on the way over," Donovan lamented.

"Let me introduce you around, Colonel. I believe you know General Bradley. Brad is helping me root out the Krauts and the *Eye-talians* here in sand land. I don't believe you know Mrs. Krantz, who, as head of the Red Cross in this part of the world, has agreed to grace us with her presence along with some of her staff. We soldiers appreciate a little prettying up of our old nasty ways, Mrs. Krantz. We are grateful. And Leftenant Binkford, one of Monty's lads. I know you know Pointer. Ah, here's Stanhope, who's a reporter with the Associated Press. He's agreed that everything he hears here tonight is off the record. Am I correct, Archie?." I was getting dizzy with the performance art that the General considered his duty as host.

At that moment, the single most beautiful woman I had ever seen entered the room. It was the same girl whom I'd utterly charmed on my way to mess the other morning. Apparently, I wasn't the only one who thought she was gorgeous. There was a noticeable lowering of the decibel count in the foyer. "General Patton", Mrs. Krantz said, "May I present to you my aide, Miss Elizabeth D'Antoni. I believe, General, that your families are acquainted."

Patton adopted his most gracious smile, which was pretty close to that of the cat who's eaten the canary, bowed, and kissed the hand of the lovely Miss D'Antoni. "My dear, I am utterly charmed. I believe that Mrs. Krantz is correct. Your father purchased the Patton family shares of Catalina Island if I am not mistaken."

Miss D'Antoni withdrew her hand, favored the General with what seemed to me to be a radiant smile and answered, "Yes, General Patton. I was able to spend one glorious summer there before I accepted this posting with the Red Cross."

Patton's family, together with his wife's uncle, had owned the island of Catalina off the Southern California coast.

"Miss D"Antoni, if you and your family are half as happy on Cat as I was growing up, then your future is absolutely assured. I learned to ride and shoot and sail there in my formative years."

"Well, sir, we are off to a good start there," Miss D'Antoni assured him. "I, too, ride and shoot on the island."

God! What a woman! I thought.

"Miss D'Antoni, your charm has caused me to neglect my duties as host. Please let me introduce you to my guests," Patton said with his Cheshire smile which said, 'actually, my dear, you and I both know that this is a social dance, and no one knows the steps better than I.'

"Elizabeth. Please call me Elizabeth, sir."

"Of course. Elizabeth, may I present..." Patton whirled around and the first face he saw was mine. "Pointer."

"Just...Pointer?" she said with what I read as a mischievous smile.

"Pointer works just fine, Miss D'Antoni" I said.

"Elizabeth."

"Yes. Elizabeth." I was in love.

"And what should I call you?"

I was almost in a trance. "Pointer. Elizabeth." I searched for something to say, anything to keep her focused on me. But Patton touched her elbow and led her about the room providing more introductions. It was funny—she seemed to be the guest of honor, not Donovan.

I ambled over to Binky and asked if he had received his summons to the meeting tomorrow with Wild Bill.

"Yes, of course. Do you suppose we'll receive orders for Sicily?" he wondered.

"Well, it's a briefing on Sicily for sure. I'm just hoping he'll let me stay in on the action."

At that moment, Colonel Donovan ambled over. The big man addressed Binky. "Leftenant, you've seen action here against Rommel?" It was an invitation for Binky to hold forth.

"Yes sir. At Tobruk and Kass Pass."

"And the Germans? Stout fighters?"

"Absolutely, sir. They know their tanks. It's only when their supply lines get stretched that they have trouble. One gets the impression that if their generals let them, the men would go on fighting even without supplies."

"My thoughts as well," Donovan agreed. "Tell me, Leftenant. Being in battle as you have, you've fought alongside some brave chaps, I presume?"

"Of course, sir."

"Well, I want you to bring me a list of four or five intrepid types to whom you would entrust your life. Tomorrow, Leftenant. As for you, Pointer, we need to find some righteous GIs to accompany your party into Sicily. I'll take care of that."

Righteous GIs? Huh.

"Yes sir. May I suggest that you look among the Marine contingent, sir."

"You may suggest, Pointer. You may always suggest. Now, if you will excuse me."

I turned to Binky and said, "What was that all about?"

Binky snagged two flutes of Champagne from a passing waiter, handed me one and said, "I suppose it means we are going to Sicily with a small band of men, some of them our chaps and some yours."

I had never taken my eyes fully off Elizabeth as I tracked her progress around the room. Not surprisingly, it seemed that I was not the only man in the room who was smitten.

A small man in an odd white uniform with green piping, a pill box hat and a little bell began circulating among the guests, announcing that dinner was served. As we entered the dining room,

I watched as Patton led Elizabeth to the seat to his immediate left, and Donovan took his place of honor to Patton's right. I tried not to be too eager scanning the place cards for my name, all the while thinking how I could work a trade with whomever was seated next to Elizabeth. But—there *is* a God!—I spied my name at the seat to her left. There's a reason Generals are Generals; gotta know how to position your troops. This was the type of combat I most enjoyed—winning the heart of the damsel over about twenty other interested parties in the room.

The General and I moved simultaneously to hold Elizabeth's chair. With a small bow, I stepped back, ceding the honor to Patton. Live to fight another day, I always say. Or at least know when you're seriously outranked.

No dinner party of General Patton's was complete without a speech and a series of toasts. The General remained standing after his guests had all taken their seats. He did look resplendent in his dress uniform; he'd even left off his Colt Peacemaker for the occasion. In his reedy, raspy voice, he began, "Ladies and gentlemen, soldiers from the Romans and the Carthagenians to Hannibal and Alexander the Great thought it fitting and proper to combine the culinary arts with those of the military. And while we are not tonight on the eve of battle, our time will come soon enough. Tonight, we welcome our distinguished visitors from the homeland—Mrs. Krantz and Miss D'Antoni of the American Red Cross and Colonel Donovan of our still-new Office of Strategic Services. This occasion marks the first time that an OSS Chief has ventured into a war zone. And, ladies and gentlemen, you are aware that I like to be in on firsts." He paused here to let a gentle tittering wash over the table.

"So, ladies and gentlemen, I propose a toast to the brave souls of the Allied Forces who have gathered in this distant land to vanquish—no, crush!—the forces of evil. May God grant us victory." This last was said not in a rousing battlefield cry; rather, it was a benediction. "And so we dine!"

Wow. Not exactly like Sunday night hash back in South Hill.

Across the table from me was General Omar Bradley whom Ike had appointed to serve under Patton. His mien was saturnine and I had always had the impression that he chafed under Patton. Their personalities were polar opposites. Where Patton was brash and shoot-from-the-hip, Bradley was calm, cool, and studied. If some day he ascended to become Patton's superior officer, few would be surprised. Bradley began chatting with me about supply trains and how to get corned beef into the hands of a GI at the front. Meanwhile, Patton was bending Elizabeth's ear.

To my left was Archie Stanhope, the AP reporter. I said to him, "Are you one of *the* Stanhopes? The Archibald Stanhopes?" I was goofing on him.

He looked at me, then smiled. "Yes, my father's name is Archibald, so I suppose that makes me one of *the* Archibald Stanhopes...of Newark, New Jersey."

Archie continued, "What is your situation here, Pointer? Pretty big stuff snagging an invitation to the General's table."

"Situation? I suppose I know Colonel Donovan, so I was included."

"Donovan? Are you an OSS man?"

"Off the record?"

"Off the record, yes."

"I'm not saying," I answered.

I knew that dinner parties were an elaborate dance. A minuet. At unspoken cues, dinner partners finished a conversation to their right and began a new one to their left. I was determined that evening to bend the rules of equal conversation and cheat in favor of the beautiful creature to my right. But I was patient.

Almost simultaneously, Bradley finished his corned beef soliloquy and Patton seemed to be wrapping up a tale of rabbit hunting on Catalina Island, so Elizabeth and I turned our attention to each other.

"Tell me, Pointer, what are you doing over here?" she opened.

"Well, I'm assigned to General Patton's army as a kind of Italian liaison." It was a white lie, but I couldn't tell her about Lucky.

"I am, you know, of Italian descent. You're not referring to me, are you?"

Will you marry me and have my children?

No, I didn't say that. But I was thinking along those lines.

"There's a thought. Are you up for some liaising?" I smiled.

"There's a war going on, Pointer," she reminded me." Besides, how will I know that I wouldn't just be a wartime fling...an affair."

"But aren't the best love affairs the ones where everyone is stressed out and think they could die the next day?"

"What about the house with rose trellises and the little white fence? No, wait, you're going to tell me that's what we're fighting for. And if you do, I'll have to agree with you."

"That's part of it. The rest has to do with stopping the Hun from advancing to our shores and raping and pillaging," I said, trying to keep it light. Way to go, Pointer, rape is such a light touch.

"You mean deflowering virgins and all of that?" Elizabeth said this with a little twinkle in her eye. Oh, man, I think we're flirting, even if the topic is on the taboo side.

"How come men don't ever get deflowered? Did you ever think of that?" I asked.

"As a matter of fact, I have. More than once." Again with the twinkle. God, I already loved that twinkle. "And Leftenant Binkford. Is he in the Italian liaison business as well?"

Don't even *think* about deflowering Binky. "Yes, we are partners in crime."

"Seriously, Pointer. Do you think we'll win this war?"

I glanced over at Patton, Donovan, then at Bradley—three of the most important cogs in the Allied war machine. Thank God *they* weren't flirting with anybody. "Yes", I said. "I do believe we will. If you look around this table, we have three reasons why. We have a great warrior in the General, who believes he's been reincarnated from a mortally wounded soldier from a battle in ancient times. But he also believes he's been put here for the sole purpose of killing as many of our enemies as one man can or one man can direct. In General Bradley we have one of the best logicians ever. He can get a GI a corned beef sandwich at the front 50 miles away. And in

Donovan we finally have a spy. Who was it that said one good spy is worth 10,000 soldiers?"

"Aristotle?"

"Maybe. We have the warriors, the tacticians and the spies. And we seem to have the will to stay with it and make the sacrifices. It helps that Hitler is so damned evil and such a caricature of evil. And it helps that no one any longer underestimates him."

"What about Mussolini? Is he a serious player?"

"I don't think so. He waited to get in the war until he saw which way the wind was blowing, after Dunkirk. I think his convictions are a mile wide and an inch deep. At the first major defeat he'll cut and run. Or his own people will get rid of him."

"He'll be, uh, deflowered." Twinkle Twinkle. "But there are a million Italian soldiers in Libya. They outnumber us by a wide margin."

"Yes, but they are not committed like the Germans and the Japanese. Not to mention the Brits, the Americans, the Russians and the rest of the Allies."

"My dad used to say that in the barnyard, the chicken is involved but the hog is committed. The chicken gives us eggs, but the hog becomes a ham sandwich," she said.

I laughed at this.

"Do you think it's smart for Hitler to have a second front in Russia?" she asked.

"Didn't work out so well for Napoleon, did it? Apparently, Hitler believes he is under Divine guidance when it comes to making war. First he bombs the hell out of London; then he stops before he finishes them off. Then he sends troops here. Now he's re-diverted many of them for a run at Russia. Hard to figure."

Patton jumped in to the conversation. "Best goddamn move Hitler's made is to invade the Russkies—best move for the Allies, that is. Goddam Stalin will be our next Hitler, I guaran-damn-tee you! If they can beat each other to a pulp, that'll be good for the rest of the Allies."

Patton voiced what many said privately, but would not venture publicly. "Let the Krauts wear themselves out in Russia. We'll come at 'em through Italy from the south and, sure as hell, Ike will come at 'em from the north. If they're screwing around in the east, what'll they do then? Eh? They're already getting their behinds kicked over there." Patton had gotten worked up and seemed to be challenging the entire table to defy his logic.

"Give me an army, and I'll go through Sicily and Italy like it was Kansas on a pretty June morning. I'll keep pushing north and before you know it I'll be across the Rhine! Ike and I both know that this is an inevitable truth!" Patton almost roared.

"Now, Mrs. Krantz," Patton arched his head toward the opposite end of the table, adopting his Cheshire smile once again and lowering his voice. "Tell us about the work you and Miss D'Antoni are doing with the Red Cross."

After Mrs. Krantz had finished holding forth, I turned my attention back to Elizabeth. I thought about the now-famous Pointer family story about how Mother and Father met and just knew. They knew that they were, well, right for each other. After that time, neither looked at another person *that* way again. I found myself wondering if that's what was happening tonight.

I produced my most winning smile and said, "Elizabeth, I would love to continue our conversation in the very near future. Are you free for dinner tomorrow night?"

Elizabeth put an elbow on the table and placed her chin in her hand and stared thoughtfully at me for a long beat. With a half-smile on her face, she said, "That would be lovely, Pointer." Lovely? Did she say that?

Chapter Six

A Spat

Although it was late, and we both had an early call in the morning, Binky and I decided to hit one of the local wine bars for a nightcap. Youth is invincible and hangovers don't slow us down.

The bar was going strong at midnight, populated mostly by U.S. sailors with the odd Aussie and Brit thrown in. Most were drinking bust-head whiskey. I ordered a beer, and Binky had a cognac. We were both a little drunk.

"So, Binky," I opened. "What do you think?"

"About what, dear boy?"

About life. Love. War. Death." Deep stuff. I was in a mood.

"I know that Cousin Friedrich believes in the right and might of the German cause as deeply as we believe in ours", he said.

"You have a German cousin?"

"He's on Himmler's General Staff. Before the war, we had many political discussions regarding the German economy, German expansionism and the possibility of a thousand year *Reich*. He was slow to come around to Hitler, but he became one of the *Fuhrer's* leading proponents. He is of the aristocracy, of course, so he has some considerable influence."

"What kind of chap is your cousin Friedrich?"

"Freddy is passionate, compassionate, brilliant. A great man, really. I actually admire those qualities in him. We spent many summers together in the Bavarian Alps. I know him quite well. He's always been one to adopt causes, so when he saw Hitler as a way out of the economic mess in Germany, he threw heart and soul behind the *Reich*."

"And what does he have to say about the way the rumor of the mistreatment of the Jews?"

"A means to an end. Unfortunate, but necessary. He believes that the exigencies of war justify extreme measures. He also believes that wealth should not be concentrated in a minority."

"Sure. As long as the minority in question is not the aristocracy," I said.

"Freddy, it will not surprise you, does not see it that way. I will confess that sometimes I have sensed doubt from him about Hitler, but never about the justness of their cause."

"Well, if half of what we hear about the Nazi treatment of the Jews is true, it is an abomination. I know that Wild Bill and his bunch know more than they are saying, not that I could tell you why they would hold back. Do your people have anything to say about it?"

There was a horrific image that was burned into my consciousness. It was a classified photograph that I was not meant to see at OSS HQ in Washington. The photo was of a terrified Jewish lawyer whose pants had been pulled down by his Nazi tormentors. He was a chubby, balding man of about 40. He was running for his life through a Square in Munich. His younger pursuers, uniformed Hitler Youth, were whipping his bare buttocks with sticks; they had fiendish grins on their faces. There was a crowd in the square, urging the mob on. The look on the lawyer's face reminded me of "The Scream" by Edvard Munch. The rest of the commentary on the photo caption stated that the lawyer had been sent to the concentration camp in Dachau. It would forever haunt me.

"Nothing that I can talk about, no," Binky replied. "People in England have their own worries. They still fear more of the *Luftwaffe.* There are shortages of just about everything, from petrol to flour and tea. And, dear boy, you know what an Englishman is like without his tea." Binky was deadly serious.

"I can only imagine", I said. "Mad dogs and Englishmen and all that. Almost as bad as a Gin-deprived bloke in summer."

"It won't kill our people to have some deprivation. We've gotten soft." Binky was clearly drunk now.

"We've had our way in the world for decades," he continued. " The last war brought us up short. We're finding our way. Before that, under the Queen, we ruled the world. In my father's world, British domination was not a question. It was the answer. Like the Romans before us, all roads led through London. Certainly economically, but also culturally. But now…" Binky looked wistful.

I had been observing a sailor at the next table out of the corner of my eye for the last few minutes. He was showing more than passing interest in our conversation. He was clearly drunk. I watched as he nudged one of his buddies and nodded in our direction. Suddenly, he stood up and lurched toward us.

"You fellas some kinda German sympathizers? What the shit, man?" His three buddies also wobbled to their feet and stared at us in as menacing a fashion as they could muster.

Oh, boy, I thought and stood up. "Easy there, sailor. We're on the same team here", I said. But the sailor had a different view and took a swing at me. I ducked and his fist landed on my shoulder.

The other three jumped on top of me as we crashed onto and collapsed the table.

Where was Binky? I didn't have to wait long as Binky had swung around behind my attackers and grabbed two of them by their cute little sailor suits, picked them up and knocked their heads together. So, it was two against one twice over with Binky and me. I was holding my own against my two guys; they were so drunk that I easily dodged most of their parries.

Binky, meanwhile, was literally pounding his two guys. One of them was out like a light and he didn't take long to finish off the other one. Then, he came to my aid. One roundhouse sent the original aggressor sprawling halfway across the room. Then, Binky grabbed me and pushed me hard out of the way. He began with a straight right to the remaining sailor's face, breaking his nose. He followed that with an uppercut to the jaw. Blood completely obscured the sailor's face as he went down in a heap. Binky kept at it, though, kicking the fallen man first in the ribs and then in the head.

I jumped up and with a lot of difficulty pulled Binky off before we had a dead man on our hands. Binky didn't seem to recognize me as I pulled him from the scene of the melee. He tried to punch me, but had no leverage since I had him in a hammer lock from behind. Then he stomped his foot down on top of my foot and, with a howl, I let him go. He charged back at the fallen sailor and only when he reached the poor guy did he seem to realize that the man was unconscious and not likely to move for a while.

With heaving chest, Binky turned to me and seemed to focus for the first time since the fight started.

I said gently, "Binky, we need to get out of here. The MPs will be here soon and it won't do for us to be at this scene."

Binky nodded, threw a pound note in the general direction of the bar and walked out with me.

I decided that I'd just seen Binky overcompensating and decided to say nothing about it, at least that night.

March 20, 1943

My Dear Robert,

You are well? I know that you receive letters from home irregularly and in batches, and will read my missives in the order that I sent them.

Your mother is well as am I and, of course, we continue to pray for your well -being and for the safety of the troops with whom you serve. We read here about General Patton. One article from the AP reporter assigned to II Corps says that he is the ideal fighting General but that when it comes to strategic planning that it's best to leave that up to others. At least that's what I infer from between the lines. It would be difficult, I think, to have someone else plan for a battle and then ask another soldier to lead that plan. I pray that Eisenhower, Marshall, Churchill, Roosevelt, et al, know what they are about. The press is generally favorable to them.

Old Bishop Pointer used to say that men plan while God laughs. There is a lot of truth in that as we have seen time and time again. Did not Patton himself, when he was stationed in Hawaii in the 30's, write a contingency plan in the event that Pearl Harbor was suddenly attacked? I believe he did, and I believe that plan sat gathering dust in a file drawer somewhere on Dec 7, 1941.

Meanwhile, you will remember that I wrote to you about the group that is called the Tuskegee Airmen. I have looked into them further. Despite long odds and big obstacles, there have been startling developments for this all-Negro force. Some of the obstacles they have faced include policing their unit. As they are located in Alabama, the local authorities refused to grant them the ability to have their own MPs as white units do. It may require a black man to occasionally have police jurisdiction over a white man, and that just wouldn't do, don't you know. Then there's the issue of surgeons. I suppose this is a silver lining as the Army finally allowed integration in a Texas facility so that Negro surgeons could receive training so that they may operate on their fellow Negroes who might be injured in combat.

They got a big public relations boost when First Lady Eleanor Roosevelt took a ride in one of their aircraft. The papers reported her saying to the pilot, "You can fly alright"! She also arranged for a large sum of money to be donated to the building of some of their facilities.

From what I can determine, the very first all-Negro aviation squadron has been assembled and trained at Tuskegee and are awaiting deployment. The great irony, son, is that they may be headed your way. The rumor is that their first posting will be North Africa. So, if you see a Negro bombardier walking around the base, remember, you heard it here first!

I have not seen young Gaskins since I last wrote to you. Perhaps he has decided after all to enlist and become a cook or a laborer in the Army, which seem to be his only choices. Tomorrow

I may take a drive over to his house and see what has become of him.

Your mother and I went on Saturday to see the wonderful movie Casablanca. *It's finally come to South Hill. You can guess why we were especially interested in it, given the locale of the story. Your mother has (wrongly) accused me of falling for Ingrid Bergman. Well, she may be just a little correct.*

Speaking of that, are there any romantic opportunities over there? Nurses and the like? Your mother would like to know.

Once again, my dear boy, please take care of yourself and return to us safely. And write! Your mother wants to hear the news.

I remain

Your loving Father,

Robert Pointer

Chapter Seven

The Briefing

At 0 Dark Thirty I arose, showered, shaved and went to Mess for—what else—hash and a cup of coffee. Given the previous night's events, I didn't feel too bad. In fact, I was walking on air. Yep, I was in love—again. I told myself that this time it was different. Elizabeth was far and away the most beautiful girl I'd ever met. And she had a way about her that was captivating. Best news of the day—I had a dinner date with her that evening.

About Leftenant Binkford, I wasn't so sure. His reaction to the sailors was extreme, to say the least. Maybe he was overcompensating for being a homosexual. But I thought there was more to it than that. During the fight, he didn't seem to know where he was, or who he was. He might have killed that sailor if I hadn't dragged him off. I thought about his behavior in the context of where I thought we were going and what I thought we'd be doing. He could certainly hold his own in a scrap, but we weren't going to Sicily to scrap; we were going to hatch plots. Spy stuff. And spy stuff requires calm nerves and quick decisions.

And then there was Cousin Friedrich. Boy, that was awkward. I would keep a close eye on old Binky over the next few days.

It was time to go see Wild Bill, who was bunking at Patton's HQ. I double-quicked over to the briefing room and met Binky at the entrance to the building. We nodded at one another and entered together.

The room was standard stuff. A long table for the briefers set up in front of folding chairs for the briefees. There were maps of the North African Coast, Sicily and Italy on the walls, the obligatory blackboard and also a screen and a projector. There were no other soldiers present when Binky and I sat down.

At precisely 0700, Wild Bill Donovan and a Major entered the room.

"Hup!"

Binky and I stood at attention until the Major said, "As you were". We resumed our seats.

At a nod from Donovan, the Major began. "Gentlemen, I am, *ow*, Major Brownwell. I have been assigned as your C.O. for Operation Husky. I will be in charge of operations and, *ow*, training from this point forward. Colonel Donovan will, of course, have overall command, but I am day-to-day."

Brownwell had an odd way of speaking. In places where some people punctuate their speech with an "um" or an "uh", the Major uttered a guttural sound that sounded like *ow.*

He continued, "We plan to select thirty Special Forces troops to support your activities in Sicily, which we have code named, *ow*, The Sauce. As in, you'll soon be in The Sauce."

Funny, Major.

"On a date TBD, but within the next two months, you will, *ow*, lead a covert party into The Sauce. You will land here." He pointed to the map at a point on the coast of The Sauce. "If, as we suspect, you land undetected, then the men accompanying you will deploy back to, *ow*, Tunisia and you will proceed on your respective routes to your respective destinations. Colonel Donovan will brief you on that part of the mission. If you are met with, *ow*, resistance, you and your men will fight it out as best you can. If odds are overwhelming, you will retreat back the way you came. But I emphasize that secrecy and surprise is the key to, ow, success here. If you have to fight, then we haven't done a good job of planning."

Great, Major. We'll be in The Sauce and you'll be back here saying, "Better luck, *ow*, next time."

"Colonel Donovan?" Donovan crushed out his cigarette. The Major sat while

Wild Bill walked over to the map of The Sauce.

"Pointer, Binkford, you were chosen for Husky because of unique circumstances and some unique qualifications you possess. You both speak Italian and are fluent in Sicilian dialects, and you each bring a perspective on the, er, civilian leaders of The Sauce. Pointer, you debriefed Husky personally and know the Mafiosi there from his point of view. And Binkford, your doctoral thesis on the Sicilian Mafia demonstrated your knowledge of the local customs."

He speaks Italian? Thesis?

"Your mission is to make contact with the two most powerful Mafiosi leaders—one in the central part of the island and the other on the east coast-- and persuade them that it is in their best interests to support us. It should not be difficult because it *is* in their best interests."

"As you know, since Mussolini came to power, one of his policies has been to crack down on the Sicilian Mafia. And he has done this with surprisingly good results. In fact, no authority has ever had so much success against this traditionally powerful group. The Mafia in Sicily is virtually underground now, and they yearn for a return to the *status quo.* If they can be convinced that when—not if—the Allies take over their island in the near future and that Mussolini's days are numbered, then we believe they will cooperate."

Donovan paused to see if we were tracking with him. I gave a little involuntary nod, as if to say, "Proceed, Wild Bill".

"That's the easy part. Husky and other sources tell us that they believe an Allied victory will be in their best interests. The harder part will be to convince them to get actively involved in defeating the Germans there. Best case, we get them to sabotage and disrupt supply lines coming down-island from Palermo. Sabotage armored vehicles. Get in positions to kill Germans with sniper fire. Use explosives to blow up roads and bridges in strategic places. Assassinate officers. All of that and more. The *more* will be up to you. You will assess their resources and willingness to use them, and help plan the best sabotage tactics you can."

"Major..."

Brownwell took up the briefing without a pause. "We will also depend on these Mafiosi for intelligence on German troop placements and movements. Pointer, you will proceed up the center of the island and Binkford you will be responsible for securing, *ow*, the east coast route. As of now, the plan is for Patton's forces to drive north through the center and for Montgomery to go up the east coast. You will have three days to accomplish your tasks in your first insertion."

First insertion?

"Our goal is to get you out of, *ow*, The Sauce one month before the invasion so that the Mafia leaders have time to plan and organize. You will then go back in with the first wave of the invasion, make your way back to your respective staging areas and do what you can to assist the efforts of the locals. As the invasion plans unfold, we'll have more detail on Phase Two."

Donovan stood. "Questions so far?"

We had none, so he said, "We do not expect that your efforts alone will make this invasion succeed or fail. But Sicily is a land unlike any in the world. As you both well know, it is clannish, its people resent authority. Hell, they resent their own Government's authority, let alone a foreign power's. They are secretive and they can be damned mean when they want to be. Compare it to any other theatre in this war. The people here, if their leaders can be persuaded to actively fight against their oppressors, can be more effective at helping us win than anywhere else I can think of."

He paused.

"I don't mind telling you that the highest authorities—and by highest,

think Prime Minister and President—
are aware of this part of the plan, and
heartily endorse it."

Well, if he didn't have my attention
before, he did now. Churchill and
Roosevelt were in on it? Well, *damn.*

The Major piped up, "We have
updated briefing papers, local maps
and Sicilian nationals recruited to help
educate you on the lay of the land.
Gents, you'll be logging a lot of
classroom time, but we also want to be
sure you're fit. So, we've planned a
special, *ow*, regimen for you that starts
tomorrow at 0500. I'll make sure
you're put through your paces,"
Brownwell said with what can only be
described as an evil smile.

Well, between falling in love, getting in
shape, and studying up on The Sauce,
sleep would be a distant fourth on my
personal North African agenda.

Binky and I spent the remainder of the
day buried in briefing books and
meetings. Busy as I was, thoughts of
Elizabeth were never far away.

Meanwhile, Patton had assumed command of the 3rd Army and had joined forces with Montgomery's I Army to push the Germans and Italians all the way back into a small area of Tunisia. It now only remained to "push them the goddamn hell across the Med to where they fucking *belong*!" as Patton was overheard to bellow more than once.

Chapter Eight

Love

Finally, seven pm rolled around. I knocked at the nurses' barracks where Elizabeth was staying and asked the matron for Elizabeth D'Antoni. She was summoned and I watched her descend the stairs in a navy blue shirt waist dress. A faint hint of perfume preceded her and almost made me swoon.

"Hi". I had a big old grin on my face that we used to say back home was something unprintable. She looked so damned pretty.

"Hi back, Pointer. You look very handsome in that uniform."

"And you, Miss D'Antoni, look...stunning."

"Thank you. Where are we headed?"

"I thought the hotel dining room would be a nice place. Get a corner table and enjoy some quiet time. OK with you?"

"Yes. Perfect."

I had requisitioned a jeep from the barracks supply so we had wheels. I drove slowly through the roads of town. The lights were all blazing, the townspeople were hanging in the streets. War had not yet touched down here.

We arrived at the hotel and I gave the Maitre d' my name and he escorted us to a table toward the back of the room. There were several dining rooms, all white washed and pristine looking. The lights were bright, the aromas were of roasted meat and garlic. I didn't recognize any of the other diners, but Elizabeth stopped by a table of four young women to say hello. Nurses night out. The room was decorated in a Colonial motif from the Continent, and the food was supposed to be spicy, local and tasty.

We ordered cocktails. Scotch rocks for me and an *aperitif* for her. As we were waiting, she asked me, "How was your day?"

No, she didn't call me 'dear'.

"Fascinating, to tell you the truth. I was learning all about a foreign land and their customs. Rather like Geography class back in high school. And yours?"

"We're organizing a blood drive. I hate to think of it this way, but we're trying to stock up on our supply for when the fighting begins again. Of course, it'll be the first time fighting for many of the Americans."

We both were quiet for a moment.

"Tell you what," I said. "Let's have a war-free conversation, at least until dessert. Deal?"

"Deal", she agreed. "Now, tell me about growing up in Virginia."

So I did. I told her about my parents and my sister. How Father was my moral compass and how Mother was the, uh, Enforcer in the family. If I signed up—at her insistence—for the church choir, then by God, I was going to be in the choir no matter what.

Once you were in on something, you were *in.* No quitting, ever. What determination I have in life I got from her. What ethics I have in life, I learned from him.

I told her about South Hill, how everyone seemed to know everyone else, how kids—boys and girls both—transported themselves exclusively by bicycle. Or by foot if there was, say, snow on the ground. How we got cherry Cokes at the drug store and got change from a nickel in the bargain. How the World War I vets had no sooner finally settled in than talk of another Great War started. How the mayor of South Hill was a philanderer and crooked as a ram's horn to boot. And everyone knew it, but reelected him anyway. How race relations worked—mainly whites and blacks avoided each other unless they intersected in commerce. And that was usually a maid in your house. Or the guy who picked up the trash on Thursdays or the Negro who came around the neighborhood and sold you veg-e-TAH-bles from the back of his truck.

You never really knew anyone from the other race except as hired help. And it seemed to work out, at least for the white folks, as long as the colored folks stayed in their places.

She listened to all this with an elbow on the table and her beautiful jawline supported by her hand, a bemused smile on her face. Her gray eyes seemed to have gotten a little bluer.

"I visited my cousin in Richmond once," she said. "They seem a little obsessed still with the Civil War. The gas stations were giving away commemorative glasses with funny looking 'Yankees' on them with a fill-up."

"You are referring to The Great Trouble. Yes, if you grow up there, you're taught that Yankees are stinky."

"Stinky?"

Smooth, Pointer, real smooth.

"Sorry, hope I didn't offend you. Californians smell like orange blossoms, I always say."

Pointer, just shut up now!

"And you have a law degree and you were a Marine." It was a statement. Had she checked me out?

"Yes, I am. I learned to fight in law school. The Marines were just practice."

She gave a little giggle.

"And you know several languages?"

"Si. Oui. Yes. And you?"

"A little Italian," she said.

"And Californian."

"And Californian", she agreed. "I'll bet when you and Leftenant Binkford are on leave, the girls are in great danger. Do you have a special girl back home?"

"Other than my mother? No. I really haven't had time for romance."

"And you, Elizabeth, what about you?" I sipped my Scotch.

She chose to take my meaning as a general question about her formative years. "My upbringing in California could not be much more different. My father was strict, sent my sisters and me to Catholic school where we had to wear those dreadful uniforms. But we were sheltered from the world. Dad was a Republican of the Orange County variety and made a fortune in land speculation in the San Fernando Valley. We had movie people at the house quite often, but never the actors. They were the hired help, even the stars. Just the studio mogul-types. Dad even invested in some films."

We paused to look at the menus.

"When I was eighteen, one of those moguls came on to me when we were out on our patio and Dad and Mom were inside making cocktails. It was really quite funny. He told me how beautiful I was and wouldn't I like to meet him at his villa in Palm Springs some weekend—on the QT, of course—and he was fairly certain he could make me a star."

"What did you say?"

"I told him that Mom had never been to Palm Springs and had always wanted to go and when she brought the drinks out we could ask her if she wanted to go too. He looked like he was going to have a stroke, looked at his watch and said he had an emergency casting session that he'd forgotten, please make my apologies to your parents-I've got to be running."

I chuckled at this.

"Bet you've gotten lots of propositions along the way", I said.

"Yes, certainly my share. But I seem to be intimidating to lots of men." She paused and studied me.

"Not to you though. Why is that?"

"Well, I can't say you've intimidated me. But can I tell you something?"

She nodded.

"You are the most beautiful creature I've ever met. And not to rush things, but I think I could fall for you given half a chance."

"Well, Pointer, that *is* bold. But it's also a pretty good thing for me to hear. I may look like I can handle just about anything, and I don't lack for confidence, but underneath, I'm just a California girl who wants what most girls want", she finished softly.

"And what is that?"

"Love. Security. Safety. A soul mate. And someone who can make me laugh," she brightened.

The waiter chose this propitious moment to appear and ask for our orders. We both went with the lamb stew, the *specialte de la maison*.

Pursuing the line of the conversation, I said, "I have to tell you, Elizabeth, that I am often the life of the party, I can tell a mean joke."

"Right, Pointer, but you're not applying for the court jester job," she smiled.

"No, but if I were, you'd be forced to employ me 'cause I'm damned funny. Just not right now maybe."

"You're doing just fine."

And there it was. As I looked at her I felt it. Tension. Not just tension, but *sexual* tension. One of the most delicious feelings on God's green earth. And I think she felt it too because she gazed at me with a very thoughtful expression that I read as, "I want to: Eat. You. Up."

Well, that was my interpretation. It could also have been, "Who is this rube from South Hill?"

I chose to believe the first impression and pursued it.

"Have you ever been in love, Elizabeth?"

She frowned. "I thought so back in California. I was engaged to marry a man who was considerably older than I. He owned orange groves, inherited them. He wooed me and would not take no for an answer. Certainly not one of the intimidated ones. After a while, I felt that it was a game for him, that he wanted to possess me like a prized piece of land."

She looked at me for a beat, then decided to press on.

"We talked about deflowering the other night. Well, he was the one who I gave myself to. I discovered two things: One, he wasn't very good at it and, two, even though he didn't know what he was doing, I knew that this was something that I could really get used to, that this was a wonderful, blessed act and that with the right person, I would like to do it early and often. Does that make me sound like a slut, Pointer? Maybe I was too.."

"No! No, it doesn't. No, of course not."

Cool now, Pointer. Easy, big fella.

"It does evoke some nice images in my fertile imagination though," I smiled.

I was right! It *was* sexual tension.

"Let me hasten to add that he was my only, uh, experience to date," she said not in the least bit hastily.

I knew what was coming.

"What about you, Pointer? You are an extremely attractive man and you do have that wicked sense of humor," she grinned.

"Oh, well, yes, I've been around. For sure."

If she only knew. A hasty coupling in the bathroom at the beach with a girl two years my senior, as friends were outside the room hooting at us to come out. A tryst at a high school reunion in the back seat of my Father's car. And, oh yes, my college sweetheart. Or at least one of them.

"Well, that's a relief. An experienced lover." She flashed a wicked smile.

It occurred to me how different this was than my other experiences with women. They were mostly flirty encounters with giggly girls, and I wasn't exactly Clark Gable myself. This was new, it felt more...mature.

"Would you like to dance?" The orchestra had started up and I thought that if I didn't get to at least touch her in the next five minutes, a seriously embarrassing incident might ensue.

I took her in my arms and we began to glide around the room. Thank God Mother had signed me up for Cotillion at the church so I was reasonably proficient. This was certainly the first time that I had held Elizabeth and I knew I would never forget it. Yes, I am a romantic fool. I admit it. But, *damn,* this was nice. Her body just kind of fit mine. My angles and her curves...melded. She was tall and lithe; I was taller, and she just fit. Like peas in a pod, as Mother would say.

I noticed that our entrees had been delivered to the table and the waiter was staring at us, wondering if we were going to let it get cold. It can freeze, I thought. I'm not going to be the one to stop. And neither was Elizabeth. We danced straight through three numbers. The orchestra took a break, so we repaired to our table. The food had been taken away and when the waiter saw us he hustled back to the kitchen.

"That was nice, Pointer," Elizabeth smiled. "No wonder the girls have thrown themselves at you."

I didn't correct her.

The waiter reappeared with hot bowls of stew and pita bread and a heretofore unseen grin on his face. Everyone loves a lover.

We ate, we talked, we danced and we drank some. I thought, incongruously, of Mother. Would she like Elizabeth? I know Father would. Even if he didn't like her, he'd like her, if you know what I mean. I wondered if I had at long last gained a measure of maturity myself, a circumstance I knew that my parents had been patiently awaiting.

I had lost track of the time and glanced at my watch. Midnight. I thought, for the first time, of my 0500 call the next morning and suggested that we have a nightcap and head home.

As we left, Elizabeth took my hand as though she'd been doing it for years. We got in the jeep and I turned to her and kissed her right there as we sat in the parking lot. I knew I'd never forget *that* either. She kissed me back with passion. I finally broke the kiss and hugged her hard, both of us panting a little, out of breath.

"Darlin'", I said. (If you leave the 'g' off this early in the game, it's a perfectly acceptable term of endearment. But, frankly, I was pretty close to going all the way to 'darling'). "If I don't get you home, we're going to have to go back in and get a room."

"Mmmmm." She nuzzled me.

"What are you doing tomorrow night," I asked.

"What are *you* doing?" she replied.

"It's my fervent hope that it'll be something with you," I said.

Elizabeth stirred and lifted her face from my shoulder. "Roger that," she murmured.

And so ended the most perfect evening of my life—to that point. And so began one of the toughest days I would ever have.

Chapter Nine

Dead Man Walking

GERMANY

March 1943

Adolf Hitler was a dead man walking.

Hitler had been at his easternmost headquarters in East Prussia obsessing over recent catastrophic defeats in Russia. On his way back to Berlin, his plane was scheduled to make a stop at the headquarters of Army Group Center at Smolensk. If Colonel Henning von Tresckow and his confederates had their way, Hitler's next flight would be his last. Tresckow had asked Lieutenant Colonel Heinz Brandt, a Hitler staffer, to take a parcel with him on the flight. It was a box that supposedly contained two bottles of Cointreau. The liquor was payment for a bet that Tresckow had lost to his friend, General Stieff. Would Brandt mind very much delivering the package for him to his friend?

Inside the package was a bomb, set to blow Hitler's Focke-Wulf 200 *Condor* out of the sky about 30 minutes after take-off. It would happen near Minsk, close enough to the front to be attributed to Soviet fighters. The ambitious plan called for Tresckow's co-conspirator, General Friedrich Olbricht, to use the crisis to mobilize his Reserve Army network to seize power in Berlin, Vienna, Munich and other power centers. Their main task would then be to defeat Heinrich Himmler's vaunted *Schutzstaffel* or the SS, Hitler's personal army.

As was customary, the *Fuhrer* fell asleep almost immediately upon boarding the plane. The last few weeks had been horrifically stressful. He knew that victory—and vindication of his world view—was but one major battle away. Yet, for months now, that final victory had eluded him. He was not discouraged, but he was exhausted.

Thirty minutes later, in the freezing cargo hold of the *Condor,* the British-made chemical pencil detonator inside the Cointreau box went off. But the bomb did not explode. The percussion cap had frozen and had saved Adolf Hitler's life. Again. Hitler did not know it, but this was the second bombing assassination attempt he had survived, and it would not be the last.

Chapter Ten

The Spy

ENGLAND

1937-1939

It was Friedrich von Furstenberg, or Cousin Freddy, who had recruited Leftenant Edmund Randolph Symington Binkford to become a double agent for the Nazi spy organization, the *Abwehr,* after the first serious assassination discussion on Hitler in 1939. As in most defections, there was a complex ethical and moral equation that all parties had to work through. Agents didn't become double agents for the money. They did it for deeply held beliefs, and Binky was no exception.

For as long as he could remember, Binky had considered himself an unofficial citizen of Germany. He had not one, but two Fatherlands. His birthplace, and his adopted summer home in the German Alps. He appreciated the one homeland, but he deeply *admired* his adopted country. And he deeply admired the old Prussian ways of Cousin Freddy, his mother's second cousin. Growing up in the von Furstenberg family chateau during the summers of his youth, Binky came to accept that the German Way was the superior way. Germans had the courage of their convictions; their belief system began and ended with the concept that they were stronger than others. That their ways were superior. That their heritage was richer, and more meaningful than their European counterparts. France was consumed with the pleasures of the grape and the café and the world of Bohemian arts. Italy? What could one say about the indolence of the Italian male? The Poles, the Czechs, the Austrians? One had only to compare the relative industrial and, yes, artistic advances of the Fatherland to those of their smaller neighbors.

The loss in the Great War was an anomaly. It could never be repeated, and it must be avenged.

And what of the great island to the north? The von Furstenbergs and their ilk were not blind to the advances of the British Empire in the Victorian Age. But the Great War had weakened and fractured the Empire so that Britain was in decline. It was as though the savageness of their Celtic heritage was reasserting itself. And despite the braying of Churchill, and a few others, it was the feckless Prime Minister Neville Chamberlain who really represented the moral fiber of England. Didn't Chamberlain display his cowardice in the face of German rigor and toughness? One had to look no further than his policy of Appeasement to understand the will, or lack thereof, of the British people.

Adolf Hitler's rise to power was remarkable in every way. He was wildly popular throughout Germany, but most especially with the vast middle class and their University scions. His ascent during the '30s was marked by one triumph after the other as his popularity grew ever greater. Yes, there seemed to be excesses in some of his policies, but Germany had been unjustly marginalized after the Great War, and Hitler was the answer that the Fatherland sought to reclaim its rightful place as the preeminent power in Europe.

But there was one faction of German society that was not so easily swayed by Hitler and the Nazi Party. And that was the relatively small, but still-powerful, aristocracy. Those to the manor born and with a "von" in their names. And this was one of the complexities for people like the von Furstenbergs. They, too, desperately wanted Germany to rise from the ashes of World War I. But Hitler was not one of *them*. He had been a Corporal in the Army. He was crude, he was brash and he was dangerous. But it was he who had seized the day; it was he who had articulated the frustrations of the people; and it was he whom the people adored.

Many aristocrats believed in Hitler's ends but not his means. And then there was the military whose officer corps included many members of the aristocracy. And many of those had their doubts. Likewise, the *Abwehr* had officers who wanted greatness for Germany but did not believe that Hitler was the answer. In fact, in 1938 there was a strong contingent in both the Army and the spy community who believed that Hitler was leading Germany deeper into an unwinnable war.

These anti-Nazi sentiments in the aristocracy, the Army and the *Abwehr* by no means represented the majority opinion. They were small pockets, but they were highly influential pockets. There were daily discussions about what could be done. Careful overtures were made to influential officers to gauge where they stood. And despite the rise in power of the SS and its domestic police arm, the Gestapo, not one officer betrayed the confidence of another right though the attempt on Hitler's life on the *Condor.*

Adolf Hitler's stunning role as the leader of Germany was deeply confusing to Binky. Before the war, he had remained in close contact with Freddy, albeit through carefully worded letters, and he could sense that Freddy, too, was conflicted. Binky saw with clarity where Hitler was headed. There was little doubt that he would invade Poland, Czechoslavakia, and maybe even France. There was also no doubt in Binky's mind that Prime Minister Chamberlain would do nothing to stop war from breaking out. For Binky, it was the perfect metaphor for the two societies: one was aggressive and had the will to seize what they believed was their right; the other was weak and lacked the will or the vision to see where events would lead.

But the grand plan for the Fatherland was being led by this strange little man with the funny Charlie Chaplin mustache whom the masses seemed to love. Like many in Germany, Binky believed—or rather, hoped—that the *Fuhrer* would rattle his sabre, conquer a couple of his smaller neighbors and then relinquish the running of the war that would surely follow to others who were actually qualified. And like others who were dubious of Hitler within Germany, Binky adopted a wait-and-see attitude.

Leftenant Binkford had started his military career as an officer in the Horse Guards. When Lt. Colonel Stewart Menzies assumed command of Section D of the British Secret Intelligence Service (SIS), he recruited Binky, a family friend, to join him there. Section D was the branch that conducted political covert actions and paramilitary operations in time of war. Binky was vetted and sent to the training base in Beaulieu, Hampshire.

His vetting for the SIS and Section D had been largely perfunctory. Naturally, his connection with Cousin Freddy had come up. Binky had been perfectly honest about his close relationship with the von Furstenbergs, and that relationship was deemed to be potentially helpful to Section D.

Binky had known for some time that in one way or another he would aid the

Germans, but in 1937, hostilities had not yet broken out, and, besides, Binky was unsure of how things would play out with Hitler in charge. He found the work of Black Ops and the training for paramilitary duties fascinating, and he excelled at Beaulieu. He always knew that he would be useful to Menzies in either Italy or Sicily because of his focus on the language and culture of those countries while he had been at Oxford.

His father had been, as ever, cold and distant during this period. Binky had learned to expect nothing in the way of praise or affection from the old man, and in this he was not surprised. His mother who spent most of her time at the Oxford estate, away from St. James Place, was not a major influence.

He had always adored the household of the von Furstenbergs, on the other hand. The patriarch of the family, Freddy's father, was a warm old Prussian, and had treated Binky with affection—and even love—throughout their long acquaintance. When Binky reflected on his hard work at Beaulieu, it was the elder von Furstenberg that he thought of and how proud he would have been of Binky.

At long last, events in Germany helped to clear up Binky's confusion and indecision about where his loyalties and his future lay. In the summer of 1938, a school chum from Eton, Thomas Dowderwell, invited Binky to dine at his Club near Piccadilly. It was a warm July evening in the City, and Binky agreed with some pleasure to the meeting.

Dowderwell had been among his first lovers while they were at Eton. And he had accompanied Binky one summer on a visit to Cousin Freddy. Binky wondered if the dinner would turn into more than just a dinner.

As he walked through the park toward Piccadilly for the meeting, Binky noticed couples and family groups with picnics enjoying each other in the lush summer grasses. This short season was what Londoners lived for—warm summer breezes, sunshine and parks with ponds and ducks to feed.

He wondered how things might have been had he been born with the desire for the opposite sex. He rarely dwelled on this aspect of his life. His father would certainly never understand, nor would he ever know. It's just how he was. He wondered what it would be like to be in love with another person, male or female. He was certain that one day he would find out. He was not without passion.

The closest he had ever come was a boy at Oxford, a fellow student. They had spent hours together, supposedly concentrating on their studies, but in reality obsessing about each other. After making love on many occasions, Binky began slowly to feel a special attachment which he thought might be love. Naturally, he wondered if his feelings were returned. When he had returned early from a weekend at St. James Place, he found they were not. He found his lover in the passionate embrace of a young graduate assistant.

Binky was furious. He lifted the interloper from the bed, shoved him toward the stairway, and threw him down the stairwell. For many minutes his rival lay at the bottom of the stairs, motionless. At that moment Binky hoped that he was dead. But the man roused himself and, clutching at his broken ribs, limped away. For his part, Binky could hardly remember what had happened.

The two old friends embraced in the foyer of the Club. The Butler showed them to a private table, and the chums began the process of catching up. Binky had not seen Thomas since he had become a member of Section D, although it appeared that his friend knew a surprising bit about Binky's assignment. Dowderwell was a trim young man, dressed impeccably in a tweed suit. Yes, it was summer in England, but one had to guard against the chill at night,

The waiter appeared and asked for their drinks order. Dowderwell ordered a Stout. For Binky, a Scotch and Soda.

At length, Dowderwell ventured, "So, old chum, what have you heard from our Freddy?" Thomas lit a cigarette.

"Oh, a letter here and there." Binky was noncommittal. There was an odd look on Thomas' face, so Binky posed, "You have spoken to him?"

"As a matter of fact, I have been in regular contact with Freddy and some of his friends. Would it interest you to know more?"

Why the crafty approach? What was all this?

"Why, of course it would. You know my affection for Freddy."

Dowderwell exhaled smoke. "As you know, Freddy is a member of your counterpart agency, the *Abwehr*."

As a matter of fact, Binky *didn't* know that. And how did Thomas know of Binky's involvement with Section D? But he let his friend continue.

"He is involved in certain highly sensitive, um, extra-curricular activities there. Are you familiar with *widerstand*?"

The Resistance movement inside Germany.

"Of course. One knows that it exists."

"Our Freddy is deeply involved and he wishes me to tell you this."

"Thomas, what is it you are trying to convey to me here?" Binky wasn't sure where this was going.

"Freddy and his friends are certain that Hitler will mobilize soon and proceed with plans to take over neighboring States. There are many pieces of *widerstand,* none of which, importantly, have to do with jeopardizing the fortunes of Germany. But Freddy and his friends' concern is very much in jeopardizing Hitler's personal future." Dowderwell said this very slowly as if to emphasize the import of the statement.

Binky immediately understood the significance. His friend was not talking about what might be good for England; rather, the topic was what would be good for Germany. It was a distinction between a treasonous discussion and a potentially patriotic one.

"Do you understand, old friend?" Dowderwell wanted no room for misinterpretation.

"Yes, Dowderwell, yes I do," Binky replied slowly.

"And dear Freddy, at some personal risk, would like to know if perhaps you, Binky, would like to know more," he continued.

Binky sat quietly and thought. Freddy is involved in a plot to overthrow Hitler, but at the same time would like to see Germany succeed in its expansion. It precisely aligned with Binky's own views. The triumph of the Fatherland, but a triumph led by honorable men.

"What does Freddy see as the chances for success?" Binky had one foot in the pool.

"He assures me that there are allies at the very highest levels of the *Abwehr* and the Army. Candidly, he admits that there are differing motives among different factions. There are people who detest what Hitler's doing to the Jews; there is a Catholic faction who is disgruntled with what they see as Nazi heathenism; there are people who believe that Germany cannot win a war under Hitler's leadership; and there are people in high places who simply hate the man. Even the Chinese are weighing in for what they see as Hitler's betrayal for aligning with the Japanese."

"And Freddy's faction?"

"Not surprisingly, he's with the Army and the security service who largely believe in the right of Germany to reclaim territory lost in 1918, but who believe they will fail with the current leadership and their timing. Almost all of the factions, it can be said, agree that Hitler is an old dog who cannot be taught new tricks, and that he must be eliminated."

The waiter appeared and refilled their drinks.

"And what does Freddy want from me?" Binky understood that he was venturing further into treasonous territory.

"Freddy and his friends know that you are well connected in the SIS. It would be invaluable to have such an ally as you. It *will* be invaluable. We all assume that you will be posted to Italy or Sicily. And we all know that those will be important theatres in the not too distant future."

"Who are 'all of us'," Binky narrowed his eyes.

"Ah, good question, old friend. There are many of us who want Germany to succeed, but who do not like Adolf Hitler. Many of us are disaffected and feel disenfranchised by Britain's policies and the direction our leaders are taking us. There are also many who believe that Germany was treated unfairly after the war. But Hitler himself does not represent us. His policy against homosexuals, for example, is *Draconian.* So, in our movement, we believe in Germany, but not in the *Fuhrer.*"

"Are you saying that your movement is comprised largely of homosexuals?"

"No, not at all, dear boy. People like us are represented, of course. But only as a percentage, probably, of the population. The common denominator is people who believe that Great Britain's time has passed. It is a time to choose sides as we always did in cricket, and that those who choose the wrong side will be lost."

"Alright", said Binky thoughtfully. "What does Freddy want me to do, and how will he communicate with me?"

Binky realized he had just put both feet in the pool. He now knew about the conspiracy, he knew what the aim was and he knew that he would, in a very real sense, be joining the German war effort. What would Menzies think? He knew what Menzies would think. He knew that he would be in a position to pass military secrets to the Nazis, and that, when asked, he would do it. Menzies, his father, his friends and his Section D mates would all think one thing: treason. And they'd be right.

"For now, I will be your primary contact. That could and probably will change. As for what you should do, sit tight. They will let you know when they want something."

Binky reflected on how easy it had been to start the process of betraying his country. A simple dinner at the Club, and an hour later, he'd made the most important decision of his life. He looked at Dowderwell and thought of what other activities he'd like to do that evening. He looked around him and slid his hand across the table, put it on top of Thomas' and squeezed.

Chapter Eleven

Training

NORTH AFRICA

April 1943

I woke up with a start. It was 0400 hours and I knew there would be a long day ahead. I had kissed Elizabeth just hours before and I still could feel the excitement of her body, her lips, her hair, the smell of her. It was a spectacular feeling.

But then my thoughts turned to what lay ahead that day. I knew, by Major Brownwell's malicious grin that we were in for some punishing physical exercise that day. I felt that I was still in pretty good shape. I had been running and lifting weights when I was able. At 6'3" and 195 pounds, I knew I was not a pushover. In fact, I was proud of my athletic prowess; I was big, strong and fast.

The balance of the day would be spent in the classroom, learning the intricacies of The Sauce, the "civilian leadership" there as Donovan had termed it, and my role in setting up the invasion. I certainly hadn't known what Luciano had taught me. Of the *dramatis personae* in Sicily, I knew whom to trust and whom not to. At least I thought I did.

Then I had another thought. At the moment of truth, could I kill another man? If someone was aiming a Luger at me with deadly intent, then sure, I would defend myself. But I was now a spy. It may become necessary for me to kill in cold blood. Just because the man on the other of his gun was a German, would that be enough for me to pull the trigger, or thrust the blade, knowing that I would destroy a life. Could I do it? Could I make someone a widow or kill someone's father? I honestly didn't know. I hoped I'd not have to find out, but it seemed to me that I needed to know before I went into The Sauce. Hesitancy could be fatal. And hesitancy could mean that others, later, could pay for my indecision. I had received plenty of instruction in Marine basic training on killing the enemy. But that seemed impersonal. Shooting someone who was shooting at you.

Maybe it was Father's influence. He had always taught me tolerance and the Christian values of love your fellow man, including your enemies. This whole slice-someone's-throat-if-you-needed-to thing was confusing. Father, what would you do in my boots? I thought I knew about Binky or Brownwell or Patton or Donovan. None of them would hesitate.

I just didn't know about an up-close-and personal killing. But I knew I'd better figure it out, and soon.

I had breakfast—eggs today—and made my way over to HQ and the briefing room. I got there five minutes early and there were about a dozen GIs as well as some Brit troops there. I spotted Binky across the way. It was the rainy season and, sure enough, it was coming down in buckets. I had on my foul weather gear as did the grunts who were milling about, awaiting our C.O.

Major Brownwell arrived.

"Hup!" We formed into a semblance of lines and stood to attention.

"Men!" the Major shouted. "This is a joint Company specially formed for a special operation. We will train together, we will learn together and, if necessary, we will die together."

Come on, Major. That seems overly dramatic at 0500 on the first day.

"Each of you draw a rifle and a pack."

"Sargent! Form the men up and double quick it over to the parade ground!"

One Sargeant Smythe began directing us into neat ranks. Once that was accomplished, he led us at a trot to the adjacent field where we would begin our training.

"Raise arms!" Smythe shouted. We raised the rifles over our heads.

Major Brownwell stepped in front of the ranks as we stood with the rifles in two hands over our heads.

"Men, get used to this position because that's how you're going to be, ow, carrying those weapons for the best part of the morning. Now, let's take a little jog."

Smythe began to jog off to the left and we followed, rifles over our heads. We ran through the rain in ponchos, helmets and full packs for the next thirty minutes. After the first five minutes, the rifles began to feel like bags of lead. Arms ached, heads were down, mud splattered. Every third lap, Smythe allowed us to lower the rifles to port arms.

After that torture, we formed up into lines and began to do calisthenics. Starting with jumping jacks, we did leg lifts, up-and-downs, push-ups, and sit-ups. After each pair of exercises, we picked up our rifles, raised them skyward and ran laps. It was deep torture. We were all winded and our muscles screamed. Meanwhile, the rain intensified and the mud deepened so the running became twice as difficult.

When we took a breather, at last, I looked over and saw Binky standing a bit off to the side. He seemed detached as though this were a minor inconvenience to his morning.

That gave me some heart. Actually, it pissed me off. Most of us had our hands on our knees, panting and gasping for breath. Was Binky tougher than I? If he was, he'd never get the satisfaction of knowing it by my actions, by God.

The Major who had been watching from a platform that doubled as a band leader stand, ordered us to divide up in two equal groups. Time for one on one hand-to-hand exercises. Binky and I went to opposite teams. The first two combatants were given panji sticks, wooden staffs with balls of padding on either end. The first opponents were a corporal and a private, both Brits. They beat each other up pretty thoroughly until the private knocked down the corporal and stood over him in triumph.

After a couple of other jousts, Brownwell called out, "Binkford! Pointer! Get in there!"

The exercise reminded me of my football days and the Oklahoma drill. The coach would draw a circle of about ten yards in diameter. There would be a lineman in a 3-point stance, a runner with the ball and a tackler. The idea would be to beat the ever-loving crap out of each other in those close confines.

Binky and I both grasped the sticks, our hands about three feet apart on the staffs. What was this, Robin Hood and Little John?

Binky feinted left and brought the right padded ball with a sweeping hook aimed at my helmet. I ducked a the last second, but about a quarter of it caught me, knocking me off balance. I recovered and lunged at him straight ahead. He blocked my staff with his so that we were locked together momentarily. I still didn't know if I could kill anyone at close quarters, but I'll be damned if I didn't feel like murdering Binky at that moment.

We were evenly matched physically. We weighed about the same, but Binky was shorter and more squat at about 5'10". And powerful. I waited to see if he would lose it like he did the other night, but he seemed to have his wits about him.

Binky got through my defenses and bloodied my lip with a clever thrust. The rain splattered down and washed the blood down my face so that pink rivulets ran down my neck into my uniform.

Time to end this, I thought, or I'll be in trouble. I bull-rushed Binky, whacking him with my left, then my right, using my superior reach. When he was off balance, I swung the stick as hard as I could, connecting with the lower half of his helmet and half with his forehead. Binky went down. I stood over him and felt as though I had just knocked out Heinrich Himmler or somebody.

After a few more jousts, Brownwell called for a chow break. We double quicked over to the mess hall, doffed our panchos and settled down for some good ol' stew. Food never tasted so good, even with my split lip. Feeling good about knocking the snot out of Binky.

The afternoon consisted of a map briefing for the entire squad, focusing on where we would depart and land. That was followed by another long run, with rifles raised straight in the air. Finally, at 1600 hours we were dismissed with a return engagement promised for early the next morning.

I hustled back to the barracks with my rendezvous with Elizabeth on my mind. But first, a nap. When I arrived, I was handed a note by the duty officer. I ripped it open and saw that it was from Colonel Donovan.

"Pointer, you will report to II Corps Headquarters at 1400 hours tomorrow," it read.

"Huh", I thought. That would be just after the fitness part of the training, and before classroom time.

Chapter Twelve

Dowderwell

That evening, Binky, too, had an assignation. He was to meet for the first time his new contact from the conspirator group as Binky thought of them. Their last serious push to eliminate Hitler had been in 1939. From then until recently the fortunes of war had favored the *Fuhrer*. But after serious defeats in the invasion of the Soviet Union, the forces of *Widerstand* led by the *Abwehr's* Canaris and Oster were regaining momentum. This enabled Binky to believe that at least part of his motive was to relieve the world of Hitler instead of exclusively being about defeating the Allies.

The message to Binky had suggested that they meet at one of two places: the same wine bar that he and Pointer had torn up the other night or a restaurant in the center of town. The form of communication was simple, yet effective. Binky was to pass a piece of paper to a goat herder who would be outside the barracks at 5 pm. One if by land, two if by sea. In this case, he was to scrawl the numeral 1 or 2. The number 1 meant the wine bar was preferable, 2 meant the restaurant.

Binky wanted no part of the wine bar, so he had scrawled the number 2, ventured outside at the appointed hour, spied the Arab and handed him the slip of paper after checking the surroundings for prying eyes. The meet was on.

Binky was tired. The training has been exhausting, stressful. He had hated being bested by Pointer. He was in good physical condition, was strong, was a good athlete. He wondered about Pointer. On the one hand, Pointer seemed naïve, part frat boy, part Marine. He seemed to have fallen into this assignment. Binky knew about Pointer's path to his role in conquering The Sauce. Pointer had been given the Luciano interview because the OSS had believed it to be a dead end. But it was now an important part of the strategy for the invasion.

Was that luck, or was it something more? Was there more to Pointer than it first appeared? Binky had learned, from his Eton days through his training at Beaulieu, not to underestimate his fellows. Had he fallen into a trap with Pointer? Binky silently vowed to keep an eye out for his partner cum rival/enemy.

I had my nap, feeling sore but a bit refreshed. No doubt the prospect of seeing Elizabeth produced a bit of adrenaline in my worked-over body. I had spoken to a Captain from Georgia who had been there for a few months and had gotten a couple of ideas about places to go that were in my budget, but would be suitable for a date. The most promising place was a restaurant in the center of town that catered to Brits, Americans and other officers of a foreign stripe. I checked out one of the jeeps and went to pick up Elizabeth.

I bounded up the steps to the Women's Quarters and confronted a very large and very dour Duty Matron.

"Hiawatha!" I said.

Mrs. Balesford, as her name tag read, looked at me with a combination of suspicion and hostility. "Hiawatha?" she repeated with emphasis on each syllable.

"Or is it Sitting Bull tonight?"

The matron looked like she was deciding to either call a medic or an MP.

"The password", I said. "Hiawatha, Sacajawea, Crazy Horse. I know tonight it's an Indian name."

A scowl.

"I'm just playing with you, Mrs. Baleful, I mean Mrs. Balesford. Lieutenant Pointer to see Miss D'Antoni."

Then Elizabeth duly appeared, looking even more ravishing than she had the night before.

"Hi Pointer", she said.

"Hi." I stared at her, forgetting myself for a moment. Gotta stop that, Pointer, I chastised myself.

"Ready to go?" I recovered.

We drove through the evening with the city looking very much as it had last night except that the sky had cleared and it was cool and pleasant tonight. We arrived at the restaurant and ordered the same drinks as we had the night before. No band here though.

"Pointer, how much can you discuss with me about what you're doing here," she asked.

OK, this was a serious start. "Not too much of the substance. But I can tell you that today was on the stressful side. I described the regimen that Smythe had put us through and worked my way up to the joust with Binky.

"Oh, dear. It must be awkward to have to fight with a friend" she said.

"Well, I'm not so sure he's my buddy. I suppose we are comrades in arms and on the same team and all. But there's something about him I can't quite put my finger on that makes me withhold all of the old Pointer munificence."

"And do you withhold your munificence from me?"

"What do you think?"

"Well, I'm not sure yet. We'll see. Pointer, is what you're doing here dangerous?"

I thought for a moment. I could simply deny that there were any perils in my assignment or I could be more truthful. I decided that I liked Elizabeth too much just to slough off her question.

"There's some danger, yes, as there is in any wartime assignment. Is it more dangerous than the men who have to face Rommel's tanks? I don't know. It's a war, y'know?"

She reached across the table and took my hand. "Pointer, I've become quite fond of you in a very short while, and I don't want to see anything happen to you."

How many conversations between a man and a woman like this had transpired over the last few years? Millions? The whole world was at war. Everyone trying to kill everyone else. If the Nazis didn't get you, then the Italians might. And that didn't include any grumpy Sicilian Mafia Dons.

"I appreciate that, darling." We both noted the inclusion of the 'g'. "The way I see it, your being here gives me that much more incentive to come back in one piece. Besides, what I'm doing is not *that* dangerous."

She looked at me skeptically.

But before she could reply, we both noticed one Leftenant Binkford enter the restaurant and begin consulting with the *Maitre d'*.

"Isn't that..?" Elizabeth began.

Binky was led across the room to a
table at which sat a British Army
officer. As he walked through the
restaurant, Binky's eyes seemed to
dart around, taking in his surroundings.
When he reached his table, he
appeared to spot us. He literally did a
double-take as he looked first at us,
then at his companion and then back
at us. Something told me that Binky
was not only surprised to see us, but
also not pleased.

Binky didn't seem to know what to do
first. Greet the officer or acknowledge
us. I made the decision for him by
giving him a little wave as if to say,
"Think nothing of it, old boy. Happens
all the time." Binky waved back and
turned to greet his friend.

"Thomas! I had no earthly idea..." Binky
stammered.

"Yes, Binky, sorry for the start, but I
only recently arrived at my new
posting. I've joined the Army, as you
see." Binky had not seen Dowderwell
since their meeting in London three
years before. They had corresponded

for a time and then the letters had stopped coming. Binky had received the occasional coded letter from a correspondent somewhere in Germany. Most of the substance had been to advise him to keep vigilant, keep the faith...when we need you we will contact you.

Dowderwell continued, "I believe in the concept of hiding in plain sight. Since we know each other and are known to know each other, what could be more natural than two old chums dining? How are you, Binky?"

"Why the cloak and dagger with the note and the Arab?"

"To establish a practice, old sport. We may need our code someday."

Across the room, Elizabeth's attention had returned to Pointer. She stared at him for a moment, then said, "Pointer, I know that what you are doing happens to be extremely dangerous. I know that the Sicilians can only be trusted insofar as their self-interest will allow. And I know that you will be entering a strange and new country undercover. I'm sorry, but I do know."

Pointer stared at her in disbelief. "You know? But how?"

"Actually, I too work for Colonel Donovan. The Red Cross is my cover. Wild Bill isn't the Chief for nothing. He sensed that you and I were headed for a personal relationship and called me in. We discussed the viability of such a pairing. At first, he told me that I was to have nothing to do with you on a personal level. I was to call you today and break our date, and not accept any future dates with you. I didn't know what to do, what to say to him." Were those tears forming in her eyes?

"But you're here."

"Yes, I'm here. As we talked it through, I told him that I could help you. I could be your steady contact back here alongside Brownwell. I speak Italian, I know a lot about Sicily, about Italy. Donovan was still skeptical because he sees that it is already personal with us. But as we talked it through, he began to appreciate the positive side of the argument. He can't stay here much longer and he needs a trusted liaison to feed him information in his absence. Brownwell can do it from a military, operational perspective. I do it from a...different perspective. Part operational, part political. You know, spy stuff."

"But why didn't you guys let me in on it from the start? We're all on the same team here."

"You know how Donovan likes to work. He likes compartmentalization. He believes that he gets better intelligence if his subordinates are reporting to him completely independently of each other." She paused. "Pointer, I hope you're not angry at me. I couldn't say anything, I know you understand that. But this morning after my meeting with the Colonel, I got the green light. You'll have to forgive me for not blurting it out right away. But I wanted to see how you answered my questions about the dangers of, uh, The Sauce. I worry about you...dear Pointer."

"And what else are you keeping from me?"

"Not a thing that has anything to do with our current circumstances. Nothing personal, nothing business," she replied. "I will say this. Donovan may be correct in his first instinct that it's best not to mix business with pleasure. Can I make decisions that are not clouded by my feelings for you? Can you?"

I thought about that. "I'm betting that it won't come to that. Donovan's betting on it too. We all know that the OSS is still new and that we're building our capabilities, and experienced agents are hard to come by. Wild Bill can't afford to move us out of our current responsibilities just now. He has to take some chances."

The waiter came by and I ordered a double Scotch.

Binky and Thomas were also drinking Scotch.

"Have you heard from Freddy?" Binky asked.

"Yes. From and about him. He is now working under Himmler with some significant responsibilities for the Jewish Question. It puts one of us in a nice position to keep an eye on the SS. Since the defeat at Moscow, our boys inside are gaining new support for the elimination of Lightning." Binky knew that was the conspirators' code word for Hitler.

"Still operating under the philosophy of 'cut off the head and the snake will die'?"

"Yes. Things have gotten too far for there to be any other solution. The Army officers swore an oath to him and they take that deadly seriously as one example. And you know the rest. With Lightning alive, we'll always have to contend with Goring, Himmler and his SS thugs."

Thomas sipped his Scotch. "I asked to meet with you to both convey information and to receive some. As

161

you know, our friends want more than ever to win. Their concept is to retain territory already gained, win as much new ground as they can, eliminate Lightning, and sue for peace under a new regime. Roosevelt seriously gummed up the works by coming out of the Casablanca Conference with Churchill and Stalin and declaring that only unconditional surrender would be acceptable. Our friends wish to retain their gains. There are many who believe that in a post-Lightning world that peace with honor is still possible. But that with Lightning at the head, the Allies will never accept anything except unconditional surrender. All the more reason to eliminate him."

He continued, "Now that it appears that the fall of the Soviets is no longer a foregone conclusion, and that war will drag on for perhaps years, our friends cannot afford to lose more ground or they will begin to lose their leverage for an honorable peace. Which brings me to the question of Sicily."

Ah, The Sauce, Binky thought.

"How shall I put this," Thomas continued. "Sicily's strategic importance is far out of proportion to its size and population. One cannot control Italy, for example, with an enemy force stationed in the middle of the Mediterranean literally at the back door. One cannot control shipping in the Med without controlling Sicily. And Germany cannot afford to lose Italy because it is the back door to the Fatherland."

"And that's one large reason that you, dear boy, have become so important to our movement," Thomas looked straight at Binky.

Binky knew what was coming. Up to this point he had not actually betrayed any real military secrets, so, technically, he had not yet entered treasonous territory. Several notorious spies throughout history flashed through his mind with one major image settling in: a hangman's noose. How much did he really love Germany and their cause? Was he willing to give his life for it? It all seemed rather abstract at the moment. All except that noose.

"Our friends would like to know what you know about plans for North Africa and for Sicily and beyond," Thomas said, and there it was.

"As for North Africa, I am in no position to know the plans. But as to Sicily, I know quite a lot. And am destined to know even more. There will be a pre-invasion force—a very small one—that will penetrate the island and make contact with the local leaders for the purposes of sabotage. I will be among that group." Binky began to tell all he knew, including the landing site and invasion routes of the Armies as he knew them to be at that point.

"I suppose the Germans will want to ambush my force and nip the entire plan in the bud. We will get very short notice as to the date of the commencement of our mission, but I imagine it will be at least 24 hours. I'm sure I could pass the word in enough time," he posited.

"But you say that your initial foray will be weeks in advance of the real invasion?" Thomas asked.

"Correct. We want to give the Mafia leaders time to prepare. My American counterpart, Lieutenant Pointer, even has letters and intelligence from a noted American mobster to help us out."

"Knowing how our friends think, they may very well let you make your arrangements so long as we know what those plans are. The big trap can be sprung when the real invasion comes. That would be my guess as to how it will unfold."

Binky felt a bit of relief that his initial push onto The Sauce would not be met by an ambush as he thought might be the case.

"Yes," Binky said. He tried not to let his relief show. "Yes, I see the wisdom in that. Let the first mouse go free so he brings back his big brother."

"Tell me about Colonel Donovan and also this Pointer chap," Thomas asked.

"I met Colonel Donovan at a dinner that General Patton gave at II Corps Headquarters."

"You met Patton?" Thomas was astonished. "You know that our friends fear him far more than any other General—Brit or American. They fear that Eisenhower will appoint him to lead the eventual invasion into northern France. How did he seem?"

"Very like his reputation. It was a dinner party, not a war council, but one could not escape that he is all about war, devastation of his enemies and killing—even in a social setting. As for Donovan, he seems to know what he is about. He personally conducted much of the initial briefing on our Sicily mission."

Dowderwell could not let go of the Patton subject. "Tell me he wore his pistols to dinner! Did he keep his helmet on?"

"No, old boy, he didn't go that far. But one sees him careening about in his staff car, sirens blaring, insignia front and center and women, children and goats get out of the way."

"Hmm. I wonder if our friends will want to arrange a special, personal surprise for the General when he reaches Sicily. Do you suppose, Binky, that you will be privy to his whereabouts there?"

"No idea, Thomas. We are to be reinserted along with the invasion and are to reestablish contact with the locals. I am more likely to be along Monty's route than Patton's."

"Yes, we'll have to arrange good communications between you and your German contacts."

Pointer looked across the room and noticed that Binky and his friend were in deep conversation.

"Would you happen to know, Elizabeth, why Donovan wants to see me tomorrow afternoon? Must be something important for him to interrupt my training."

"Yes, I do know something about it, and the Colonel has authorized me to speak to you on the subject. We will be meeting with Dr. Mark Hopkins, a European history scholar from Princeton. Dr. Hopkins has been recruited by the OSS to focus on the question of Jews and their treatment by the Third Reich. His base of operations will be out of II Corps for now. As the Allies advance into the Continent, he'll probably stay with them so that he will retain access to Army assets as he needs them."

"The Jewish Question?"

"Yes, we are learning more and more about the Nazis' plans and treatment of the Jews in all of their conquered territories. Frankly, it is difficult to believe some of the atrocities that are being committed. But they seem to be getting bigger and worse by the day. It appears that things are escalating from round-ups and deportation to something even worse. What is being called the Nazis' Final Solution."

"That sounds ominous," I commented.

"It *is* ominous," Elizabeth said. "There was a conference last year on the subject at a place called Wannsee, a suburb of Berlin. It included most of the heads of *Reich* Government Departments. It was an important Conference in that all of these Government departments were co-opted into the overall plan. They will never be able to claim that they were ignorant of the *Reich's* policy on Jews. We know that Hitler and Himmler really call the shots on the policy toward Jews. Perhaps the most important figure at the meeting was Himmler's personal representative, a fellow named Friedrich von Furstenberger."

At that moment, Binky asked Thomas, "Tell me. How much does Freddy know about yours and my dealings? How involved will he be in our plans for Sicily and beyond?"

"I am not certain about that, but I suspect that he is not involved day to day since his transfer to Himmler's staff. He is in an extremely dangerous situation there and must keep a very low profile with respect to the plot against Lightning. I can tell you that our main control in Berlin is Colonel Oster of the *Abwehr*. But dear Freddy is no longer under the direct protection of Oster and his group." Dowderwell said all of this with a lowered voice.

I excused myself to go to the restroom. On my way, I decided to be social with Binky so I stopped by their table. They were still in deep discussion.

"Evening Binky!" I almost shouted above the din in the room. The restaurant was now completely full.

Binky jumped. I swear his ass lifted three inches off his chair.

"Pointer. Gave me a start, old boy," Binky was recovering quickly. "Yes. Right. May I present my friend Thomas Dowderwell. Thomas, this is Lieutenant Pointer whom I told you about."

Both men stood and we shook hands all around.

"Thomas and I were old school chums all the way back to Eton. Just heard today that he was in-country." Binky seemed nervous.

"My pleasure, Captain," I said. And how have you found things here thus far?" And don't tell me you used a map, I thought. That's *my* line.

"Oh, a bit confusing, but Binky here is showing me the ropes. Grateful for that, quite lucky, really."

"Well, if we Yanks can help you out in any way, I hope you'll ask." Back to the old Pointer munificence.

To make conversation, Binky said, "We've ordered the Bananas Foster for dessert. Thomas' grandfather invented it, you see."

"Oh?" I said. "Was he Bananas or Foster?"

Binky just looked at me.

Dowderwell said, "That's a lovely companion you have with you this evening. Special friend?"

Something told me not to share. "Oh, we're just getting acquainted," I said. "Well, Binky, don't stay up too late. I want you fit for tomorrow in case we have a re-match," I gave him the old wicked Pointer grin.

Binky just smirked.

When I got back to our table, I said to my dinner companion who was, indeed, lovely, "Where do you and I fit in with this Dr. Hopkins?"

"The President has asked Wild Bill to develop as much intel as he can on the subject of persecution of the Jews and to help develop a plan of response. Dr. Hopkins is leading the effort. Our role is to assist in any way we can. Obviously, you have a full plate, but while Donovan is here, he wants to make sure that you hear about it first-hand. As for me, assisting Dr. Hopkins will be my first priority."

"And where, Elizabeth, am I on your list of priorities?" Wicked smile again.

"Pointer, you are a master of the *non sequitur.* But I have been thinking about that. One of these days, we're going to get some leave. I think that I will be able to fix it so that it's at the same time. I have heard about this little town on the coast that used to accommodate Italian tourists and is now under Allied control. Some of our officers have been known to take their R&R there. I hear that it's still lovely. And romantic."

"Is that an invitation?" I smiled again, but not my wicked version. Probably my lascivious version.

"Yes, Pointer," she said. "That's an invitation."

April 15, 1943

Dear Pointer,

Meyer got in touch with the autorities and got certain insurances that this letter would get to you without too much sensership. You let me know if they held up there end of the bargin for I will be miffled if they don't.

Things here at Great Meadow are fine if you got to be in jail. Betillo is still doing the pasta and poring the vino. I guess it could be worser. I been thinking about you Pointer. Ive give you important and _personal_ information about whats going on in XXXXX. Don't XXXX it up you hear. These people are my blood. They will do what you say if you tell them that I said so. I say again. Don't XXXX it up.

Now the real reason for this letter is to tell you to tell the government that I am a patriotec guy. I have sacrifised myself for this Crowt war and I deserve some concideration for what I done. I aint asking for a medle. I aint asking for FDR or whoever to come see me. I aint

*asking for the fist lady to give me roses.
But I want concideration for my part. I
got 30 more years in this joint and yeah
I like my food and certin visitors but I
deserve to be on the outside. And I
don't mean outside the country
neither. I mean back in new york. You
tell your friends that, capiche. I saved
the docks when they needed saving. I
called off the unions when they needed
to be called off. I gave you anything
you want to know. Give me a XXXXXX
brake.*

*Anyhow I hope you are doing ok
wherever you are. I am fine,*

Your pal,

XXXXX XXXXXXX

April 17, 1943

My Dear Robert,

*Mother and I are fine. She and your
sister join me in sending our love and
best wishes for your safety.*

In my last letter to you I mentioned that I was going to go 'round to see the Gaskins boy. I have done this and found him at home. He was in a bad state. He was morose and, it's safe to say, bitter against circumstances in general and our Government in particular. I cannot say that I blame him. He lives at home with little or nothing to keep him occupied.

It seems that he approached the local Draft Board on his own. I wish to the Almighty he had let me represent him. Perhaps I should have followed up with him sooner. At any rate, he was at the very least impolitic with the authorities. Apparently, he demanded to be accepted in a role that would allow him to be on the front lines in a combat position. The Board explained to him that the Army is not set up for integration and that he could join but that he would be likely assigned to be a cook or a laborer or some similar function.

According to young Gaskins, he lost his temper and tried to assault the

Sergeant at the Board. He was subdued, but the local police were called and he spent two weeks in jail. The Army is deciding whether or not to press charges, but Gaskins' military career is over before it started. I will, of course, represent him should there be further legal action.

The irony of this, dear Robert, will not be lost on you. Most of our young men have readily signed up for duty. Blacks and whites are doing their part and the country seems united behind the war effort. But this cursed Jim Crow sentiment! More than sentiment— there are laws that we are supposed to follow that keep the Negro forever in a place that is inferior. We fought the bloodiest war in American history over the right to enslave another race. And we lost! It is now 75 years later and I cannot be proud of the progress we have made in race matters. In fact, I am deeply embarrassed.

Speaking of minorities, do you remember Rabbi Smith? He attended one of our Sunday evening soirees several years ago that your mother jestingly calls the Pointer Salon. I ran into him the other day at The Dixie. We had a cup of coffee together and had an opportunity to catch up. As always, the talk turned to the war. Rabbi Smith and the Jewish community here—small though they may be—are deeply concerned about the plight of the European Jews. There are loud rumors here of a burgeoning persecution campaign. There is talk of murder, which we know for certain has happened. But this talk is of murder of Jews on a large scale. No one knows for certain how large.

The Rabbi is joining with other American Jewish leaders in an effort to lobby the Congress and the President to at least acknowledge the problem. And to do something about it. They believe that it is far too easy for our elected officials to say, "Well, we are fighting a world war. What more do you want us to do?" Rabbi Smith and others believe that a human rights campaign needs to be mounted to put a spotlight on what the Nazis are doing to the Jews of Europe.

So, dear son, it seems that our military forces are not the only ones fighting battles. There are wars over minority issues and rights here at home as well.

Your mother asked me to ask you—again—about romantic opportunities over there. I have tried to explain to her that 99% of the people you come into contact with are soldiers, all of whom are male. She simply will not accept that. Please write and put that misconception to rest once and for all.

Please, Robert, look out for yourself and return to us safely.

As Ever,

Your Loving Father,

Robert Pointer

Chapter Thirteen

The Shoah

Binky rose before dawn to get ready for Day II of training for The Sauce. His heart was deeply troubled over the events of the previous evening. He wondered for the thousandth time whether he was doing the right thing. The Soviet victories of the past few months had made him wonder whether he had chosen the winning side in this war. On top of that were these damned Yanks. People like Patton, Donovan and Pointer seemed so sure of themselves. They seemed so blasted positive, so can-do. Binky believed that the Germans had every reason to fear Patton. The man seemed to be a killing machine, and, worse, he seemed to inspire everyone around him to kill, kill, kill. The Italians couldn't be counted on; the Japanese—who knew? It seemed to be Germany against the world. If Freddy and his friends were successful in assassinating Hitler, then maybe, just maybe peace with honor could be won.

But Freddy was serving under Himmler now, the conspirators' deadliest enemy outside of Lightning himself.

Stop it, Binky, he told the voice in his head. Hadn't Germany conquered all of her neighbors? Didn't we still occupy France? Aren't we in control in Italy, Africa, Greece and Turkey? We are still at Moscow's front door. And who knows, maybe the *Reich* will decide to invade Britain after all. Before the Allies invade France. Binky noticed not for the first time that the voice in his head said "we" when referring to the Germans.

After chow, Binky headed to the Parade Grounds for fitness training. He spied Pointer before he could be spotted. Look at him. Typical American frat boy jock. So cocky. Well, maybe Binky would have the opportunity to wipe that superior smile off Pointer's face before this was all over.

"Morning Leftenant. You and your pal have a pleasant evening?" Pointer seemed unusually cheerful.

"Yes. It was nice to catch up."

"Come on, ladies! Time to put away your make-up cases!" It was Smythe.

The squad formed up and began a long morning of grueling exercise.

After mess at 1200 hours, the squad repaired to the briefing room while I reported to a different room to meet with Donovan and crew.

Elizabeth and I arrived at the same time. I knocked and was told to enter. Wild Bill was seated at a conference table with another gentleman whom I assumed was Dr. Hopkins. Both men stood as we entered.

"Pointer, this is Dr. Mark Hopkins. Hopkins, Lieutenant Pointer. I know you already have met Miss D'Antoni," Donovan started.

We shook hands and Dr. Hopkins said, "Call me Mark. May I call you Pointer?"

"Of course. Everyone else does", I said.

"So I've been told," he replied. "And Miss D'Antoni, if I may have the privilege of calling you Elizabeth? Everyone calls me Mark."

"Of course, Mark."

"Well, that's settled," said Donovan. "Let's get to work."

As the Colonel began, I studied Hopkins. He was fortyish, wore tortoise shell glasses and what looked like the beginning—or was it the end—of a beard. Withal, he appeared boyish with dark, unkempt hair. He wore a tweed three-piece suit and a rep tie. He had a lean, muscular physique and looked like he could hold his own out there on the jousting field. Not what Rabbi Smith would call a *nebbish.*

"Hopkins has compiled a timeline of significant events surrounding the Jewish Question, which I think you'll find interesting and compelling. Hopkins?"

"Thank you, sir. Yes, the *Shoah* as it is known to the Jews, has been underway for many years. In fact, anti-Semitism in Europe is as old as history itself. But, of course, since Hitler came to power in '33, it has slowly but steadily become institutionalized and in recent years has turned more and more deadly to millions of people in and around Germany. Moreover, we now have evidence that Hitler not only wants to wipe out the Jews of Germany, Poland and other States that he has subdued, but his ambitions go far beyond that. He already has murdered huge numbers in the Soviet Union, but countries like England, Ireland and all of Scandinavia are in his sights."

"I'll give you a few moments to study this timeline," he said, handing us each a document marked "Classified".

A Timeline of Nazi Activities and Atrocities Against Jews, 1933-1942

*Denotes low to moderate level of certitude

1933

January-Hitler appointed Chancellor of Germany. Jewish pop. 566,000

February-40,000 SA and SS men sworn in as auxiliary police

February-Hitler granted emergency powers

March-Dachau (Munich); Buchenwald (Weimar); Sachsenhausen (Berlin); Ravensbruck (for women) Concentration Camps open

March-German Parliament passes Enabling Act giving Hitler dictatorial powers

April-Nazis stage boycott of Jewish businesses

April-Nazis decree definition of a non-Aryan as "anyone descended from non-Aryan, especially Jewish parents or grandparents. One parent or grandparent classifies the descendant as non-Aryan especially if one parent or grandparent was of the Jewish faith."

April-Hermann Goring creates the Gestapo

July-Nazis pass law to strip Jewish immigrants from Poland of their German citizenship

July-Nazis pass law allowing for forced sterilization of those found by a Hereditary Health Court to have genetic defects

September-Nazis establish Reich Chamber of Culture and exclude Jews from the Arts

September-Nazis prohibit Jews from owning land

September-Jews are prohibited from the position of Newspaper Editor

"Lord," I said aloud. "Those bastards moved fast, didn't they?"

Hopkins replied, "The Germans are not known for their efficiency for nothing. But they'd waited a long time to implement these policies."

"Shhh. I'm concentrating," Elizabeth said.

1934

January-Jews are banned from the German Labor Front

May-Jews are not allowed national health insurance

July-Jews are prohibited from getting legal qualifications

August-von Hindenburg dies, Hitler becomes Fuhrer

1935

May-Jews banned from serving in military

August-Nazis force Jewish actors/performers to join Jewish Cultural Unions

September-Nuremberg Race Laws against Jews decreed

1936

March-SS Deathshead Division established to guard concentration camps

June-Himmler appointed chief of German Police

1937

January-Jews banned from certain occupations such as teaching Germans or being accountants or dentists. Also denied tax deductions and child allowances

1938

March-Nazi troops enter Austria. Jewish pop. 200,000

March-SS placed in charge of Jewish affairs in Austria. Adolf Eichmann establishes Office for Jewish Emigration in Vienna

March-Himmler establishes Maulthausen concentration camp near Linz, Austria

April-Nazis prevent Aryan "front ownership" of Jewish businesses

April-Nazis order Jews to register wealth and property

June-Nazis order Jewish businesses to register

July-In Evian, France, U.S. convenes a League of Nations conference to aid Jews fleeing Hitler. No action ensues as no country will accept them

July-Jews prohibited from trade and many specified commercial services

July-Jews over age 15 ordered to apply for identity cards from police

July-Jewish doctors prohibited from practicing

August-Nazis destroy synagogue at Nuremburg

August-Jewish women required to add "Sarah" and men to add "Israel" to their names on all legal documents, including passports

September-Jews prohibited from all legal practices

October-all Jewish passports must be stamped with large red letter "J"

October-Nazis arrest 17,000 Jews of Polish nationality living in Germany, expelling them back to Poland. Poland refuses them, leaving them in no-man's-land for several months

November-*Krystallnacht*

November-Jewish pupils expelled from all non-Jewish schools

December-Goring takes charge of the Jewish Question

1939

February-Jews forced to hand over all gold and silver items

March-Nazis seize Czechoslovakia. Jewish pop. 350,000

April-Slovakia passes own version of Nuremburg Laws

"So, they want to wipe out all European Jews? I asked Hopkins.

"Clearly," he said. "Including England and Ireland if they get the chance."

April-Jews lose rights as tenants and are forced to move to Jewish houses

May-The *Saint Louis,* a ship with 930 Jews is turned away from Cuba, the U.S. and other countries and returns to Europe

July-German Jews denied right to hold Government jobs

July-Eichmann appointed director of Prague Office of Emigration

September-Nazis invade Poland. Jewish pop 3.35 million

September-Jews in Germany forbidden to be outdoors after 8 in winter, 9 in summer

September-Polish Jews are to be resettled in ghettoes near rail centers for future "final goal". Establishment of

Jewish councils to carry out Nazi
policies and decrees

September-German Jews forbidden to
own radios

"Radios," I said. "Radios? I suppose it's
their only form of communication with
the outside world."

"Right", said Hopkins.

"Shhh", said Elizabeth.

September-Nazi newspaper, *Der
Sturmer,* publishes statement, "The
Jewish people ought to be
exterminated root and branch. Then
the plague of pests would have
disappeared from Poland at one
stroke"

October-Nazis begin euthanasia on sick
and disabled in Germany

October-evacuation of Jews from
Vienna

October-Forced Labor Decree issued for Polish Jews aged 14-60

November-yellow stars required to be worn by all Polish Jews age 10 and over

December-Eichmann takes over section of Gestapo dealing solely with Jewish affairs and evacuations

1940

January-Nazis select Auschwitz in Poland for new concentration camp

January-*Der Sturmer* opines, "The time is near when a machine will go into motion which is going to prepare a grave for the world's criminal-Judah-from which there will be no resurrection"

February-first deportation of Jews into occupied Poland

April-Nazis invade Denmark (Jewish pop 8000) and Norway (Jewish pop 2000)

April-the Lodz Ghetto in Poland is sealed off from the outside world with 230,000 Jews locked inside

May-Rudolf Hess chosen as kommandandt of Auschwitz

May-Nazis invade France (Jewish pop 350,000), Belgium (Jewish pop 65,000), Holland (Jewish pop 40,000) and Luxembourg (Jewish pop 3500)

July-Eichmann's Madagascar Plan presented, proposing to deport all European Jews to Madagascar off the coast of east Africa

August-Romania introduces anti-Jewish measures restricting education and employment. Later begins Romanization of Jewish businesses

October-Vichy France passes its version of Nuremburg Laws

October-Nazis invade Romania (Jewish pop 34,000)

October-deportation of 34,000 Jews from Baden, the Saar, and Alsace – Lorraine into Vichy France

November-Krakow Ghetto sealed off containing 70,000 Jews

November-Warsaw Ghetto sealed off containing 400,000 Jews

1941

January-*Der Sturmer* quote, "Now judgment has begun and it will reach its conclusion only when knowledge of the Jews has been erased from the earth"

January-Pogrom in Romania results in over 2000 Jewish deaths

February-430 Jewish hostages deported from Amsterdam after a Dutch Nazi is killed by Jews

March-Himmler visits Auschwitz and orders Hess to begin massive expansion to be built at nearby Birkenau to hold 100,000 more prisoners

March-Nazis occupy Bulgaria (Jewish pop 50,000)

March-German Jews ordered into forced labor

March-German High Army Command orders creation of SS Murder Squads in Poland

April-Nazis invade Yugoslavia (Jewish pop 75,000) and Greece (Jewish pop 77,000)

May-3600 Jews arrested in Paris

June-Nazis invade Russia (Jewish pop 3 million)

June-Romanian troops conduct Pogrom in Jassy killing 10,000

July-in Berlin, Himmler informs Hess of Hitler's order for the Final Solution and tells Hess that Auschwitz has been chosen for this purpose*

July-SS troops follow German advances into Russia, conducting mass murders of Jews in seized lands

July-Ghettos established in Kovno, Minsk, Vitebsk, and Zhitomer

July-Majdanek concentration camp in Poland becomes operational

July-3800 Jews killed in pogrom by Lithuanians near Kovno

August-Jews in Romania forced into Transnistria. (By December 70,000* perish)

August-Ghettos established in Bialystok and Lvov

September-the first test use of Zyklon B gas* at Auschwitz

September-German Jews ordered to wear yellow stars

September-first general deportation of German Jews begins

September-Vilna Ghetto established containing 40,000 Jews

"How much do we know about this new gas," I asked.

"Only that it's lethal in the extreme. If you really want to know the chemical compounds, I can oblige," said Hopkins.

"No. that's fine."

September-SS troops trailing the Army murder 33,771* Jews near Kiev

September-23,000 Jews killed at Kamenets-Podolsk

October-35,000 Jews shot at Odessa

October-Jews forbidden emigration from the Reich

November-trailing SS troops report another 45,476 Jews killed

November-Thereisenstadt Ghetto established in Prague. Nazis to use it for propaganda

November-mass shooting of Latvian and German Jews

November-Chelmno extermination camp near Lodz, Poland, becomes operational. Jews there are taken to burial grounds in mobile gas vans as carbon dioxide from the exhaust is funneled into the rear compartment, killing them

December-the ship *Struma* sails for Palestine with 769 Jews on board. British authorities deny entrance. *Struma* sails back to Black Sea where it is sunk by a Russian U Boat

1942

January-mass murder of Jews using Zyklon B* begin at Auschwitz in Bunker I. Bodies are buried in mass graves in nearby meadow

January-Wannsee Conference to coordinate The Final Solution

January-SS troops report tally of 229,052* Jews killed by them

March-Belzec extermination camp in Poland becomes operational. It is fitted with permanent gas chambers which use CO_2 piped in from diesel engines

March- mass deportations of Slovak
and French Jews to Auschwitz begin

April-German Jews banned from using
public transportation

May-Sobibor extermination camp in
Poland becomes operational

May-*New York Times,* on interior
pages, reports that Nazis have
machine-gunned over 100,000 Jews in
Baltic States, 100,000 in Poland and
twice as many in western Russia

June-gas vans in Riga used

June-Eichmann meets with
representatives from France, Belgium
and Holland to coordinate deportation
plans

June-at Auschwitz a second gas
chamber, Bunker II, is opened to keep
up with huge demand

July-*New York Times* reports that over
1 million Jews have been killed by Nazis

July-Swiss representatives of the World Jewish Congress receive info from a German industrialist regarding plans for the Final Solution. They pass the info to Washington and London

July-Himmler grants permission for sterilization experiments at Auschwitz

"Does this Himmler know no bounds? Is he actually human?" I asked.

July-beginning of Dutch deportation of Jews

July-12,800 Jews of Paris are rounded up for deportation to Auschwitz, Majdenek and Sobibor

July-Himmler orders Operation Reinhard, mass deportation of Polish Jews

July-Treblinka extermination camp opens. It is fitted with 10 gas chambers, holding 200 persons each

September-open pit burning of bodies begins at Auschwitz to prevent buried bodies from fouling ground water

September-food ration restrictions for German Jews begins

"Food restrictions. Sure. They're not human anyway, right? Wouldn't treat a dog like this," I muttered.

October-Himmler orders all Jews in concentration camps in Germany to be sent to Auschwitz or Majdenek

During my reading of this hideous document, I would occasionally glance at Elizabeth. Her concentration seemed total and I never caught her eye. Donovan and Hopkins seemed lost in thought as we read.

When I finally finished, I saw that Elizabeth was waiting for me to catch up. For the first in memory, I was speechless; I could think of nothing to say. I just stared dumbly at the others, and they back at me.

"You want a glass of water, Pointer? Elizabeth?" Donovan asked.

I nodded, and the Colonel rang a bell and a steward appeared with a pitcher and glasses.

As I swallowed my first gulp, Elizabeth asked, "Why? Why would Hitler want to slaughter an entire race of people? And what can we do?"

"Two huge questions. Hopkins has been assigned to the OSS to find those answers," Donovan replied. "We *are* fighting an all-out war against these people. And if we needed more incentive, this would certainly provide it. The President has seen this document and is thinking about how to deal with it politically. Our job is to advise on military options."

I finally found my voice. "Why haven't we heard about this?"

"Well, we have heard about some of it. You noted the two *Times* articles in the timeline. One theory is that the public has been overwhelmed with this war and all of the information and concern it has generated. We know that we are fully engaged, and our national concern is naturally about us, not what's happening in a far off land. After all, a report of the murder of hundreds of thousands of people doesn't even make the front page," Hopkins theorized. "Beyond that, the Nazis have been pretty effective about keeping a lid on it."

"In December, British Foreign Minister Eden noted to the House of Commons that Hitler was pursuing a policy of extermination of European Jews and our State Department vowed revenge."

"But what about those ships that were turned away?" Elizabeth asked. "Is that anti-Semitism? What if they were shiploads of Presbyterians?"

Donovan took this one. "Anti-Semitism in the U.S. is certainly a possibility. The people responsible for denying safe harbor, of course, did not admit to that. Their reasoning had more to do with the exigencies of war. We were not prepared to accommodate them, we had our hands full, we were not willing to take on someone else's problems."

"It will be left to history not only to judge the Nazis, but also to judge the rest of the world in our responses," Hopkins said.

"History will indeed judge us," Donovan said. "And since we are playing a part in history, I intend for us to do everything in our power to end these atrocities sooner rather than later. We've got a hell of a lot of catching up to do, but the President has put this right at the top of the OSS' priority list."

"But before we get into formulating our options, I think it wise to answer as best we can why Hitler and his goons would want to do this. We also need to understand something about Himmler, Goring, Eichmann, Heydrich and other SS leaders who are involved. That is why we have brought in Dr. Hopkins."

I interrupted. "What's so striking to me is that when you sit down and read the timeline from '33 on, the Nazis did not make a secret of their intentions. They did it within the German judicial system, legalizing anything they damned well felt like doing to Jews. The whole German population went along with it. And the Jews themselves. Why haven't they done anything? Like leave the country!"

"They have attempted flight as we've seen in the two ships that were rejected. There are some underground railroads, not unlike with the slaves in the American Civil War. There have been heroic efforts, but the Germans are unbelievably efficient in carrying out their policies against the Jews. The German people, it must be said, *are* complicit. One has to conclude that they want this, this marginalization of Jews," said Hopkins.

"Marginalization?" I said. "How about mass murder? They're efficient, are they? They're brutal murderers, godamnit."

"No one here would argue with you, Pointer," said Donovan. "We don't have the luxury of getting emotional."

"Bullshit", I said. "When you try to exterminate a race, it tends to get emotional. If you're not going to get emotional about that, when are you going to get emotional?"

Donovan said, "I think we should take a break." He arose and left the room. Hopkins followed.

Elizabeth and I were left alone. She came over to where I was sitting, pulled a chair next to me and hugged me around the neck.

"Darling, I know how you feel. I feel the same way."

I took a deep breath, found my maturity and replied, "I know, Elizabeth. It's a shock to the system. A religion being turned into a race in the eyes of the Nazis. And—what— genocide, nationalized genocide, being perpetrated against them."

"Is Donovan nuts?" I continued. "Filling my head with this, on top of my other, more immediate mission?"

"I'm sure he has an overarching plan. He always does."

"Yeah, well, if he wanted me to head north and crack Himmler in the head personally, mission accomplished. On the other hand, if he wants me in The Sauce..." I couldn't finish the thought.

"Pointer, I think that Himmler and his crowd are perhaps in your future. And while he's here, Donovan wants to brief you himself."

"What did *you* think, Elizabeth?"

"Of the document? I was horrified. Most of what shocked me was what's going on. But some of it is that it's been going on right under our noses. I wonder, though, what we could have been doing? I also wonder about our Government. Have we done everything we could?"

"It's hard to control the world, y'know? Much as we want to make everything right everywhere, we can't. We're just one country." I was now taking the other side. "We're just people. Hitler is just a man, Himmler is just a man. If we are lucky, we get put into extraordinary places where we're able to do good against evil. Hitler's way ahead of us on the evil balance of the scales. We—and I mean the Allied 'we'—are going to have to catch up. I suppose Hitler is grateful for his chance to do evil."

Donovan and Hopkins reentered the room.

"Shall we proceed?" Donovan said. He looked at Hopkins.

"Yes. Right," said Mark. "As I was about to say, Hitler and his views on Jews were not produced in a vacuum. Far from it. I defy you to name a single group, association of groups or press or any institution throughout Europe who has declared solidarity with the Jews. There are none. Whether out of fear, apathy or agreement, for the past ten years there is no one in Europe—and precious few outside—who have stood up and said, 'This is wrong.'"

"But of course the seeds were planted long ago," Hopkins continued. "The second half of the last Century and the first part of this one produced the emergence of a movement called

Volkish which produced a form of racism that views Jews as a race locked in mortal combat with the Aryan race for world domination. Notice I said that *Volkish* views Jews as a race, not a religion. It's like Catholics being seen as a race. In speeches in the *Reichstag* back in 1895 Jews were being called 'predators' and 'cholera bacilli' who should be 'exterminated'. There were *Volkish* leaders like Heinrich Class who urged that all Jews be stripped of their German citizenship, forbidden to own land, hold public office, or participate in banking, journalism, or other businesses. Sound familiar?"

"How widely was this accepted in Germany?" Elizabeth asked.

"After the German Empire was proclaimed in 1871, these notions were broadly accepted, especially within the educated classes. Even with the *Volkish* parties being defeated in the 1912 *Reichstag* elections, their brand of anti-Semitism survived their fall. In fact, it was incorporated into the major party platforms. The National

Socialist German Workers Party, the Nazis, was an offshoot of the *Volkish* movement. The Great Depression only exacerbated the problem. Even the medical community began to support a policy of euthanizing the mentally and physically disabled so as to have more resources to cure the curable. It was but a short leap to policies that saved the racially 'valuable' and to dispose of those seen either as enemies or less 'valuable', which is to say, the Jews."

I thought about what Hopkins said. "So, what you're saying is that Germany's elected officials were espousing radical ideas about Jews, and insofar as they were *elected,* they must have been representing a majority viewpoint among the populace. But it's a long way from prejudice to wiping a whole people off the face of the earth."

"Ah," said the doctor. "That's where Hitler and his Nazi party come in— against a backdrop of prejudice and extremely radical ideas that have been voiced publicly and have not been shouted down by the people. Remember what swept Hitler into power. It was a tide of national anger. They felt that they had been unfairly treated after the first war; the economy was in shambles; they had lost territory to which they believed they were entitled; and here is a man who, in fiery oratory, gave voice to this anger. If the people are angry, it's nothing compared to this man's rage. And who better to blame than those shadowy Jews who manipulate the financial markets to their own gain and who have a conspiracy to challenge Aryan supremacy. Or so they postulate at every turn."

"And the people eat it up with a spoon," said Donovan.

"More like a shovel", answered Hopkins. "The people seem to be saying, 'I don't like the Jews either. You're in power. Whatever you do is fine by me, I just don't want to know the details.' There are, of course, exceptions among the German people. Many of them. Just not nearly enough to stand up to the Nazis, who, for the most part, have been wildly popular in Germany."

"But you haven't answered my question," I said. "How did they get to extermination from prejudice?"

Hopkins looked at me, probably trying to judge if I were just persistent or if I were just an asshole.

"Pointer, the Nazi leadership—specifically Hitler, Himmler, Goring and others—are like kids in a candy store. They view their time at the top as a unique opportunity to rid the world of a problem that's been plaguing them for millennia. That's their mind set. There is nothing more important to them than implementing the Final Solution to the 'Jewish Question'. If they have their way, the fact that they slaughtered millions of Jews will be on their tombstones. It will be the first thing they want said about them in the history books. It will be their crowning achievement. Does that help you?"

It was difficult to wrap my head around something that I found so utterly abhorrent that another group considered to be a triumph.

"Yes," I answered slowly. "Yes, it helps. Thank you," I finished quietly.

"The only reason that they are being quiet about the implementation of this Solution is that they know the world will not understand. They fear that it will further fan the flames of enmity against them. They also fear that their own people may think they've gone too far. It's one thing to consider genocide in theory, but the practicalities of massive, massive numbers of murders are horrifying, even to people who don't like Jews."

"Better to ask forgiveness than permission, eh?" I said.

Donovan weighed in, "Doctor, speaking of practicalities, it will be helpful if you would speak to the continuum of the process. The OSS has been tasked with formulating plans for disruption and sabotage in this matter."

"Right sir," Hopkins said. "The, er, continuum goes something like this. First there are the definitions and laws. Who, exactly, is a Jew? After all, it could be the difference between life and death. The Nuremburg Laws handled most of that definition, and the Wanssee Conference wrapped a bow around it by clearing up any remaining ambiguities in the definition."

"For example," Hopkins continued, "What about people who are one-quarter or one-half Jewish? Under Nuremburg, their status was ambiguous. At Wannsee, it was announced that "Mischlings", Nazi slang for mixed-race, of the first degree, or those with two Jewish grandparents, were to be treated as Jews. This would not apply if they were married to a non-Jew and had children by that marriage. They would instead be sterilized. Mischlings of the second degree are persons with one Jewish grandparent. They are treated as non-Jews *unless* they are married to Jews or Mischlings of the first degree. *Or,* and get this, they have a 'racially undesirable appearance that outwardly marks them as a Jew or have a political record that shows he feels and acts like a Jew.'"

"Yeah, I can see it now", I said. 'Hey you! I don't *care* that you're a Catholic. You *look* like a Jew. Get into the van.'"

"Yes, that's not far off the mark," Donovan said.

"In occupied territories, such fine distinctions are usually ignored. If you're living among Jews, you are rounded up with everybody else and herded off to a camp," Hopkins continued.

"Once definitions and laws were established, the Nazis began marginalizing Jews by means you see in the timeline—prohibition of owning property, holding certain jobs, forcing them to wear yellow stars, shuttering Jewish businesses, etcetera. But perhaps the biggest impact has been what can only be called bullying. Before deportation, Jews' lives are made miserable by other Germans. They are taunted, teased, beaten on a daily basis while the police stand by. Or the police join in. it's an intolerable existence for Jews in Germany and occupied territories."

"Why don't they fight back?" Elizabeth asked.

"Good question and a tough one. There have been some pockets of resistance, but in the first place, any sign of resistance is crushed immediately. In the second place, Jews in Europe have suffered persecution throughout history. They have found that the best policy has been to wait it out and hope that the tide turns in their favor politically or socially, if not culturally. It's worked, more or less, for centuries. What they haven't seemed to grasp, though, is that this time is different. This time the Nazis are bent on their total destruction and elimination. What we know as the Final Solution. Most Jews don't know that they're about to be killed until the gas gets turned on. Many are living in denial, hoping against hope."

"Shit", I muttered.

"The next step is physical marginalizing, throwing Jews out of their homes and herding them into Ghettoes where they await deportation to the East. At this point, most believe they are going to be transported to labor, or concentration camps. And that's what happened for the first couple of years. That still happens, but more and more, they are transported to death camps like Auschwitz where they are gassed. CO_2 was the poison of choice at first, but that required engines and valuable fuel that could be better used at the front. We now believe that most death camps have converted to a new poisonous gas developed by German scientists."

Donovan said, "If you think of the stupendous logistics involved in housing, feeding, transporting and-yes-killing millions of people, you begin to understand how the entirety of

German industry, transport, agriculture, science and building trades have to be involved."

"So their final destination is Hitler's Final Solution," I stated.

"That's it," said the Colonel. "Now, it's our job to figure out where our entry points could and should be. Early stages, middle or late. In addition to Hopkins and Elizabeth here, I have a team in Washington working up scenarios. Any early thoughts? Elizabeth? Pointer?"

"My early thought is that they are most susceptible to disruption and sabotage when they're on the move, on the trains," said Elizabeth.

"Pointer?" prompted Wild Bill.

"That's certainly true, but maybe a stationery target like a camp would be easier to approach. But, sir, aren't we getting ahead of ourselves? All of this activity is deep in enemy territory. I am not aware that we have assets that far east."

"Mostly correct, Pointer. We're obviously in early planning here. Secretary Stimson tells me that best predictions of Allied forces penetrating Germany is 18 to 24 months out. We— this operation-- would like to be somewhat ahead of that timetable. At the rate the Germans are killing these folks, every day counts."

"What about the Russians?" I asked.

Donovan said, "They are certainly closer to the death camps in the east. And their own Jews are being slaughtered by the thousands, mostly by firing squads. I have feelers out to some of Stalin's men to see if we can do some coordination. But I'm not holding my breath. They have their agenda, and we have ours. Our respective interests meet at Hitler's front door. But their priorities and ours, politically, don't match up very well."

"With all due respect, sir, I need a drink," I said.

"You'll have to hold that thought, Pointer. Major Brownwell is waiting for you to give you the briefing on The Sauce that you missed this afternoon.

April 23, 1943

My Dear Robert,

I pray that you are well, son. As ever, your mother sends along her love and her admonishments to write more frequently.

Life here is consumed with selling War Bonds, bandage wrapping, Draft Board meetings (yes, I've been appointed to the local Board), and worrying about the War and our boys overseas. At the Dixie yesterday, I saw Rabbi Smith again, and his mission to Washington to bring attention to the plight of the Jews is gaining momentum. He and his colleagues believe that we know only a fraction of the atrocities that are being committed by the Nazis. They are determined to shine a light on the issue.

I also paid another visit to Gaskins only to find him in a terribly morose state. Poor boy wants to fight, but his country won't let him. Now that I'm on the Draft Board I'll see what I can find out.

I have asked around to my National Guard and Draft Board friends to find out more about the Tuskegee Airmen. Best I can tell is that they are still slated for deployment in the next few months and they are probably headed your way, dear Robert.

I have enough time on my hands these days to do some serious reflecting. You know, son, that I do enjoy my quiet time! My practice is slow. The occasional will, the odd domestic dispute, fixing a speeding ticket here and there. My thoughts have been mostly about our capacity to inflict pain on one another. It seems that the entire world, from Asia to Africa to Europe is engaged in trying to kill one another. And to what purpose? More territory? More power? Yes and yes. Hitler was certainly the aggressor in Europe, and the Japanese certainly made the first move on us at Pearl Harbor. To what end? What was so important to put so many boys on both sides in harm's way? Now, there's no turning back until one side or the other cannot get off the mat.

As you know, President Roosevelt declared that nothing short of unconditional surrender would do in Europe. That seems to have removed from the equation any notion of an early, negotiated peace. I wonder if that was the best move.

After the Great War, President Wilson and his fellow idealists believed that we had a global structure in place that would ensure peace for decades, if not longer. What a folly that turned out to be! No League of Nations or other type of peace-loving organization can foresee the rage that had built up in Germany. What a perfect person for an era is Adolf Hitler! An army Corporal from an unstable background rises from the personal ashes of a jail sentence to become the Fuhrer! How does this happen? It only happens when a leader is able to capture either the darkest or the most hopeful thoughts—or in this case both—of his countrymen, articulate them and then act. Hitler did all of this. He turned his peoples' inner rage into some kind of hope for a better future. And when he saw that he had won their hearts and minds, in a tremendous bout of hubris, he moved to export that rage and hope to other countries. And the rest of the world reacted. They had no choice. And the consequences for our entire world have been cataclysmic.

Enough of my philosophizing, dear Robert. I know that you do not have that luxury. Yours is a world of action, no doubt. If I could, I would gladly, joyfully trade places with you. Not a minute of a day goes by that your mother and I don't think about you. Please take every precaution to stay safe.

I remain,

Your Loving Father,

Robert Pointer

Chapter Fourteen

Billingsley

For the next two days I was unable to
see Elizabeth. Our squad spent an
overnight on a training exercise
through the desert. We took only what
we could carry, including a single
canteen ration of water and one ration
of food, consisting of a tin of beans.
Sergeant Smythe led us on a hike—
more like a run—beginning at 0500
hours. We didn't return until the next
afternoon. Often, he had us running
through the desert with our hands
raised, holding our rifles aloft. After
this, The Sauce was going to be a cinch.

The thing that kept me going was
thoughts of *her.* The way she looked,
the way she smelled. How she talked.
Her beauty, her brains. I was, as they
say back home, over the moon.

One of the GIs, Corporal Billingsley
from Omaha, was the weak sister
among us, the runt of our litter. We
were about an hour into our trek, all of
which was spent on the run, when

Billingsley tripped over a rock and went down with a nice 4-point landing on his face. His canteen top came flying off and out poured his water. Binky was trailing him and did a nice hurdle over his prone body and didn't break his stride. I saw all of this out of the corner of my eye and pulled up to try to help the poor devil.

"You okay, Corporal," I huffed.

Billingsley looked like he was going to cry. "I didn't sign up for this shit, Lieutenant," he wheezed. He was trying unsuccessfully to show bravado.

"You signed up for whatever shit I decide to dish out!" Smythe had overheard. "Now get off your weak little ass and double-time it up that hill!"

I gave Billingsley a nice long pull from my canteen, helped him up and we got back into rhythm. I decided I'd better keep an eye out for the young Corporal. As we ran, I could see snot running out of the kid's nose and his eyes tearing up as he stumbled along half-blinded.

When we stopped for a break at 1200, I sat down next to him and began a conversation. "You're from Omaha, right Billingsley? Farm boy?"

"Yessir. Raise hogs and grow corn. All I ever known til this hitch." He took out his tin of beans and made as if to open it.

I grabbed his arm. "Kid, you wanna go easy on the beans. It's all we've got for two days. Wait until this evening before you open them."

"But I'm hungry, Lu. Had the shits for the last two days. I'm starved."

"Not yet, Billingsley."

We spent the afternoon in formation alternating between walking and running. The scenery was numbingly brown. The little track we were following was rutted with tank and truck tracks from Patton's army passing through a few days previously.

It was still the rainy season so they'd made quite deep cuts, and made the footing treacherous. Many of the men stumbled, but Billingsley fell at least four times that afternoon. At about ten minutes before sundown we came upon a tiny settlement of goat herders and their flocks. Goats equal water, I thought. Because of sharing my ration with Billingsley, my canteen was almost empty.

I also thought: Goats equal food.

Smythe ordered us to settle in at the settlement. We were going to sleep "rough"; that is, no tents. I prayed that it wouldn't rain, but I knew that the desert got very cold at night, so we began to gather what fuel we could find to build fires. Smythe set about setting the watches and placing our men at strategic points around our camp. While he did this, I approached one of the Bedouins and asked him how much for a goat, by saying in Arabic, "How much for a goat?" Clever.

We haggled for a bit as I knew we would and eventually settled on 25 rounds of ammo for one prized goat. Fifty for two. The deal was sealed, the goats were delivered and I asked for volunteers for the slaughter and the dressing of said goats. A couple of the boys from Pennsylvania were deer hunters back home and stepped right up. We had those goats ready for the spit in under 30 minutes. I thought Smythe would be pleased with my leadership and initiative. Binky had warned me when I started the project that Smythe wanted us to survive on a tin of beans.

"Man cannot live on beans alone," I replied. "Leave Smythe to me."

"What in the goddamn Sam Hill are you doing, Pointer?" Smythe gently questioned when he returned. I was his superior officer, but this was his show.

"Why, hunting and gathering, Sergeant, hunting and gathering. Roasted goat will make a fine side dish to our main course, don't you think? Wish we had a *Chateauneuf du Pape* to complement the fare. As it is, we'll have to boil some of that dirty water."

Seeing that he was outranked and outfoxed, Smythe wisely commented, "Pointer, we need more initiative like this in this man's army. Well done."

"I insist on medium rare, Sergeant." I couldn't resist.

I invited Billingsley to be my dining partner, and we sat together on a rock a few feet from the roasting goat.

"Billingsley, this is likely to be one of the finest meals you've ever eaten. You know about context, don't you?"

"No sir, I don't. What's context?"

"Well, if you were home in Nebraska and your sweet mother served you a meal of beans, goat and water after a hard day of farming, how would you feel? How would you like it?"

"Not a little bit, sir. Ohhh, I see. You mean 'cause we're out here in this godforsaken wilderness and we're having goat, we should feel blessed."

"Very good, Billingsley. And what if instead of being here, you were staring down the muzzle of one of Rommel's tanks?"

"I get it, sir. Context."

"Right. Now enjoy your goat. And don't eat all of your beans."

I noticed Binky staring in our direction with a not-nice look on his face.

Chapter Fifteen

Wild Bill

Washington

April 1943

Wild Bill Donovan instructed his driver, "White House. West gate."

He thought about his trip to Africa and what he had learned, preparing mentally for his report to the President.

Patton was ready, he thought. Ready to take North Africa and after that, Sicily. Old Blood and Guts was, as they say, born ready. If anything, Ike had to hold him back. But with George, it was ever thus. He had shaped up II Corps; the men seemed to love him and were ready to follow him anywhere. Like everyone else in the Allied camp, Patton was looking forward to the Fatherland and taking on the Nazis where they lived. Donovan was confident about North Africa. The Brits had softened the German Panzer

Divisions over the past two years so that there needed only a final, deadly assault to drive them out. Hitler had inexplicably divided his forces with what now appeared to be an ill-conceived invasion of the Soviet Union. Both sides there had sustained massive casualties, the numbers of which were unprecedented in the annals of warfare.

About The Sauce, Donovan was not quite as confident. First of all, it was an invasion. Troops had to travel over water and land. That was always dangerous. Yet the Allies had no choice. They couldn't bypass the island because of its strategic location.

And so much depended on stealth and surprise, not least Pointer and Binkford's expedition. If they could at least neutralize, if not completely turn the Mafia leaders and their followers, then the invasion would go much smoother with a lot less potential for casualties. Donovan felt ambivalent about leaving this mission up to a 29-year old, but it had been too late and he was too shorthanded to find someone more experienced. Besides, Donovan found that he liked the kid. Just before he'd left Africa, he'd heard from Brownwell about Pointer's little escapade with the goats in their desert trek. Donovan smiled ruefully to himself and thought, 'that's something I would've done'.

No, I think we'll be alright there. I've got Brownwell and Elizabeth looking after things, he thought. The Colonel's mood suddenly darkened as he pondered the "Jewish Question", thinking of the Nazi euphemism for racial genocide. That had been put on the OSS' plate just a few weeks ago. He'd spent the entire day strategizing with his task force over how to handle that. Donovan knew that they had a long way to go before they had formulated a viable plan.

"Here we are, sir," the driver announced. The Marine sentry ID'ed Donovan visually and waved them through the gate.

It was late winter and there was still snow on the ground from the previous week. But this late afternoon was cold, clear and windy. He knew that FDR wanted a private meeting with just him and Secretary of War Stimson. But afterwards, Donovan would be expected to stay for cocktails, a nightly ritual with the President. Donovan didn't drink, but he enjoyed Franklin's company and had done since they were at Columbia together. He wondered if the mysterious Mrs. Mercer would join them.

The Butler showed Donovan upstairs to FDR's private study. The President was sitting in his wheel chair in front of a roaring fire, smoking and pensive.

"Ah, Wild Bill! There you are!" He was as effusive as ever.

We shook hands as he lied, "Mr. President, so nice to see you looking so well." He didn't.

"Now, Bill, you know what I told you about addressing me. It was Franklin at Columbia and it's Franklin today."

At that moment, Secretary Stimson was shown into the room. They shook hands all around. Donovan had known the Secretary for years.

"Bill, I appreciate your dropping by. We want to hear all about your trip." As though he were doing the President a favor.

"Well sir, where to begin."

"Begin with General Patton. How is the old rascal?"

"Full of piss and vinegar, sir, as always."

"Ha!" FDR roared as though this was the funniest thing he'd ever heard. "You hear that, Henry? Old Blood and Guts hasn't lost his fastball."

"Sir, I get the feeling from talking to Patton that he and Montgomery have a winning plan to push the Germans out of North Africa. It's going to take some doing, but their plan is solid, and I don't think the Germans have the heart or the manpower to resist for long."

"Splendid, splendid. Is that what you believe, Henry?"

"Yessir," replied Stimson. Our boys have enough men and firepower to do the job. And remember, Omar is there to make sure everybody's taken care of."

FDR lit a cigarette. "Where are my manners? Do you gents need something to drink? Coffee, tea?"

"No thank you sir", they both answered.

"Fine, then. Tell me about preparations for Sicily, Bill."

"I believe, Franklin, that we have a solid, if a bit unorthodox, plan in place for the invasion. Thank you again, by the way, for calling Dewey off of Luciano. He's been quite cooperative. Luciano, I mean."

"Bill, you'd better explain the unorthodox part of the plan to Henry."

Donovan laid out the piece about Luciano helping with the locals and his intel. He told them about the incursion that Pointer and Binkford would lead and how they hoped to clear the way for Patton and Montgomery.

"Ha! See what we mean, Henry, about an unorthodox plan?" FDR was enjoying himself. "This is why we needed the OSS. Cloak and dagger stuff like from a dime novel. Ha!"

Donovan suddenly remembered why he liked FDR so much, even though they were from opposite sides of the political spectrum. The President had the knack of making anyone who entered his personal orbit feel like he was the only person in the President's life at that moment. Even if FDR countermanded an idea you put forth at a later date, which he often did, it was difficult to stay angry for long.

"Tell me, Bill, what kind of fellows do you have running the operation? By the way, Henry, it's called Operation Husky. Is that not a splendid cloak and dagger name?"

"I've got a young lieutenant running it from our side and we've borrowed a chap from Monty. Lieutenant Pointer made the contact with Luciano and I've got him following through on the operation side. He's young but smart— and seems fearless."

"Young, smart and fearless. Hmm. Sounds like Cousin Teddy in his youth."

"Well, not quite, sir, but I have a lot of confidence in him."

Donovan then told the story of the goats.

"Ha! Hear that, Henry? An enterprising young sprout! Just what we need in this blasted war."

The talk then turned to the Jews and their persecution, and the mood darkened as it always did when that topic was raised.

"I've spent all day with my task force on the problem and expect to devote many more days and weeks on it," Donovan said.

"Bill, Henry and I both are deeply concerned about this issue. We read the report from—what was his name, Hopkins? And it's bad and getting worse. There will come a time when we invade Germany and hopefully get to the east as well. If the Russians don't get there first. I want us to do everything we can to save as many of those wretches as we can. I don't want our GIs getting to one of those camps and being totally surprised at what we find there. I want, well, what I want and what is possible is for you to tell me, Bill."

"Yessir. We're working on it around the clock."

They talked more about Africa, Sicily and Europe—and then about the Pacific side of the war. At 5:30 the Butler knocked and escorted Mrs. Mercer and the President's daughter, Anna, into the room.

Stimson and Donovan stood up and the President went into his host mode.

"Henry, Bill, I believe you both know Mrs. Mercer and my dear Anna. My dears, welcome to our little soiree. I will mix the cocktails while you four get reacquainted."

Donovan knew that FDR and Lucy Mercer had been conducting an affair on and off since about 1918. Eleanor Roosevelt had discovered love letters between the two sometime around that time and had delivered an ultimatum to Roosevelt. Either stop seeing her or she would file for divorce. Roosevelt's mother, Sara Delano Roosevelt, had intervened and declared that divorce was out of the question. It would ruin both the family and Franklin's political career. Roosevelt had indeed stopped seeing her for a time, but she was now back in his life. Some said that Anna actively participated in helping her father carry on with Mrs. Mercer.

The President took great joy in the ritual of cocktail hour. He awarded

Mrs. Mercer and Secretary Stimson martinis and Anna and Donovan were presented with Club Sodas with a twist of lime. He mixed his own martini last.

"What shall we drink to?" the President asked. "I've got it! Wild Bill Donovan's successful sojourn to Africa!"

We clinked glasses and all took a sip.

"You know, Bill and I have known each other since school days. I was in the stands watching him crash and thrash around the football field one game against Harvard when someone shouted out, 'Go get 'em Wild Bill!' The sports man from the *Times* was there and printed the nickname in a headline that read something like, 'Wild Bill Donovan Wreaks Havoc on the Crimson'".

"Excellent memory, sir, but I believe it was I who was knocked cold that day, not the fellow I ran into."

"Yes, yes. But you got right back in there and tore them up. Magnificent display of manhood!"

And there was joy there in the President's study for at least that hour. Mostly, the President talked about their college days. They laughed at his anecdotes and enjoyed the reminiscences as much as he did. Donovan knew that this was an important respite for the great man. He also knew that when they left, he and the other men would get back to the business of slaying their enemies.

Chapter Sixteen

Briefing From the Top

II CORPS

NORTH AFRICA

May 1943

I was walking slowly up a dusty road in The Sauce. It was a hot summer day, and I saw a figure dressed in a black suit ahead, his image shimmering in my vision. If I was correct, the man was Mafia Boss Calegero Vizzini, my point of contact. The figure slowly raised his right arm as if to welcome me. In my peripheral vision, I saw, to my right, a glint of medal in the fierce sunlight. I squinted in that direction and saw a man with a carbine raised toward Vizzini. I drew my revolver, but it was too late. The man --it was Thomas Dowderwell—fired four times directly at Vizzini. Inexplicably, the Mafiosi didn't go down. Then I saw Binky draw up behind Dowderwell and gently pull him backwards out of my range. I began to run toward Vizzini, but the harder I ran the farther away he got.

I awoke with a start. The vision was still just in front of me, but it faded and all I saw was the whitewashed wall of my room. I tried to clear my head, and slowly the realization of where I was began to crystallize.

"I gotta get this mission over with," I said aloud. "It's making me nuts."

Today was to be the final day of preparation before we had a three-day leave. I hadn't been able to see much of Elizabeth for a solid week except for one dinner out. We had had another training exercise in the desert, this time two nights and three days. Again, I had looked after Billingsley. I noticed that Binky had looked after only himself. The morning was to be physical training and the afternoon further briefings. The rumor was that Patton himself was going to make an appearance. My hope was that I'd get the chance to pound the snot out of Binky in a punji stick joust.

We gathered, as usual, on the parade grounds and went through our grueling set of exercises and then for a nice 3-mile run with rifles raised above our heads. After a break, it was punji time. But this time I drew a private from New Jersey. He didn't give me much of a fight, and I was able to dispatch him quickly with a left-right combination, followed by a thrust right in the old bread basket, which put him down.

Binky drew Billingsley, which I was sorry to see. Billingsley wasn't a complete disaster at fighting; he just lacked confidence.

They circled each other, each feinting at the other. Billingsley landed the first blow to the left side of Binky's head. Binky went down, but it was mostly a stumble rather than a result of the force of the blow. But when he came back up there was murder in his eyes. He rushed Billingsley, who should have sidestepped, but instead tried to hold his ground. Binky smashed the middle part of the staff directly into the smaller man's chin, which is patently against the rules of the joust. You only hit with the padded ends of the stick. Blood gushed from Billingsley's face as Binky pursued his advantage by smashing the fallen man's head three times before I jumped in front of Binky, grabbed the staff and jerked it free from Binky's grasp. Binky then charged me and I was able to smash the left padded end against his jaw, knocking him to the ground. Smythe intervened and positioned himself in front of me before I could do any more damage.

"Well," I thought, "I did get to knock the snot out of Binky today after all. I'm a grateful lad."

After chow, it was briefing time. Billingsley had been patched up by a medic and had taken five stitches to the jawline. I was still angry at Binky, who acted as though nothing had happened.

Major Brownwell took up where he had left off the day before—the terrain, vegetation and the climate were that of the southern coast of Sicily during the summer months when the invasion was targeted to happen. It was April now, the rainy season was over, and it was hot. It wasn't unusual to lose 5-10 pounds during a training exercise as we ran and worked out in full uniform, complete with 30 pound packs, rifles, pistols, knives and ammo.

Twenty minutes into the briefing, there was a commotion outside in the hallway. Since it had been preceded by the sounds of the General's siren on his staff car, we knew it was Patton.

"Ten-HUT!" We rose as one and stood at attention.

Patton's aide led him to the front of the room. "As you were. Enlisted men, dismissed!" announced the aide. By previous agreement, we knew that Patton would be covering sensitive information, not meant for the ears of the Grunts. That left Brownwell, Binky and me.

The General slowly removed his helmet. He was attired in khaki riding breeches, knee-high boots, a brown tunic and, of course, his pearl handled

Colts. He had half an unlit cigar clenched between what seemed to me over-sized teeth. His white hair was slicked straight back. He looked every inch the aristocrat-soldier.

"Be seated, gentlemen," he commanded. He glanced at his aide who hustled over and pulled down the roll-up map on the wall behind Patton.

"Pointer, Binkford," he growled. He looked straight at us, temporarily ignoring Brownwell. "The American 7th Army and Montgomery's British 8th Army will lead the largest amphibious assault to this point in history. There are approximately 300,000 Italian and German personnel defending the island of Sicily; there are a number of airfields that harbor close-air-support aircraft; there are also a number of panzer divisions, including the famed Panzer Division *Hermann Goring*.

"Supreme Allied Commander Eisenhower and Land Forces/Army Group Commander General Sir Harold Alexander are working closely with Montgomery, me and other Allied

Commanders to coordinate, land, air and sea forces so that we are assured of obliterating the defenders. Our objective is to drive their armies all the way north to Messina where we will capture their men, their armaments and their supplies. Our next stop will be Italy."

"Now. Beachheads are under discussion. But we know for certain that we will land here and here." Patton used his riding crop to point to two spots on the southeast and south central coast. "My contention is that we should also land at Palermo in the northwest, and squeeze the bastards right in the middle. But field commanders don't always get our way. Goddamnit."

"The invasion will be preceded by bombing sorties to knock out the airfields as well as extensive Naval bombardments from the south. However, we will not bomb the beachheads so we don't tip off the enemy as to where we intend to land. In fact, we don't want them to know that Sicily is a target at all. We want them to believe that our targets are Greece and Sardinia. We are working on plans of deception to make the enemy believe this," Patton continued in his raspy voice.

"Any questions so far?"

"Yessir," I stood up.

"Sit down, Pointer. I can hear you perfectly well."

"Yessir", I said. "May I ask, sir, what kind of plans of deception have been considered?"

"Plenty of them, Pointer, but not one worth a tinker's damn."

"You said you want them to believe that we are going to attack elsewhere, not Sicily. You will remember, sir, that McClellan's forces recovered General Lee's orders for attack before Antietam."

"Correct. A Union man found the orders wrapped around three cigars that were meant for Lee. Where is this going, Pointer?"

"Well sir, in McClellan's case, the orders were authentic. What if we arranged for the Krauts to 'discover' orders from the Allies that were directing us to invade Sardinia and Greece?"

"Go on."

"It would have to be believable, some way to get the fake orders into their hands that would be beyond reproach, some way for them to find them like the Yankees, I mean the Union, found Lee's orders. Like they, uh, captured them. The problem with that is we would sacrifice a soldier's life." I paused and thought. "Unless the soldier were already dead."

"You're proposing that we plant false orders on a dead man? Might work." Patton's mind was whirring.

"Yessir. What if we planted the papers on a corpse and had him, say, wash up on shore somewhere where the enemy

253

would find him? They might just take the bait."

"Not bad, son, not bad at all. I'll run it up the flagpole at HQ."

"Now, where was I?" the General growled. "Ah, yes, your roles in the invasion. Brownwell has briefed me on your operation. I want the Mafia to be our eyes and ears on the island. I want strategic on-site sabotage. I do not want our men to be targets of enemy snipers. I am more than happy to slug my way north. But I want the way to be as clear as possible. And if there are ambushes—and there will be—I want to know about them in advance. I'm sure that Montgomery feels the same way. Winning the hearts and minds of the locals has been vital to invasions since Julius Goddamn Caesar! You *will* make this happen. Is that *clear?*" The General was getting overheated.

"Yessir," Binky, Brownwell and I chorused.

"Fine then." And Patton exited without another word.

254

Chapter Seventeen

Bliss

I didn't quite know how to handle it.
Elizabeth had invited me on a jaunt
into the countryside. An overnight. I'd
rather face a joust than a jaunt. At the
same time, I was really excited. I really
liked this girl. But I wasn't at all sure
that I wasn't "over mounted" as one of
my buddies, using a barnyard analogy,
used to say back home. I thought she
was unbelievable. I was pretty sure she
liked me. But was I ready for a real,
grown-up romance? I didn't know for
sure, but I knew that I wanted to give it
a shot.

"Hi," I said in my most clever and suave
way.

"Hi back, Pointer", she said. "Are you
all set?" She put her hand behind my
neck, drew me in and kissed me.

That was the perfect move. It gave me
a jolt of confidence, as though I were
really in charge, like a young Cary

Grant. I kissed her back, but didn't go crazy. A Cary Grant move.

Once again, I had commandeered a Jeep and we were off. Our destination was only 50 miles away, but it would take most of the day. The roads were bad and there were lots of check points along the way.

As we bumped along the dirt road out of town, I said, "How much do you know about this place?" I meant our destination.

"I've only heard that it's a wonderful Mediterranean fishing town. It's been occupied over the centuries by the Romans, the French and the Italians, so it has all of these influences, especially in the food." She had to raise her voice to be heard over the open air Jeep.

"Can we go fishing?" Smooth, Pointer, smooth.

"Maybe", she said. "You know how to sail, right?"

"Yep. But it seems odd to go sailing while there's a war on."

"I know what you mean, but it's something we could tell our grandchildren. We went sailing in the middle of a war..."

Our grandchildren? Our grandchildren together, or just our grandchildren?

"Elizabeth, what do you want to do after the war?"

"My parents are upset that I'm not already married with a couple of babies. Most of my friends are. I'm 29, which is getting to be Old Maid territory. But I love my work. I know how fortunate I am as a woman to have this job. And I know that it was family connections that got me the job. So, the way I see it, I have a lot to prove. I suppose what I'm saying is that I want to help us win this war. Afterwards? No idea. What about you?"

"Father would like me to join his practice in South Hill though he's too polite to say so. But I can't see it. Colonel Donovan is hopeful that the OSS will become permanent after the war, but there doesn't seem to be much political appetite for it. If General Patton is right, the Soviets are poised to become our next great enemy, and if that's the case, count me in on that fight."

"Me too," Elizabeth said. She reached over and squeezed my hand.

Four hours later, we arrived at our little seaside hideaway. We had gone through five Army checkpoints and had seen enough goats and camels to start a zoo. I grabbed our bags and rang a bell in the inn. A swarthy woman in her sixties appeared, smiled and welcomed us to what passed in a war as paradise. She spoke no English so we conversed in Italian.

The inn was simple, but beautiful. The floors were Mediterranean white tiles with sea-blue highlights. Beyond the front desk, we looked past an indoor seating area to a terrace which was literally hanging out over the Mediterranean.

"Will that be one or two rooms, Lieutenant Pointer" asked our host.

With a quick glance at Elizabeth, I said, "One room with a double bed if you have it."

"Of course."

We carried our bags up two flights of stairs to our room. It had the same tiles with an area rug spread at the foot of the bed. The bathroom, as was the custom, was down the hall to be shared with other guests. But there were French doors opening out to a small balcony overlooking the sea. I could see fishing boats below, beached at the low tide. Very picturesque.

I was a little nervous, though I detected no such emotion in Elizabeth.

She hugged me and said, "Pointer, this is more perfect than I imagined. I am at this moment thoroughly happy. I'll just nip down the hall and freshen up. Then a drink?"

"Sure", I said.

We went down to the terrace and noticed several Brits, Canadians and a couple of American officers on R&R, all male. We found a table, sat and gazed out at the Med. We held hands. We ordered Gin and Tonics. I supposed that they'd had quite a few Brits as guests over the years. And I began to feel a deep sense of relaxation come over me.

"Here's to R&R," I toasted.

"I'm trying to remember the last time I actually sat down in a non-war setting and didn't think about Hitler, Mussolini, The Sauce or any of that stuff," she said. "Probably back in California."

"Hello? Elizabeth? My God, it's you!" An American Major had approached our table.

Elizabeth looked up and said, "Johnson, what are you doing here?" She stood and they gave each other a little hug.

"I'm assigned to the 3rd Army as a liaison to the Canadians. We're having a small conference here this weekend. How've you been?" Johnson said.

"Oh, fine, fine. Johnson, this is my friend, Lieutenant Pointer. Pointer, Johnson is a friend from back home."

Seems like everyone was on a last-name basis.

"My pleasure," Johnson said as I stood and shook hands.

"Elizabeth, did you know Palmer is coming to Tunisia?"

Uh-oh. Palmer had the distinct ring of an old boyfriend.

"No, I didn't know that. When?"

"In a few weeks. He asked me if I'd run into you." Johnson glanced at me. "I suppose now I can tell him I have."

It was that time in the game where you invite the unexpected old friend to sit down and join you for a drink. Damned if *I* was going to cave. Elizabeth didn't either. So, after a moment of awkwardness, Johnson announced that he'd better get back to his friends.

Elizabeth took a deep breath and let it out. "That is Palmer's best friend and, yes, Palmer is my ex."

"Swell," I said.

"Pointer, there is no reason on God's green earth why this should affect us in the least, let alone cast any kind of pall over our time here."

"No, of course not. Why should it?"

"Look, darling. I think I'm falling in love with you. OK? There I said it, and I don't care if it embarrasses you. Palmer is in my past and he's going to stay there. Yes, he'll hear about this from Johnson, but what difference does it make?"

Well, if you put it that way.

We left the inn to take a stroll down the beach. It was a fine late spring afternoon, about eighty degrees with a soft sea breeze. We took off our shoes and walked around the big oval that described the beach. A fisherman was untangling his net and I had an inspiration.

"Ciao, Signore", I tried Italian.

Blank stare

I tried broken Arabic and hand gestures. "Will you be going fishing tomorrow?"

"Yes," he nodded.

"How about you skip the fishing and take the lovely *signorine* and me on a picnic tomorrow. I will happily pay you what you would've earned plus ten percent," I had to repeat this several times, using what little Arabic I knew and filling in the rest with sign language.

We haggled a bit more until I agreed to fifteen percent commission. We were all set for eleven am the next day.

Elizabeth and I dined that evening on the terrace. We had filet of sole, a salad, and homemade bread and butter, accompanied by a *con brio* Italian Sauvignon Blanc. We talked about everything under the sun except the war, Hitler, The Sauce, Donovan, Patton or the Casablanca Conference. I had a pleasant buzz going from the *vino* and we finished the meal off with a Remy Martin cognac.

It was bedtime.

We walked up the stairs, hand in hand and when we got to our door I pulled her to me and kissed her like I meant it. She excused herself and went down the hall with a travel bag. Fifteen minutes later, there was no Elizabeth. Just as I was beginning to think that Johnson had kidnapped her and taken her back to California, she appeared.

I didn't gasp aloud as she dropped her silk robe, but I couldn't swear to that.

She was attired in a black lacy-something. She was the most gorgeous sight I had ever seen. She approached me, took my hand and led me to our little patio overlooking the Sea. The wind was still blowing softly and we could hear the waves lapping on the beach below. There was a gibbous moon shining over the water, its reflection seeming to lead right to us. We kissed, and I led my lovely Elizabeth to bed.

Making love to Elizabeth is something I'll never forget. I just hoped that it would last forever. It didn't. But after a short time we were ready to try again. And then again. At sometime around four am, I drifted off to sleep with Elizabeth draped around me. I had told her that I loved her and I had meant it.

At 0930 I woke up with the African sun streaming through our windows. Elizabeth was sitting on the edge of the bed with a tray of coffee and croissants next to her, wearing the robe. But one side had slipped off revealing a naked shoulder. She was lost in thought and hadn't noticed that I had one eye open. I reached up and tugged the silk off of both of her shoulders and pulled her to me.

"Mmmmm," she murmured.

To say that Elizabeth's and my experience was unlike my other lovemaking experiences is like saying there's a personality difference between Patton and Billingsley. Everything about it was deep and moving. Unless I missed my bet, she seemed to think so too. Based on what she had told me about her experience with Palmer, I believe this was another Billingsley/Patton comparison. But who's comparing, right? Guys never do that.

A half-hour later I realized that Abdul would be waiting for us with his boat. Elizabeth wore shorts, sandals, a sleeveless top and her long hair was pulled back in a ponytail. "Damn," I thought. "That girl can't look anything but terrific in any setting, any outfit." I put on khakis and a white tee shirt and kept my dog tags on. You never know, right?

We arrived at the beach and, as we'd agreed, we brought the beer. Abdul was to supply everything else. There was one small cardboard box on board so I assumed we'd be eating light. The boat was a modified Egyptian dhow, about 16 feet in length. She had a main, a jib and a tiller. We had to wade out to the anchorage in just under hip deep water. Abdul tipped the boat toward us as we clambered aboard. He was grinning in his toothlessness and said something in Arabic I didn't catch. The only items on board were a single paddle and a homemade spear.

Abdul shoved us forward and hopped aboard, raising the main, all in a single movement. Guess he'd done this before. He then raised the jib and off we went. There was one bench amidships on which Elizabeth and I perched while Abdul knelt by the tiller. The winds were moderate out of the southeast and Abdul set a course more or less parallel to the shoreline.

"Where are we headed?" I asked in Italian with a gesture toward the Sea.

"The island!" he replied. Or at least that's what I thought he said.

We were cranking along at about five knots with seas of about two and a half feet. The shoreline was still in sight. I couldn't help but look northward as though I might catch a glimpse of The Sauce. The sea seemed to be teeming with life. Flying fish were everywhere and, about an hour in to the voyage, porpoises began to frolic at the bow. Spray routinely breeched the boat and we were pleasantly misted by the salt water.

After another hour or so, we spotted land, which turned out to be the island in question. As we got closer, we spotted a couple of old stone houses, some sheep and several men tending them. Abdul had done *this* before too as he abruptly turned the tiller over, brought the boat into the wind and dropped the sails. After he dropped anchor, he said, "You like to go for a swim?"

I looked at Elizabeth. She had not brought a bathing suit. Who had a bathing suit in a war?

Abdul grinned and gestured, "Go ahead! I won't look!"

Sure, and I have a camel I'll sell you. But Elizabeth surprised me by jumping in the water fully clothed. I stripped to my skivvies and jumped in after her. We frolicked. Yes, that's the word. Frolicked. I hadn't frolicked since high school. Who frolicks during a World War?

Abdul had anchored. While we were messing around in the water, he grabbed his spear, took a deep breath and dove in the water. We watched him through the crystal clarity until he finally disappeared from sight. I actually began to worry about our new friend as no one I knew could hold his breath for that long. At length, Abdul popped up about 200 yards away with something wiggling on the end of his spear. A fish—a red snapper. Lunch! He swam back to the boat, deposited the fish, took another deep breath and reappeared many minutes later with both hands full. Prawns. More lunch!

We all got back in the boat and sailed around the north end of the island, the uninhabited side. Abdul sailed the boat straight up on the beach and didn't bother to lower the sails. He began gathering brush and wood for a fire. An hour later, we had consumed the best lunch either of us would ever have. It was made more special as Abdul dug into his little cardboard box and withdrew his stash of special seasonings for the seafood. The beer was lukewarm, English style, but it was perfect.

After lunch, Elizabeth and I repaired to a spot under a juniper tree and in five minutes were down for a siesta.

Chapter Eighteen

Plans

II Corps Headquarters

May, 1943

Binky was nervous. He'd gotten another message from Dowderwell seeking a rendezvous. He'd not heard from his friend since their first meeting downtown in the restaurant. By their crude system, they'd agreed to an assignation at the same place.

"Hullo, old boy," Thomas said as he lit a cigarette. They'd ordered their Scotch and Thomas seemed to want to get down to business. Binky had half-hoped that this would be a social visit.

"Thomas. Glad to see you."

"Right. Well, Binky, it seems that things are heating up to the north. There was an attempt on Lightning that, for some blasted reason, went awry. It was a perfect plot. We could've blamed it on the Soviets. Well, bad luck for us, but

Lightning's luck won't hold out forever. The disasters in Russia have shown the people that Lightning is not invincible, much as they want to believe to the contrary. What a blasted fool to open up a second major front! Everyone knows that it's a matter of time before the Allies invade from England. Fool!"

"One of the things I wanted to speak to you about is your friend Pointer," Thomas continued. "My contacts up north are having a difficult time believing that the Americans are actually relying on a mobster—a gangster—for intelligence. This...Luciano chap. They are wondering if the Yanks are on to you and if this is a disinformation ploy."

Binky sipped his Scotch and regarded his old friend over the top of his glass. Of all the things Binky was worried about, this wasn't one of them. "No, Thomas, it's not disinformation. For one thing, Pointer is not that smart. For another, the Yanks wouldn't go to all of this trouble just to throw me off the scent in such a minor way. There *have* been some new developments, however. Patton himself came and spoke to us."

Again, Dowderwell was amazed at Binky's association with the great General. "And what did he say?"

"That Sicily is definitely the target and that the Allies would like us to think that Sardinia or Greece is the point of the exercise. Pointer even suggested a strange plot to plant false orders on a dead man. Further, that the southeast and south central coasts are definite entry points and that Palermo as a third beachhead is still under consideration."

"And the timing?"

"All we know is summer."

Dowderwell let the smoke drift out of his nostrils as he thought. "Tell me, Binky, you've been training with these chaps. Are they ready for this mission?"

"Quite unimpressive as soldiers, I'd say. There's the Pointer-type who's an overgrown college kid. He has a certain physical prowess, but doesn't understand strategy. More often, their skill level is represented by a certain Corporal whom I put down in a joust the other day."

"A joust?"

"Quite. It's a contest of strength and fighting-- *mano a mano.* Poor fellow won't be going anywhere soon without looking over his shoulder."

"Mmmm. Right. My friend, mainly what I wish to discuss is Cousin Freddy. The poor chap is in a most awful spot. As you know, he has been assigned to Himmler's staff, and he has been working on what they call the Jewish Question. It seems that Lightning and Himmler are bent on killing every Jew in Europe."

"Right. One hears outrageous rumors," Binky nodded.

"They are probably not just rumors. The SS has apparently kicked the campaign into high gear, moving from labor camps to extermination camps. There's a camp in Auschwitz, for example, that Freddy has visited with Herr Himmler on multiple occasions that was built with one thing in mind. Killing Jews. My information is that thousands per week are being gassed at this one facility alone. And you know our Freddy—such a moral chap. He's having great difficulty on that score, but politically, it's even worse for him. He knows that if the Allies find out the extent of the persecution that it will be extremely difficult to negotiate a separate peace, even if Lightning is gone."

"Poor Freddy."

"Indeed. Canaris and Oster of the *Abwehr* have even showed signs of distancing themselves from him so as to not be too closely associated with the genocide. Freddy's argument is that he can operate from the inside of the SS and is in a position to pass along intelligence on Himmler and Lightning. It is, one may say, a good argument. And so far, it's holding up. If our group cuts him loose entirely, Freddy will be on an island, committing atrocities and not being seen as part of the cabal that's working on the removal of Lightning. At least that is how it would appear from the outside."

"I see. A conundrum," Binky commented.

"The good news is that with the defeats on the Eastern Front, there is renewed momentum for *our* Final Solution."

"You mean eliminating Lightning."

"Yes. But in the meantime, we have to win every battle, fight for every inch of turf. Lightning needs to get the hell out of Russia, and consolidate forces in the South and in the West. But now he's stirred up the great Russian Bear, and they'll be coming for us. Imagine it! Communists! Finally, we'll have something in common with the Americans. We both hate the Reds."

Chapter Nineteen

Jumping

II Corps

May 1943

I could feel it. We were getting close to going. Brownwell hadn't said so, but I could sense it in the urgency of the briefings. In fact, Brownwell had hinted at a major tactical change in our mission.

And Smythe! Lord, Smythe! He was working us half to death.

At that day's briefing, Brownwell had sprung the change on us. We were not to land on The Sauce's beaches. Instead, we were to land from the heavens via parachute. Things just got a little more complex. There would be more of us on the initial incursion, in addition to just Binky and me. There would be caches of supplies dropped along with us— food, along with bombs, ammo for the locals and even vehicles for us to use. Binky and I would be each joined by two men on the first incursion. The entire squad would go with us when we accompanied the main invasion.

"Binkford, Pointer. I see no evidence of parachute training in your files. Am I missing something?" Brownwell asked.

"Other than my extreme acrophobia and vertigo? Not a thing," I replied.

I didn't really say that.

"No sir," we both said.

"Then you are done-ski with Smythe. From now on, mornings will be a crash course in parachuting. You should pardon the pun." Brownwell smiled wickedly.

"I see that squad members with parachute experience include Parsons, Jameson, Goldstein, and Billingsley. You're in."

Billingsley? Lord, let him be assigned to me.

"Parsons and Jameson, you'll be with, *ow*, Binkford. Goldstein and Billingsley, you're with Pointer. Any questions? Good. Report to the airfield at your regular time. There are some new pilots in country who'll take you up."

Those pilots proved to be the newly-deployed airmen from Tuskegee.

But first there was training on the ground. The Army had pioneered the training of combat paratroopers beginning in 1940 in Ft. Benning, Georgia. Why bases in the U.S. were still called forts I couldn't fathom. At Ft. Benning, candidates are put through a 3-week course consisting of "Ground Week", "Tower Week" and "Jump Week". In other words, progressively terrifying. Brownwell let us know that we would be combining the normal three weeks into eight days. He also let us know that what he meant by Billingsley and the other selectees having parachute training was that they had all washed out at Ft. Benning. Otherwise, they'd be paratroopers. Made sense.

Our instructor was Lieutenant Ryder, the proverbial grizzled veteran from New Jersey. He'd trained at Ft. Benning and had graduated to become an instructor as his superiors deemed him too old for combat.

"Alright, ladies, line up over here," Ryder said when we reported the first day. Love it when the crusty vets call you "lady".

"Before we do any real jumping, you gotta learn how to land. You will be using the T-10D round shaped parachute that gives a descent rate of 23.5 feet per second for a 250 pound load. That's a 200 pound man with 50 pounds of gear. If you jump out of a plane and hurt yourself in the fall, it doesn't do us any good, am I right? So, you gotta learn how to land. So, you will learn to perfect the Parachute Landing Fall, the PLF."

What's an army procedure without an acronym?

Ryder continued, "You will learn how to transfer the shock of the landing up the sides of your lower legs and knees, all the way up the side of your upper body. Now, we don't have perfect props here like they do at Benning, so we're going to have to improvise quite a bit. Follow me."

We walked around the other side of the hangar and saw a ladder propped up against the roofline. Ryder climbed the ladder to the roof and waited while we followed suit. We were about 12 to 15 feet from the ground. Someone had dug a pit and filled it with sand below us.

"I am going to jump down into the pit below. When I hit the ground, watch how my knees go into a controlled buckle and how I roll with the momentum."

Ryder did just that, popping up after a 360 degree roll, good as new. We each tried it and no one was hurt, although my landing was certainly more of a jolt to me than Ryder's had been to him. We spent the rest of the morning jumping off the roof. I predicted that there would be six sore soldiers the next day.

As a change of pace, we spent the afternoon jumping out of a jeep that Ryder was piloting across a field at about 20 miles an hour.

"That's what it's like, boys, to land from thousands of feet, long as the parachute works," he said over and over.

For two and a half days we worked on landings. Then, it was time to graduate to "Tower Week", or "Tower Days" in this case. Ryder and his boys had rigged a cable from the top of the control tower to the concrete-side of the hangar. The tower was about 35 feet high. We donned real parachutes, clipped an O-ring to the cable and slid down to near the bottom. The trick was to unbuckle and drop into the sand pit before you hit the side wall of the hangar. A couple of the guys failed to do this in time and hit the wall full-on. Because we didn't have the equipment, we were unable to simulate opening the jump door and feel the impact of the wind and weather conditions as they would be in a real operation.

At last, it was time to jump. We were introduced to the crew who would take us up. They were indeed Tuskegee Airmen, from pilot to co-pilot to bombardier. It was odd to see Negroes in such a position of authority and power. But they didn't seem to think it was odd. They behaved as though they belonged. Colonel Kittridge was the pilot and he would be with us all the way through the mission.

We were schooled in how to pack our chutes, what to do in the event of a malfunction and what to do in case we, say, landed in a tree. Short answer: that's what our knives were for. We also practiced, on the ground, at pulling the guy lines which would change our course. We learned that we would be dropping into The Sauce at night. Made sense, but added to the degree of difficulty in a big way.

So we were ready to jump. More or less. Like a lot of people who are afraid of heights, mine is situational. I don't mind flying. But when I went on the hangar's roof, just a few feet up, I felt my glutes clench. So, I hoped since we were jumping at night, even in practice, that I wouldn't be affected since I couldn't see below.

I had spent a little time with Colonel Kittridge. We'd had coffee in the Mess on our second day. I told him that my father had told me to expect the Tuskegee Airmen in Africa.

"Yeah, Pointer, it's been a long road for us. We been shut outta more places than you could shake a stick at. What I mean is, it took a lot of doing to get this gig together. When we travel, for example, in the States, we gotta find rooms that will let us in, not just the whites. It's not as bad over here. Folks used to seeing colored. It's like they never seen a black soldier back home. They feel bad, but they're used to custom. And some of 'em don't feel bad at all, uniform or not. The Tuskegee men, we go about our business. We got a war to fight."

I didn't know what to say. So I said, "There are a lot of us, sir, who are grateful to you and glad you're here. I am glad you'll be the one flying that plane."

We finished our coffee and headed out to work.

The plane was a Douglas B-18, basically a flying rail car. It would fly at 1200 feet and at a speed of about 130 miles per hour. The crew does their pre-drop and slow-down checklists, half of us get up, line up and jump according to the green light. The pilot then does a U-turn and returns on the same course and the second group of three jumps out the other side of the plane.

Our first jump was in daylight, which suited me fine. We packed our chutes, boarded the plane and Kittridge took us up. Ryder was our mother hen, yelling last minute instructions over the drone of the aircraft. As leader of my team, I was to go last behind Billingsley and Goldstein. I requested of Ryder that we go before Binky's team. And because I requested, Ryder ordered the opposite. Binky *et al* would go first. And they did, without incident, not that I allowed myself to look. I stared straight ahead at the other side of the fuselage, not daring to look at my squad and certainly not out the open hatchway.

The pilot circled the "race track oval" and returned to roughly the same position from which the others had jumped to their certain deaths (not really, they were fine, I was pretty sure), and Ryder screamed, "Goldstein! Go!" He did. Billingsley! Go!" And he did. "Pointer! Off with you now!" I closed my eyes and jumped out into space. I kept my eyes closed and counted to ten as they'd advised, and then ripped the chord. With a jolt that had my kidneys coming out of my mouth, the parachute opened. I opened my eyes and saw the checkerboard of the landscape below along with the tiny toy buildings of the hangars, the control tower and the parked aircraft. I was drifting, blown sideways by the wind currents. It was so quiet, just the sound of wind. First, I smiled, then I began laughing out loud, deep, joyful barking that I was sure they could hear on the ground. I pulled the wires this way, then that way, marveling that I had some control of my direction. At length, I spotted the bullseye of the Drop Zone, and it occurred to me that I should be the closest of everyone. Just because.

I saw one, then two, then four and five of the jumpers as the ground rushed up to me. I pulled to starboard as hard as I could and drifted closer to the bullseye. When I finally hit ground, I was five yards off dead center, but much closer than the others.

I hit the ground, rolled and popped up on a perfect 3-point landing. I was grinning from ear to ear without being conscious of it and shouted, "Let's do that again!"

And we did for the next few days. Billingsley had some serious problems with it. The second time, he refused to jump until we had passed the point of no return. We did three more passes until Ryder shoved him out of the plane. By this time, I was nervous all over again, but once I jumped, I was fine. Billingsley never did get comfortable, especially with night jumps. He spent every moment in the plane and every moment leading up to getting on the plane terrified. No amount of coaching or cajoling could ease his fears. I could see that I'd have my hands full when we did the real thing in The Sauce.

Chapter Twenty

An Understanding

It was nearing the time when we would go. Brownwell had told us how we'd get *in,* but he hadn't told us yet how we'd get *out.* He addressed it at that afternoon's briefing.

"We would prefer to extract you by air, but we cannot trust that we can land and take off safely. There are too many, *ow,* bad guys around. Therefore, along with ordinance and other supplies, we will be parachuting in a vehicle for each team. If the vehicle is damaged in the drop or it is somehow captured, then you will make your way to here on the southern coast as best you can. Our hope is that the, *ow,* locals who you have befriended will provide transport if need be. Otherwise, it's about 60 miles for both squads, and you'll have to do the best you can"

He continued, "You will be radio-silent for your three days in The Sauce. When you get to within about 30 miles of the southern coast, the pick-up Zone, you may radio to our Naval craft off the coast and they will be able to relay messages back to us. You will be due at the Zone at between 1600 and 1900 hours on the third day after the drop. Early is fine, late will be a problem."

"You will be pleased to learn that the very latest in Landing Craft, the, *ow*, DUKW, will be awaiting you to return you to Tunisia." Brownwell gave us a paternal smile.

"Any questions?"

"Yes, what if we're late?" I asked.

"If you're late then we will deal with it at that time. We should be in radio contact at that point, so we'll do an *in-situ* assessment."

Love those *in-situ* assessments.

Then the Major announced, "You will have R&R for the next 24 hours and then we go. Friday night at 1700 hours. Further questions? If not, dismissed."

Afterwards, I sought Binky out. I'd been thinking about him quite a lot. I'd even confided in Elizabeth that there was something about him I didn't trust. I knew I didn't like him, but trust was another, more serious matter when you're going into combat. I knew he was a bully; that was clear from his treatment of Billingsley. What a jerk, I thought. But how should I confront him?

Elizabeth, being a woman, said to just "talk it out". Me, being a man, wanted to go at him head-on. And say what? Hey, Binky, there's something about you that I don't like and don't trust. Can we talk about it? Please? So, I decided to approach him with the old Pointer subtlety.

"What do you think about the mission, Binky?" I opened.

"What about it?"

"You comfortable with everything? Your guys? Your mission? You feel like you can make headway with Russo?"

Binky looked at me skeptically. "What do you want, Pointer? What are you trying to say?"

"What I'm saying, Binky, is that you and I are going into The Sauce together, and I want to know if you've got my back. We have to depend on each other. You're not the most giving fellow I've ever met, you know. If you have an agenda other than the one we both know about, I want to know about it. As in now."

"Pointer, I am trying hard not to be insulted. What, exactly, are you implying?"

"I'm not *implying* anything, Binky. I'm *saying* that there're things about you, things I've seen in our training, that give me pause. I am wondering if you are about Binky, or are you about the team?"

"Pointer, is this about my being homosexual?"

I was flabbergasted and flustered. "No, Binky. Why in hell would I think that at this late hour? I don't question your toughness, just your commitment."

"You act as though I were some kind of Nazi sympathizer, Pointer. Is that it? Am I a spy?"

"Jesus, Binky, no one said anything about being a goddamn spy! Where is that coming from? I just need to know that I can depend on you; that the men can depend on you."

"I'll play my part and you play yours".

"Binky?"

"Yes?"

"Anyone ever tell you you're an asshole?"

Hey! That went great, didn't it? Glad we got that straight.

Chapter Twenty One

Getting Close

It was Thursday afternoon. I was in the best condition of my life, thanks to Smythe's special brand of torture. I knew more about Sicily than I'd ever need to know. Likewise, I was now an expert on one Don Calegerro Vizzini. I expected that Binky was similarly educated on his target, Frankie Russo. I actually had absorbed quite a bit on Russo as well. You might want to have dinner with either Don—they seemed to be affable enough—but you wouldn't want them to stay the night, especially if there were women and children about.

Neither was a true *capo dei capi* like Lucky was in New York. But Vizzini did have the nickname "The Pope". Russo and Vizzini were in fact rivals, albeit in neighboring territories. Both lived in relative splendor and both had small armies of men at their disposal. Luciano had gotten word to them, supposedly, that we were to drop in, you should pardon the pun. I also had correspondence from Lucky to take with me and, if all else failed, we both had Lucky's personal pennant that he had designed: a yellow silk rectangle with a black "L" in the center.

We had been taught all about Mafia customs. *Omerta,* the code of silence, was something they viewed as a solemn vow. *Omerta* literally means manhood, and in the Mafia context it referenced a man taking care of his own problems. The last place to go was the authorities. Then there was the concept of *vendetta.* A *vendetta* could, and often did, last for decades and generations. It was valuable to know who hated whom, and we had been schooled on that as best our tutors knew. So, we knew that someone in Vizzini's family hated someone in Russo's family, which, of course, meant that both families hated each other in their entirety.

The plan was to find our respective Dons, befriend them, and explain why it would be in their best interests to help us win. We would also enlist them to be the Allies' eyes and ears on the island during the invasion. If we were convinced that they would cooperate, we would arm them with enough bombs and firepower to seriously disrupt the Italian and German defenders. Speaking of the defenders, our biggest challenge by far would be to avoid them. We figured that the most dangerous times would be between landing and making contact with our targets and then again afterwards when we made our way south to the pick-up zone.

Leaving The Sauce, Binky's group and my group were to rendezvous about half-way to the pick-up zone and travel together the rest of the way. Brownwell had assured us that that part of the island was sparsely attended by the enemy.

Define sparsely.

What I wanted now was to be with Elizabeth one last time before we left. We'd agreed that we would have dinner and spend the night together once we knew the plan. I telephoned the best—and only—hotel in town, and booked a room. I also made reservations at the same restaurant where we'd had our first date. Elizabeth had announced that it was "our place". I went back to the barracks and showered and shaved and put on my best after-shave stuff. I was ready.

That evening, Elizabeth and I had a tasty dinner of fish and prawns, which, she told me, was "our dinner".

"Pointer, I'm not going to pretend that I'm not over-the-top nervous about this mission of yours. Billingsley and Goldstein are the ones who've got your back? Geez."

More like the other way around. I again reflected on how many women had similar conversations with their men over the last few years. Men go to war while others can only stand and wait. To me, it was easier to be the one going to war than to have to pace the sidelines.

"Donovan's returning tomorrow, you know," she said. "It's a further indication of how important this mission is."

"Yes, I'm aware. Listen, if anything should happen to me—and I'm sure it won't—will you contact my folks in South Hill? Please tell them, Elizabeth, that I love them. And while you're at it, tell them about us. That I love you. I've hinted to them in letters that I've met someone, but they don't know how serious I am about you." I was getting into mushy territory, which was about as familiar to me as central Sicily.

"Darling, you're right. It won't be necessary."

"I know. But just in case."

We spent that night together. I had the rest of my life to sleep. Good thing, too.

Chapter Twenty Two

Deception

Spain

May 1943

Little Maria Sanchez and her brother
Jose Maria were picking their way
along the shoreline of the Costa Del
Sol. Their father was out at sea with his
nets while their mother was at home
hanging out the laundry. Franco had
kept Spain out of the war, which was a
minor miracle. But then Hitler had not
made aggressive moves his way either.
Life for a fisherman and his family
hadn't changed much over the past
decades. It was a good life. Good
climate, a Catholic atmosphere, a
decent school for the children—and
the price of fish was currently very
good.

Maria was gathering shells while Jose
Maria contented himself with skipping
the stones he picked up across the flat
water. Maria spied the glint of a shell—
a conch?—a few yards away. As she

ran toward it, she realized that the shell was attached to something larger. Then she noticed that it was not a shell at all; it was a button. And it was attached to a tunic which was wrapped around the horribly bloated body of a corpse.

Maria screamed and Jose Maria came running. He took one look, turned on his heel and began sprinting for the house. It was only when he saw his mother in the yard that he realized that he'd left little Maria behind.

It took an hour for the *soldados* to arrive. They dragged the corpse, which was dressed in an English Army uniform, to the waiting ambulance, and, sirens blaring, drove away to the garrison in town. When they presented the corpse to the *commandante,* he found a packet of papers, which he hoped would identify the poor soul. Instead, they appeared to be orders. The words Sardinia and Greece were two words that he immediately recognized.

Chapter Twenty Three

Into The Sauce

Sicily

May 1943

The distance from Tunisia to our drop zone was about 350 miles, about a three hour, fifteen minute flight. We were ready. Even Billingsley swore he'd have no problem jumping out of the plane this time. We'd been preparing for this mission for months. I looked over at Binky. His jaw was clenched, betraying no emotion. My teammate Goldstein seemed determined and also had his jaw set. Ryder was aboard and was uncharacteristically silent.

There was a trailing aircraft with two jeeps and crates of ordinance aboard, also in line to be dropped.

The plane's droning tempted me to relax, but in reality there was little chance of that. We would execute our jump, hit the ground, find our Jeep and other supplies and lie low until dawn.

We had been equipped with little clickers that sounded like crickets so that we could communicate with each other, or at least identify friendlies in pitch black darkness. And it *was* dark, no moon, which was exactly why the date was chosen.

My team's destination was the south central town of Caltanissetta, Binky and his boys were headed for the east coast town of Catania. We were targeted to land outside of the towns on farmland so that we could hide until daylight. We would be busy locating and corralling our supplies. Binky and I were given maps showing the homes of our prospective hosts. I hoped that my arrival would not interfere with the Don's weekend plans.

All of us were heavily armed. For pistols, we all carried the FP-45 single-shot, a new design that had at first been supplied exclusively to the OSS. The thinking was that it was light weight, easy to use and ideal for individuals who wanted to resist their conquerors like we hoped the Sicilians felt. We were also dropping crates of FP-45s to distribute to the locals. I chose to carry a Thompson submachine gun while others carried M1 Carbines. We all sported Ka-Bar combat knives, binocs, canteens and other essentials. We were dressed as civilians—Sicilian civilians, which meant black pants, jackets or suit coats and white shirts. We'd been instructed to keep our coats buttoned up around our shirts to help avoid detection when we landed.

As we neared the first drop zone, which was to be my team's, I huddled my guys up and went over the plan one more time. Of course, it was loud in the plane so I had to shout. "We'll jump out fast one after the other. Goldstein, you're first, then you Billingsley and I'll be right behind you. The equipment will come next. Watch out that you don't get squashed by a jeep or a crate of bombs. I'm serious about that! Goldstein, you'll be on the look-out for the two of us. We'll meet up in the field and go find the supplies. Then we stay put til dawn."

What could go wrong?

"Goldstein, get ready! Go!" shouted Ryder. And Goldstein jumped. "Billingsley! Go!"

But Billingsley froze. "Goddammit Billingsley, go!" Ryder and I both grabbed him and began wrestling him to the hatchway. Precious seconds were ticking by until we were finally able to shove him out into space. As a last desperate act, Billingsley had shoved me to the floor before he departed. More seconds passed.

"Pointer, we're past the drop zone," Ryder shouted. "You'll be separated from them!"

"I'll find them!" I shouted back. And I jumped.

Just like practice, I thought, as I ripped the chord and the chute deployed. I tried as best I could to steer back to where I imagined the drop zone would be. Below was pitch black, a big nothing-burger. I had to be getting close to the ground though and I tried to be ready for impact. Suddenly my boots hit something solid. I braced for the ground, but I experienced an unexpected jolt as I was jerked to a stop with my feet dangling in midair. I bounced crazily up and down and side to side, with my left side banging into something hard and solid. A tree? Didn't feel like it; there were no branches or leaves. No, it was a structure of some kind, a building. As the torque from my sudden stop subsided, I was able to reach out to my left and grasp an outcropping of some sort from the structure and still myself.

My eyes began to adjust slowly to the dark, but there was almost no visibility. The surface next to me was broken stucco over stone. I looked up and could make out my chute caught and tangled on some kind of structure. I thought hard. A church. Or a town hall. Some kind of building with some architectural feature on top that my chute had tangled with. I knew that it couldn't be a farm house. Which meant I was in a town, no doubt Caltanissetta. So, I'd made it, but not in the way I'd wanted to. Maybe the Don would poke his head out of window in his nightcap and welcome me to The Sauce.

It was now 0400, one and a half hours until dawn. I considered what to do. It *wouldn't* do to be dangling here when the townsfolk started their morning rituals. But how to get free? I could cut my way out with my Ka-Bar, but I couldn't see the ground below me, so I didn't know how far I would fall. Probably far enough to break an ankle. How about pulling myself up the wall to the top? I could stand on the bell tower, or whatever was up there, and try to rappel down the face of the building to the ground. That would be difficult and time-consuming, but I couldn't come up with a better plan.

Suddenly out of the eerie quiet of the town I heard a noise below me. Faint at first, but getting louder. It was a rumbling, and as it drew nearer, I identified it as the rumbling of a cart's wheel on the cobblestones below. Then I saw it, a lantern swinging up on the bench of a buckboard, a man in the driver's seat and two oxen pulling the cart and heading right for me. A farmer going out to his fields. Would he be able to see me? I calculated that when he came adjacent to my position if he looked up, he would spot me. Nothing to do about it except stay still and pray. As he drew up to the building, he pulled on the reins and stopped the cart. He was about twenty feet directly below me. I held my breath. He was fumbling in his pockets for something and, at length, drew out a match. He struck the flame on the seat beside him and lit a cigarette.

"Hup!" He grunted at the oxen and rolled his way toward the outskirts of town.

When he was out of sight, I began pulling myself up the sheer face of the wall, grasping the chute lines hand over hand. Every few seconds I had to stop and untangle myself from the mess of lines that obstructed my path. With 35 pounds of equipment on my back and belt, the going was slow and exhausting. What were Goldstein and Billingsley doing? That damned Billingsley! I loved the kid, but what a fuck-up. I felt exactly like an older brother who had to protect his well-meaning, but incompetent sibling.

When I stopped to rest, which was every few seconds, I considered what to do when and if I ever reached the ground. It all depended on getting out of town before dawn. I wasn't in uniform, but nor had I changed into my civilian guise. A strange man humping a pack with a submachine gun through town wouldn't be confused with a traveling salesman. On the other hand, if I didn't make it before daylight, I could leave my gear on the roof, sneak down to the ground and try to bluff my way out of town. Not a great option.

I kept pulling myself skyward, foot by foot, inch by inch. If this was a church or even a cathedral, as I suspected, I tried to imagine the trappings inside. If it was a medieval structure, which seemed to be the case from the material that I was scrabbling on, it could have taken a century to build. There would be the long nave crossed by the transept before the altar forming a cross. I remembered from a course I took in college that Christians believed that the Church was the Body of Christ. The altar was the head, the transept the arms and hands and the nave and aisle was the rest of the body. Scholars believed that the long length of the nave was a reminder of longsuffering, which endures adversity. The breadth was Christian love. And the height was a hope for future reward. These thoughts flashed through my mind in a second.

Those beliefs fit my situation precisely. If I could gain the height of this structure, then I would have a shot at the future. Otherwise, there could be a lot of suffering in my near future. Maybe I could talk my way into the Don's good graces, but what if there were Italian or German troops in the vicinity. After all, the island was under their occupation. I wanted to approach the Don on my terms.

I began to sense the false dawn. I had perhaps 45 minutes, and I still didn't know exactly how far I had to go. I struggled for another 15 minutes and my right hand came in contact with what felt like a ledge, maybe six inches wide. At least it was a break in the sheer stucco, stone and mortar that had dominated the façade. A few more feet and there was another, wider ledge. This energized me so I redoubled my efforts to climb. Soon, I was able to stand on a slim parapet just a few feet underneath my chute. I cut one of the guy lines where it attached to my harness and then felt my way to its other end at the top of the chute and severed it there. I repeated the process with a second line and tied a surgeons knot to connect the two. I now had my rappelling line. I scrambled out of my harness and began feeling along for a place to attach the line. I found what felt like a gargoyle head protruding and tied a bowline around the head. Next, I had to ball up the chute and the other lines. I tossed them over the top of the parapet so they were out of sight. I rigged up the rappelling line and in a flash bounced my way to about fifteen feet above the ground. There, I stopped and shrugged out of the rappelling harness and cut the line. I then let go and dropped the remaining distance to the ground. It could be hours or it could be weeks before anyone noticed a line from the top of the church hanging down its side to fifteen feet from the ground.

Fifteen minutes or so to dawn. I peered at my compass and began double-timing it south through the ancient streets of the town. In a few minutes I had reached the edge of town and I followed the dirt road out into the countryside, alert for signs of life. The road was lined with cedars on either side, protecting me from being seen from the fields. When I judged that I'd run five miles along the road, I exited the road and entered a field where I believed Goldstein and Billingsley to be. The sun was just coming up so visibility was much improved. I crossed the field toward a copse of trees on the far side and as I approached I heard a 'click-click'. I stopped in my tracks and extracted my clicker and answered.

Goldstein appeared at the edge of the trees and beckoned me to join him.

"Hullo, boys," I said. "Have a good night's sleep?" Billingsley appeared, looking sheepish.

"Not much in the sleep department, Boss," said Goldstein. "But we sure are glad to see you, sir."

"Lieutenant, I sure am sorry about what happened in the plane," said Billingsley softly. "I just kinda lost it, sir."

"We'll forget about it. Let's just say our days of jumping together are done. Did you find the jeep and the supplies?"

"Yessir. The jeep's good as new and we rounded up the ordinance. It's packed up in the jeep and ready to go. We stashed the parachutes where nobody'll find them until we're long gone," Goldstein answered.

"Billingsley, it's your watch."

I pulled out my blanket, spread it out, dropped to the ground and promptly fell asleep.

Chapter Twenty Four

Don Vizzini

I consulted my map. The Don's compound was on the far side of town from where I'd made my escape. In case there were unfriendlies, I decided to skirt the town and approach Don Vizzini's place from the other end. I got in the driver's seat of the jeep with Goldstein riding shotgun. Billingsley sat on one of the crates in the back.

The island of Sicily has a long history of conflict, beginning with its occupation by the Greeks in 750 BC. Over the centuries, the Carthaginians, Germans, Byzantinians, Romans, Italians Spaniards and Arabs had fought and occupied the country. And now six Americans had dropped in. The terrain was rolling hills with almost all of it covered by plantings of some sort in the rich Volcanic soil—grapes, lemon trees, olive trees, almonds, citrons and orange groves. We passed the Greco-Roman ruins as we drove toward Vizzini's.

In under an hour, we were approaching the Don's compound. I stopped the jeep about 100 yards away and waited.

Within five minutes, four men armed with shotguns and knives had surrounded us.

"*Stop! Buttare giu le armi*!" said the one I'd already picked out as the leader. "Stop. Throw down your weapons."

"*Siamo venuti in pace per verdere Don Vizzini*," I replied. "We come in peace." But we didn't drop any weapons.

"Don Vizzini is not at home," said their leader. "What is your business here?"

"I am Lieutenant Robert Pointer, U.S. Marine Corps, and I come on official business to see Don Vizzini. I was sent by a friend." I pulled out my Luciano pennant and waved it.

With that, our new friend looked frantically around and gestured for us to follow him. He and the others broke

315

into a trot toward the compound. The gate swung open, and we entered the courtyard. The gate swung shut behind us.

"If you are who you say you are, you are in great danger from the Germans who are everywhere. If you are not who you say you are, you are in even greater danger from us. Wait here."

He disappeared into the house while the others pointed their shotguns at us. I smiled at my new companions and even gave them a little wave.

A few minutes later, our friend reappeared with a large white haired man dressed in black pants, a white undershirt and suspenders who trailed our greeter. It was the Don. He held a towel and was still wiping shaving cream from his face. Not at home, eh?

"You are a friend of Don Luciano?" he asked and held out his hand.

I handed him the pennant along with a letter from Lucky. Vizzini took a moment to read and said, "You are very welcome in my house, *Signor...*"

"Pointer," I said. "Everybody calls me Pointer."

Goldstein and Billingsley had watched these exchanges, not understanding a word. But they could read body language, and they relaxed as the Don did.

"Come in my house. Are you hungry? Thirsty?"

"*Si*, Don, we could use some refreshments and some cleaning up."

One of his men led us upstairs where there was a sitting room and a washroom. We took the opportunity to wash, shave and change our clothes from our single travel bag.

When we came downstairs, Don Vizzini greeted us as honored guests. He'd had servants lay out a feast in the main room. There seemed to be just about every food imaginable—fish, lamb, crab, rice, spaghetti, sauces, bread and butter and on and on. Carafes of rich-looking red wine were spread along the table, which the Don himself began pouring for us. He raised his glass and we followed suit.

"To Pointer, to Don Luciano and to my new American friends." We drank and the alcohol hit my tired body immediately. Watch it, Pointer.

"And to you, Don Vizzini, our host. May our association yield profitable results for both of our countries." I returned the favor.

I peered out into the courtyard and noticed a man leading a cart crammed with four goats. I turned and looked at our host, who was also watching the cart. Don Vizzini was gazing upon the goats with what looked like pride.

"Is there some significance to the cart full of goats?" I inquired.

Don Vizzini peered at me as though I were a visitor from another planet. No, just another world.

"Yes, Pointer, there is significance in the goats. The Germans and Italians were not the first to occupy our homeland. We have a long list of invaders, one of which was the Greeks. It is from them that we take this tradition."

"What? Goats?"

The Don smiled. "Not goats, *per se*, Pointer. It is a tradition that when you invite honored guests to dine at your table that you bring live goats in view so that they understand that no matter how much they may consume, there is always more."

Ah.

"Now you must eat. And then we will talk," said our host.

"Tell me how my great *compadre* Don Luciano is faring in the New World, my friend."

"Well, he doesn't seem to be any the worse for wear," I started. "He has all the comforts of home, including any visitor who wants to see him. Oh, and he has an excellent chef. Not to worry about your friend, Don Vizzini."

"Excellent! You know we still do quite a lot of trading, he and I. His businesses continue to thrive even though his movements have been halted. Tell me, Pointer. Do you think your Government will pardon him and set him free because of his magnificent patriotism?"

"No sir, I do not. I do think they will let him out of prison. But you have a better chance of seeing him here than they do in New York."

At that moment, the Don's *consigliere,* or at least who I assumed was his *consigliere,* entered the room and urgently whispered in the Don's ear.

"Ah, gentlemen, it seems we will be having unexpected visitors from the local garrison. Colonel Haas of the German Army has requested an audience with me. It would be wise to oblige him. And it would be wise if you were to take your espresso in my special room. Falcone will show you the way."

Falcone gestured for us to follow him. He still had his shotgun strapped over his shoulder. Probably slept with it. He led us down a flight of stairs and through three rooms to a reasonably comfortable salon. I noticed that he locked each door as we passed through. He left and returned a few minutes later, rolling a cart with espresso and cups.

Boy, this guy does it all, I thought. Gotta remember to leave a nice tip.

We cooled our heels down there for about an hour when Falcone returned to fetch us.

When we returned to the dining area, the Don bade us follow him to what I would call a family room. Lots of pictures of the Don's descendants as well as a couple of newspaper shots of Lucky that he'd had framed.

"Our Gestapo here is led by Colonel Haas of the SS. It was not, as I'm sure you suspect, a social call. Although I do know him. We've done some business together since the Island has been occupied. I make sure his supplies don't disappear, and he donates a few *lira* for me to spend on my grandchildren. Now, Pointer, you must tell me what I can do for you. The Colonel was asking questions that I did not like to hear. It is not safe for you to stay here for long."

"Don Vizzini, the United States Government believes that it is a matter of time before we drive the Germans and the Italians out of Sicily. You have suffered under Mussolini's rule, and it is a matter of time before his own people get rid of him. The Allies are coming, sir, and when they come, they will 'come heavy'." I'd heard Lucky use that phrase so I hoped it would be especially effective on the Don.

"The Allies would like to have you, Russo and the other Dons on our side in this fight," I continued. "Don Luciano, too, wants you to prosper by helping us, as he said to you in his personal letter."

"And what do the Allies want me to do? And Russo? Hah! He may as well be Mussolini himself! What I say is what I will do, but not him."

"Again, Pointer, what is it you would have me do?"

"For starters, sir, those German supplies could start disappearing. And certain arms depots could catch fire or even blow up. And you could get word to us about any rumors you hear or see on your Island. For example, troop movements, new fortifications that might get built. And your men could be very helpful with their marksmanship, which I understand to be superb."

I then informed the Don about the bombs and guns we'd brought. This seemed of special interest to him.

"And when should we be expecting your troops?" asked Vizzini.

"I don't have a date for you, but you've got at least thirty days to prepare…and to disrupt. I've been authorized to tell you that General Patton himself is grateful for your assistance."

Vizzini's eyes narrowed as though this was too fantastical to be believed. "The great fighter Patton? He will be leading?"

"Yes. He is personally invested in liberating Sicily."

"You may tell the General that we will do all in our power to help. And if he comes this way on his march, he will receive the minimum of resistance. I would also advise that he not take the eastern route through land controlled by Russo. Now, I have things I must attend to. You, Pointer, and your men should rest and be prepared to depart tonight. The Colonel will be back."

Chapter Twenty Five

Flight

At 1700 hours we ate a cold supper, attended only by Falcone. We had accomplished our mission a full 24 hours ahead of schedule. We couldn't stay with the Don as the SS had sniffed us out and suspected our presence. I thought of breaking radio silence and checking to see if Binky was ready, but discarded that idea because our transport back to Tunisia wouldn't be available.

Falcone solved our dilemma by telling me that the Don had arranged for us to stay at one of his country houses to the south. He would lead us there this night. We would form a two-vehicle caravan for a two-hour journey. Falcone knew where the Nazi checkpoints were. *"No problema"*, he said.

Falcone and three of his men piled into a 1938 Fiat, and we boarded our Jeep. No lights, Falcone had warned. Just follow. We pulled out of the Don's compound and Falcone roared off. This was going to be exhilarating, I thought.

Falcone soon hit speeds of 50 miles per hour, which was akin to 90 on a normal road. This one was twisty and turning and heavily rutted. I watched as the Fiat bounced, at times all four wheels leaving the dirt at once. We fared no better; I just concentrated on keeping on the track. Fortunately, the Fiat's brake lights worked, and Falcone was working them hard, so I had some visual reference in the pitch black dark. Goldstein, Billingsley and I all had our weapons at the ready and, of course, Falcone and his men had their shotguns, I had noticed that they were already sporting the FP-45s as well.

At around midnight, I saw two lights in the rear view. A car. Then, the lights split into two discrete beams. Two motorcycles! I wondered if Falcone had spotted them although it didn't really matter because we could not go any faster.

I yelled back at Billingsley, making sure he saw the lights. "Billingsley, you're in the best position to take them out. But wait until you can get off a good shot!" I was assuming that these were unfriendlies. If I was wrong, we'd ask forgiveness later.

The motorcycles were gaining on us. When they were about 300 yards behind us, they turned on their sirens and emergency lights. Definitely unfriendly. I could see Billingsley setting up with his M1 Carbine resting on a bag in front of him. But with the jouncing, he had little chance of accuracy. Goldstein had turned 180 degrees and was getting his submachine gun ready. Goldstein's weapon was better for close-in work so I was grateful for Billingsley's M1. Ahead of us, Falcone's brake lights came on—and stayed on. Then they disappeared momentarily. He was fishtailing to a stop. I slammed my brakes and swung the wheel hard to the left, narrowly avoiding a collision. Billingsley was nearly thrown out of the back but managed to barely hang on. We were going to make a stand right here.

All four doors of the Fiat opened and Falcone and his men jumped out. We had to kill these guys before they could radio in. We too jumped out of the jeep, taking positions behind it. The motorcycles had slowed noticeably and were moving cautiously toward us. They were out of shotgun and machine gun range.

"Billingsley, do you have a shot?" Don't fail me now, son.

In answer, he squeezed off a round and we saw one of the cycles careen off the road into a ditch. Billingsley carefully sighted the other pursuer, who had now stopped altogether and was turning around. He fired, but the rider was now hightailing it back up the road.

"Let's go!" I shouted at Falcone. We had now killed or at least seriously wounded an enemy and there would be hell to pay.

We roared ahead at an even faster clip if that was possible. In another hour, Falcone turned off the road to his right.

We traveled two or three miles up a track and up a rise to a cottage on a hill. Falcone went in first and lit a lantern and some candles. It was a three-room building equipped with a wood stove and four cots. This would be our home for the next 24 hours.

"Falcone, who knows about this place?" I asked.

"The four of us and, of course, Don Vizzini. No one else. You are safe here. There will be patrols out looking for us so we will stay here tonight with you."

We settled in for a long night. Falcone and his men stationed themselves outside among the trees as sentinels. I offered our services to relieve his men, but he declined.

My thoughts turned to Binky and his men. Brownwell had said our route south would be "sparsely attended" by the enemy. If two motorcycle troopers was a sparse representation, I supposed he'd been right. Binky would have to travel a similar distance to our rendezvous and I hoped he would make it. I wondered if he'd had success with his dealings with Don Russo. Vizzini had no use for Russo, but that was probably Mafia rivalry. Binky also had Luciano's pennant and a copy of his letter, so if Russo was anything like Vizzini, that would have carried weight. I didn't much care for old Binky, but I hoped his mission was a success.

The next morning, we risked a fire in the wood stove and made coffee and heated up some beans for breakfast.

"What's the plan, Boss?" Billingsley asked.

"We wait for dark and head south. Our rendezvous with Binky is for midnight. Our pick-up is for tomorrow. By the way, Billingsley, that was some good shooting last night."

Billingsley beamed. "Thanks, Boss. Figured I have some making up to do after the jump. There was a reason I washed out at Benning, but I was tops at marksman class. Squirrel hunting back in Omaha, y'know."

"Your folks would be proud."

"Hell, my dad's never been out of Nebraska. He wouldn't know The Sauce from the sauce, if you know what I mean. But I love the old codger. Me and him got plans for the farm when I get back. By the way, these beans are great, considering the context."

We spent the day playing Liar's Poker with Sicilian currency and catching naps. At last night fell. It was time to go.

Chapter Twenty Six

Betrayal

We loaded the jeep and made our way back to the main road. No headlights, so I was able to do only about 20 mph. Falcone would've done 50. It was another moonless night and a soft wind was blowing out of the south. Very comfortable. The terrain had turned to sparse vegetation and big rocks in the fields. Every now and then we would pass a farmstead or a ruin, but only rarely were there any lights on. Falcone had assured me that there were no towns or checkpoints on this route. In a couple of hours we would arrive at our rendezvous point.

I thought about Elizabeth. If I made it through this war I thought that I'd want to spend my days with her. Father would say that this was a sign of my maturity. I'd turn thirty next October, five months from now. Maybe it was time to settle down. I doubted that the war would be over that quickly. We probably had at least a couple more years to go. I had meant what I'd said to Elizabeth about a career either in the military or the OSS if Wild Bill could convince Congress to keep it going. I'd missed seeing Donovan when he returned to Africa, but I expected to see him when we got back. I didn't want to let him or Patton or, hell, FDR down. The Colonel had entrusted this mission to me under the skepticism of many, and I was determined to prove him right.

Goldstein had the job of navigator and interrupted my thoughts. "Our spot is just up here off the road, sir. We'll hang a left and go overland for about a mile until we see a lemon grove. That's where the meet will happen."

We bumped across a field until we spotted the grove. I stopped the jeep and told the boys to get out. We'd approach the grove on foot, spread out, so if there were some kind of ambush, we wouldn't be sitting ducks. We all took our clickers out and as we neared the trees we clicked away. There was no response. I was the first to breech the grove and could find no sign of life.

"Goldstein, go back and get the jeep. We'll park in here and wait."

And we did. I stationed the men on opposite sides of the grove and I took the point where we'd entered. We were pretty well concealed, the jeep was well into the small forest, and we communicated by whisper. When we spread out, we agreed that if anyone saw something, he would use his clicker.

An hour passed before we heard the soft rumble of a vehicle. We all three clicked to indicate that we'd noticed. The rumble grew louder and then stopped. We could see nothing from where the noise had emanated. A few minutes went by in utter silence. Then I heard it. "Click". I clicked back and was answered by a second click. Had to be Binky. And it was. He came close enough for me to see him so I stepped out and hissed, "Binky!", and I could see him relax. "Pointer!"

We embraced. Binky and I actually hugged. Never thought I'd be so glad to see my comrade. Jameson and Parsons joined us and we all began to whisper at each other at once. When the initial excitement died down, I asked Binky about Russo.

"Oh yes. He was most cooperative. Agreed with the entire plan right away."

"Great to hear. Tell me, Binky, what did he have to say about Don Vizzini? Seems the two don't see eye to eye."

"Don Vizzini? Oh, of course, your Don. Um, no, no, there appears to be no love lost."

I told Binky, Parsons and Jameson about how we'd made contact with Vizzini, the suspicious SS Colonel, the flight from the house and the fight with the troopers.

Binky said, "I decided to approach Russo very differently, old boy. I felt that stealth was paramount, so I left Jameson and Parsons at the drop zone and made contact on my own. After I showed him the pennant, he was sweetness and light."

Sweetness and light? It didn't seem in character for Binky to take such a risk.

"The skids are perfectly greased for Monty and his boys," Binky concluded.

"That's terrific, Binky," I said slowly. "We should get a move on to the coast, don't you think?"

"No!" Binky said hastily. "I think it's better that we wait here until dawn and then move out. We're ahead of schedule so we'll have to kill some time either here or on the coast waiting for the DUKW. Might as well be here where we know we're safe."

"But that means we'll have to travel in daylight," I pointed out.

I noticed the men were looking at their two leaders a little anxiously.

"Yes, true. But we'd be perfectly exposed in daylight if we had to wait at the beach."

I looked at Binky for a moment and made a decision. "Alright, we'll do it your way, Binky."

We spread out around the perimeter as best we could. Binky moved off about 40 yards to my right. Something was wrong here, but I couldn't figure out what. Why would Binky want to stay put? Did he and his men need rest? Was he right about daylight exposure being better on the move than on the beach? I didn't think so, but I didn't want to argue in front of the men.

The time ticked by. One hour to dawn. I nodded off a couple of times, but I knew that Billingsley was next to me and awake. I told him to wake me before dawn. As soon as I'd issued that order, or so it seemed, Billingsley shook me awake.

"Almost dawn, Boss," he said.

I shook myself awake and poured a little water into my hand from my canteen and splashed it on my face. I began to be able to make out the shapes of the landscape and then the men spread around the copse of trees. Something had been nagging at me all night, and it was Binky's actions in Catania. It didn't seem in character for Binky, a bully and a coward, to undertake meeting Don Russo alone.

I called over to him. "Binky," I hissed. "Step into my office here for a chat."

He moved over next to me.

"Let's go through your meeting with Russo again. You approached him alone, and then what happened?"

I could see that Binky was exasperated with me. "Yes, Pointer, I met him at his farmhouse. I pulled out Luciano's pennant and gave the Don his letter. He invited me in for breakfast and we made plans for the invasion. I already told you this."

"And he was cooperative? And there were no visits from the Germans? They are, after all, stationed there in Catania. Wonder how they knew about us and not about you?"

"I've no idea. Now, if your interrogation is over, I'd like to get back to my preparations to leave."

He moved off to the flank of the copse of trees, but I smelled a rat.

The sun was now over the trees in the distance. We would be traveling through Nazi territory in broad daylight, and it didn't make sense to me.

Something moved over to my right. It was Binky and he was tying a bright red bandanna around his neck. Bandanna? And it hit me. This was a set-up.

"Men! Get down! Get down!" I screamed.

Billingsley turned and lurched toward me, and as he did, I heard a blast. Billingsley was thrown into me, knocking me down as he landed on top of me. I looked down at him. His face was a red mass of blood and tissue.

I held him in my arms. He looked up at me and muttered, "Pop. Tell Pop..." And he died.

I pulled my Thompson up and began raking the area where the blast had come from and from where now steady fire was ripping through the lemon grove. It sounded like a brigade out there. Three troopers got up and charged my position, crossing open ground about twenty yards away. Jameson, to my left, and I were able to mow them down. But Jameson, in exposing himself, took multiple rounds to the gut and went down screaming. To my right, I could see Binky sprinting through the field, red bandanna streaming behind him. I had a shot, at least for a second. I had to expose myself, but it was worth it if I could bring the lying bastard down. I aimed the Thompson, led him by a couple of feet and let go a burst of fire. But it was too late, he was too far away.

There was a momentary lull in the firing. Then, an amplified voice called out, "Surrender! You are surrounded by fifty men! There is no escape!"

I frantically reviewed our options. Billingsley and Jameson were dead. The jeeps were behind us in the center of the grove. Could we reach them and charge our way out? I didn't think so. We were done. All I could accomplish at that point was to get the remaining men killed. Shit!

"*Jawohl*! We surrender! Men, put down your weapons!" I shouted. And I threw out my Thompson and my pistol. The others followed suit as the Germans closed on us cautiously. When they reached us, they shouted, "Down! Down! Hands behind your back!" We complied as they cuffed our hands behind our backs.

As they marched us to their vehicles, I caught sight of Binky climbing into the lead truck even as a Colonel got in on the other side. Another trooper got into Binky's jeep and drove off.

Bastard! I was feeling some extreme hate toward my former comrade-in-arms. I swore to myself that if I ever got the chance, I would personally shoot him.

We were taken back to Catania and led to the rear of a concrete building and locked in a cell.

"Sir, is what I think Leftenant Binkford did really what happened?" asked Parsons.

"Yes. He's a traitorous coward, he set us up. I'm certain that he never saw Don Russo. He came straight here and met with Colonel Haas instead. I should've figured it out."

"What do you think they have planned for us, sir?" asked Goldstein.

"No idea, but I'm not keen on going back to Germany with these folks," I said.

At that moment, Colonel Haas appeared with two guards. "Which one is Pointer?" he demanded.

I stood. "I'm Pointer. Who wants to know?"

"Come with me," he said as a guard unlocked the cell and pulled me along down the hall.

I was led into an office which clearly belonged to the Colonel and told to sit down. The armed guard stood at attention at the door.

"You were sent here to make contact with Don Vizzini to clear the way for the invasion." This wasn't a question.

"Not at all. The Don invited me to his hacienda to compare notes on medieval Italian church architecture. He's quite a scholar, you know. But I never made it there. I, uh, got hung up."

"Your General Patton will be coming through Caltanissetta and Montgomery through Catania."

"Look, Colonel, no offense, but if you've got all the answers, why are you asking me?"

"Because, Lieutenant, we have credible intelligence that Sicily is not the target at all. Rather, you will be invading Sardinia or Greece instead. This may be a ruse to throw us off the scent. You, Pointer, will answer my questions, or it will go very badly for you and your men."

"Tell you what, Colonel, I'll trade you some information. You tell me what you're doing with Binkford, and I'll tell you what we're doing here."

The Colonel smiled. "Binkford? Or, Binky as you call him. Binky has an appointment to keep. He has to get to the south, get in radio contact with your superiors and tell them the unfortunate news about the ambush that killed all of his compatriots. Then, I believe he has an appointment with a boat to return him to Africa where he will resume his duties."

"Now, Pointer, it is your turn. What are you doing here?"

I looked at Haas for a moment and said, "Colonel, fuck you and the horse you rode in on."

Chapter Twenty Seven

Revenge

They beat the snot out of me for that.

Afterwards, Haas said, "They'll love you in Auschwitz." I'll admit that sent a chill down my spine.

I was thrown back in the cell with the boys and I slumped in the corner as Goldstein tried to minister to me as best he could. I wasn't sure if my ribs were broken or just bruised, but my midsection hurt like hell.

As soon as I could speak, I told the guys what Binky was planning. "If he succeeds, he'll get back to Africa and spin his yarn and be in a position to screw up all of our plans."

"What can we do, sir?" said Goldstein.

As I was pondering that, we heard a deafening explosion. The vibration made plaster rain down around our heads. I lurched to the bars looking out to the hallway. No sooner had I reached the window than another massive explosion hit. Again, plaster rained down, this time in big chunks.

The hall was empty. But then I saw two of our guards backing down the corridor with their submachine guns trained to the far end. The door burst open and there was Falcone blowing away the guards with two shotgun blasts. He and his three men rushed down the hall, picked the keys to the cell out of the guard's belt and opened our door.

"Falcone! I hoped you'd come!" I screamed in Italian. In fact, I'd counted on it. Don Vizzini wouldn't leave one of Lucky's boys to be shipped off to a death camp.

"Come on, Pointer. We have to get out," said Falcone. His tip was getting bigger and bigger.

We hustled down the hall with Falcone and his men leading the way. There were two guards waiting on the other side of the exterior door. They pumped rounds of machine gun fire into the two Mafiosi who were leading us. Falcone, having reloaded in our cell, took both of the guards out with a single blast. We were out. There was Falcone's Fiat and at first I thought he wanted us to ride with him. But he gestured at the two motorcycles parked next to the Fiat. I jumped on one and directed Parsons and Goldstein to the other one which had a sidecar.

I saw that half of the building had been blown away, no doubt with ordinance that we had provided. Patton's going to love these guys, I thought.

I realized that Binky probably had an hour's head start on us. But we knew where he was going, and he didn't know that we'd been liberated. So, Advantage Pointer.

We roared out into the road and hit top speed within seconds. No sign of Haas or his men. Had they been killed? I didn't know, and I didn't care. I had eyes only for Binky. We gunned our motorcycles and raced back the way we'd come.

There were about 40 miles until we were in range of communications with our offshore ships. It wasn't certain that they'd be there to answer every call as they were obliged to dodge Axis Destroyers and bombers. But, I thought, Binky has the same problem. In any case, I didn't much care if Binky told Brownwell *et al* that we were dead as long as we had the chance to correct him. I only cared that we stop Leftenant Binkford from doing any more damage to our cause.

No one was following us. Falcone and his boys had done a thorough job back in Catania. We passed the point where I judged us to be in radio contact, but I decided not to stop. One problem: my gas tank was showing that I had less than a quarter tank. This wasn't South Hill where we could stop at the friendly Esso station and fill 'er up. I guess Falcone couldn't be expected to think of everything. Still, he deserved a massive tip.

After another twenty minutes, my engine began to sputter. *Damn!* Out of gas. I pulled off to the side and Goldstein followed. I jumped into the sidecar behind Parsons, sitting with my legs straddling his and smacked Goldstein on the shoulder as a signal to rev it up again. "Go!" I shouted.

My ribs were aching, but I was operating on adrenaline without being conscious of it. I was hell-bent-for-leather to catch Binky. We were only a few miles from the coast and catching Binky was all that mattered. I heard a pop and Goldstein lost control of the cycle. I realized that the front tire had been shot out. Goldstein grappled with the steering, lost control and plunged us toward the ditch paralleling the road. At the last second, he jerked the wheel back so that we didn't hit the wall of the ditch head-on; rather we glanced—hard—against the side of the embankment. More shots rang out, ripping through the scrub at the side of the road and whistling off the rocks.

But we were on the move, away from the road. We scrambled across the scrub until we were behind a massive rock.

"You guys ok?" I breathed.

"Good, sir," said Goldstein, and Parsons nodded.

"Pointer!" It was Binky. "We can make a deal! You let me go back to Catania and I'll let you get to the landing zone. I've got you pinned down! You have no chance." And with that, he loosed a fusillade of bullets which ricocheted all around our position.

He's up there on the high ground, I thought. Smart. Binky was an asshole, but he wasn't stupid. Falcone had tossed us an M1, three knives and an FP-45 as we'd busted out of Catania.

"You just leave, Binky," I shouted. "We won't stop you. We'll declare a truce."

"Why don't I believe you, Pointer," he shouted back.

"I don't care if you believe me or not," I shouted. "It's the best I can do."

Binky fired again, but we were dug in now and the bullets sailed over our heads.

"Pointer, Haas and his men will be here soon! It's in your best interests to take my deal!"

"Fuck you, Binky!"

I gestured to Goldstein and Parsons to give me the pistol and the knife. This would be close-quarters combat, so I wouldn't be needing the M1. I whispered to Goldstein to continue the dialogue. He'd have to do his Pointer impression.

"Come on, Pointer. It's your best chance." He unleashed another fusillade of bullets to emphasize his point.

I had a pretty good idea of his hiding place so I crabbed my way to my left for about twenty-five yards and then began an ascent up the hill.

"No way!" I heard Goldstein respond, doing his best Pointer imitation. Was Binky buying it?

I continued to scrabble my way up, trying not to make noise, but my foot slipped on a loose rock and it went tumbling down the hill, making a racket. This prompted Binky to swing his rifle around at me and fire shots that hit very close.

I held my breath and waited.

Goldstein shouted, "Let's go, Binky, we don't have all day!"

I began my climb again. In a few moments I'd made my way high enough to where I judged Binky to be. When I paused I glanced back down the hill and I saw him. He was crouched behind a rock, his total focus down the hill.

"Binky!" I shouted. He swung his rifle up toward me and fired, but I had anticipated this and ducked behind a rock. Now, I would finish the bastard off. He was a sitting duck there below me; there was nowhere for him to hide from an assailant from above. I flattened myself on my belly, waited a beat and in one motion, stuck my head and my pistol out on the right side of the rock about six inches off the ground. I got Binky dead in my sights and pulled the trigger, aiming right between his eyes.

Click.

Nothing happened. The gun had jammed. *Oh shit.*

Binky immediately realized what had happened and fired up at me, but I'd ducked behind the rock again. Now I was the sitting duck, and I wondered how he would come at me. As long as I was behind the rock, he'd have to come get me. Then I heard him as he began to laugh. It started as a low chuckle and escalated into a full throated belly laugh.

He at last got enough breath and shouted up to me, "Isn't this a fine mess, Pointer? You have the strategic advantage, but I actually have a gun that is in perfect working order with enough ammo to hold off a small army. Right now, I'm wondering if you have a back-up weapon. Another pistol, perhaps? No, I don't think so. You'd have used it by now. But maybe a knife? Yes, probably a knife. If not, you could try throwing rocks at me."

This produced another round of guffaws, which ended after a moment. Then silence. Then scrabbling. Binky was climbing up the fifteen feet to my position. I risked a peek and watched as he crabbed his way up the sheer cliff, rifle held in both hands in front of him. I couldn't let him get to the top or it would be me and my Ka-Bar against him and his carbine on equal footing.

I emerged from my hiding place and sprinted the few feet to the edge. Binky heard me coming just as he had a good foothold on the hill. He raised his rifle against me and was preparing to fire, but I was already airborne, Ka-bar in hand. I landed with my full weight on him, and we rolled back down the steep hill. I grabbed hold of his rifle, which discharged into the air. As I did, he rolled me over and he was on top, pinning my arms with his knees. But his rifle had gone flying. Sweat and spittle were rolling down his face as he punched me in my cheekbone. After the punch, he went for his pistol, which was stuck in his belt. The Ka-Bar had been jostled out of my hand, but it was lying within reach so I grabbed it and in one swift motion drove it upwards into the soft part of his throat. Blood spurted from the wound, covering me. But Binky was deader than dead.

Chapter Twenty Eight

Reunion

When the three of us—Goldstein, Parsons and I—arrived in Tunisia, we were met by Brownwell... and Elizabeth.

She held back as Brownwell congratulated us and shook each of our hands. When I turned to her, she lost her careful reserve and gave me a bear hug that affected me to the core. In fact, she wrapped her legs around me as I twirled her in a circle. Was this any way for a Red Cross official to act? Let alone an OSS agent.

"Pointer, we heard that you were dead. We got Binky's transmission, and there was no reason to doubt his account."

I looked at her. She had tears in her eyes.

"There was a lot of reason to doubt him, but, like me, you hadn't worked it out."

"I thought I'd lost you, and that was something I couldn't bear. Darling."

There was no longer any question about dropping the g.

Maybe I was cocky, but I had never seriously considered that I'd die in The Sauce.

"Elizabeth, we'll make it out of this war and, whaddaya say, we keep together afterwards."

What an old romantic I am.

"I love you."

"And I love you, Elizabeth."

There. I said it.

Chapter Twenty Nine

Debrief

May 23, 1943

Mr. and Mrs. James Billingsley

Omaha, Nebraska

Dear Mr. and Mrs. Billingsley,

I know that you now know of Jim's death. I was his commanding officer on a mission that required steadiness and bravery. Jim was outstanding in both categories. In fact, Jim was a particular favorite of mine. His enthusiasm and bravery were something our entire squad admired and appreciated.

Mr. Billingsley, Jim shared with me your plans for your farm. I know that he would have made a success of it. He was so full of determination and love of the land. His last words were speaking your name, sir.

He was a brave soldier and always did his duty. I am grateful that he was

under my command, and I, like you, will
always cherish his memory.

Very truly yours,

Robert L. Pointer, USMC

There was one more item of business
to take care of. Thomas Dowderwell.
There was some urgency to this task as
Dowderwell had to know that he was
in trouble. But I wanted us to have
jurisdiction over our Thomas so at my
first de-brief with Wild Bill, I brought it
up.

Goldstein, Parsons and I were invited
to meet with Donovan and Brownwell.

"Pointer, men, I want to congratulate
you on your mission. From everything
the Major has told me, you conducted
yourselves with honor," Donovan
opened.

"Thank you, sir," I spoke for our group.
"I just wish we could've brought
everyone home."

"Yes, let's start with that. Did you have any inkling that Binkford was a traitor?"

"None, sir. Looking back, I don't know how we'd have known. But when he refused to leave the rendezvous point until daylight, I should've known something was up. For that, I am sorry."

"You personally killed him, did you not, Pointer? I imagine you feel some sense of vindication, yes?"

"It's complicated, sir. It's going to take me a long time to sort that out."

"Don Vizzini. That part of the mission was, I understand, a success. But we can conclude that Binkford never made contact with Don Russo. You agree?"

"Yessir. He spent his entire time in Catania with the Nazis, it's safe to assume. There is a loose end, sir, that I'd like your permission to pursue." Donovan nodded, so I continued. "I met Binkford at a restaurant in town as he was dining with someone he said was an old pal from London. A Thomas Dowderwell, British Army. Binky didn't plan all of this on his own. He had to have some help, perhaps communication with the Nazis. I know from Binkford first-hand that he is close with a cousin in Germany, a Friedrich von Furstenberg, who is fairly high up in the SS. Maybe Binkford was in touch with him, and maybe Dowderwell was some kind of conduit."

"You realize, Pointer, that an OSS officer's investigating a British Army officer presents a ticklish situation," Donovan observed.

"Yessir, I've considered that. What I was thinking is that I interview him off the record and, if I consider him to be suspicious, we deal with the politics later."

Donovan looked out the window in thought. "If we have a spy in our midst, then it's our job to root him out. The 'book' says that we turn him over to British Intelligence. As it is, we'll need a full report on Binkford's treachery. But

I am disposed to agree to your plan, Pointer. Dowderwell has got to be expecting that someone will be looking to talk to him. May as well start with you."

"I'll get right on it, sir."

Chapter Thirty

Freddy

I was able to find Dowderwell quite easily. Binky's commanding officer, who still believed that Binky was killed in the line of duty, looked him up and even arranged the meeting. I was to see Dowderwell the next day at the same HQ office at which I first met Binky.

"So nice to see you again, Pointer. Such a shame about Binky. Poor chap." Dowderwell was cool.

"Yeah, a tragedy," I agreed without passion.

"Are you here to commiserate, or is there something else I can do for you, Pointer?"

"Do you know Binky's cousin Freddy?"

"Why, yes, yes I do. Spent a wonderful summer with Binky and Freddy in the Alpine home of the von Furstenbergs.

Fine family. So sorry this blasted war has come between us all."

"When's the last time you were in contact with Freddy?"

"You see, Pointer, the thing is, I don't recall. Freddy is such a complex fellow. One could spend a lifetime understanding Freddy and what motivates him."

Well, OK. Here's something.

"What do you mean, Dowderwell?"

"It's just that Freddy is such a moral chap, and I believe that he's not all in with this whole Nazi movement. Just my speculation, of course. My belief is that if Hitler were to, say, die in an airplane crash, Freddy would perhaps see the bright side of the thing. Same if something were to befall his immediate superior, Himmler."

"Freddy is with Himmler?"

"Quite. Himmler is a busy fellow. In charge of the SS, the Gestapo and, of course, the Jewish Question. I believe Freddy is on his general staff. One hears rumors."

"And what else does one hear?"

"Oh, this and that. It would seem that not everyone who wears a Nazi uniform is enchanted with the way the leadership is conducting the war. If one could lend a hand to these chaps, it could end up to the benefit of the Allies."

"And how do you know these things, Dowderwell?"

Dowderwell stared at me and paused before replying. "Oh, one hears rumors if one listens in the right places."

I thought about confronting him about Binky, but I was getting the strong sense that he would back off with direct questioning.

"Dowderwell, have you reported any of these rumors to your superiors or to British Intelligence?" I thought I knew the answer to that.

"No, Pointer, they are, after all, just rumors. And if I were to repeat them to the wrong chaps, then, well, then I'm afraid they wouldn't understand, and it could get sticky for me, you see."

"But you're repeating them to me."

"Yes, so I am," he said thoughtfully. "Perhaps you will know how to treat them. And me."

All my doubts about collusion between Dowderwell and Binky were erased. A large part of me wanted to jump across the table and strangle the supercilious bastard to death in revenge for Billingsley and Jameson. But I managed to keep my cool.

"You're not thinking of going anywhere, are you Dowderwell? Like to another posting in another country?"

"Heavens no. I believe my highest and best use is right here. With you, Pointer."

Chapter Thirty One

A Volunteer

May 1943

Patton Pushes Axis Powers Out

Operation Torch Complete Victory

By Archie Stanhope (AP)

General George S. Patton's 3rd Army, in collaboration with General Bernard Montgomery's British I Army, have successfully driven the Germans and Italians out of North Africa. In a stupendous display of cooperation, logistical mastery and fighting skills, the two armies hounded the Axis powers to the very last.

The Supreme Allied Commander, in overall command of Operation Torch, pronounced himself well pleased with the outcome.

"General Alexander and I wish to commend Generals Montgomery and Patton for their battlefield skills and

relentless pursuit of Axis forces during Operation Torch. It is an important and vital victory in our war against Nazism and Facism."

Speculation now turns to where the Allies will strike next. Now that Allied control of the Suez Canal is assured, control of the Mediterranean Sea becomes more strategically important than ever. Axis forces now operate out of bases in Sicily, Greece and Sardinia as well as Italy. This reporter has searched for clues as to where the next strike will come. But Allied commanders in North Africa are keeping mum on the subject.

One thing seems clear, however. With their victory in Operation Torch, it is a sure bet that both General Patton and General Montgomery will be tapped to lead the next invasion.

The day after my meeting with Thomas Dowderwell, I was scheduled to see Donovan again to report my findings. The other members of the North Africa OSS contingent, Elizabeth and Hopkins, joined the conference.

"The bastard is a spy, a double agent. He's as responsible for our guys' deaths as the SS men who pulled the trigger," I said.

"He admitted it?" Donovan questioned.

"In so many words, yes. There's no doubt."

"I'd recommend immediate arrest and we'll sort out the jurisdiction issues later, "Hopkins said.

I said, "Unless we can turn him to our advantage."

Donovan was silent and thoughtful.

"What do you mean," asked Hopkins.

"What he means, Mark, is that from the sound of it, Dowderwell may very well be willing to use his Nazi contacts to our advantage," Donovan said.

"So, he'd be, what, a triple agent." Elizabeth weighed in.

Donovan said, "From his tone and his words, Pointer, is that a possibility? A probability?"

I thought about what Dowderwell had said and how he'd said it. I answered, "Yes, I believe that's exactly what he'd like to see happen. It'd be a way to save his own neck. He all but admitted to being in touch with von Furstenberg, who's very high in Himmler's command and is no doubt in some kind of contact with Hitler himself. He also hinted that von Furstenberg would not be at all disappointed to see Hitler—or Himmler—dead. He said that there were a lot of Nazis who didn't like the way Hitler was conducting the war.

"That suggests a cabal or some kind of anti-Hitler conspiracy," Donovan observed.

"Yes", I agreed. "If one can trust Dowderwell, that's exactly what he was saying."

Hopkins weighed in, "The two leading proponents of the Final Solution are Hitler and Himmler. We know this with certainty. If one or both were assassinated, then perhaps some of these wretches who are being led to the slaughter could be saved. I say we do whatever we can to join forces with von Furstenberg and whoever else in Berlin and Munich is likewise disaffected."

"Not to mention the entire Nazi war machine would be crippled," added Elizabeth.

"I agree that we have a potentially important contact with a high-up in the Nazi command," said Donovan. "The question is how to exploit it."

"Well, sir, I've been thinking about that," I said.

"Why am I not surprised," Wild Bill observed wryly.

"Yessir. If von Furstenberg were to prove amenable, we could send someone to Berlin under deep cover to make contact with him. We could have one of our own agents in the inner circle, helping the conspirators pull off their plans, and, at the same time, be our eyes and ears there. It'd have to be an excellent, fool-proof cover, and it'd be dangerous as hell, but I think it's doable."

"And might the agent to pull this stunt off be someone we know?"

"Yessir. We all know him quite well." I smiled.

"Pointer, why don't you invite Dowderwell to come see us. Say, tonight?" The Colonel was intrigued.

Donovan and Hopkins left the room. Elizabeth said to me, "Pointer, when I fell in love with you, I didn't realize you had a death wish. Why can't you be a back-office agent like Hopkins and be a planner, not an executor."

"Sweetheart, I am fluent in German. I've studied their culture. I'm the perfect candidate."

"Yes, but you'll be the Lone Ranger. You need some help, you need another agent to observe and help report what you see, to widen the net for you."

"Darlin' it'll be hard enough to get a cover story for one agent, let alone two."

"Unless", she said thoughtfully, "the second agent is already connected to you. Like, say, your wife. Yes, your recent Italian bride. That could work."

Chapter Thirty Two

Cover

I got a message to Dowderwell through the same channels I'd used before for him to report to II Corps HQ that evening at 1700 hours. Colonel Donovan, Hopkins, Elizabeth and I scheduled a dinner meeting to discuss plans before he arrived. We were able to commandeer the conference room for our sit-down. I knew that Wild Bill didn't like to miss a meal, and I doubted that he'd done so in his adult life.

Navy stewards brought a platter of hot roast beef, mashed potatoes, cabbage and green beans for our dinner. Beat hell out of mess hall hash. After they'd closed the door, Donovan began thinking out loud.

"To say this would be a dangerous operation is an understatement. Someone, an agent, would be in a veritable nest of vipers in Berlin. That's one big challenge. But another would be that Dowderwell here would have us by the short hairs. Pardon my French, Elizabeth."

"Let's say he does have a way to be in touch with von Furstenberg. If we, say, locked Dowderwell up so he couldn't communicate, then von Furstenberg would know. And the other thing is, we don't know who else he's in contact with up there." Donovan nodded his head vaguely toward the north.

"Bottom line is that we would need to trust Dowderwell. He would hold the life of our agent, and our plans, in his hands. Now, of course, we have something on him. We could make it clear to him that if anything should happen to our man, even if he slipped on a banana peel coming down the *Reichstag* steps, that we would hold him personally responsible."

"Sir." I jumped in. "I believe that would be effective. Like Binky, Dowderwell doesn't strike me as being eager to die for this cause."

"Would you bet your life on it, Pointer?" Donovan stared straight at me.

"Yessir. Yessir, I would."

We discussed the pros and cons, the ins and outs of the plan. Elizabeth and I had agreed not to introduce her participation in the scheme until later. I wasn't crazy about the idea of her risking her life. The only reason she'd be doing it is because I'd volunteered in the first place.

"Pointer, we'll need a good cover for you," Elizabeth said. "For starters, if you're a German national, why aren't you in the Army. We need a reason why you're a civilian."

"Right. Something manly, like I hurt my knee hunting wild boar in Africa."

"I'm not sure they have wild boar in Africa. I was thinking more along the lines of flat feet", said Donovan.

"No, no. Flat feet would never do. How about an injury suffered while playing futbol in Bavaria or someplace like that."

"Have you ever played soccer?" Hopkins asked.

"Well, no, but it's better than flat feet."

We discussed why I would be classified 4F for the next while without coming to any conclusion. I was secretly happy that my going to Berlin seemed to be a foregone conclusion.

"Assuming von Furstenberg agrees to a plan, we need a cover for you, a reason why you need to be in Berlin," Donovan said. "Any ideas?"

"Von Furstenberg is on Himmler's staff, assigned to the Jewish Question and the Final Solution," Elizabeth pointed out. "An engineer? A chemist? An arms dealer?"

"Too easy to trip him up," said Hopkins. "Assuming he has no training in any of these fields. Do you, Pointer? Have training as an engineer or chemist?"

"No."

"Then it should be some kind of supplier to the camps. Something basic. Like food," Hopkins said.

Elizabeth said, "A food broker. But make him more important than that. He could be the supplier of food for the camps, but he could also supply food, wine and liquor for the officers. That would elevate his importance a bit."

"Great," I said. "A grocer with flat feet," I said.

"Not a grocer, Pointer. A food and wine supplier. Or, more simply, a wine supplier," Elizabeth said.

"OK. A wine supplier. But I'm not going up there with flat feet."

It was time for Dowderwell to join us. A Sergeant knocked on the door and announced our visitor. We knew that Donovan would take the lead.

Dowderwell entered the room and, at the Colonel's invitation, took a seat. He seemed nervous as he lit a cigarette. He glanced around the room at each of us in our turn and adopted an attitude of "come on and get what you think you can".

Again, I wanted to smack him in his upper class, public school jaw. I thought of Billingsley dying in my arms. If you weren't presenting such a golden opportunity, I thought, you might have to deal with my Ka-Bar. Not for the first time, I thought about how I'd evolved from someone who wondered if he could really pull the trigger to someone who was a pissed off, half-murderous cowboy.

"Welcome, Leftenant," Donovan said. "Pointer here has told us that you have some knowledge of certain Nazi people in Berlin. We are interested in knowing more."

"What would you like to know, Colonel Donovan?" Dowderwell drew on his cigarette.

"Everything you know."

Dowderwell considered this and evidently decided that it was time to offer something.

"I know Friedrich von Furstenberg and some of his friends. I believe that they would welcome a dialogue with the Allied Forces. I believe that some of their goals align nicely with your, *our*, goals."

"Such as?" Donovan pressed.

"Such as if you cut off the head, the snake will die."

"You are speaking of Adolf Hitler?"

"And some of his people, yes. There has long been a faction of the Nazis who would like to see the head cut off."

"And how could we facilitate that?"

"I don't know that you could, Colonel. But this faction is very interested in the Allies seeing that the, uh, faction is doing the right thing. When it comes to the subject of death camps, for example. The faction would be open to a dialogue of creating a separate peace."

"You know, Leftenant, that I am not authorized to make political deals on behalf of the Allies."

"Yes, Colonel, I am aware of this. But we also believe that you are in a position to influence policy."

"'We'"?

"My friends in Berlin and I."

"Dowderwell, what is in this for us?" Donovan asked the very question that was in my mind.

"You may find yourselves in a position to cut off the head of the snake. And you may very well pick up intelligence from being in such close proximity to the higher-ups in the Nazi command. It is a golden opportunity for you," Dowderwell said, echoing our own thoughts.

"And how do we know that we can trust you. How do we know that you're not saying all this to deflect blame from you for your treasonous activities with Binkford."

"You'll never be one hundred percent certain, sir. But consider this. I have been the personal conduit for Binky to my contacts in Germany. I am the one who alerted Colonel Haas and his men to Binky's arrival and plans, as an example."

There it was. Would we make a deal with the devil? This was positively Faustian.

Donovan looked at the double-agent, wondering if he could turn him into a triple-threat in our favor.

"We'll get back to you, Dowderwell. In the meantime, I will make arrangements with your C.O. for you to be stationed right here with us."

Chapter Thirty Three

An Accomplice

"You want me to write a story about Pointer marrying an Italian aristocrat. And Pointer is a second generation wine merchant from Bavaria?" Archie Stanhope was incredulous. "And publish the story in *The International Herald Tribune?*"

"That's about the size of it, Stanhope," Donovan said. "We're bringing you in on this to help us create a cover for Pointer who's going to be going on a mission."

"Where's he going?" Stanhope asked.

"Can't say," said Donovan. "And now you're going to want to know what's in it for you. Other than doing something good for your country. Am I right?"

"Well, yeah, yeah I am," said Stanhope.

"We'll give you the exclusive on the mission. When it's safe to do so."

"Colonel, I'm an AP reporter, not a spy, for Christ's sake."

"You'd be surprised how many journalists do double duty, Stanhope."

After we had dismissed Dowderwell, the four of us had talked long into the night about the proposed mission to Berlin. We had decided that the wine cover would do nicely. We compromised on the reason for my 4F Draft status: a punctured ear drum. If I wanted to invent a macho story around that, then the rest had no problem. We brought up the issue of communications and how we could stay in touch and relay information. We all agreed that that would be very difficult to pull off and very dangerous. We knew, though, that Dowderwell had some sort of system already in place, so we resolved to learn more about that and, if feasible, hook into that system.

We then explored the idea of an accomplice. Bringing another agent in on it at this point was rejected for a number of reasons—not least timing and training. At that point, Elizabeth nominated herself. She laid out the plan of her being an Italian who had met and married a wine merchant who had been in Rome on business. It had been a whirlwind affair, her parents had been not happy, and they had eloped. They had settled in "Fritz's" home in Bavaria. She made the case that Pointer would benefit by having an extra set of eyes and ears, a back-up, and perhaps she could do the communications back to OSS.

We could see that Donovan was struggling with this concept. Putting a woman, indeed, a family friend at risk like that was not to his liking. I stayed out of the discussion because I, too, was conflicted. It was Hopkins who broke the logjam.

"Sir, I think it's a solid idea. I wouldn't like it so well if it weren't this particular set-up, a husband and wife. But that's natural enough, and it will help Pointer to have an accomplice. She can be an extra set of eyes and ears for him. Watch his back."

"Alright", Donovan said. "We'll proceed with the husband-wife idea as a working scenario. I haven't mentioned this before, but we do have some assets in Germany. Berlin, Munich and, yes, Bavaria. We'll need their help in setting this up, although not any one of them will know the whole plan. Just enough to execute their parts."

June 4, 1943

My Dear Robert,

We appreciate your letters. We received a batch of them yesterday. What joy they bring us! Just to know that you are alright is plenty good enough for us at this moment.

I am sure that you are being circumspect for good reason, and I would never pry. But I confess that curiosity sometimes gets the better of me and I wonder what it is you are training so hard for. We loved your story about Billingsley and the goats. You must continue to watch out for that boy. And you met a Tuskegee airman! Smythe sounds like a perfect tyrant. And we loved your description of General Patton. What an honor to sit at the same table as the great warrior. The newspapers here mention him frequently, along with Montgomery, Ike and Marshall. We feel as though the leadership is superb in Europe and Africa.

*Now, you mentioned a young lady—
Elizabeth whom you met at General
Patton's soiree. You know perfectly
well that your Mother will require more
details on her. I admit to being more
than a little curious myself.*

*South Hill continues to be quiet. There
are so few young men here. Only those
home on leave and the few who were
not drafted for one reason or another.
Speaking of that, young Gaskins has
gotten a job. He's delivering groceries.
He was here last week with the day's
supplies and I happened to be the one
at home. I asked him how he felt. He's
doing much better as evidenced by his
employment. He even talks of trying to
enlist again. With the trouble he got
into, I fear he will need my legal help to
succeed.*

*Rabbi Smith and some of his colleagues
around the state are talking about
organizing a march on the White House
to bring attention to the plight of the
Jews in Europe. So much is rumor and
so little is fact. They circulated a
petition which your mother and I*

signed. We are considering going on the march if it comes off.

Dear son, do you suppose there's any chance of your getting enough leave for a visit home? If it's this summer, we could go for a sail on the Bay. Or, we could just relax around here.

Send more news, Robert! And thanks for the previous letters. They mean so much to us. I pray for your safety.

I remain,

Your devoted father,

Robert L. Pointer

Chapter Thirty Four

Preparations

As we planned for infiltration into Germany, the Allied forces planned their invasion into Sicily. It was baking hot in the summer African sun. Most of my time was spent indoors trying to stay cool. I was involved in both missions to one degree or another. In fact, I was scheduled to brief Patton and Bradley that afternoon about what I'd found in Sicily. I had, of course, written a report and had personally been debriefed by Donovan. But Patton had always liked to personally interview soldiers who had been in the field. He liked to say that everyone had an opinion, a theory. But if you were able to begin a sentence with the words, *"I was recently in enemy territory and..."*, then you went right to the front of the line outside Patton's door.

So, I was waiting in his outer office. High ranking officers of the American, British and Canadian Armies bustled to and fro. I felt as though I were in the way. But then Patton's Chief of Staff came out of the inner sanctum and beckoned me.

"Lieutenant Pointer, the General will see you now."

"Ah, Pointer! Welcome back! You've become quite the warrior since we last met. You've met Brad, haven't you?"

He indicated Omar Bradley who was seated on a divan opposite an easy chair where Patton sat straight upright.

"Yessir. We met at your dinner party a couple of months ago."

"Brad" had established himself as the ranking expert on getting a corned beef sandwich to a soldier who could be in the middle of nowhere.

"Fine then," Patton barked. "Tell us everything, and don't leave a thing out."

"Well, sir, Major Brownwell and Sergeant Smythe prepared us mentally and physically for our mission. I wanted to be sure you knew that. As you know, we parachuted in on a Friday night, my squad to Caltanissetta and Binkford's group to Catania. I was able to make contact with Don Vizzini the next day."

"Hold on, son. You're leaving out the good part." He looked over at Bradley. "Brad hasn't read the report."

"Oh, that. Yessir. Well, we had a mix-up in the jump and I was late getting out of the plane so I ended up spending the night dangling from a church in the middle of town."

Patton gave his "KKKKKHaaa!" laugh, slapped his knee and said, "If that isn't goddamn something, Brad! Spent the night on a church, not in a church."

Bradley smiled politely.

"Tell me, Pointer, is it true that the outfit that flew you over were the Tuskegee Negroes?"

"Yessir."

"Well, as I live and breathe. This man's army is finally showing some goddamn sense. And some goddamn balls!"

The General continued, "Tell us about this Vizzini character. Can he be trusted? Do you believe he'll do anything that'll help us?"

He glanced over at Bradley and explained, "Vizzini is the local muscle on our route north."

"Yessir on both questions. When you are ready to invade, he'll give us a sit rep of the area. He's also prepared to kill their snipers with his snipers. And, finally, sir he should now be in the process of sabotaging the enemy's supply lines and ammo dumps."

"Excellent", snarled the General. "But it didn't go so well over in Catania, did it? Goddamn cheating, yellow sumbitch..."

"No sir. I don't believe we can count on any help from Don Russo in Catania."

Patton looked over at Bradley, then back at me. "You killed him personally." It was a quiet statement.

"Yessir, I did."

"Ran him through with a Ka-bar, Brad. How many times have you wanted to do that, even to some of our own people. Just kidding, Brad. But we've got a brave boy here, a brave boy."

Patton got up and started pacing the floor. "Son, when we absquatulate from here I want you positioned with the 7th Army's advance. I want you whispering in the ear of the Colonel leading that squad, and I want you communicating with Vizzini the whole way up the Island. Understood? "

"Understood, sir."

He scrawled out some orders on a pad, signed them, ripped the page off and handed it to me.

"Now, see my Chief, give him those orders and tell him to put you on the invitation list for my next big throw-down dinner. And bring that pretty girl with you."

Chapter Thirty Five

Fatherland

Bavaria

July 10, 1943

Freddy had a ten day leave and had rushed to the family home near Passau in the Bavarian Alps. There, his wife Marta, his three children and his parents greeted him with the affection they'd all long held for one another. When he looked at his beautiful family, he had a difficult time separating the realities of Berlin and this one here in Bavaria. He knew that he was commanded by a mad man. No, two mad men. Aldolf Hitler and Heinrich Himmler.

The contrast between his two lives was dizzying, disorienting. The things he'd done and seen in the war were beyond horrific. The men, women and children he'd seen being led to their deaths at Auschwitz and Treblinka were images that were burned on his soul forever. He'd accompanied Himmler on an

inspection tour of Auschwitz the
month before, and Himmler, upon
witnessing the gassing of thousands,
had ordered a promotion for the camp
commander to commend his efficiency
at killing. Freddy had excused himself
and had barely made it to the lavatory
before he threw up.

But now he was with his family. He
really didn't think he could return to
the nightmare that was his daily life
since he'd received his orders to
transfer from the *Abwehr* to Himmler's
command. The *Abwehr* under Canaris
and Oster was the center of anti-Hitler
sentiment, and as the fortunes of the
Nazi war effort rose and fell, so did the
chances of a successful assassination of
the *Fuhrer,* in reverse proportion. That
is, when the war was going poorly, as it
had now started to do, the chances of
eliminating Hitler rose. More
influential people in both the Army and
the *Abwehr* became amenable to a
plot.

There were really only two people on
earth who would understand how he

felt. Marta and his father. After his welcome-home dinner, he knew they would want to discuss things. But first, a hike in his beloved mountains to clear his head. His family understood and anticipated this ritual of his. He needed some time to make the transition, to decompress.

Freddy chose his favorite route—out the front drive which was lined with perfectly groomed cedars, taking a right and find the old farm track that led down the mountain and eventually alongside a mountain stream. The day was clear and warm. The birds were in full throat. When he gazed up into the distance, he could see the snow-capped Alps. The stream emptied into a lake that stretched as far as he could see. Deep azure blue, it almost hurt his eyes to look at it.

This was the land of Freddy's youth. Where he had romped as a boy during summers with Cousin Binky. They had grown up together, trading stories of their respective homelands. They'd both been born shortly after the Great

War that had first divided their nations. But they had learned of the trench warfare from Freddy's father that had slaughtered so many of his contemporaries.

Freddy's favorite story was of The Christmas Truce on the Western Front in France in 1914. His father had been among the Germans in their trenches facing the British in their trenches across No Mans Land. Suddenly, that Christmas night in frozen France, a young German voice rang out, singing a carol. He was soon joined by his comrades in song. A group of Brits from Kent then sang "God Rest Ye Merry Gentlemen". The Germans followed with a rendition of *"Stille Nacht"* and were joined by their enemy singing in English. No one knew quite how to feel until a lone German, unarmed and with a flag of truce, walked out into No Mans Land. A thousand rifles were trained on him, yet no one fired a shot. Soon, he was joined by soldiers from both sides who began exchanging gifts of chocolate and cigarettes and showing each other photos of loved ones from home. A German with a violin and a Brit with a squeezebox began to play. Someone had the idea to play a game of soccer so flares were launched so they could see. And that is how December 26, 1914 dawned, the most remarkable day in that long war.

His father said that the men were disoriented for a time after the experience. When dawn came and they returned to their trenches, they were expected to recommence killing each other, these men whose enemies seemed so much like themselves.

And now the world had been plunged again into a great war. What did we learn, Freddy thought. As horrible as the Great War had been, there had not been the genocide of this conflict. The systematic murdering of a race of unarmed men, women and children. Freddy doubted that there would be a Christmas Truce in this war. And now, dear Binky was dead. And Freddy had been complicit, recruiting him into his strange cabal. Using him for his own ends.

Freddy sat down on a fallen tree trunk by the lake and began to weep. He wept for all of the innocents, he wept for his family and the dreams of a thousand year *Reich* that he had shared with his countrymen. And he wept for how it had all gone so wrong.

After dinner, which had been subdued with just a few gusts of forced gaiety, Freddy retired with his father to the older man's study.

"Friedrich, how are you faring?" asked his father.

"I am not sure how much more I can take, sir. My job is not fighting a war, it's murdering innocent people. It is not what we envisioned at the beginning. The *Fuhrer,* Himmler and a few of the others are mad. Everyone else, like me, are keeping their heads down and following orders. They are not going to rest until they've exterminated the entire population of Europe of Jews, gypsies, homosexuals, and others they find objectionable."

His father stared out the window. "Yes. That's clear. What about the plans against Lightning?"

There was a knock on the door. It was Marta. Both men rose.

"The children are in bed. May I come in?" she said.

"Of course," I replied. Marta and I had no secrets, even like the ones we were then discussing.

"Since the bomb on the plane failed to detonate and that lone chap tried to kill him, our friends have been lying low. But there *has* been one new development that could be significant," Freddy said.

He continued, "Just before I left Berlin, I got a message through the usual channels that the Americans may wish to join in with our efforts. It seems there is a plan to send us an undercover emissary who may be able to provide assistance."

"Interesting," said von Furstenberg.

"Yes, they are awaiting a response. I had an opportunity to meet with Wolf before I left. Naturally, the Americans are being circumspect at this point, so we don't know much of what they have in mind. Only that they are willing to send two agents under certain pretexts who are aligned with eliminating Lightning. Wolf and I discussed whether this could simply be a trick for the Americans to infiltrate our high command. But we think that's unlikely since it would be I who would be their sole contact. At least at first. We should certainly be able to partition them off from any information to which we don't wish them to have access."

"Oh, Freddy. Aren't you in enough danger as it is? Now you'll be hiding Americans under Himmler's nose." Marta said.

"Yes, but Wolf and I agree that we need something to galvanize our plans. If we can co-opt an American into our plans, then we will have established a channel for future negotiations with the Allies. Plus, he, or they, will see that we are utterly opposed to the Final Solution, and that one of our primary goals is stopping the slaughter."

"Yes, I see that," said von Furstenberg. "Is Wolf authorizing you to proceed?"

"Not yet. We have responded cautiously, but favorably. We want to know a bit more about their motivations. As you know, I am able to receive these special messages when I travel as well as in Berlin. So I am expecting a communiqué in the next few days."

There was a knock at the door. A servant entered and handed the elder von Furstenberg a note. He opened the envelope and took a moment to read. He took off his spectacles and looked at Freddy and Marta and said, "Last night, the Allies invaded Sicily."

Chapter Thirty Six

Invasion

July 1943

The largest amphibious invasion in history had begun. Lieutenant General George S. Patton commanded the Western Task Force, which consisted of the American 7th Army. The 7th Army initially consisted of three infantry divisions commanded by Major General Omar Bradley. The logistics were beyond complex. The U.S. 1st and 3rd Divisions sailed from Tunisia, while the U.S. 45th Division sailed from the United States via the port of Oran in Algeria. The U.S. 2nd Armored Division, also leaving from Oran, was to be held in reserve at sea.

The British 8th Army under General Bernard Montgomery faced similarly complex logistics with four infantry Divisions and an independent infantry brigade. Those Divisions and Brigades sailed from diverse ports such as Suez, Tunisia, Malta and the U.K.

There were two Allied naval task forces as well as the Mediterranean Air Command (MAC) which was comprised of units from the U.S. 12th Air Force, 9th Air Force and the British Royal Air Force (RAF) operating out of bases in Tunisia and Malta.

The Axis defenders consisted of about 270,000 Italian and German soldiers along with 30,000 *Luftwaffe* ground staff. The panzer divisions had about 150 tanks at their disposal.

Patton's 7th Army was to land in south-central Sicily in the Gulf of Gela. This is where we had exited The Sauce two months previously. The U.S. 82nd Airborne Division was to drop behind the Axis defenses. Montgomery's troops were assigned the landing 25 miles to the east of the Americans and were to proceed up the eastern part of the island.

Allied strategic bomber forces had been bombing airfields in Sardinia, Sicily, southern Italy and the ports of Naples, Messina, Palermo and Cagliara in Sardinia for the past month. These attacks were diffuse enough to spread confusion as to where the landings would come. Northern Italy and Greece were added as targets in the weeks leading up to the invasion. Notably absent in the bombing were any ports in the south of Sicily.

The invasion started in disastrous fashion. Just after midnight, the American 82nd Airborne Division's aircraft, intending to drop paratroopers five miles inland from the Gulf of Gela, were shot down by friendly fire. A nervous Allied ship's gunners fired upon the formation as it neared the Sicilian coast. Other ships joined in, and most of the planes were downed with over 300 casualties. The rest of the paratroopers were blown off course by heavy winds so that the troops were widely scattered by the time they hit the ground. Nonetheless, many of these troops found one another and were successful in creating confusion and panic in the defenders.

It was Zero Dark Thirty. Colonel Bates and fifty men, including yours truly, were ready to land at the Gulf of Gela. The winds were "blowing like a stink" as the sailors liked to say, and we counted on the fact that no one in his right mind would attempt a crossing and landing in such weather. But, apparently, we weren't in our right minds because cross and land we did. At least half of the Grunts in the DUKW were barfing their guts out even as we leapt from the craft and waded in to shore. There was no enemy fire so we rallied on the beach around Bates.

"Pointer! Make your call!" he shouted to me as we ran inland.

"Muscle, this is Spear. Come in," I said into the radio in Italian and using our prearranged code. "Muscle, this is Spear. Come back."

"Spear, this is Muscle." It was my old buddy Falcone.

"Muscle, great to hear your voice. How do things look up north?"

"Heavy concentrations three miles from you on the way to Licata." Licata was one of the first objectives of Patton's force. "Recommend skirting east and then turning toward your objective."

"Roger that, *compadre.*"

I translated for Bates and we took off to the northeast. In the middle distance we could hear gunfire. A battle. Paratroopers? Had to be. We rushed in that direction and came in from the rear of an Italian squad firing at our guys in the darkness. We had them between our pincers and inside of ten minutes they took off with about a dozen killed or wounded. We paused to talk to the paratroopers. They were in the process of finding each other, concentrating their forces and then heading for a bridge they'd been assigned to capture. This skirmish happened when they stumbled into those Italians.

Not wasting time with niceties, we hustled toward our destination. When we judged that we'd gone four miles, we turned to the northwest. I was hardly winded thanks to Smythe's making me run all those miles with my rifle over my head.

"Spear, this is Muscle. New information. Licata is heavily guarded. Recommend you come home and await reinforcements. Clear here." Home was the Don's place in Caltanissetta.

I again translated for Bates. He nodded, so I replied, "Roger that, Muscle."

By dawn, we had made our way to the Don's. Bates set up a perimeter around the grounds and posted sentries at all points of the compass outside of the town. We had effectively captured Caltanissetta without firing a shot. I liked to think our earlier mission had something to do with that.

It was time to see Don Vizzini again. And Falcone. The Don had insisted that Bates and I stay in the house. The men bivouacked around the grounds. I made my fourth report via radio back to Patton's command, telling them what we'd seen-- and heard from Falcone. It gave Patton's boys some direction on the path of least resistance on their move inland. Thinking back to the long night just past, we'd skirmished once; I'd fired several bursts with my Thompson but wasn't sure if I'd hit anyone. From what I could tell through the typical fog of war, the American part of the invasion, at least, had gone well. But, really, it was hard to say with the one small piece that I knew about. Patton's boys on the other end of the radio transmission weren't exactly reporting in to *me*. Not surprisingly, it was quite the other way around. I did know that Patton's main Divisions were still well to the south, slugging their way northward. And other than the paratroops, we were in the vanguard.

I wondered about Monty's progress to the east and if Binky's betrayal and lack of assistance from Don Russo had retarded his progress.

As Bates and I were shown to our quarters in the Don's house, one of Vizzini's men approached us and said, "Don Vizzini bids you and your men welcome. He desires that you rest and hopes you will join him for lunch if conditions permit."

Yeah. Those damned conditions.

Bates and I retired, and I slept the sleep of the truly exhausted for what seemed to be five entire minutes. Vizzini's man gently shook me awake and told me it was lunchtime.

When Bates and I came downstairs, there was the Don. We embraced and kissed each other on both cheeks, old-school style. I introduced Bates, and we sat down at the table, which was not laden quite so lavishly as last time.

"You are most welcome here, Pointer, and you too, Colonel Bates. You may stay here as long as you wish, which, I fear will not be long."

Falcone had stationed himself to the Don's right, still standing as usual. He and I nodded at each other, which seemed to be all Falcone wanted or needed. I noticed that, aside from his ever-present shotgun, he wore a holstered FP-45 and a Ka-bar knife, courtesy of the U.S. Army.

"What news do you have, Don Vizzini," I asked.

"There are Italian and German Divisions, as well as a Panzer Division, located about 40 kilometers northeast from here. We expect them to arrive here by nightfall, at least some of them. We have snipers positioned along their route, and we will slow their advance, but, alas, we do not have the firepower to halt it."

I nodded. "What do you hear from the east?"

"The defenders there are much better organized and concentrated against Field Marshal Montgomery's troops. Don Russo—curse his name—has done nothing to help you. They will have a much more difficult time of it than you Americans."

I translated for Bates, and took a helping of pasta and a piece of the Don's delicious bread.

"And what will you do, Don Vizzini, when the Axis Divisions arrive in Caltanissetta?"

"I believe they are aware of my activities these past two months since your visit, Pointer, so it would be best if I were not here to greet them."

I addressed Bates, "Colonel, I will check in with the Command, but it seems we should make plans to evacuate our men this afternoon. We will probably be wanted in Licata to rendezvous with Patton."

"Makes sense, Pointer."

We nonetheless took our time in this relatively luxurious setting. The Don talked about his sabotage activities over last two months. He'd been successful at blowing up three ammo dumps. He'd hijacked numerous supply trucks crossing inter-island, enriching his own coffers. One failed attempt had been a kidnapping caper. Falcone had spotted an outpost of just twenty Italian troops. He and his men had attempted to sneak into the camp and abduct the Major in command. Their plan had been to ransom him. However, an alert sentry had spotted them and raised the alarm. Falcone and his boys had had to shoot it out, and two Mafiosi had been wounded.

The Don paused for effect. "One hopes, Pointer, that one's efforts will be remembered and rewarded when this trouble is over."

"And what, dear Don Vizzini, would you consider a suitable award?" I asked.

"For me personally? Only the thanks of your government. But for my people, there is much I could do if I were, say, a Mayor."

"Of Caltanissetta?"

"Ah, there is only so much that can be accomplished in a backwater like this town."

"Then what did you have in mind?"

He smiled. "Palermo would do. Yes. Palermo."

Bates led us that afternoon to Licata. There were skirmishes still going on between some Italian hold-outs and Patton's guys, but it was in its wind-down, mop-up phase. I had been asked to report directly to Patton's command, which I did as soon as we arrived. I told the duty officer everything we had observed and learned, all of which he wrote down in shorthand.

For the next several days, I followed Patton's command as they worked their way up the island. When there was an obstacle, human or the elements, Patton refused to admit it was even there. He drove Bradley to drive the men. There were rumors that Bradley was chafing at the General's aggressiveness. The men needed more rest, there were too many casualties. I was allowed to attend Bradley's officer briefing every day. But I was neither fish nor fowl. I was trained as a Marine, but I was an OSS officer. I tried to get Bates to put me out there with the infantry, but he refused. I think he was confused about just how to use me.

I had some time to reflect. I thought about the Pointers' history in American warfare. Father had been a Reservist in the First World War and had not seen combat. But there were other Pointers in U.S. military history. There was our Virginian ancestor, Powhatan Pointer, who fought with Lee at Petersburg, the Wilderness and was with Lee at Appomattox. He was famously mentioned in Douglas Southall Freeman's seminal work on the Civil War, *Lee's Lieutenants,* as being seen hiding behind a tree during the fiercest fighting at The Wilderness. His mama didn't raise a stupid boy. I used to joke that he was so famous that they named an Indian after him.

But the fact is I was a little restless. I wanted to do something beyond re-report Falcone's intel. My chance came in early August. Patton's Army was busy cutting off an east-west highway vital for Axis resupply purposes. Sure enough, Montgomery's push had been slower than that of Patton and if I knew Patton—and I think I did—he wanted to reach Messina, the ultimate destination, before Montgomery did. But first he had to secure Palermo.

At that day's briefing, Bradley began to speak about Palermo and what needed to be done to get there and to drive the bad guys out. There was the matter of the harbor, which was heavily mined. He spoke about a special naval force which he called Frogmen, specially trained underwater divers who knew how to dismantle explosives like mines. Bradley emphasized the danger of this mission. His Frogmen would enter the harbor under cover of darkness, locate the mines and dismantle them one by one. Without blowing themselves to high heaven, it was hoped. They were set, but because of the stealthy nature of the mission, they couldn't risk using any of their own motorized craft. So they had requisitioned the best fishing vessel they could find. The only problem remaining was none of the Frogmen knew how to sail, besides which, their regular pilot was in the hospital with shrapnel in his gut. The Navy couldn't find anyone qualified at this late hour. Patton wanted that harbor cleared now. Enter Pointer, I thought.

As soon as the briefing ended, I approached Bradley's aide and presented myself as the answer to their prayers. Any port in a storm, you know. I was told to wait, which I did for over an hour. The aide finally returned and told me to follow him. He led me to a villa where the command had settled and told me to wait again. At length, a Colonel named Voorhees came out into the dining room, which was now a waiting room, introduced himself and beckoned me to follow.

"So, Pointer, you know how to sail," he said. Two more officers were in the room. Presumably Frogmen.

"Yessir, been sailing my whole life."

"You prefer a beam reach or a broad reach, Pointer?"

This was a test. "Depends, sir. If there are heavy seas and comfort is a concern, definitely a broad reach. But if I need to get somewhere in a hurry, I like a good beam reach."

"I'll have to take your word for it, Pointer. I wouldn't know a beam reach from a flashlight beam. Let me tell you what we have in mind." He unrolled a chart of the northwest coast of Sicilian waters which included the Palermo harbor. "Tomorrow night, we will shove off from here." He pointed at the harbor town of Marsala, which was just below the northwest tip of the island. "We'll sail around Cape San Vito and approach Palermo from the west. You can see the shoals around the Cape here so you have to keep a wide berth around them. But the fun really starts as you enter the mouth of the harbor. Rocks here, shoals over there and the Nazis have removed all navigation aids, so you have to basically dead reckon your way into the harbor."

"How much does the boat draw, sir?"

"Eight feet. Now, we have a very good idea where the mines are placed so it'll be more like an Easter egg hunt than a crap shoot. There are six of us. Your job will be to sail around the harbor at my direction and drop each of us off near where we believe mines to be. We will dismantle them and tread water until you make the circuit back to each of us. Here's the chart showing the believed locations of the mines."

He unrolled a second chart, showing mine placements every 100 yards or so.

"Sir, how good is your information on the locations of these mines?"

"Good enough, Pointer. Any other questions?"

"Yessir. Can we paint the sails black?"

The rest of the day and into the night I studied the charts. The next day I went to have a look at the boat, and I noticed that the sails had been painted black. She was a standard rig for this area. She had a long boom and a correspondingly large main sail. She had a single foresail and a tiller for steerage. I personally removed all of the fishing gear—nets and the like, and only kept on board the essentials for sailing. The cockpit was large so that the fishermen had plenty of space to maneuver. Below were two berths and a small galley consisting of a one-burner stove. I realized that I would need a deck hand to help me with the sails. It'd be helpful to find someone with experience.

I hustled back to the villa which housed Bradley's staff and asked for the aide. This time, he didn't keep me waiting. I explained to him my need for a crew member. He said he'd get right on it, so I told him to send someone down to the docks double quick.

As I was rearranging the gear below back at the boat, my crew showed up. He was a boy of about fifteen, obviously a local. Philip was the son of the owner of the vessel.

"You know how to sail?"

"*Si.* This is my papa's boat. I go with him every day."

"Alright. Let's take her for a spin." The winds were light as they usually were this time of year in the Med. We hoisted the main and we pushed ourselves out of the slip until we caught the breeze, heeled over and off we went to sea. I was mainly getting a feel for her. I tacked upwind, coming about every twenty seconds to test her maneuverability and to brush up on my own skills. We tested jibing; we practiced reefing the main so we'd be ready in the unlikely event of heavy weather. And every other trick I could think of. Philip was so comfortable as crew that we barely had to speak. He anticipated most of my commands.

Voorhees, the men and I had chow together to discuss the mission. Voorhees confessed to me that this was their first mission in underwater combat, which was the term of art. "In fact," he said, "this is the first time for any American underwater combat unit. We were rushed out of training from

Ft. Pierce for this invasion. But the Italians have been doing this since the '20s," he concluded.

Another military first for Patton, I thought.

"Colonel, what are the likely pitfalls in this mission? In the darkness there's plenty of room for error. How will I find you guys after I drop you off? I could follow the same chart, but you will have drifted from your original position with the current. It's not like you can shout, 'Hey Pointer, over here!'"

"We'll take small buoys with us which will be tethered to our belts. It'll be your job to know which way the current is moving and make an educated guess as to where we are. You *do* know about currents and tides, Pointer?"

"Of course I do. It's just that strength of current and tides are not uniform. I'll have to gauge it *in situ.*" I used my new favorite military phrase.

"Go get some rest or commune with your God, or whatever it is you do before risking your skin. I've got to check our gear. See you at the boat at 1900 hours."

We departed the harbor right on schedule. There was a soft breeze blowing from the northeast, so we had a nice port tack heading up and around the Cape. When we turned east and set the course for Palermo, I fired up the engine, doused the headsails, sheeted in the main and we motor sailed our way along the north coast of The Sauce, making about eight knots.

Voorhees and his men appeared to be in peak physical condition. I had heard that their training made Smythe's look like child's play, not least because a lot of theirs was conducted in the water. And not just any water. The snake and alligator-infested swamps and canals of South Florida, as well as the ocean. I'd always considered swimming the toughest sport. Turns out we're mammals and don't possess gills, so there's the matter of fighting to breathe when you're swimming. Hey, I was just driving the boat on this one. If I had to get wet, something was very wrong.

Maybe because we were at sea, I thought about another Civil War ancestor, Lt. Conway Pointer, CSA Navy. He was smuggled aboard a Confederate warship in London (the Yankees were watching) with orders to sail to the Bering Sea and, there, to destroy the Yankee whaling industry. This they did with such fervor that they were still sinking Yankee whalers months after the war ended, unbeknownst to Conway and his men. When they put in to San Francisco for supplies, they heard the news and knew that they were in deep whale blubber. They sailed back to London and narrowly avoided being hanged. They eventually received a full pardon.

Voorhees interrupted my thoughts. "How we doing, Pointer?"

I showed him our position on the chart, which I had spread out in front of me. Philip was at the helm. "We're about

90 minutes out from the mouth of the harbor, sir. Making good time."

"In your opinion, which of Patton's quotes is best. I have my favorites." Voorhees and just about everyone else associated with the 3rd Army were familiar with "Old Blood and Our Guts'" sayings.

I considered this. "How about, 'In war just as in loving you must keep on shoving'."

Voorhees smiled. "How about, 'A good plan violently executed now is better than a perfect plan executed next week'. Or, my all-time favorite, 'The object of war is not to die for your country, but to make the other bastard die for his'."

"'A pint of sweat saves a gallon of blood'," I countered.

"'Better to fight for something than to live for nothing,'" Voorhees continued.

"Better to dismantle the bomb than have it dismantle you," I said. Voorhees frowned. "I'm just jerking your chain, Voorhees, he didn't say that. That's a Pointerism circa July, 1943."

As we neared the harbor entrance, Voorhees and his men began to don their Frogman gear, which consisted of a dry suit, fins, mask and snorkel. These mines were right at the surface, anchored in place, so the men would be able to hold their breaths to do their work. They each had a waterproof bladder strapped to their waists, presumably carrying the tools of their trade.

Philip and I redoubled our efforts to scan the horizon, looking for the shore, but also for enemy vessels. It was a moonless night; I had killed the engine long before, and when we spoke, it was in whispers. I stared at the chart and directed Philip, who remained at the helm.

"Course, 265 degrees," I whispered.

"265 degrees."

As we turned toward the mouth of the harbor, we had the wind on our starboard beam and were now making about 5-6 knots. I knew that we would be alongside a shoal and some rocks jutting out from the starboard headland, so I ordered Philip to steer a little more to port. The port of Palermo was dark, no doubt under a blackout. The only sounds were the wind and the water rushing alongside the hull. I reduced sail as Philip continued at the helm. Speed was no longer important. Maneuverability became paramount.

"Colonel, we're approaching Target 1, port side," I hissed.

"Jones, get ready," Voorhees ordered.

As we peered into the murk, we at last made out the top of the mine bobbing slightly in the swells. Jones, sitting on the port gunnel, dropped almost soundlessly, back first into the water. I steered for the next target. This time, a Frogman named Simpson dropped over the side. We repeated the process until at last it was Voorhees' turn.

We continued to look for signs of trouble coming from the port as I jibed the boat and began making a long circle toward Target 1. Voorhees had told me that it would take each man about 15 minutes to complete his work, so by the time I got back to Target 1, Jones should be ready for pick up. I was now steering and ordered Philip to make ready the swimming ladder. As we approached the position I thought Jones should be, I turned the boat into the wind so that she stopped dead in the water. I did not see Jones until after he saw us. In the quiet of the night, I heard a thump on the port side. My heart leapt into my throat. Had I hit something? No, it was Jones, who now appeared at the top of the ladder.

We then collected Simpson, the third man, and the fourth man. The fifth Frogman, whose name I recalled as Blundon, was our next target. Voorhees would be last. As we were still about 50 yards away from Blundon, a massive explosion ripped the waterline and sent a geyser of water high into the air. The blast was deafening and the shock waves knocked us all to the deck of the boat.

"Shitfire!" I screamed. Blundon had detonated his mine. He was gone, but the Coast Guard would be coming.

I was the first to recover. "Philip! Head for Voorhees while I raise the main all the way up. Start the engine. I'll raise the genoa too!" No sense being quiet now. We hauled ass over to Voorhees. I ordered Philip to put the gear in neutral and turn into the wind. Where was Voorhees? All hands began searching the water for him. Had he been injured in the blast? "Voorhees!" I hissed.

We heard the sirens and saw the light of the port as the garrison mustered their vessels to race to the site of the explosion.

After three or four minutes of scanning the dark water, Simpson said, "Pointer! Over there!" He pointed about 20 yards off the starboard bow. I saw nothing, but I put the engine in gear and followed Simpson's pointing finger. There, at last, was Voorhees, floating on his back. Once again, we came up into the wind and the men pulled their leader aboard.

"Let's get out of here!" I hollered. "Full speed, Philip!"

I scrambled up to the bow and finished raising the genoa. Now all sails were hoisted and the engine was full throttle, but I knew it would not be enough to outrun the Nazis' motorized craft. Our only chance was to get through the mouth of the harbor and somehow get lost. We made it past the headlands as we saw boat lights moving from the distant docks. They were on their way.

I hung a left and cut across the shoals, praying that we had enough water at high tide. We bumped bottom once and my heart froze, but our momentum carried us free. I handed Philip the helm once again and began frantically scouring the chart. It was either open sea for us, which would surely not end well, or find someplace to hide on the coast. I thought about scuttling the boat on the rocks and swimming for shore. It was huge longshot, but seemed to be our only option.

Then, I spotted it. About five miles west on the coast was a tiny bay, more like a cove. But it showed 6 feet of water at mean low tide. It was high tide now, which would give us, what, two feet of clearance. I grabbed the protractors and gave Philip the course for the cove. This could work if we got there before we were spotted. The wind was now on our aft quarter, which was giving us a nice lift.

"Come on, baby, come on, darling," I urged our vessel on. I looked back and could now easily see what appeared to be three boats, each with searchlights and each zigzagging around the mouth of the harbor. It would not be long before they determined that there was no one there and would come out to sea. We needed to be well away before that happened.

I looked over at the men who'd been working on Voorhees. He was sitting up now and seemed to be alert. Probably got the wind knocked out of him from the blast.

The wind had picked up over the past few minutes, giving us a much needed lift in speed. The chase boats had now exited the mouth of the harbor. One turned east, one headed straight out to sea and the third turned toward us. I estimated that we needed about ten more minutes to enter the cove and be protected from the chase boat's sight lines. If worse came to worse, I was prepared to turn the boat toward our pursuer and shoot it out. But that would attract the other boats so it was best to avoid that tactic.

Fortunately for us, the chase boat continued its zigzag pattern, buying us precious seconds, but she was still gaining fast.

"How we doing, Pointer?" It was Voorhees.

"We're running like hell, sir," I replied. "We've got a shot."

We were now only about fifty yards outside of the range of our pursuer's searchlight. But we were close to the protection of the cove. A few more minutes. Go baby! I screamed inside my head.

At last, we reached the entrance of the cove just as the searchlight was catching up to us. Had they seen us?

"Kill the engine and hard alee!" I shouted to Philip. We glided past the near point of the cove and headed slightly to the port so that the point hid us from the searchlight. I scrambled up to the bow and threw the anchor out. The wind pushed the boat backwards until I could feel the anchor catch. We held our collective breath while we watched the beam of the searchlight sweep the arc of the cove's shoreline. Fortunately, we were tucked up in the northeast crook of the arc and were just out of view.

The chase boat steadily moved further west down the coast. My next thought was how long we had there before the tide turned and we'd be aground. I hoped that the searcher would return home first and allow us to be on our way. I figured we had about an hour and a half of the deeper water.

An hour passed until we saw the searchlight again. The boat was reversing its course, heading back to Palermo. But this time she was headed straight for our hiding place. Had they decided to take a closer look at the cove? The boat slowed and was idling offshore about fifty yards away, and Voorhees and his men got ready for a shoot-out. We could hear a heated discussion from the boat as though they were arguing about whether to come in to the cove or not. The boat began inching closer into the mouth of the cove. Because we were tucked up under the near corner, we would be spotted only when they got into the little bay itself. By now, I could see the sailor on the bow manning the machine gun there. Their searchlight flicked the shoreline. Another ten yards and they would have an angle that would enable them to see us. I held my breath; I heard a series of metallic clicks as Voorhees and his men slid shells into the breeches of their rifles.

And then the boat turned for the open sea. The captain gunned the engine as they raced off looking for the bandits who'd ruined their mines.

When we got back, the Army was preparing to pull out and head to where we'd just left: Palermo. The fighting still raged, but the outcome was no longer in doubt.

Chapter Thirty Seven

The Race

Sicily

August, 1943

The battle within the battle was that between Patton and Montgomery. Patton believed that General Alexander had handcuffed his 7th Army in favor of Montgomery's 3rd Army. Patton believed that American Army prestige was at stake. He had flown to Tunisia within days of entering Sicily to plead his case with Alexander. He did receive some concessions so that beating Monty to Messina was now a possibility. Monty was, after all, bogged down on the east coast south of Catania. American forces had now entered Palermo and were poised to move east and take Messina.

Monty and Patton engaged in two near comical meetings. Patton flew cross-island to Syracuse to meet with Monty and Alexander. Monty was cordial, but did not accord Patton the military pomp and circumstance to which Patton felt entitled. The final insult was Monty's gift of a five cent cigar lighter to the great General. "Someone must have given him a box of them," Patton remarked to an aide. But at that conference, Monty surprised Patton by suggesting that the 7th Army be the ones to take Messina. Patton doubted the motives, and redoubled his efforts to be first to the prize.

When Montgomery visited Patton at Palermo a few days later, he was met by a delegation at the airport and was received at headquarters with martial music by a full military band. Patton wrote to a friend, "I hope Monty realized that I did this to show him up for doing nothing for me."

During the first two weeks of August, Axis forces began evacuating its men and materiel across the Strait of Messina to Italy. It must be said, they were amazingly successful in accomplishing this massive logistical feat. But the race to Messina was still on, even if only Patton was interested in winning it. Monty had finally broken through Catania, but the Germans were fighting a brilliant rear-guard action in retreating toward Messina, slowing their progress toward the prize.

Coming from the west, Patton ordered two separate amphibious attacks in order to bypass Axis defensive positions. The first, on August 7th and 8th, led by Major General Lucien Truscott, put his troops behind enemy lines and twelve miles closer to Messina. Then, Patton ordered the second landing. Truscott balked because he didn't have time to get his infantry up for support. He asked for an extra day, and he had Bradley's backing. Fearing that another day would mean losing the race, Patton ordered Truscott to proceed. Truscott's men were pinned down by enemy fire for thirty hours until reinforcements arrived. It was a high cost for the ground gained. Axis forces, pursued by the Brits, continued to flood into Messina in preparation for evacuation.

Finally, late the night of August 16, parts of Truscott's 3rd Division entered Messina. Patton notified Ike, Alexander and Bradley that the moment of triumph was at hand. Patton himself would enter the city at 1000 hours the next morning. The next morning, he gathered with Truscott and other commanders on a hill overlooking the city. Notably absent was Bradley who'd become disenchanted with what he saw as Patton's unseemly haste in beating the Brits to the prize. Nonetheless, as they gathered, Patton barked, "What in hell are you all standing around for?"

At 1030 Patton reached the city square. Minutes later, Brigadier J.C. Currie of the British 4th Armored Division rumbled into town. Currie's troops were equipped with bagpipers so they could celebrate their victory. Instead, Currie graciously congratulated the General, calling it a "jolly good race".

Patton's victory did have consequences for the Americans. Previously viewed as inferior to the British forces, they had now defined new standards for speed of an Army crossing hostile territory. While he'd gained grudging respect from his enemies and allies, Patton had never doubted his own abilities. He wrote to his wife, "Of course, had I not been interfered with in July (by Alexander), I would have taken Messina in ten days..."

PART TWO

VALKYRIE

Chapter Thirty Eight

Herr und Frau Moeller

Tunisia

August 1943

Wild Bill Donovan had departed North Africa at about the same time the invasion had begun, leaving Dowderwell under virtual house arrest under the auspices of Brownwell. Now that Sicily was under Allied control, we could again plan for our infiltration into Germany. Donovan had been working on it with his people back in Washington, creating false personal histories for Elizabeth and me. We decided to reconvene in Tunisia as soon as I could get there.

Hopkins and Elizabeth had concentrated their efforts on understanding as much as they could about the Final Solution, which was not particularly fruitful. The SS had done a good job of throwing a blanket over the whole mess. They had also, with Donovan's approval, been communicating with Freddy via Dowderwell and his intermediaries.

I hitched a ride with an Army cargo plane to Tunisia on August 20. I was met by my beautiful Elizabeth who had rented a room at a local inn for the occasion. We dined and spent a long, blissful night together before reporting for duty the next morning.

When we walked in to Donovan's commandeered rooms at 0800, Hopkins greeted me with, *"Guten Morgen, Herr Moeller."* Herr Moeller? Oh, I get it, my new identity. "Or may I call you Fritz?" he asked.

"Fritz works all day long," I replied.

"And who is this young *Frau*?" I asked, nodding toward Elizabeth.

"This is Elizabeth D'Alessandro Moeller," Hopkins said. "Late of Rome, the city of her birth. You met her during your frequent business trips there in your capacity as a wine importer, and you fell in love."

"At least part of that is true," I observed.

"You were married in a civil ceremony in Rome last month. Unfortunately, due to the exigencies of the war, you have not yet been able to take your honeymoon, but you look forward to doing so the minute the future of the Thousand Year *Reich* is secured."

He continued, "Your business reputation has been growing, and it has come to the attention of Lieutenant Friedrich von Furstenberg who is assigned to Heinrich Himmler as a special assistant dealing with logistics of the Nazi camps. Your specialty is in the high end of wine. Therefore, you are not involved with the prisoners; rather, you will be supplying the officers both at the camps and those who are in Berlin. *Verstehen?*

"Jawohl. I understand," I answered. "What else?"

"This cover should bring you into close proximity with the camps and with high ranking officers in Berlin."

"And, aside from being blissfully married to me, what is *Frau* Moeller's role?"

Elizabeth answered. "You've been unable to keep good help in your business during the war. I have volunteered to temporarily be your secretary-assistant. It's imperative that I travel with you, attend meetings, be present to keep track of your business dealings. Got it, Fritz?" she grinned.

"But you don't speak German. How can you be in business?"

"You'll be there to translate."

"As you know, Pointer, Mussolini has been deposed, and Italy is suing the Allies for peace. The timing couldn't be better for us. We think we can get you two into Rome so that you can take a train from there to Berlin. Just like a businessman would do," Hopkins said.

He continued, "Over the past month, in Washington, our people have been busy constructing identities for the two of you. If, for example, someone in

Berlin wanted to speak to Elizabeth's parents, they could do so. They'll be speaking to two Romans on the OSS payroll. Likewise, in Bavaria, if they want to check up on you or your business, there will be records and some 'friends' of yours to whom inquirers will be directed. We frankly don't expect much in the way of questions since von Furstenberg has already 'vetted' you, but just in case. You will, of course, be supplied with full documentation of your identities."

"What could go wrong?" I said.

"We have also been talking to von Furstenberg's people about how we get you out of Germany if something goes awry. There is no plan that is foolproof. The best they can tell us is that they have some safe houses around the country. These houses have been used to smuggle Jews out of the country, believe it or not," Hopkins said.

"We need to sharpen up the focus of this mission," Wild Bill Donovan stated. He had joined us in the conference room. He waved his cigar at Elizabeth and me. "These two are going to be in a hell of a lot of danger. What's the reward for us—and for them?"

Hopkins answered, "I've always thought of this mission as learning more about the death camps. Giving us a chance of getting there early and disrupting things."

"Too broad," Donovan said.

Christ, I thought, we shouldn't be talking about this now.

"Dowderwell has said that von Furstenberg and his cohorts have been plotting to assassinate Hitler for years. They are excited that our presence there will be seen as a signal that the Americans want to support them and that they will have some influence in a post-Hitler Germany. So," I concluded, "the reason for this mission is to do everything we can to help *their* mission. And in so doing, we'll bring an early close to the camps.

"I believe Pointer has it right," said the Colonel. "That's the focus. If you can learn something about any of their strategic plans, including information on the camps, you will let us know."

Chapter Thirty Nine

Interlude

February 1944

Newlyweds Fritz and Elizabeth Moeller checked into the Da Vinci Hotel three blocks from the Spanish Steps. The Da Vinci was oozing with charm with a beautiful mahogany paneled lobby, tapestries on the walls and one of the prettiest Orientals I had ever seen. My family had stayed there years before in one of our visits to Rome.

We had run into a serious snag in getting this far. Dowderwell had reported that his contacts in Berlin had indicated that they were not sure that our presence there would be such a good thing. In fact, they told Dowderwell directly that our deal was off. So, Elizabeth and I had been ordered back to Washington until things were straightened out between the parties.

We'd taken a merchant ship from Algiers to New York. It took much longer than it otherwise would have, as the ship ran across the ocean in a zigzag pattern, as all ships did. The crossing was uneventful and would have been tedious if I hadn't been with Elizabeth. Turns out she enjoyed my sense of humor and—hey—you can't beat a pretty girl laughing at your jokes. By now, I was "over the moon" as Mother would say. We spent over half of our time in our tiny cabin getting to know each other more and better.

We spent a couple of nights in New York and splurged on the Waldorf. We saw movies, ate and drank and walked the city in the Indian Summer weather. Central Park was a daily favorite as we walked among other wartime couples who were lucky enough to be stateside. Elizabeth liked to hold hands and I even got used to that; in fact, I preferred it to just walking solo as I'd done for the nearly thirty years of my life.

We took the train down to Washington and disembarked at Union Station. We couldn't believe the crowds. Soldiers, sailors, airmen and Marines everywhere we looked. It seemed as though everyone were engaged in the war effort in one way or another. We knew that we'd be assigned to single-sex quarters when we settled in at Fort McNair on the DC waterfront, so we splurged again—this time at the Mayflower on Connecticut Avenue where we stayed for three nights. As in New York, we spent our time just walking the streets and being a normal couple. We did play a spirited game of tennis at the Army Navy Club with another couple we'd met on the train coming down. Life was normal, life was good. I tried hard to forget about Binky, Dowderwell, Don Vizzini (he had, in fact, been named Mayor of Palermo by the Allied Forces), and that poor Frogman bastard who'd gotten himself blown up. I wasn't entirely successful. But the one thought I could never shake was Billingsley and his dying in my arms. It seemed to be a thousand years ago, but it had been only a few months. More than once, I woke up screaming and sweating until Elizabeth calmed me down.

After our stay in DC, it was time to board the train for South Hill where we would spend a few days with the folks. Elizabeth was nervous, but I assured her that she would be a huge hit. And she was. My sister came over from Norfolk where she was working as a secretary in the shipyard.

On the way down, Elizabeth asked me what I thought about children. I knew what she meant, but I said, "The little tykes are adorable, except the bratty ones who cry and puke and poop."

She smiled and said, "No, really, Pointer, do you want children someday?"

"You mean a little Pointer? Or Pointress? Or a Pointerette?"

"Yes. A little Pointer."

"Well, sure I do," I said slowly. "How about you? Would you like a little Pointer?" Suddenly, I was nervous.

"A child or a Pointer child?" she asked.

"A Pointer," I answered.

"Yes." And she grabbed my hand and put her head on my shoulder so I couldn't see her smile.

My parents put on the dog, as we say in South Hill. There was a "Welcome Home Robert" sign over the front door and both Mother and Father hugged me in their turn until I thought they'd never let go. Then they hugged Elizabeth as though they'd known her for years. My mother waited twenty whole minutes before she asked me if we were getting married. She said it *sotto voce* as Father and Elizabeth were chatting in the living room.

We had dinner that night and the next two and were treated as conquering heroes. Sister Sally told us all about her work in the shipyard while Elizabeth and I related what we could about our work, which wasn't much. During the day, I provided personal tours of South Hill and environs to Elizabeth in Father's Packard. I showed her the railroad tracks where my buddies and I used to hop freight trains and ride them through town until just before they resumed speed. I even put a penny on the tracks for old time's sake and we watched as a passing train pancaked it. Such fun! The baseball diamond at the high school where I had maintained a .316 batting average my senior year. Our church where I was made to go each and every Sunday so that my attendance medals made me look like a decorated Brazilian General. The drug store where Louise behind the soda fountain remembered my name and smiled for the first time since I'd met her in 1931. We parked in the local Lovers Lane and necked until I thought we'd better get out of there before we did something in semi-public that we'd regret.

Father and I had some time to talk while the ladies were doing some lady stuff. I assured him I was fine and that my work was no more dangerous than the average spy's. We were, after all, stateside, but I told him there was a good chance that we would be going back to Europe at a point to be determined. I think he deduced that Elizabeth was in my line of work even though we maintained that she worked for the Red Cross.

The day came for us to return to Washington as we were due to meet Colonel Donovan at his office the next morning. We said our goodbyes—and Mother, in particular, made it hard. She tried to put on a brave face, but didn't quite manage it, and wept quiet tears. Father even misted up as they hugged us both and begged us to be careful.

"Robert, you write to us even though you're only in Washington. And you tell your Colonel that that's where you should stay. There is no reason for you to be gallivanting all over Europe. And that goes for you, too, Elizabeth," Mother admonished us.

The next morning we sat in Wild Bill's office on 16th Street in Washington. He told us that there had been no further progress with von Furstenberg and his group, but that we should be ready to move out at a moment's notice. In the meantime, we would be translating German and Italian documents and analyzing intercepted cables. Donovan hinted to us what everyone assumed to be the case: the Allies were preparing to invade France. Perhaps even he did not know when or where. But it was coming. So, most of our work would be reading decoded transmissions that had been intercepted and then giving our analysis of what it all meant. What did the Germans know, and what did they *think* they knew. We were also to continue to stay physically fit and be regulars at the Fort McNair shooting range. A tutor was assigned to me so that I could brush up on my German, particularly the dialect of Bavaria where I supposedly had come of age.

Two weeks into our stint, Elizabeth's parents made the trek from California. On their second night in town, I was invited to dinner to meet them. Mr. D'Antoni reminded me a little bit of my pal Lucky except he didn't have the lazy eye. I thought he was a total windbag, frankly. He held forth about Generals, Senators and Adolf-goddamn-Hitler, as Patton would call him. As a Californian, he seemed more interested in the war in the Pacific, which I found at least bearable because he actually knew some things that I didn't. The mother seemed very sweet and spellbound by just about everything Old Windbag had to say.

A few weeks later, Elizabeth decided that we should go out for drinks to celebrate our nine-month anniversary. Any port in a storm, I always say, and any excuse for a fine cocktail. We went to the Red Robin bar at the Willard Hotel, and I ordered a Martini and Elizabeth had Champagne. As usual, the bar was filled with military-types, Congress-types and the usual self-important types from business and, as far as I knew, the Supreme-goddamn-Court (as Patton would call it). We were halfway through our first round when an Army Major tapped Elizabeth on the shoulder. She looked up and blushed visibly.

"Palmer. My God, what are…"

"Hello, Elizabeth. I saw you across the room and I thought the right thing to do was to come and say hello," Palmer announced.

The right thing to do? My antenna was buzzing. Palmer was in his early forties with a dark buzz cut, glasses and a cleft chin. But I was taller, I judged. I was already thinking, "mine's bigger than yours".

Elizabeth seemed to recover some of her composure. "Darling, this is Palmer Minter from back home. I believe I've told you about him. Palmer, this is Pointer."

I stood up and shook hands. Yep, I was taller.

"Just Pointer?" Palmer asked?

"Everybody calls me Pointer," I said.

"Well, Palmer, this is a surprise. Will you sit down?"

Palmer paused for a beat and said, "Yes, that'd be nice. How have you been, Elizabeth? You look wonderful."

"Never better," she smiled.

God, I loved that girl. Did you hear that? Never better.

"Are you still in the, uh, Red Cross?"

I didn't think he was buying that cover.

"Yes, I am assigned to the national headquarters here," she said.

"How about you. Pointer?"

I kill enemy spies and eat them for breakfast, you brush-headed sumbitch, I thought.

But I said, "I'm assigned to the OSS here under Colonel Donovan. We're working on codes, the usual secret agent stuff. And you, Major?"

Palmer seemed just a little too happy to answer that one. "I'm assigned as a military attaché to the White House. I deal with Ike's ETO command in

London. Pretty interesting work, actually."

Yeah? Going to Ber-fucking-*lin* anytime soon?

Palmer continued. "Actually, I'm aware that you've been in North Africa, Elizabeth. You, too, Pointer. At least I presume it was you who my friend spotted at the resort on the Med." He looked at Elizabeth and smiled, "I have spies everywhere, my dear."

Spy on *this,* brush-head.

Elizabeth said, "Yes, we saw Johnson briefly. Pointer and I were enjoying a little R&R, relaxing you know. In fact, we had a *blissful* few days." She smiled sweetly.

Oh my.

Palmer looked uneasy at this, which, of course, was the point. "Well, I should get back to the others. It was nice seeing you, Elizabeth. And meeting you, Pointer."

He and I stood up and shook hands. I was still taller.

I turned to Elizabeth and said, "You're pretty good in the clenches, darlin'."

"I realize now how much I dislike him. Pointer, you've spoiled me for everyone else," she said as she took my hand.

As autumn turned to winter, we settled into a routine. We reported to the 16th Street offices every day. We read cables, dispatches and decoded messages. The good news was that the Germans seemed to be very unsure about Allied plans for the invasion. We knew that the disinformation campaign by the Allies coming out of London, some of which originated on 16th Street, was intense. I thought about reprising the dead soldier washing up on shore with fake orders trick, but rejected it ultimately. I was starting to think like a spy. If we planted orders on a corpse, the Germans would have probably figured out that we'd tricked them in Spain. But maybe they'd know that we knew that they knew, and

we'd never try it again. Therefore, this
time it might be authentic. I got dizzy
with the permutations.

We both continued an intense physical
regimen and we both improved our
marksmanship at the firing range.
Maybe I'd get a shot at the *Fuhrer*. You
never knew.

We were able to slip down to South Hill
for a couple of days over Christmas,
which was great fun. Mother harbored
the hope that a) we would spend the
rest of the war in Washington and b)
that we would be announcing our
engagement any minute. We attended
midnight services at Saint Paul's and
sang Christmas' greatest hits, including
my favorite, *Silent Night.*

I recalled a Christmas when I was ten
or eleven when my major gift was a
bow and arrow set. For the next year I
had hunted squirrels in the
neighborhood, never so much as
wounding one. Like Captain Ahab and
the Whale, I hunted the Great Albino
Squirrel, which lived in a tree down our
street. Every week or so I would catch

sight of the critter and fire off a shot. I was obsessed with that pale aberration. I noticed Elizabeth looking at me strangely as I told her this one.

We spent New Year's Eve partying with other OSS people, and a smattering of Marines and sailors at the Mayflower. When Elizabeth and I kissed at midnight as we saw in 1944, I was as happy as a boy from South Hill could be. But neither of us could shake a feeling of foreboding because we knew that we'd most likely spend the next holiday on the calendar in the belly of the enemy beast.

The call came in early February. Our code specialists had taken over from Dowderwell, who was now under arrest by the Brits in London. They had managed to reestablish contact with Freddy's people, who had recently become more receptive to us. We figured it was because the war continued to turn against the Nazis and Freddy and his group were getting more and more desperate to get rid of

Hitler once and for all. They needed something to galvanize the effort, and

Lieutenant Robert L. Pointer aka *Herr Fritz Moeller* could be it.

And so Elizabeth and I found ourselves in Rome.

We had agreed to speak Italian to each other, and I would speak German otherwise, as it was my "first language". That first evening in "enemy territory" was nerve wracking. We constantly were looking at the other guests, wondering if they had guessed that we were interlopers. I had to think before I spoke to her in public to make sure I used Italian, not English or German. The hotel was populated mostly by German and Italian officers. The Italians had to be confused. They were negotiating a peace with the Allies, but were still in political No Mans Land.

Before dinner, we took a stroll around the neighborhood. We were, after all, supposed to be on our pre-honeymoon. The crowds were light, the mood a bit dark in the Eternal City. We sat in an outdoor café and ordered Camparis and watched the Romans hustling by. The offices had closed and the men and the secretaries were heading home for their pasta. I thought again about the nature of this war. It was indeed global. Other major cities like Berlin and London had sustained heavy bombing damage and loss of life. Paris had been occupied. Islands in the Pacific were being contested by Japanese and American forces as if they held great treasure. And they did. Because if you controlled a patch in the middle of the ocean, you controlled the ocean itself. But here in Rome, hard by the Borghese, little had changed outwardly. The same could be said for Washington and New York. But behind the closed doors of the apartments and homes in all of these places, there were few families who were not either in mourning for a lost son or father, or terrified that an Army officer would be knocking on the door with terrible news. I thought of Patton's dictum about "killing the other dumb bastard first".

"So, Pointer, tomorrow we go. And we meet von Furstenberg?"

"Yes, we are to have dinner with him and his wife Marta. A business dinner, of course. I have a case of the new Chianti line that I will be presenting him."

She leaned over and adjusted my blue silk tie. "Well, you look very successful, quite the businessman. I'd buy all of my wine from you if I could," she smiled. "What's Berlin like?"

"We won't really know until we get there because of the bombing campaign of the Allies. But the Berlin that I remember is beautiful—great architecture, food and lots of forests throughout the city. We'll be staying in the *Mitte,* which is the borough in the center of the city. Most of our business will be conducted in the *Reichstag* or the *Bendlerblock* unless they have been too damaged by the bombing. I hope we'll be able to take in some of the sights. I have good memories of the Brandenberg Gate, the Charlottenberg Palace, the Tiergarten and some terrific restaurants and even some nightclubs. I'd also like to see the Olympic Stadium."

"Sounds like a lovely extension of our honeymoon."

"Right. I wonder if Lucky knows any German Dons."

Chapter Forty

Cabal

Berlin

February 1944

The most important conspirators were gathering in Friedrich von Furstenberg's Berlin apartment. Marta was out visiting her aunt and uncle, not because she wasn't privy to the men's plans, but she made some of them nervous by her presence. Women and children were to be kept in ignorance of important military matters, not to mention secrets like this one. The von Furstenberg children were in Bavaria, in school, with their grandparents looking after them.

Freddy had important news for his collaborators that evening. And this was the meeting at which Lieutenant Colonel Claus Schenk Graf von Stauffenberg would be formally introduced to the group. Count von Stauffenberg had been badly wounded in North Africa, and had been recuperating while working with the general staff in Berlin. Stauffenberg was a conservative Roman Catholic, a zealous nationalist with extreme moral views.

In 1942 he had begun to believe that the *Fuhrer* was leading his beloved Germany to disaster and needed to be removed from power. After the Battle of Stalingrad, his beliefs evolved from removal of Hitler to assassination. Death was the only way. Like many Germans, Stauffenberg strongly suspected that Hitler and Himmler were murdering Jews by the trainload in the East. But unlike most Germans, he made it his business to confirm the facts as thoroughly as he could. What he learned appalled him to his core. He was deeply offended as a Christian and as a German. Yes, Hitler—and Himmler—must die. And, if necessary, he would gladly pull the trigger.

The chimes rang in Freddy's apartment. It was the first of his guests, Colonel Henning von Tresckow. There was no more ardent oppositionist than Tresckow, who had nearly succeeded in blowing Hitler out of the sky the year before. It was Tresckow who had recruited the newest member of the cabal. Freddy shook hands warmly with his old friend. In short order, they were joined by General Friedrich Olbricht, head of the General Army Office headquarters at the Bendlerblock in Central Berlin. Olbricht was their most important recruit to date because his command controlled an independent system of communications to reserve units throughout Germany. Finally, Stauffenberg arrived.

Introductions were made to Stauffenberg and drinks were served in Freddy's study.

As host, Freddy inquired after Stauffenberg.

"Count, how is your recovery progressing?"

Stauffenberg looked at his host before answering. He was a handsome man with a strong jaw and deep set, piercing eyes. His dark, pin-straight hair was parted on the left and appeared to have a bit of gel plastering it into place. His angular features were rarely interrupted by a smile.

"I am recuperating nicely, Lieutenant. *Danke.*"

"Please call me Freddy. Everyone does."

Stauffenberg made no reciprocal gesture for Freddy to be on a familiar basis.

Drinks were really just *a* drink so the men repaired to the dining room where a dinner of roasted goose, roasted potatoes and assorted vegetables awaited them. Not a word of politics or plots had yet been uttered. It was bad form to speak of such things while cocktails were being served.

When the servant retired to the kitchen, Freddy conspicuously cleared his throat and began, "Tomorrow, *Herr* Fritz Moeller arrives in Berlin by train.

He will be accompanied by his wife, Elizabeth, who is Italian. As you know, *Herr* and *Frau* Moeller are American agents who are sent to us by our British contacts in North Africa. He is posing as a wine wholesaler who will be among the suppliers to our officer corps here in Berlin and at the camps. She is his wife and assistant."

Freddy continued, "His presence here has significant symbolic value for us. His being here suggests that the Americans have given us their imprimatur. The question for us tonight is how best to use him. Shall we include him in our plans only in a symbolic sense, or shall we find a real role for him to play?"

Tresckow spoke up. "The intelligence from our friends indicates that Moeller is not the type to be content just being a symbol. Did he not personally slay our agent in Africa, your dear cousin?" Tresckow looked at Freddy.

"Yes, he did. Strange bedfellows and all that," Freddy said. "But the question remains: what shall we do with him?"

Olbricht offered, "Let's feel him out first and make our plans accordingly."

Stauffenberg spoke for the first time. "I believe his political views will be important to our group. For example, how do the Allies view our chances of winning the war. Of course, the more confident they are in their own victory, the worse our position. There will come a time, in the next year I believe, that an assassination of Hitler and a *coup d'etat* will have much less meaning to the Allies. With each German defeat our position gets weaker and the urgency of our mission grows greater. If the rest of you believe, as I do, that the war is not now winnable, it doesn't necessarily mean that the Allies believe the same. It is important that we understand his unadulterated views of our respective positions in the war. And to what extent do his views reflect the views of his leaders?"

The other men considered the wisdom of the Count's words.

"Whatever else we may think, it is vital that we make our plans and execute them with all due haste," Olbricht agreed.

Freddy said, "Based on what we know of Moeller, he is not a *dumkopf*. Like the General, I think we should proceed with caution with him, but I also believe that we should give him every benefit of the doubt when it comes to his being an active participant in our plans."

"We are in full flight on the Eastern Front. How long will it be before the Soviets are knocking on our doors here? A year? Two? Also, it is a matter of time before the Allies invade from England. We must act soon," said Tresckow.

"Our main problem", he continued, "is that the *Fuhrer's* public appearances are becoming extremely limited, and in private he is always heavily guarded. We need a way to get close to him."

Freddy said, "I am in personal contact with Himmler frequently. There are signs that he will look the other way when it comes to a coup. In August, Finance Minister Popitz made a direct overture to him about the opposition supporting him if Himmler would make a move to remove the *Fuhrer*. Not surprisingly, he did not agree to do anything, but nor did he arrest Popitz or any of his supporters."

"*Sheist*!" exclaimed Stauffenberg with vehemence. "I am not here to remove one mad dog only to replace him with another!"

"I am only saying that Himmler seemed neutral about the idea," Freddy said quietly.

The General said, "I believe we are all agreed that the best plan would be to kill Hitler and Himmler at the same time. Goring, too. We *are* agreed?" He glared at the others and each in his turn signified their assent.

Freddy said, "It would be an honor if I could be the one to put a bullet in the brain of Himmler. He *is* a mad dog. His Final Solution is a crime against humanity. He has the blood of millions on his hands. There will, you know, come a time when Moeller will be asked to go to the camps in his capacity as a businessman. It would be best if I could accompany him, which I believe I can arrange."

"Freddy, do you harbor ill will against Moeller for his role in your cousin's death?" Tresckow broached the subject that had been on all of their minds.

Freddy had done a great deal of soul searching on that very topic. He was about to join forces with the man who had killed his dear Binky. But Freddy was a soldier and this was war. At length, he had come to the conclusion that he would have acted exactly as "Fritz" had done had he been in the same position. He had hardened his heart to not take it personally and had mostly succeeded in doing so.

"Of course not," Freddy said. "*C'est la guerre.* He was only doing his duty. All of us would have done the same."

"And when do we get to meet *Herr* Moeller and his charming wife?" Olbricht asked.

"*Sehr bald*," Freddy said. Very soon.

Chapter Forty One

The von Furstenbergs

We arrived on the 4pm train from Milan. Both the train stations were massive structures. In Milan we'd gotten thoroughly lost in the station and almost missed our train. But once we'd settled in, we were treated to breathtaking sights. The vineyards of Northern Italy, the Lake Country, then the Southern Alps. Every vista was a postcard, even in the dead of winter. We'd occupied a car with two other travelers, an Italian gentleman of uncertain provenance and his *signora.* They were pleasant enough, but kept to themselves. He had the smell of dirty money about him. Arms merchant? Maybe a plant from the Freddy's group?

At length, we arrived in Berlin. It was bitterly cold when we stepped out of the train, and it looked as if snow were in the offing. As arranged by von Furstenberg, we were met by a Corporal from Freddy's unit (I had been mentally calling him Freddy ever since I

481

first heard his name a year ago from Binky).

"Herzlich wilkommen in Berlin," greeted Corporal Heinsohn.

"Danke, *Stabsunteroffizier,"* I responded. "You will retrieve the bags?"

"Jahwohl, Herr Moeller."

As we expected, the platform was crowded with Nazi soldiers, many of whom had German Shepherd dogs on leather leashes. They all seemed to be scanning the crowds for suspicious behavior. As the saying goes, just because I'm paranoid, it doesn't mean they're not out to get me. We saw a group of poorly attired, bedraggled people being herded by SS men off to a train on the west platform. Refugees from the East, I thought. Better to be coming *from* the East these days than going *to* the East.

Heinsohn led us to a car that was idling outside the station just as the snow began to fall. I guess the SS doesn't worry about parking tickets. We drove away from the station toward the *Mitte* where we would be staying. There was quite a bit of traffic in mid-afternoon Berlin. We passed block after block which seemed to be undisturbed. Just when I was thinking the Berlin Chamber of Commerce had dictated our route, we came across three city blocks that were nothing but rubble from the bombing.

"How often do you see the bombers?" I asked the Corporal.

"Ah, it seems to come in waves. There will be weeks of peace and then four days of strikes," he said. "Our squad leaders tell us it is to keep us off balance."

"Civilian casualties?" I asked.

"It is a close secret, but the rumors are 50,000 to 60,000 so far."

I thought about this. Usually when you visit a foreign city you're asking the cabbie about the weather, the best restaurants, what new shows are in town. Here, we were talking solely of death and destruction.

We reached the Bavarian, our hotel, and the Corporal handed us over to the hotel staff. Before he departed, he handed me an envelope, which I opened while the porter was handling our luggage.

"Herr und Frau Moeller, *Wilkommen.* Please make yourselves comfortable in your rooms. We will meet at 9 pm at the *Kaiserplatz* for dinner. In the meantime, do not hesitate to ring the number below should you require anything. My wife and I eagerly look forward to making yours and *Frau* Moeller's acquaintance. Friedrich von Furstenberg."

Elizabeth and I settled into our suite. It had a bedroom and a sitting room in which we could receive guests. We decided to take a walk and stretch our legs after the long train ride. It was still snowing, but only lightly. We walked out of the hotel and turned south, with no particular destination in mind. The pedestrians who braved the storm were all walking with their heads down against the wind. As we traversed the streets, gazing at the classic architecture of the *Mitte,* I sensed a presence to our rear. I grabbed Elizabeth's hand and pulled her across the street and then doubled back the way we'd come. I noticed that a man in a long trench coat on the opposite side of the street was gazing into a shop window. Who does that in a snow storm? Someone who's following you, that's who. Freddy's man? The SS? I would be sure to question my host tonight at dinner.

We dressed for dinner, me in my best double breasted gray pinstripe suit and Elizabeth in a straight A-line skirt with a silk top. *Herr* and *Frau* Moeller going out for a business dinner with an SS officer and his wife to get acquainted as we begin to do business. We arrived at the *Kaiserplatz* promptly at nine, and I spotted who I thought were Freddy and Marta at a prime table across the room. Almost everyone there was in uniform. This was obviously an Army hangout.

The Maitre d' led us to Freddy's table.

"Ah, *Herr* Moeller. And you, of course, are *Frau* Moeller," Freddy said, rising.

We shook hands and introductions were made. Marta was yin to Elizabeth's yang. Where Elizabeth was tall, dark and willowy, Marta was short, petite and light-skinned, Germanic to her core. She had freckles showing where her décolletage dipped on her gown.

"How was your journey, *Herr* Moeller? And your accommodations?" Freddy inquired.

"You must call me Fritz. Everyone calls me Fritz," I said. "And this is Elizabeth."

"So it is. And we are Freddy and Marta."

After more pleasantries, Freddy got down to business. "Tomorrow you will meet me in the Bendlerblock and meet some of the other officers with whom you will do business. Say, 10 o'clock?"

"We are at your service, Freddy," I replied. I noticed that Marta seemed preoccupied with her cocktail and wasn't leaning into the conversation. Every so often I would pause and translate snatches of the dialogue in Italian for Elizabeth.

"And whom will we be meeting," I asked.

"Count Stauffenberg and General Olbricht for certain. And I am hoping that Colonel von Tresckow will join us as well."

"These gents are involved in the food and wine side of things?" I arched my brows.

"They are indeed involved in your line of work, Fritz."

I looked around briefly. "Freddy, on the *strasse* today near our hotel, I noticed a man who was following us. Is he also in our line of work?"

Freddy frowned and thought for a moment. "We have no one from our group assigned to such a duty. Are you certain about this?"

"There's no doubt," I said.

"Well, that is interesting and, yes, a little alarming," he said. "What do you think, my dear?" he asked Marta, attempting to draw her into the conversation.

"I would say that's very alarming," Marta said at once, her reticence gone. She in fact looked alarmed.

"We will discuss this with the group tomorrow," Freddy said. Now, Fritz, there will be some travel involved. In two days, we are scheduled to go to Auschwitz in the East. After that, we will both go home to Bavaria for a few days. I'd like you to meet my father— and our children."

At this, Marta stiffened just enough for me to notice. I watched her as I translated for Elizabeth. She didn't seem to want to be there at the table. We'd known in advance that, like Elizabeth, she was privy to all of the plans. I couldn't decide if I was comfortable with that. It seemed a little extravagant to have yet another person in on the secrets

As we were being served our entrees, an SS Colonel stopped at our table. Freddy fairly leapt to his feet, clicked his heels together and saluted crisply. "Good evening Colonel Schmidt, sir."

"Good evening, Furstenberg," the Colonel said rather languidly, not looking at Freddy, but eyeing Elizabeth and me instead. "Won't you introduce me to your friends?"

"Of course, sir. May I present *Herr* and *Frau* Moeller from Bavaria. *Herr* Moeller is in Berlin to meet with us about wine for the officer corps and some of the camps. He is a new supplier."

"I see. How fortunate for you, *Herr* Moeller. It must be a very large contract. How were you able to secure it?"

"I have a small, family-owned company, *Herr* Colonel, very little overhead, so we were the low bidder this time out. Very fortunate indeed, sir."

"*Herr* and *Frau* Moeller are recently married, *Herr* Colonel," Freddy said in an effort to change the subject.

Colonel Schmidt kept his gaze fixed on me. "I shall ask my clerks for the records for this contract first thing tomorrow. I want to see all of the money that the *Reich* is saving through your company, *Herr* Moeller. You must come and see me when you come to the Bendlerblock." With that, he nodded to the table and went on his way.

"Friend of yours, Freddy?" I said.

"Hardly. I sometimes think his idea of fun, other than pulling the wings off of flies, is to spy on me. Somehow I don't think his being here tonight is a coincidence."

Marta appeared to be stricken. "Are you alright, my dear?" Freddy reached across and put his hand over hers.

"I am not feeling well, Freddy. Would you mind terribly if we skip dessert and go straight home. I am so sorry, Fritz and Elizabeth."

"Not at all," I said. "It seems we'll have plenty of opportunity to be together in the next few months."

Chapter Forty Two

The Bendlerblock

The Headquarters for the Ministry Of Defense and the General Army, the Bendlerblock, was located near the *Tiergarten.* For my purposes, its importance was that it was the epicenter of the plot to assassinate Adolf Hitler. General Olbricht, Count Stauffenberg, Colonel Tresckow and Freddy all had their offices there. Freddy was a high ranking officer in Logistics Command and reported to Colonel Schmidt, who reported to Himmler himself. Colonel Stauffenberg was under the command of Olbricht. The conventional wisdom was that Tresckow was about to be transferred to the East, which was not good news. The other rumor was that Stauffenberg was in line for a promotion, which would put him in war planning sessions with the now-reclusive Hitler. That would give the conspirators a man close to Hitler and one close to Himmler. And they were the primary targets.

At 1000 hours Elizabeth and I reported to the Bendlerblock, a building of classic design angled around a gigantic courtyard. The duty officer left to alert Freddy of our arrival.

For the past twenty-four hours we had been exposed closely to SS officers and their uniforms. I had to admit to myself that they were well designed. The Nazis, and the *Fuhrer* and *Reichsfuhrer* Himmler in particular, were keen on the appearance of the SS officer corps. Himmler had famously said, "I know there are many people who fall ill when they see this black uniform; we understand that and don't expect that we will be loved by many people." Talk about an understatement.

Most of the SS uniforms by 1944 were no longer black; they were slate gray. But they still struck fear in almost everyone who encountered them. The uniforms I saw that morning had the Army-style shoulder boards with SS collar patches trimmed in silver or army-style silver-grey braid around the collar. Sleeve chevrons and pips on the collars denoted rank. There are more eagles on an SS uniform than they have in the aerie at the Bronx Zoo, I thought. And, of course, there were the Death's Heads worn by officers and guard in the camps. Death's Head, I thought. Nice touch.

When Freddy appeared, I asked, "How is Marta feeling? Better I hope,"

"Yes. Just nerves, I think. She hates being away from the children, you know. She will return to Bavaria when we go to Auschwitz, and I will join her there after our trip. I have some unpleasant news for you, Fritz. Colonel Schmidt would like to see you in his office immediately."

"Do you know why?" I asked.

"He didn't say. But then he wouldn't, you know. Come on, I'll show you the way. I'm afraid he said for you to come alone. Elizabeth can wait here."

I translated for Elizabeth, and she immediately became worried. We doubted this was a social call. Freddy led me down the hall to the corner office. There were double doors and a male secretary was busily typing and answering a phone that never seemed to stop ringing.

"*Herr* Moeller to see the Colonel," Freddy announced.

The secretary nodded to a sofa where I was to sit. I sat for nearly an hour. Every ten minutes or so I asked if the Colonel may have forgotten about me. The secretary just peered over his typewriter and gave me a little smile as if to say, "You obviously don't know how it works around here. This man is very close to being God, and he *is* God in this office. Sit and be silent."

At last I was buzzed in. The great man was seated behind a desk the size of a Volkswagen. By now, I was fuming. I hate to wait. Cool, Pointer, I told myself, but I knew I was close to the edge.

"*Herr* Moeller, *guten morgen.* Tea?"

"No thank you, Colonel," I replied. I sat up straight in one of the visitor's chairs which was strategically lower than Schmidt's enormous, high-backed swivel chair, positioned so I had to look up to him. I didn't like that so I stood and said, "If you don't mind, Colonel, I'd like to stand. The train ride and my back..." I shrugged apologetically.

"Mmm. Yes. Well, *Herr* Moeller, I have been reviewing the records of your company. It seems that your experience consists of supplying restaurants in Bavaria. Your biggest account has been, let me see... Hotel Brindle." He began shuffling papers.

"No sir, that is incorrect. The Rhineland has been my biggest account," I countered.

"Quite so, quite so. But there is a period here where you had a hiatus in '41. Can you tell me why?"

"They closed for renovations in the New Year of '41."

"But by the standards of supplying our Army, you have had no experience in doing anything on that scale. And your business records show only a few small hotels and restaurants apart from the Rhineland. Why did von Furstenberg choose you for such a large assignment, do you suppose? Does he owe you something? Are you a relative of his?"

I stared down at Schmidt and thought hard about how to play this. "Colonel Schmidt, I resent your implication, sir, that I have won this assignment by anything other than hard work and skill. The records will show that I was the low bidder on this job; in fact, sir, it is my opinion that you were being gouged by the previous vendor."

Schmidt smiled in his "I-am-God" way and said, "It is the previous vendor who has lodged a complaint against you, Moeller. He claims that there must be some funny business going on. For one thing, he's never heard of you or your company. For another, he claims that no one could deliver the wine and spirits for the low price that is in your bid. How do you respond to that, Moeller?"

I smiled back and tried to appear as though I were relaxing. "Ah, my competitor! He is a wily old crook. Did he also tell you that when I won the account for the Rhineland that he told *them* that he had never heard of me and that my prices were impossibly low?"

"No, he did not. But I intend to ask him. Now, tell me why you are really here, Moeller?"

"What do you mean, sir?"

"Why you've come to Berlin? To the Bendlerblock?"

"To meet with Lieutenant von Furstenberg, of course. About quantities, timing, deliveries."

"Quite so, Moeller. We shall see about that, won't we. Now you may leave. I am busy."

"How did it go?" Elizabeth asked me when I returned.

I told her that Schmidt had tested me, that he seemed suspicious and that we needed to keep the eyes in the back of our heads open and look out for the SS Colonel.

Freddy assembled Stauffenberg and Olbricht. This was to be a brief meeting under the auspices of their meeting with a new supplier. It was not unusual for officers to want to meet the wine guy and get their favorite vintages recorded. Tresckow had been called away. We repaired to a conference room off of Olbricht's office which he had swept daily for listening devices. Even though he was a General, he had to be mindful of prying eyes and ears from other SS-types. Especially SS-types like Schmidt. He made it clear that we were to meet for no longer than thirty minutes.

Introductions were made and I was made to feel important by Stauffenberg and Olbricht. It was the first time I heard the term *"Valkyrie"* used to describe the plot against Hitler.

"Colonel Stauffenberg is to be assigned to Hitler's war council staff so that he will have personal contact with the *Fuhrer,"* Olbricht said. "We rarely see him any more since the war has turned against us. Very few public appearances. He rarely leaves the *Wolfsschanze* or visits Berlin. He goes only to his mountain retreat on a regular basis."

The *Wolfsschanze* was Hiltler's Wolf's Lair.

"Therefore, we must go to him. The Count's promotion opens the door for us to get close." Olbricht continued.

"I will do the deed at the earliest opportunity," Stauffenberg said.

I looked at him and saw the intensity of a zealot. I did not doubt him.

Olbricht said, "We have a pre-existing plan in place code-named *Valkyrie,* which can be quite useful, indeed, vital for our plan. It was originally put in place in anticipation of massive disruption by Allied bombing, which may cause a breakdown in law and order in our major cities, or in the event of an uprising among forced labor. It is a communication plan so that we may inform the Reserve Army what has happened in the event of Hitler's assassination and a subsequent *coup d'etat.* We will use *Valkyrie's* communications network to issue new orders from a new government in the wake of our take-over."

"This *Valkyrie* network already exists?" I asked. "Who controls it?"

Freddy said, "The commander of the Reserve Army, General Erich Fromm, is the only one who can put the plan into effect. We are working on him to join us."

"He's not on board?" I was a little surprised.

Stauffenberg said, "No, he is not. But he will be, or at the least he will be neutral and we will step in." Again, the old Stauffenberg intensity. His eyes were burning holes in the paper on the table at which he was staring.

Olbricht said, "One more thing, Moeller. You and Freddy are going to Auschwitz tomorrow. You will see things there that are horrible and will affect you to your core. Your Government should know that there are those of us in the Army who are deeply ashamed of what's happening there and elsewhere, and it is the chief reason why we are trying to rid Germany and the world of this madman who is our *Fuhrer*. See everything you can; you will, no doubt, report it to your Government. The world will soon know it anyway." He trailed off.

Chapter Forty Three

Darkness

Elizabeth was denied permission to go with us to Auschwitz. Freddy explained that this was non-negotiable. Part of me was glad as at least only one of us would have nightmares. The irony of me—supposedly a merchant of fine wines—going to a death camp to supply the officers with drinks they could enjoy after a tough day of exterminating people was almost too much.

We flew from Berlin to Krakow and were met by a car which drove us through the Polish countryside to the gates of what was known as Auschwitz I. There were two other main camps— Auschwitz II, or Birkenau—and Auschwitz III. Besides these three, there were forty-five sub-camps as part of the Auschwitz system. Killing millions of Jews, Gypsies and other undesirables was a huge industry for Himmler, Hitler and their henchmen. Thousands of SS men and women were posted to the complex.

Freddy had filled in some of the gaps for me on the way from Berlin. Before the Wannsee Conference in early 1942, when the Final Solution had become policy, Himmler had ordered the construction of this camp, originally a Polish army artillery barracks. The Police Leader of the region needed a site for a concentration camp to house prisoners in the Silesia region as the prisons there were overflowing. Himmler named Rudolf Hess to oversee its development and to serve as the first commandant. One of Hess' first orders of business was to expel all the citizenry of the surrounding towns, creating a "Camp Interest Zone" of isolation for many miles around the camp. They were then free to conduct their business in privacy.

"It started as a work camp, but Auschwitz I was soon being used to exterminate prisoners who began arriving by the trainload," Freddy had explained. "Early in the decade they began imprisoning Poles by the thousands—the intelligentsia, dissidents, anyone who represented a threat. And, of course, Jews. People think that there was no gassing and torture done that early, but 'people' are wrong. Block 11, for example, was the 'prison within the prison'. Sinners, at least in the eyes of the guards, were made to work all day, then spend their nights in standing cells."

"I can only imagine what a standing cell is," I said.

"No. You can't. A standing cell is a 16 square foot room in the basement where they put four men, all standing, where they are forced to sleep. Then there are the starvation cells where prisoners are given no food or water until they simply expire from starvation."

"When did the gassing start?"

"On a relatively small scale in '41. Apparently, there was some experimentation with pesticide. About 600 Russian POWs and 250 Polish prisoners were taken to the basement on Block 11 and were subjected to a cyanide-based pesticide called Zyklon

B. After that, the SS were in business as you Americans say. They converted a bunker into a gas chamber, built a crematorium and began the killing in mass numbers in '40 and '41. That original bunker-turned-chamber is now an air raid shelter for the SS."

This was going to be depressing. "Kill the other poor bastard before he kills you", I remembered Patton's admonishment. But these poor bastards, once they got here, didn't stand a chance.

"So, there's enough demand for two more big branches and 45 smaller camps?" I asked.

"Yes. They constructed Auschwitz II—Birkenau—in 1941. Today, more killing is done there than any other single location. They went operational there in '42 with what they call the Little Red House and the Little White House, two brick cottages converted for the purpose. In '43, they greatly increased capacity for gassing at Birkenau. What is called Crematorium II was originally a mortuary with morgues in the basement and ground-level furnaces. They sealed up the door, added vents for the Zyklon B and ventilation equipment to evacuate the gas and had themselves a grand-scale killing factory. By spring, they had three more of these gruesome death chambers. Since '43, they have stepped up their killing to a point where it is at a fever pitch now."

"What about III?" I wasn't sure I wanted to know.

"III, or Monowitz, mainly provides slave labor for industry and the mines. There are about 12,000 prisoners there, mostly Jews. It's not much more than a death camp itself though. The life expectancy for a worker there is about three to four months. For miners? One month. And if you are deemed unfit for work, you are sent to Birkenau for the Final Solution."

We sat in silence in the plane flying over the Polish countryside. Below was nothing but clouds, but for the moment we were above the cover and the winter sun was shining. Millions of people exterminated? Chambers and crematoria designed and constructed to handle mass murder? A cyanide-laced pesticide used to gas women and children. It was too much to get my head around. I tried to think of one person at a time being murdered. Our culture says that is the worst thing one human can perpetrate on another. Binky had told me that Freddy was just like him, only they held different political beliefs. Well, he did seem like a normal chap, but he is part of this immoral, abhorrent, horrific process. This wasn't political, was it? Systematic, mass murder isn't a political act. Only by targeting a religion, or as the Nazis would have it, a race, does it take on the dark sheen of politics. In the end, I just didn't understand. Did Hitler or Himmler understand? This was not, of course, an accident. There were conferences, plans, budgets, chemists, builders and designers involved. So, of course they understood. They were the engines behind the atrocities.

I thought about my cover. Wine supplier. Even pretending to become involved, even tangentially, was becoming an anathema to me. I had to remember my purpose there. Be a witness. Tell what I saw.

I recovered from my dark thoughts enough to ask, "We are going to Birkenau for our meetings? Are we likely to see any...activity?"

"You mean gassing? It is not out of the question. Remember, I am an officer of the SS. They believe they have nothing to hide from me. In fact, I sometimes think that they are perversely proud of their work. We have unrestricted access to the camp. Don't forget, it's like visiting a factory. It's difficult to do that without seeing the process of manufacturing. Their product is, of course, death."

When we landed in Krakow and were picked up by a staff officer from the camp, I could not help but notice the Death's Head proudly displayed on his uniform. I'd like to show you a Death's Head, I thought. It was cold, foggy, gloomy. A perfect Auschwitz day, I thought. Know what I could use right now? A letter from Father telling me that not much had happened in South Hill since we'd left. Mother had come down with a little cold, nothing to worry about. Gaskins is doing OK at his job. It hasn't snowed all winter. A little humanity.

In doing my research, I had learned the basics about the structure of Auschwitz and how things worked. Once again, Freddy filled in the gaps. The command was made up of members of the *SS Totenkopfverbande,* or SS-TV, all of whom lived on the premises. The *Gestapo* also maintained offices at Auschwitz. There was an entire medical corps whose purpose to me was unclear. It certainly wasn't to keep the prisoners alive. Freddy hinted darkly that there were certain experiments conducted on human subjects. It just got worser and worser, as my old drill sergeant used to say.

Each of the three main camps was run by members of an SS group called the

Lagerfuhrer who answered directly to the Camp Commander. Several non-commissioned SS officers called *Rapportfuhrers* reported to them, and the *Rapportfuhrers* in turn commanded the *Blockfuhrers* who oversaw order within individual prisoner barracks. Kapos were prison trustees who were at the bottom of the totem pole. Those SS who were assigned to gas chamber duty actually lived locally on site at the crematoria with usually four SS soldiers assigned to each chamber led by a non-com officer who oversaw over 100 Jewish prisoners who were forced to assist in the extermination process. These were known as *Sonderkommando.* A special SS unit known as the Hygiene Division would drive the Zyklon B canister to the chambers in an ambulance and then empty the canister into the chamber.

Freddy noted that the highest suicide rates were among the *Sonnerkommandos,* followed by members of the little bands of Kapos who were forced to play music for arriving prisoners.

Then there was external security which was under the authority of the SS Guard Battalion. They manned the watchtowers and patrolled the perimeter fences.

Freddy had told me that life among the guardians of the Auschwitz camps was actually quite pleasant. I guess they considered it another job in the Army except nobody was shooting at you. Oh, and you had to get used to mass murder.

I had a good idea about the selection process once the prisoners had been trained in to the camp. At Birkenau, about three-quarters of arriving prisoners were selected for immediate death, including nearly all of the women, children and elderly. A doctor would give the others a perfunctory examination and make further selections based on the ability of prisoners to work. Most were summarily gassed. In the late winter of '44, incoming trains brimming with deportees had reached an all-time high at Auschwitz. The more conquered territory and the more time the Nazis had to organize the camps, the more arrived on a daily basis. And the more were murdered. After the gassings, *Sonderkommandos* extracted gold fillings and other valuables and sorted the loot in an area they dubbed Canada because they thought of Canada as a country of many riches.

Against this backdrop, Freddy and I arrived at Birkenau for a meeting with the *Lagerfuhrer* and a few non-commissioned officers. It felt obscene to me to be going over selections of vintages with these people, but that's what we did. We had noticed a train arriving at about the same time we did. It didn't take much to guess what was going on outside the building where we were meeting. I did my best to play the role of wine merchant, but I doubt I was terribly convincing. I was mostly mute, sitting at the table as the *Lagerfuhrer* and his staff made their selections.

The meeting finally ended, and we walked outside, heading toward the staff car for our next meeting at Auschwitz I. We heard a loud voice over to our left toward one of the chambers. It appeared to be the SS "welcoming" the latest victims to the camp. As we got closer, we were able to hear the speech. An SS officer was addressing the larger group who had been selected to go to the left for showering and delousing. Freddy whispered to me that this was a "shipment" of Greek Jews.

"On behalf of the camp administration, I bid you welcome. This is not a holiday resort, but a labor camp. Just as our soldiers risk their lives at the front to gain victory for the Third *Reich,* you will have to work here for the welfare of a new Europe. How you tackle that task is entirely up to you. The chance is there for every one of you. We shall look after your health, and we shall also offer you well-paid work. After the war we shall assess everyone according to his merits and treat him accordingly."

"Now, would you please all go inside and get undressed. Hang your clothes on the hooks we have provided and please remember where you left your belongings. When you've had your bath there will be a bowl of soup and coffee or tea for all. Oh, yes, before I forget, after your bath, please have ready your certificates, diplomas, school reports and any other documents so that we can employ everybody according to his or her training and ability."

"Would diabetics who are not allowed sugar report to staff on duty after their baths."

What we knew and they apparently did not is that they would all be dead within minutes.

Our subsequent meetings with other officials were a blur to me. I was almost catatonic and went through the motions of the wine offerings. A couple of times Freddy had to kick me under the table to prompt a response from me. I was, I think, in a state of shock from what I'd observed at Birkenau.

On the plane ride back, I again reflected on the horrors of war. I had killed a man with my bare hands, and I knew if I had to do it over again, I would not hesitate. But here, sitting beside me, was a man who had loved the man I had killed.

"Freddy, you are aware of what transpired between your cousin and me." It wasn't a question. "He was my colleague one moment and my enemy the next. I cannot say we were ever friends, but we did have a common goal, or so I thought. At your group's behest, he betrayed us. He had to die, and I am sorry for the pain that has caused you."

Freddy sighed deeply. "Like you, Fritz, I have seen and done things in this war that I never could have imagined just a few years ago. That performance back at the camp? I have watched that happen more than once. I have gone from literally being sick at seeing it to now being just numb. I am sorry you had to see it and I cannot tell you the depth of my shame that my countrymen are perpetrating such acts. But, Fritz, there's still a part of me that resists falling in line like those at the camps and so many others have done. I and my colleagues are more committed now than ever to ending this national nightmare. Stauffenberg, Tresckow, Olbricht and many more of us are fully prepared to give our lives to end this."

I waited for more.

"As for you and Binky? It is a personal tragedy to me that my cousin died in this war. But that's just it—he died in war. This wasn't some back street mugging, it was combat, both of you fighting for what you believed in. It wasn't murder like we saw back at the camp. Now, if you don't mind, let us not speak of Cousin Binky or that episode again."

I really *did* have to do some work to get the Auschwitz camp wine ordered from the suppliers that Donovan and his crew had organized for me back in Washington. After a couple of days of dealing with vineyards in France and

Italy, it was time to go to our "home" in Bavaria. Freddy had already joined Marta, his children and his father at their home. When we arrived we were to join them for an evening there.

Elizabeth asked me how it went at Auschwitz. I decided to tell her everything, and, I have to admit, it was cathartic. When I got through, she just stared at me. "Pointer," she said, "it's not like you could've done anything to help the poor devils. What we're doing here is the best way to help. You know that, I know you do."

That night we made love with a tenderness I'd never known, and we slept in each other's arms. If I needed humanity, Elizabeth supplied it. I think she needed a little human contact herself.

There was one more chore before we left Berlin for "home". Freddy had arranged to send one of his staff to pick us up and show us the two Berlin safe houses that we might need in the event we had to exit in a hurry. Sergeant Stoessel picked us up under the guise of showing us around Berlin. That he did, but our first stop was a brick townhouse in the East Central neighborhood adjacent to the *Mitte* just to the south. Berlin was Germany's largest city with nearly 3 million inhabitants. There was a time that it would've been easy to lose oneself in such a large place. But now, the *Gestapo* and the other SS branches had clamped down. Everyone was subject to producing their identity papers and if you were found to be in a part of the city without a good reason, they wanted to know why and what you were doing there.

The townhouse was nondescript and was situated on an equally nondescript block. The family of a World War I veteran on a pension lived there. The old Colonel was sympathetic to *Valkyrie* and allowed his cellar to be used in the event the collaborators needed to hide out. We didn't go in, but Stoessel pointed out the lock to the door on the English basement style design and told us the combination. He let us know that we were not to write it down; we had to memorize it. He also told us that there were currently four Jews hiding out there awaiting transport to the west. As we slowed down to take a look, I glanced over my shoulder and noticed another car also slowing down.

"Sergeant, how good a driver are you?"

"Sir? I don't understand the question. Driving is my profession."

"Good enough. You see that car half a block down the street behind us? If you speed up, I believe they will, too. If that happens, we gotta lose them. *Capische*?"

"*Capische?* What is this *capische*?"

"Just drive."

Stoessel gunned it and the chase was on. Sure enough, the other car followed suit. Stoessel was indeed a pro. He took the first turn on two wheels and laid rubber down a side street, clipping a garbage can and sending it flying.

"Go baby, go!" The adrenaline was pumping, but I remembered to say it in German.

Stoessel had succeeded in putting a block between us, but we weren't out of sight yet. He passed a car on the left on a two-lane street and then a Mercedes on the right, which I didn't think could be done. But Stoessel was an expert at his craft and performed the maneuver when there was a rare vacant space on the curb. Actually, he may have gone up on the sidewalk a bit.

"Elizabeth!" I screamed in Italian, "Can you still see them?"

In the backseat, she craned her neck to look out the back window.

"No! I can't see them anymore."

Just as I was also looking back, Stoessel slammed on the brakes. The big sedan fishtailed to the left and came to a stop just before the roadblock. Two SS men were there with submachine guns and had sprinted to either side of our car, waving the guns at us. Out of a Mercedes stepped my pal Colonel Schmidt. Taking his time, he strode toward us. He wore a leather trench coat over his uniform as protection against the weather and was calmly smoking a cigarette.

"Ah, it's you, Moeller. What's the big rush?" he said.

"I asked Stoessel here to show me what this baby could do. He's good. I think he's ready for a promotion, sir."

"You will get out of the vehicle and come with me. Your wife also. You too, Stoessel."

"I'd rather not, Colonel. We haven't finished our sightseeing." I smiled.

Schmidt nodded to the two thugs at the side of the car, who took a step closer and raised their guns.

"Down!" I shouted.

All three of us ducked and covered our heads with our hands as the two men emptied their submachine guns into the windows, front and back, of the car. The sound was deafening and glass rained down on us. It seemed like the burst lasted five minutes, but it was in reality under twenty seconds. I finally raised my head slowly, checked to see if Elizabeth and Stoessel were OK, and peered out the front window.

"Well, since you insist, Colonel..." I said as I opened the door.

"If your eardrum wasn't burst before, Moeller, it probably is now," Schmidt smiled wickedly. "We will extract the cost of this car from your contract. Now, all of you, come with us."

The street was now utterly deserted as it seemed that the good people of Berlin knew when to make themselves disappear. We were shoved into two different vehicles, me with the two shooters and Elizabeth and Stoessel in Schmidt's car. We drove for about twenty minutes, and I figured we weren't headed for the Bendlerblock; we were going in the opposite direction. Finally, we arrived at a stone building set back from the street with a courtyard. We drove in. My two handlers hustled me into the building and we descended a stairwell into a basement area, then down a corridor and into a small room. I was ordered to sit in a hardback chair and the door closed. It looked like they were separating the three of us.

I cooled my heels in the room for an hour. Finally, I heard footsteps and the door opened. I expected to see Schmidt, but a Major in SS uniform whom I'd never seen before stood before me with a file folder in hand. He wasn't putting out warm feelings. In fact, he was as grim as the basement in which we were imprisoned.

The Major sat down opposite me and began reading through the file. What, no *schnitzel*?

"You were married to Elizabeth D'Allessandro in Rome on December 26, 1943." He stated this flatly.

"No, it was January 1, 1944," I corrected him.

"Your address?"

"24 Gunderson Street, Apartment 4, Passau, Bavaria," I answered.

"Your company was formed last November."

OK, I see where this is going. Test Pointer on his memory. Fortunately, Hopkins and crew had spent days drilling us on our cover story, even asking trip-up questions like this.

"No, my company was founded several years ago."

The Major continued in this vein for nearly an hour. I aced the quiz. I just hoped that Elizabeth had as well.

"Are you through, Major?" I inquired politely. "Because if you are, I'd like to get a message to General Olbricht that we are being held here unnecessarily and against our will.

The Major ignored this, got up and left the room. About forty-five minutes later, Colonel Schmidt walked in. He lit a cigarette and said, "You were observed slowing down almost to a halt on *Birkenstrasse*. What were you looking at?" he asked.

"A house. My wife and I are considering renting something here, as we will be traveling to Berlin quite often in the future."

"Odd. Your wife denies slowing down at all."

"Oh, you know the ladies, Colonel, she didn't care for the look of the place. Wants to forget all about it. You know how it is." I gave him my wink-wink conspiratorial smile.

But Schmidt didn't return it. "No, I don't know how it is. So, you are shopping for a house?"

"Partly. That and sightseeing. My wife's never been to Berlin."

"Moeller, I do not like you. I believe you are hiding something, and I will find out what it is. I do not care a whit if General Olbricht thinks you are the second coming of the *Fuhrer*, even though his vouching for you is the only reason you are not now in a cell. I *will* discover what your secrets are, and you and the *Frau* will hang by your toes until I know *all* of your secrets." He glared at me as though he wanted his hatred to be fully understood and never forgotten.

Chapter Forty Four

Schmidt

Colonel Claus Schmidt grew up as the son of a hardware store owner in the town of Augsburg in Bavaria. His father eked out a meager living for his family of four. He claimed that before the Jews had moved into town, business had been much better. They were a cabal, sending their jewelry and grocery customers to each other and borrowing money from the Jewish lenders at favorable rates.

In 1929, during the worldwide Depression, the Schmidt family was hanging on to their family business by a thread. In desperation *Herr* Schmidt had gone to see a money lender by the name of *Herr* Olbermann, a Jew. The lender received Schmidt politely, listened to his request, which was fairly modest, and then began asking the standard questions. How would he apply the funds? Did he bring a copy of the books? What other debts did Schmidt have? What collateral could he offer? How would he repay the loan? *Herr* Schmidt was not an educated man, but he was honest and hardworking. Shouldn't that be enough? He wasn't exactly sure how he would repay the loan, but he offered his word that he would, no matter how long it took. Olbermann denied him credit right there in his office; he didn't even need to think about it.

"Fucking Jew," Schmidt muttered and stormed out.

When Hitler came to power in 1933, the elder Schmidt had been an ardent supporter, participating in rallies and, later, leading the charge in Augsburg to, isolate, then expel the Jews. Business, however, did not improve. People seemed afraid to invest in their homes' upkeep, and the hardware store eventually went under. No matter. *Herr* Schmidt was then employed as a Nazi Party organizer, and looked forward to going to work every day. Such was his fervor.

The elder Schmidt used his connections with the Party to secure an appointment for young Claus to attend officer training school, and Claus had the drive and the wit to climb the military ladder from there. His fervor for the Cause matched that of his father's, and soon he came to the favorable attention of his superiors. Rising through the ranks had proved easy for Claus, and in 1944 he had gained the rank of Colonel in the SS.

Karl Haas was his best friend in the officer training school. Haas came from a similarly humble background and, like his friend, climbed the SS ranks with ease. They were united in their hatred of the Jews, their love of the Fatherland and their devotion to both the *Fuhrer* and the *Reichsfuhrer*. They had maintained a friendly rivalry as to who could make rank first. So far it was a dead heat as they were both Colonels assigned to General Army Headquarters in the Bendlerblock.

Karl had sent word that he needed to meet with Claus, preferably in the beer garden they both favored. So it was that the afternoon after his encounter with Moeller, Claus was hurrying through *Stankenstrasse* to rendezvous with his old friend, Karl. The weather had brightened although it was still seasonably cold. Claus loved being posted at the very center of SS activity. No, it was not Hitler's *Wolfsshanze*, but it was the next best thing. Perhaps if his current project worked out as he hoped, the Wolf's Lair would be his next stop—on the *Fuhrer's* personal staff, a trusted member of the inner circle.

"Greetings, old friend," Haas said. They had both been extremely occupied with their respective responsibilities and had not seen each other for weeks.

"How are you, *Herr* Colonel?" Claus beamed at his friend and lit a cigarette. "You are beginning the process of transporting the Hungarian Jews? That must be keeping you extremely busy."

Karl reached over and pulled a cigarette from Claus' pack. "Trying to quit. Helene cannot stand the smell, you know. Yes, the Hungarian situation is coming to a head. Production in the camps has stepped up in order to accommodate them, so we are staying busy organizing the evacuations."

Both ordered a stein of beer from the *fraulein* who gave them a welcoming smile. Their SS money was no good in this establishment.

"Tell me, friend, why did you wish to see me?" Claus asked.

"There seems to be a problem that is coming out of the General's office." Claus knew that he was speaking of Olbricht. "The problem has to do with you, Claus, and your persecution of a certain *Herr* Fritz Moeller and his wife. Apparently, the General is acquainted with Moeller and wants to know why you are harassing him."

Schmidt smiled grimly and considered for a moment. "I thought that was why you wanted to see me, old friend. Moeller? Let's just say I have good reason to suspect that he is up to no good."

"But Claus, now that you have the attention of the General, vague suspicions are not going to be enough to cause him to drop his objections. Do you have some kind of evidence of wrongdoing? We both know that quite often our suspicions are enough to instigate an investigation, but not in this case."

"Evidence? It would be difficult to term what I have as evidence. But it is more than enough to pursue Moeller." Schmidt paused to consider. "I will show you, old friend, why I am pursuing Moeller. I will let you be the judge."

Schmidt reached into his briefcase and produced some papers. "This is a mimeograph of two letters I have received quite recently. In fact, the second came to me just a few hours ago." He handed the letters to Haas.

Haas read, "*Dear Colonel Schmidt, In a few days, a Herr Moeller will appear in Berlin under the guise of a wine merchant. He is, in fact, a spy for the Allies. There is one traitor in your midst*

*who has arranged for this, a Colonel
'T'. You must believe me that I know
this from the most reliable authority.
Yours, A friend February 15, 1944."*

Haas raised his eyes to meet
Schmidt's. "How did this come to you,
Claus?"

"It arrived by mail at the Bendlerblock.
No way to trace it, I'm afraid."

"And what makes you believe it is
authentic?"

"A gut feeling. Someone knew that
Moeller was coming. Not that it was a
state secret, but it was not widely
known. Von Furstenberg is his primary
contact here, but that is his job—
logistics in food, wine and spirits, so he
is not necessarily complicit."

"And who is this Colonel T?"

"There are only two Colonels with last
names starting with 'T' in Bendlerblock.
Tosch and Tresckow. Both were out of
town when Moeller arrived so we have

nothing to go on there as of yet. We will question them when they return."

"And the second letter? Haas asked.

Schmidt produced it.

"Dear Colonel Schmidt, I am sorry to note that you have not yet apprehended Herr Moeller. I say to you again: he is a spy. His mission is no less than the murder of the Fuhrer. Also, the Reichsfuhrer if he can. You can prove this to your own satisfaction by asking him questions about his supposed 'life' and 'business' in Bavaria. Though he is very clever, you will eventually trip him up. Yours, A friend February 24, 1944."

Haas crushed out his cigarette and thought for a moment. "I will speak to General Olbricht," he said.

The General called the meeting for the next day. Freddy had had to return to Berlin just as Elizabeth and I were going to Bavaria.

Olbricht looked at his men. Stauffenberg, Freddy, Jencks, and Loggereist stared back and waited. They were in the General's conference room in the Bendlerblock.

"Gentlemen, we have a leak," Olbricht stated flatly. "Someone has been whispering in Schmidt's ear about our plans." And he told the men what he'd learned from Haas.

Freddy was stunned. It was simply not possible. By his count, only seventeen people knew about *Valkyrie,* and any one of them being a traitor seemed impossible. Yet there it was. Olbricht had paraphrased the content of the two letters that Schmidt had received, including the part about Colonel 'T'. It was undeniable. They had a traitor among them.

"What should we do about Tresckow? About Fritz?" Freddy asked.

Stauffenberg spoke up, "Tresckow is in the East and, for the moment, is out of harm's way. At least there's one other

Colonel 'T' for them to consider. Moeller is in Bavaria, yes?"

"Correct," Olbricht said. "He's well within reach of Schmidt and his goons, but if they didn't want him to leave Berlin, he would not have been allowed to go. So, for the moment he is safe. But only for the moment."

Jencks weighed in, "We all know the tactics that Schmidt and his fellows use to extract information, including their favorite—leveraging wives and children's lives to get what they want. I sometimes wonder if I could withstand that kind of treatment myself."

Freddy looked at Jencks, then at the others one by one. "Is the traitor in this room", he asked himself.

As if Stauffenberg had read his mind, he said, "We must root out the traitor as soon as possible or *Valkyrie* will be just another failed assassination attempt. My orders to join Hitler's War Council have not come through and until they do, we have no one who has access to the *Wolfsschanze*. And we know of no plans for Hitler to travel here."

Jencks said, "I hate to say this, but I've been thinking that Anschutz was never as keen on our plans as I'd have liked. And he hasn't shown his face around here for weeks. I've never fully trusted him, especially since he argued that we should take Hitler prisoner and not kill him."

"Anschutz is as loyal as the rest of us," Olbricht said. "I cannot accept that he would be the traitor." The General surveyed the members of the team. "Here is my proposal: the four of us in this room are not without resources. We have men under our command whom we can deploy in our service. Some of these men know of our plans, but those are the very ones we do not want to use. There are eleven people who know of *Valkyrie* other than the four of us, Moeller and Tresckow. That includes Marta, my wife and my secretary. We will divide up responsibility for each of these eleven people and put 24-hour surveillance on them. We will tell our people that they are suspected of liaising with Colonel Schmidt in a suspicious manner and that they are to report any suspicious behavior to us directly. We will, of course, employ the greatest secrecy in these orders. Are we agreed?"

Stauffenberg said, "Excuse me, General, but are you certain you want your wife and Marta under surveillance?"

Olbricht glared at Stauffenberg. "Yes, Count. I am quite certain. This meeting is adjourned."

They all rose and began shuffling out of the room, but Olbricht said, "Count, a minute of your time please?"

Stuffenberg sat back down and waited until the door was closed. "Sir?"

"I want you to know that I will also assign surveillance to Jencks and Freddy as well as the others."

Major Anders Jencks left the meeting in an agitated state of mind. He had a letter to write.

Chapter Forty Five

Bavaria

Spring 1944

Elizabeth and I arrived in Munich by train. Like Berlin, *Munchen* had suffered from Allied bombing as it was a center of German industry and manufacturing. The piles of rubble in the streets didn't stop me from cracking to Elizabeth, "How about a little munchin' in *Munchen?*" I was hungry.

She did a little eye roll, but then gave me a smile. She, too, was glad to be away from Berlin and the SS and the Nazis and the intrigue. Freddy had told us that we needed to keep our distance from him and the other collaborators now that our names had surfaced in the poison pen letters to Schmidt. That was fine with me on one level—let the *Valkyrie* guys do their business and let Elizabeth and me get out of here. But on another level, I wanted to be in on the action.

We walked from the train station to the *Marienplatz* in the center of town and went into a beer garden and got a table. The famous cuckoo clock, the *Rathaus-Glockenspiel*, on the town square was taking the war off as were the singers and dancers in their traditional *lederhosen*. So it was just Elizabeth, me and the beer.

"Fritz, I think while we're in Bavaria I will go back to calling you Pointer if that's ok with you," she said.

"Fine with me. How bout I go back to calling you darlin'?"

"Perfect," she smiled. "What are our next moves, Pointer?"

The beers were delivered, and I had my eye on a nice fat sausage hanging near the back of this fine establishment.

"First thing is to buy a car. Then we drive to Passau, and check in to our apartment. I need to keep up appearances in the wine business so that'll take some time. Freddy should be back at the family estate soon, so we need to figure out a way to keep up the communications with him and the rest of the, uh, group."

"I've been reading up on Bavaria in general and Passau in particular. Oh, Pointer, it's beautiful—spectacular scenery, wonderful traditions, nice people, fresh air. It'll seem like a real honeymoon to us."

"Sure, darlin', but most honeymoons aren't taken in the heart of enemy territory under surveillance by the SS and under the constant threat of arrest."

"I know, Pointer. But can't we just pretend every now and then?"

"Of course we can," I said, brightening. "Here we are sipping great Bavarian beer. Did you know that there's a law here that they can only use three ingredients in making beer—water, barley and hops. It's important enough to them to enact a *law*. Who says Germans are all bad?"

"Pointer, don't look now, but there's a man four tables over who looks like he doesn't belong in here."

I didn't look. "I know. He's our new best friend. He's been shadowing us since we debarked from the train." So much for the honeymoon atmosphere.

Munich had played a central role in Hitler's rise to power. It was here that the infamous Beer Hall *Putsch* had taken place in 1923 when the Nazis attempted to overthrow the Weimar Republic. The attempt failed, Hitler was jailed and Nazism, largely unknown outside of Munich, lost most of its momentum. But the Nazis—and Munich's place at its core—made a comeback ten years later when the National Socialists took power. All of which was why Elizabeth and I did not want to linger munchin' in *Munchen*. Or lunchin' for that matter. I couldn't help myself, I was so glad to be on our way.

Freddy had set us up with an old family friend in *Munchen* who had an old

Mercedes that we bought. It was time to hit the road for Passau.

Passau lies about 120 miles northeast of Munich on the Austrian and Czech borders. It is situated at the confluence of three rivers—the Danube, the Inn and the Ilz.

As we drove, Elizabeth began quoting from a guidebook she'd bought in a Berlin bookstore. "Uh oh, Hitler again. We can't escape him. He and his family lived there in the 1890s," she said. "But listen to this, Pointer, the world's largest cathedral organ is there in St. Stephens Church 17,774 pipes and 233 registers."

"Mm hmm," I murmured as I negotiated the winding road. I noticed that we had no tail; they knew where we were going.

"The architecture is dominated by the gothic and baroque styles...it was an important church center for Roman Catholics...the town is dominated by the *Veste Oberhaus,* which is the Bishop's fortress...let's see...oh, there's a big cabaret stage right by the town hall. Our apartment is near the center of town in the *Alstadt* District, isn't it?

"Yes, and Freddy's estate is about 20 miles outside of town in the foothills. I'm working out in my head how we will stay in touch. He should be back by tomorrow."

"Pointer?"

"Mmm?"

"Can we have at least one more day when we don't obsess about...the mission?"

I turned to her and smiled. "Of course. Sorry, just planning ahead."

Chapter Forty Six

Moral Ambiguity

The weather had turned unseasonably warm for this time of the spring, and Freddy had suggested the four of us meet near his estate for a picnic. The surveillance was loose enough that we could do so undetected.

Since Major Jencks had been caught in the Central Post Office by Olbricht's men attempting to mail a letter to Colonel Schmidt, there had been little movement on *Valkyrie.* The letter had named all of the conspirators, the locations of our safe houses across Germany and as much detail as we ourselves knew at that point. Thank God for Olbricht's prescience. Otherwise, we would all be "toes pointed up" as my drill sergeant used to say. Now, the only one who'd gone to his eternal reward was Major Jencks. He'd been taken to the rail yard that night and shot in the head by one Sergeant Stoessel. Pretty much how Lucky would've handled it, I thought.

But now Freddy wanted to meet. You had to give old Freddy points for style. He thought a picnic by a lake would be a splendid way to pass information, and who was I to argue? We drove to a country crossroads as directed and there were Freddy and Marta waiting. Freddy actually wore lederhosen and a funny looking hat with a little feather in it. When we shook hands, I barely succeeded in concealing a chuckle.

For Elizabeth's benefit, we all spoke English. Freddy and Marta were passable but several times we asked them to repeat themselves because of the heavy accents.

"May I call you Pointer? It *is* Pointer, isn't it?" Freddy began.

"Yes, everybody calls me Pointer."

After we'd hiked a couple of miles to the lake, Elizabeth and Marta began unpacking the food and the bottle of *Reisling* that Freddy had brought from his cellar. In fact, he'd brought two. There was roast chicken, potato salad and *strudel* to keep our strength up.

The mood was festive even though I knew we'd get down to business before too long. Freddy uncorked the wine and poured four glasses.

"What shall we drink to?" he asked.

Before I could think of a smart-ass reply, Elizabeth piped up, "Let's drink to the end of the war—and peace."

"To peace," we chorused.

To say that the scenery was spectacular was an understatement. The lake was a deep azure blue, the fir trees grew right up to the shore, their reflections mirrored in the water. In the distance stood the snow-capped peaks of the Alps against a blue sky with nary a cloud to spoil the perfect nature of the day. It was "sweater weather", not too cool, not too warm. The perfect Bavarian day.

Sitting on the blanket, I leaned over and whispered to Elizabeth, "This place is almost as beautiful as you."

She looked at me in surprise. I was not the "mushy" type so this was unusual for me. But I was feeling good, right there at that moment in the clear mountain air. We had spent the past few months in Passau in relative peace and calm. I had some work on fulfilling wine orders; I was actually getting pretty good at it. Since I didn't care about the sales side, it was easy work, an hour or two a day. The rest of our time was spent in town, hiking in the countryside or driving up into the mountains. Although we mainly kept to ourselves, we were starting to feel like real Bavarians. We communicated back to our handlers on a minimal basis through Freddy's network. There really wasn't much to report.

"So, Freddy, what's the news from the Front?" I broke the reverie.

Marta said, "*Liebling*, do we really have to talk about this ghastly war and your plot? It's such a beautiful day." Marta had been chatting with Elizabeth about their home, their children and things for us to do during our stay in Bavaria.

"Yes, sweetheart, I have some developments that our friends here need to know about." Freddy didn't look very happy about the change of subject either.

"Stauffenberg has at last been transferred to the *Fuhrer's* War Council staff. He has not yet been to the Wolf's Lair but expects to go at any time. The Count is champing at the bit for the opportunity, as you know. We feel that we are in a race against time with the war. Everyone expects an Allied invasion at any time from England, and many believe it is a matter of time before Germany is breeched by the Americans and Brits from the West and, even more ominously, the Soviets from the East. Our position grows weaker by the week."

"You know, Freddy, you put me in an awkward spot," I said. "Part of your reason for assassinating Hitler is so that Germany will have a better position at the negotiating table. But you will be negotiating, in part, against my country."

"Surely you and your superiors considered this before you undertook this assignment, Pointer. If you are looking for silver linings, consider this: if the Americans and the Soviets do break through, we will have little to say in any case. Most of our motivation now with killing the *Fuhrer* is to do with saving German lives as well as those we have imprisoned and, yes, our enemies' lives."

"You are correct, Freddy. We did consider all angles before we undertook this mission. It's just that it troubles me sometimes."

Elizabeth joined in, "Pointer, we are spies, we are in the business of espionage. Our world is not black and white, it is often gray, and this is one of those times."

"Agreed," said Freddy. "I believe it is called moral ambiguity."

We all thought about that concept. I knew perfectly well about moral ambiguity, but I didn't have to like it.

Marta asked, "When will Stauffenberg strike, *liebling*?

"Yesterday, if he could have. But there's one remaining obstacle, apart from getting Hitler positioned in the right place when the Count is armed and ready. General Fromm, commander of the Reserve Army, still must be won over. He controls the communications network to the field. We need to be able to broadcast to the reserves what has happened and who is in control."

"Is he resisting?" I asked.

"No, he is neutral. He is waiting for convincing evidence that we will succeed. Doesn't want to bet on the wrong horse, it appears. Olbricht, Stauffenberg and the others asked me to talk to you, Fritz—Pointer—about this."

Uh oh. I felt more moral ambiguity coming on.

"Fromm and his assets are important because if we are able to kill Hitler, we don't want *Reichsfuhrer* Himmler filling the void. And, we believe, that's exactly what he would try to do. Ideally, we would get rid of both of them at the same time, but that is easier said than done. The two are rarely in the same place at the same time. We cannot make our plans based on eliminating both of them. But with control of the communications, we can neutralize Himmler."

"So, how does Pointer figure into this?" asked Elizabeth.

Freddy stared at the tall peaks in the distance for a long moment.

"In the Great War, my father was often asked to speak on behalf of his superiors. When they wanted something from the Kaiser's people, they asked him to go. Even during the Christmas Truce, the men asked my father to ask the leaders for permission to meet the enemy. The reason was that he was different. He was an aristocrat who was fighting in the trenches alongside the men. He spoke with an authority his superiors could not match. So it is with you, Pointer. You are an American and, like it or not, you are a symbol for us of the Allies, at least tacitly, approving of our plans. So, my fellow conspirators and I believe that if you go to Fromm and explain our need for his cooperation, he will agree."

And there it was. We, or maybe just I, would be heading back to the belly of the beast—Berlin. Back to the center of the plot to assassinate Hitler, which was surely one of the most dangerous places in the world.

As I was gathering my thoughts to reply, a young woman came running up the hill to where we sat. She was out of breath. Both Freddy and Marta rose to greet her and eased her down onto the blanket.

"Gertie, what is it? What is wrong? Is it the children?" Marta was close to panic.

"No, ma'am, the children are fine. *Herr* von Furstenberg sent me." She couldn't catch her breath. "It's the

war. The Allies have invaded France."
She gulped more air. "He said to tell
you it is in a place called Normandy."

Chapter Forty Seven

Der Wiesel

Berlin

July 1944

So it was back to Berlin for us. We decided to drive this time so we could maintain some mobility when we got there. Also, it would be easier to escape Passau undetected as we departed in the dead of night. With luck, and papers in order, we would pass through the checkpoints along the way unimpeded. We drove all the first night to a small town which was about halfway of the 360 miles to Berlin. We had passed through one roadblock manned by four sleepy Nazis. I explained my business in Berlin and they waved us through.

Before we left, Freddy and I had sat together for half a day in our apartment going over possible escape routes for Elizabeth and me. He had shown me all of the safe houses across the country that he knew about as well as the concentrations of Army positions as he understood them. He had related that the safe house on *Birkenstrasse* in Berlin that we'd seen had been abandoned as soon as it had come under suspicion.

"If things go wrong, Pointer, Olbricht, Stauffenberg, Tresckow and all of the rest of us will be executed. There will be a show trial, a quick one, and we will most probably be hanged. It would be more honorable for us to be shot, but that will not happen. None of us will run; we are prepared. But you, Pointer, you and Elizabeth, this is not your country. You should run."

"Freddy, I ain't arguing with you, brother," I said. "Preaching to the choir."

During the drive, I related to Elizabeth more details that I had learned from Freddy about *Valkyrie*.

"Many more officers have now pledged their support to a coup, some of whom are very high up in the regime. There's even a rumor that Rommel himself is ready to come on board."

"The Desert Fox?"

"Yep. The most famous and revered soldier of them all. But the higher the profile members of the plot, the more people know, the more dangerous it gets. I get the feeling that our involvement is not widely known, which is good for us, but Freddy told me that one of the arguments they used to persuade Rommel was that the Americans were supporting it and that there were representatives here on the ground."

"So, Pointer, what *is* the plan to kill Hitler? Is it as simple as Stauffenberg putting a Luger to his head and pulling the trigger?"

"Almost," I answered. "At this point the key is to get close enough to do something. I gather that a timed explosive, which would give the Count time to get away, is the weapon of choice. The downside of that is that you can't be sure you nailed him because you aren't there. The upside is..."

"You don't blow yourself up, or get shot by a bodyguard. Understood," Elizabeth concluded.

Hey! We were finishing each other's sentences, just like an old married couple.

We checked in to a small inn in a suburb of Chemnitz. The place was little more than a widow's house. In fact, that's what it was: a widow's house.

It was 8:30 am. "Sleep fast", I told Elizabeth. At her quizzical look, I said, "Old Marine expression."

That evening, we drove the rest of the way to Berlin and checked in to our hotel, the same one as before. We were not there in secret, but we were avoiding being seen with officers like Fromm, considering how unnatural it would seem for a wine supplier to be seen with a ranking member of the *Reich.* That left Freddy and his staff. As for the others, it would have to be *sub rosa.*

For some unknown reason I was glad to be back in Berlin, the proverbial belly of the beast. I think it was because the end was near, one way or another. Both of us were missing that home cookin', even though we'd had a pleasant interlude in Passau. I wanted to leave this land of death and misery behind, but I wanted to leave it minus one evil *Fuhrer.* Olbrict and Company wanted me to speak to Fromm, convince him to cooperate and then get out of Dodge. Fine with me. We would go back to Bavaria and then make our way out of the country, back to Rome, on the pretext of a business trip. That was the plan at least. *Easy peasy.* And, no, my drill sergeant never said that.

We went to see Freddy at the Bendlerblock the day after our arrival. He had the group's instructions on how to approach Fromm for the best chance of success.

"I will tell you, Pointer, that Fromm is a *wiesel*." His German for 'weasel' sounded like 'VEE-sel'. "He goes whichever way the wind blows him. I would not be surprised to see him lick his finger and stick it up in the air during your meeting," Freddy warned me. "Our ranks seem to be full of such men. If he thinks for one moment we won't succeed, then he will withdraw his support. On the other hand, when he actually meets an American who is involved, he is bound to be impressed."

I considered this for a moment. "Freddy, I am a spy. But a spy is first cousin to a diplomat and, as you know, to diplomats, words are everything. My plan is to very carefully give him the impression that my Government supports me and, by extension, supports *Valkyrie.* The truth is, very few in my Government know anything at all about this. There have been hints, though, that FDR does know and approves."

"Well, you know, Pointer, that there will be chaos after we kill Lightning without a communications network."

"Hey", I said, changing the subject, "How's my old pal Colonel Schmidt?"

Freddy looked around him before answering as though Schmidt might be in the corner listening. "We have not heard much from him lately. Apparently, the poison pen letters have stopped coming."

"Well good. Give him my best when you see him."

"Your meeting with Fromm tomorrow will be at a safe house at this address." Freddy handed me a piece of paper. "Olbricht and Stauffenberg will be there as well. Now, memorize it and I will destroy the paper."

I did as he said. As we were getting up to leave Freddy's office, a Gestapo officer knocked and entered. He didn't look friendly. He said to Freddy, "Colonel Schmidt requests that *Herr* and *Frau* Moeller come with me."

With a look at Freddy that said, "Whaddaya gonna do?", Elizabeth and I followed him down the hall.

As we entered his spacious office, Schmidt was seated at his desk and did not rise as we entered. There were two flags behind his desk, one with the Swastika insignia and the other with the SS eagle, both flags were blood-red with the insignia in black. Schmidt was smoking a cigarette and looking down at some papers on his desk blotter.

"Sit," he said.

"*Herr* Moeller, we have found some irregularities in your business records that we need you to explain. Two years ago you claimed that you provided a large shipment of wine to a garrison in Passau. The officers there have no record of receiving any shipments from you. Why is that, Moeller?"

I stared straight at the Colonel and didn't blink. "They cancelled the order just as it was to be delivered." Don't elaborate. If he asks you if you know the time, just reply 'yes'.

"But your records show that you received payment."

"That's correct, sir. Under the terms of my contract, cancellations within 48 hours of delivery are payable in full. I billed the central command."

"Can you explain why you were named by an informant as a spy?"

"Probably my competitor, the same one that we spoke about before who claimed I didn't exist."

As Schmidt rose from his chair and walked around to where I was sitting. I decided to stand so that I towered over him. Elizabeth stayed seated and looked up from one of us to the other.

Schmidt said, "Moeller, you are hiding something. I think you *are* a spy. You are at the least a dishonest businessman. I have my eye on you."

"Colonel, you are in a position to keep your eye on anyone you choose, so I cannot stop you. General Olbricht will surely be interested in how you are wasting time and resources."

"Yes," Schmidt said thoughtfully. "General Olbricht. Another interesting case. Now, Moeller, get out of my office. But Moeller, do not leave Berlin under any circumstances."

Chapter Forty Eight

Poison Pen

General Olbricht sent a messenger that afternoon with word that we were to leave our hotel immediately and go to the safe house. We were in grave danger. He had called an emergency meeting of Stauffenberg, Freddy, Tresckow, Elizabeth and me. Elizabeth and I were to bring our belongings.

We hastily packed and left the hotel without checking out and drove across Berlin past the *Tiergarten* to the address that Freddy had given me earlier for the meeting with Fromm. We were the first to arrive other than our host, Olbricht. It was immediately apparent that he was in a state of agitation.

"Good evening General," I said. "Is everything alright?"

"*Nein,*" he said. "Everything is definitely not alright. What time was your meeting today with Colonel Schmidt?"

"I met with Freddy at 2 pm, and Schmidt called for me at 3. Why?"

"Because at the end of the workday, he received this." Olbricht handed me a letter. I skimmed it, then translated for Elizabeth.

July 17, 1944

Dear Colonel Schmidt,

I trust you have received my previous two missives and yet you have done nothing to curtail the assassination plot against the Fuhrer. I have told you that Moeller and Colonel T are two of the traitors. I tell you now that there are many more, and that they are preparing to strike. You must take action before these treasonous officers act.

The Fuhrer's life is in immediate peril.

A friend

I looked up at Olbricht just as Stauffenberg and the others arrived.

"It is the same handwriting as the other two letters. It is definitely the same person," Olbricht said.

"But Jencks..." I stuttered. "He was caught red-handed with a letter that betrayed us."

"Yes he was," Stauffenberg said. "But clearly he was not the original traitor." It seemed that Stauffenberg, Freddy and Tresckow already knew about the latest letter.

"Obviously, your life, Moeller, is in serious jeopardy. Elizabeth's and Tresckow's too," Stauffenberg said. "The question now is threefold. Who is the traitor, will there be more damning correspondence and can we pull off the coup before this spreads to the rest of us? There is a conference at the Wolf's Lair in two days' time at which Hitler will review plans. I am to be in attendance. Unfortunately, there is no reason to believe that Himmler will be there. But I am ready to strike, and I will strike."

One look at the Count told me that he was deadly serious. His eyes were burning as he looked around the room as if challenging the rest of us to try to raise an objection.

Olbricht went into operational mode. "The meeting is scheduled for 12:30. The Count will fly to the *Wolfsschanze* that morning. His briefcase will contain a 1 kilogram block of plastic explosive sufficient to kill everyone in the conference room. Von Freytag-Loringhoven has prepared the bomb?" He looked at Stauffenberg for affirmation.

Olbricht continued, "He will excuse himself to go to the washroom where he will arm the detonator. He has only to cut the copper tubing which contains copper chloride, which in ten minutes' time will eat through the wire holding back the firing pin from the percussion cap. He will reenter the conference room and place the briefcase under the table as near to Hitler as he can manage. We have arranged for the Count to receive an urgent phone call which will require him to leave the room. After the bomb has detonated, he will board his plane and return to the Bendlerblock where we will be putting into place the *Valkyrie* communications plan to the reservists across the country. With their backing, we will assume control of the Government. The reservists will be on our side and we expect most of the remainder of the military will follow."

"Questions?"

"Yes," I said. "What if Fromm doesn't go along with the plan?"

"He will," said Tesckow. "And if he doesn't, we will force the codes out of him and implement *Valkyrie* ourselves."

"This latest complication—the poison pen letters—means we must act on the 20th. It will probably be our last chance," said Olbricht.

"And who is the author of these letters?" Freddy asked the room.

"It sure isn't Jencks," I offered. This earned me a glare from Stauffenberg.

"I've been thinking about that," Olbricht said. "Outside of the people in this room, there are many who know of the plot. But there are only four who know of Moeller's involvement. My wife, Marta, my secretary and Major Breskind."

Tresckow said, "Someone should pay a call to Breskind. I would do it but I have to lie low for the next two days."

Freddy volunteered, "I will do it tonight. He should be at home. He's not likely to fall on his sword and confess. The best I can do is obtain a handwriting sample from him."

"Aren't Marta and your children back in Berlin?" Tresckow wanted to know.

Freddy looked at him sharply. "Yes, they are. Do you have something you wish to say, Colonel?"

"Only that we cannot take chances with anyone. I would like for both you and the General to look at handwriting samples from Marta, Liesel and the secretary."

The room went quiet for a long moment.

Olbricht broke the silence. "Of course the Colonel is correct. Unlikely as it may be, we need to check out everyone who knows of Moeller."

Stauffenberg closed the meeting. "Tomorrow is the eve of *Valkyrie*. All of our lives are at risk, and we are all willing to die for this cause. I do not care if I am exposed so long as it happens after 12:30 on the 20th. After all, then the whole world will know."

Chapter Forty Nine

A Representative of the U.S. Government

Elizabeth and I slept little that night. We had the "master" bedroom while Tresckow, the only other named conspirator, occupied a room on the first floor. Elizabeth and I talked about our meeting with General Fromm and the tactics we could use to persuade him to fully commit to our plan. We also talked about our escape plan. We had decided to flee from Bavaria, but that was before we were back under Schmidt's microscope. We knew that he and his men were out looking for us in force.

"We know where the safe houses are to the west," she pointed out. "If the coup is successful, we shouldn't have a problem, right?"

"Yes, if it's successful," I agreed. "But what if it's not? Can you imagine what will hit the fan if Hitler survives? I'm not crazy about the idea of hanging around to find out. I say that after our

meeting with Fromm, we hit the
bricks."

"But Schmidt is looking for us even
now."

"Yes, but if Hitler isn't killed—and let's
face it—the man seems to have nine
lives, Schmidt's dragnet will seem like
child's play compared to when
Himmler sics his SS dogs on everyone."

Elizabeth stared up at the ceiling where
a fan was slowly making circles ruffling
the stifling July air. "So, what do you
have in mind, Pointer?"

And I told her.

Valkyrie Eve, as we'd started thinking
of it, dawned with alternating rain
showers and sunshine as though the
day couldn't make up its mind whether
to be sunny or cruddy. We three
inmates of the safe house ate hot rolls
with butter and coffee.

I asked Tresckow to describe the
attempt that he'd made on Hitler when
he had placed a bomb in his plane. He

seemed happy to comply with the condition that we speak English. He needed the practice.

"If the goddamned detonator hadn't frozen, the course of history would have been altered eighteen months ago, and we would all be much better off today."

"What happened to the bomb? It was in the cargo hold, wasn't it?" I asked.

"Ah, yes, the bomb. I had to hustle back the next day and retrieve it before anyone could find it." Tresckow actually gave a little chuckle at this memory.

"And, of course, this time will go better, right?" Elizabeth asked.

"Of course! It's July, no ice!"

General Friedrich Fromm was a stolid looking man in his forties who looked as if he'd graduated a few years ago from the Hitler Youth Movement. He wore his blonde hair close cropped and his blue eyes stared out from under a heavy brow. I noticed, though, that those eyes were rarely at rest—they darted. They darted at me, at Elizabeth, at Tresckow, at the room. He was clearly nervous.

"May we offer you some coffee, General?" I asked.

"No thank you. I would like to get on with it if you please."

"General, I am here as a representative of the United States Government," I began. "In fact, we both are." I nodded toward Elizabeth. "We are here to support General Olbricht and you in your plan to assassinate the *Fuhrer* and to take control of the Government. The United States believes that there will never be peace until the *Fuhrer* and his closest supporters are gone."

"My Government will never forget those who were instrumental in this historic endeavor. Indeed, the world will never forget and will always be grateful to you." I started laying it on thick. "I am here today to ask you to lend your office and your critical communications network to this noble cause."

"What assurances do I have that this one won't go wrong like all the others?" Fromm asked with a nod toward Tresckow.

"We have a simple, but deadly plan. Stauffenberg has a bomb. He's been invited to a meeting with the *Fuhrer*. He places the bomb in the room, leaves--and boom. There goes the *Fuhrer*," I answered. I accompanied this statement with a hand gesture that said, 'no more *Fuhrer*'.

Fromm seemed taken aback by my American-style informality.

"Boom? There goes the *Fuhrer?*"

"Precisely."

"It is important to me and my compatriots that there is American support for *Valkyrie*. How can we be assured that your Government is actually behind us?"

Really, General. Elizabeth and I are here posing as a business couple because we just love the weather in Berlin in July.

"General, I am Lieutenant Robert Pointer, a U.S. Marine and a member of the Office of Strategic Services. She is likewise a part of the OSS. We were sent here by Colonel William Donovan who is head of the OSS. I assure you we are not here for the *schnitzel*." Again with the informality.

"And you are risking your lives. Why?"

"It's not mine to question why. I just follow orders."

Fromm's eyes again darted about the room. He glanced at Elizabeth, at Tresckow and back at me. He seemed to make up his mind.

"I will tell you, Lieutenant, that we will lend our *Valkyrie* network to this effort. May God have mercy on us if we fail."

Chapter Fifty

Marta

Marta von Furstenberg kissed her three children goodbye and gave final instructions to the nanny. She had spent this July morning writing and re-writing a letter. She knew that she had to reveal more about the plot in order for Schmidt to fully mobilize against Pointer and Tresckow. All that mattered now was that Freddy and the children stay safe.

Marta was a seer. A psychic. Most of her family believed she had extra sensory powers and was able to see into the future. She had predicted accurately the sex of each of her three children. She had foreseen the Nazi invasion of Poland, France and virtually every other *blitzkrieg* that the Nazis had executed. She was now saying that the President of the United States would soon die. But Freddy wasn't so sure although he dared not totally disbelieve because she had been right so often. But he had deep doubts. Her most recent vision had concerned Fritz

Moeller, dreaming that *Herr* Moeller would bring destruction and ruin to the von Furstenberg family.

She had wanted Freddy to turn Pointer away when he came to Germany, to keep him away from her family. She had begged him, sobbing hysterically that first day when they were to meet for dinner. But he had instead embraced the spy from the U.S. Meanwhile, her visions of her family's demise had gone from hazy and vague to becoming sharper and clearer. She dreamt that SS officers had imprisoned Marta, Freddy and all three children and were preparing to torture them. Even the children. She believed passionately that she must stop the plot and, at the same time, divert suspicion from Freddy. Pointer and Tresckow would have to be sacrificed, but that was a small price compared to preserving her own family's safety.

So she had written her final letter to Schmidt.

July 19, 1944

Dear Colonel Schmidt,

I will now present you with details that will make my claims of a plot undeniable. Herr Moeller and his wife are U.S. spies. His real name is Lt. Robert Pointer and both he and his wife belong to the OSS.

The assassination will take place very soon. You must put a stop to it.

Pointer, his wife and Tresckow are now in a home on Plankstrasse south of the Tiergarten. If you hurry, you will catch them there.

A friend

Marta had taken a taxi to the Post Office where she had posted the other letters. She knew that Schmidt would believe her this time, if he hadn't before, because of the new details she was supplying. If Freddy came under suspicion in the investigation that was sure to ensue, then and only then, she would come forward and reveal that it had been she who had alerted the SS to the plot. Surely that would engender leniency for Freddy.

As she waited in the long line, she noticed two men wearing trench coats, despite the warm weather, studying the post office patrons. When at length it was her turn to buy postage for her letter, she saw the clerk notice the addressee and that her eyes widened at what she read. She looked up quickly at the men off to the side, gave a sharp nod and stepped back from her window. Marta felt rough hands on her upper arms as she was dragged from the line.

"You will come with us, *Frau*," one of them said. And they walked her hurriedly out of the building and into a waiting car.

One hour later, as Elizabeth and I were poring over a map of Germany, we heard footsteps outside. Many footsteps. Tresckow had left early that morning for a meeting in secret with some of the collaborators.

"Tresckow! *Herr* Moeller!" a man shouted outside the front door. "You and the *Frau* come out with your hands in the air. We have you surrounded. There is no escape!"

We jumped up from the table. I grabbed my Luger from the holster which was hanging over the chair. Just as I was figuring out how to get out of there, someone or something, started battering at the door. In a flash it burst open and four SS troopers came running in, guns at the ready, led by two giant Police dogs, followed by Colonel Schmidt. Two of them basically tackled me while the other two got a hold on Elizabeth. We were made to lie down, face first, while they cuffed us. Three more troopers ran to the back of the house and two others went upstairs.

"Tresckow! You must surrender!" Schmidt called out. "Tresckow!"

He turned to me. "Where is Colonel Tresckow?"

"Colonel who?" I answered.

Schmidt put his boot on the side of my head and began grinding it so that my face was squashed on the floor. "Tresckow! We know he's here with you!"

Both of the troopers who had gone upstairs and one of the three who had searched the rear of the house returned to report in.

"There is no sign of anyone else, sir," said one.

Another emerged from Tresckow's room and said, "Someone has slept in this room, sir."

Schmidt removed his foot from my head and strode to the room. He returned a moment later and said to the others, "He is gone, but he will probably return. You, you and you remain here and wait for him," he said pointing at three of his men.

He then leaned down on his haunches so that his face was inches from mine. "As for you Lieutenant Pointer, you are under arrest. We have another letter and, this time, the letter writer. We will go back to the Bendlerblock and you will spend the rest of the day and tonight telling me everything you know about this little plot of yours. You and your so-called wife. *Herr* and *Frau* Furstenberg will round out our party. I am so looking forward to it. And Pointer, you *will* tell me everything."

I twisted around so I could look at him directly. "Colonel Schmidt...fuck you and the horse you rode in on."

Chapter Fifty One

Prison

So much for our plan to escape early. We had been taken to the bowels of the Bendlerblock and thrown into a cell-like room that reminded me of the room in Catania where I'd been hosted by Colonel Haas. Why is it that they never give you a room with a decent view?

A few minutes after our check-in to the 'Schmidt Inn at the Bendlerblock', we heard a commotion in the hall. I caught the mention of "Lieutenant Furstenberg" so I figured they'd rounded up Freddy and put him in a cell nearby. Together with Marta, we were the first four prisoners of the *Valkyrie* Plot. I had put it together when Schmidt mentioned the von Furstenbergs being prisoners and that one of them had given us up. My money was on Marta. Why the hell would she turn on us, I wondered?

Elizabeth had borne up well under the rough treatment. She was sitting on a stool in the corner of the cell which was about the size of one of Marta's closets. There was a chair, a toilet and a sink complete with a single light bulb dangling from the ceiling.

"Now what, Pointer?" she asked. We had begun to speak English since the jig was up. I figured it lessened our chances of eavesdroppers understanding us.

I lowered my voice to a whisper. "I calculate we've got to last here less than twenty four hours. The Count is scheduled to take off tomorrow morning and the conference is at 12:30. We should know what happened shortly after that. Just pray that he's successful."

"I'm praying, Pointer. I guess I know what'll happen if he fails—not sure I want to think about that. But what if he's successful? What happens then?"

I gave her a little smile. "Then we ask for limousine service all the way to Rome. We'll be heroes."

I just hoped Marta and Freddy could withstand whatever was coming from Schmidt. I recalled Ben Franklin's words, "We must, indeed, all hang together or, most assuredly, we shall all hang separately."

An hour passed, then two. I was going stir crazy.

"What do you think is on the menu for dinner?" I asked Elizabeth. "I'm in the mood for *strudel*."

No comment from Elizabeth. "Why don't you try to communicate with Freddy? He's just down the hall."

"Good idea."

I gave as loud a "sssst" as I could. Nothing. Then I banged three times on the wall. There was an answering knock.

"Freddy," I hissed.

"That you, Moeller?"

"Yes. Elizabeth and I are here." I figured I'd better keep the Moeller identity for those who might be listening. "You OK?" I hissed.

"Yes. What happened? Why were we arrested?"

Uh-oh. Freddy didn't know that Marta had ratted us out.

I said, "There was another letter. They caught the sender."

"Who was the traitor?" he hissed back.

I looked at Elizabeth and whispered, "I'm going to tell him. Otherwise, Schmidt will use it as a surprise. Better he knows."

She nodded.

"Freddy, it was...it was Marta."

Silence. I let Freddy digest this.

"Marta? That's impossible," he hissed.

"Afraid so, old boy. She's in here somewhere. Wanted you to know for the interrogation."

Another long silence.

"But the children...what will happen?"

"Stay strong, Freddy. Just for a few more hours."

Schmidt came for me at 1900 hours. One of his goons opened the door to the cell and two others grabbed me by either arm and dragged me down the hall to another room that was mostly barren except for a table, chairs and, yes, another naked light bulb.

"Lieutenant Pointer, you are a spy from the United States. Do you know what we do to spies in the *Reich*?" Schmidt opened.

"My guess is you hang them," I replied.

"You *are* Lieutenant Pointer sent by the U.S. Government to spy and wreak havoc on the Third *Reich?* You are plotting to assassinate the *Fuhrer*?"

"No. I am Fritz Moeller of Moeller and Sons Wine Distributors. You know this, Colonel."

He nodded to the goon who was stationed behind me. He pulled out a hose that was constructed of some pliable material, probably rubber, and administered a great whack to my rib cage.

"Oooof!" I belched and doubled over in pain. I was pretty sure he'd cracked a couple of ribs, which were already throbbing.

"When and where is the assassination attempt, and who is involved?"

"I've got a special on a nice Riesling, Colonel," I croaked.

Whack! More ribs gone.

We went on like that for over an hour, the Colonel asking and me not answering. After they finished with my ribs, the goon started on my solar plexus, this time with his fists. I passed out and they threw a bucket of water on me to revive me. I was groggy, barely able to comprehend what was happening. Finally, Schmidt asked, "One more time, Lieutenant Pointer, when, who and where is this attempt?"

I gasped out an answer, "If...you don't...like Riesling... I've got an...excellent... *Chianti.*" I don't remember anything after that.

They gave Elizabeth and then Freddy similar treatment. God bless her, Elizabeth is a tough *hombre* or *hombress.* She gave them nothing, despite the rubber hose treatment. I had no way of knowing what they did to Marta. If she—or any of us broke—we were dead meat.

I was beginning to dislike the attitude of the Schmidt Inn's General Manager.

They woke me up in the middle of the night for more fun. More questions, more non-answers, more beatings. As I lay on the floor, Schmidt made a promise for the next day.

"This is the beginning, Pointer. Tomorrow we will bring your wife in so that each time you are evasive, we will administer a beating to her in your presence. And don't worry, we will extend the same courtesy to Furstenberg. And if that doesn't work, we will bring in his children." Schmidt smiled.

Hang on, Pointer, I told myself. We needed to survive until Stauffenberg acted. I knew that I couldn't hold out watching Elizabeth get a beating. I didn't think Freddy could deal with watching Marta either. Lord knows he couldn't watch them hurt his children.

We waited the next morning for Schmidt's next round of torture. Every time we would hear a noise in the hall, we would jump nervously. But all that morning we were left alone. We heard no noises that would indicate that they'd come for Freddy either. We were starving. We'd been given a scrap of bread and a dish of water the night before and nothing else.

Finally our door opened and two SS goons grabbed Elizabeth and me. Oh, boy, I thought, here we go. But they didn't take us to the torture room; instead, they led us upstairs to a conference room. A photographer was there and we were posed, separately, against the wall and we were shot. Photographed, that is. I now understood why they had worked over our bodies and not our faces. We needed to look pretty for Goebbels' propaganda photos. Joseph Goebbels was the public relations mastermind behind the Third *Reich,* and we were his two prized trophies. My ribs hurt like hell and I know Elizabeth's did too, but that didn't show in the pictures that were taken.

As we were being taken back to our cell we passed Freddy, then Marta in the hall. They had taken no precautions in beating Freddy. His face looked like a dog's breakfast. Marta, though, appeared unscathed. Neither looked up from the floor as we passed.

When we got back, I said to Elizabeth, "I saw the clock upstairs. It's now about 11: 45. Forty five minutes until Stauffenberg sets the bomb. This would be a good time for a prayer."

And so we waited.

Chapter Fifty Two

Into the Wolf's Lair

July 20, 1944

Early that morning Lieutenant Colonel Claus Schenk Graf von Stauffenberg checked his gear. He had two bombs with one as a backup. He wrapped the explosives in brown paper and put one in his briefcase and the other in a satchel. His aide, Werner von Haefton, would be picking him up soon and together they would fly to East Prussia to *Wolsschanze*, the Wolf's Lair, for the military conference.

Ever intense, Stauffenberg thought about all of the planning that had gone in to this plan. There were now many officers who knew about and supported it. Amazingly, there had only been one leak—those blasted letters to Schmidt. Many of the officers were actively involved. One had constructed the bomb, another had secured the plane for today, a third and fourth were scheduled to be at the conference. "Today, I will not fail,"

Stauffenberg said this aloud to himself as he gazed at his reflection in the mirror. "Today begins a new Germany, a new beginning to the end of the war."

Haefton arrived and they set out for the airfield where they boarded a Ju-52 airplane. The weather was mostly sunny, promising to be a glorious day in East Prussia. On the flight, they went over the plan a few last times. Stauffenberg was calm, his resolve unshakable. The *Fuhrer* must die.

They touched down at 11:30 and were driven the short distance to the complex. The meeting would start at 12:30. When he arrived, there were twenty officers present, including General Erich Fellgiebel, who was in on the plot. They arranged themselves around the large conference table, and Stauffenberg placed himself two officers away from Hitler.

At the appointed hour, the conference began. As usual, the *Fuhrer* began with a monologue, which might easily last for hours. After a few minutes,

Stauffenberg excused himself to use the washroom. He entered staff officer Wilhelm Keitel's personal washroom off of his office where he used his pliers to crush the end of the detonator which was inserted into the block of plastic explosive. He placed the primed bomb back into his briefcase and hurried back to the conference. He had ten minutes before the explosive detonated. He placed the briefcase under the conference table where Hitler and the officers were discussing the defense of their positions in France. After a few minutes, an aide entered the room and informed Stauffenberg that he had an urgent phone call. Stauffenberg hurriedly left the room as did General Fellgiebel, claiming a call of nature.

At that moment, Hitler was making a particularly salient point about the armored vehicles assigned to the Western Front. U.S. troops had reached St. Lo in France just two days earlier and were on the move.

"We cannot allow General Patton and his Third Army to break through. They will be aiming for the Brest Peninsula!" Hitler was shouting now.

Colonel Heinz Brandt who was responsible for this part of the defense of France leaned in to hear better. There was a briefcase underfoot. Colonel Brandt pushed it with his foot out of his way so he could better hear the *Fuhrer*. The briefcase came to rest against one of the table legs of the big table. This particular position of the briefcase saved Adolf Hitler's life even as it caused the death of Brandt.

Stauffenberg had positioned himself next to his staff car, awaiting the explosion. His eyes were trained on the windows of the conference room. Seconds ticked by like hours. At last he heard the massive explosion and saw the smoke pouring out of the windows of the room.

"*Lassen Sie uns hier verlassen*, let's get out of here!" Stauffenberg shouted to Haeften.

They sped down the drive, reaching the first of three checkpoints. "We have been called away on an emergency," Stauffenberg barked at the guards as they raised the gates.

"*Halt hier*, stop here," Stauffenberg ordered Haeften. "Throw the other bomb out into the forest."

They continued through the other checkpoints with the same bluff until they reached Rastenberg airfield. By 1300 hours they were airborne.

Chapter Fifty Three

Dead or Alive

By 1430 hours, there was chaos in the Bendlerblock. Olbricht had received a call from General Fellgiebel that Hitler had survived the explosion despite other reports to the contrary. Minutes before, he had released Elizabeth, Freddy, Marta and me and had arrested Schmidt.

We had been in the torture chamber and Schmidt had just started in on us. We were seated side by side, cuffed to our chairs.

"I will ask you again *Herr* Pointer, what do you know about the plot to assassinate the *Fuhrer*?"

I replied with a reference to the horse he rode in on.

Whack! He backhanded Elizabeth across her left cheek. Her head flew back and tears sprung to her eyes, but she uttered not a sound. I struggled against the cuffs with no success.

Elizabeth and I had talked about what we should do if this happened. She had been brave and told me to say nothing, but I wasn't sure I could hold out.

"Again, *Herr* Pointer. Tell me what you know." Schmidt's eyes gleamed at me. He was enjoying this, I realized.

I said nothing.

Whack! This time the blow was on her right cheek. I was getting ready to say something, anything to make him stop when the door to the room burst open and one of Olbricht's men burst into the room.

"Colonel Schmidt, you are under arrest. Get down on the floor." Encouraged by the Luger pointed at his head, Schmidt complied. He was taken away by one of the men.

My cuffs, then Elizabeth's, were unlocked and I rushed to her side.

"Are you hurt badly, darling?" I looked at her tear stained face. It hurt me much worse to look at her than if he'd beaten me.

"Fine, Pointer," she muttered. "Don't beat yourself up about this. It's what we agreed to do."

We were escorted to the command center where Olbricht, Tresckow and several others were arguing about what to do next. Freddy and Marta were led in and I noticed that Marta was doubled over in pain—busted ribs, I thought. Presumably, Schmidt had gotten to the von Furstenbergs first. Fromm was present as well.

Olbricht was hovering over the seated Fromm. "Execute *Valkyrie* now! The Fuhrer is dead. If not dead, then incapacitated!"

Fromm's eyes darted around the room. He stood up. "We need to have confirmation, General. I cannot put the communiqué out until we have confirmation!"

I looked at Elizabeth and nodded to her to come with me. We got out of earshot and I said, "We've got to be ready to vamoose if things don't fall our way. I'll be back in a few minutes."

I left before she could say anything and went downstairs to find Schmidt. On the way, I saw first-hand the confusion in the Bendlerblock. Officers were running from office to office. Phones were ringing madly. No one knew whether Hitler was dead or alive.

I made a beeline for our former cell. Sure enough, there were two guards posted out front. I said to the senior one, "General Olbricht has commanded me to interrogate Colonel Schmidt. You will unlock the door."

The guards looked at each other. Sensing their hesitancy, I said, "YOU WILL OPEN THIS DOOR OR IN FIVE MINUTES YOU WILL BE ON THE WRONG SIDE OF ONE OF THESE ROOMS. NOW!"

With another glance at his compadre, the guard opened the door. I stepped in and closed it behind me.

I turned to face Schmidt. He was hunched over in the chair that I had occupied not long before.

"Hello Colonel. Having a good day?" I smiled. "Listen, uh, Colonel, I don't want to intrude at a bad moment, but I need a big favor."

Schmidt looked up at me, a glum look on his face.

"I need to borrow the keys to your staff car. See, the missus and I might be taking a little trip and, what with the chaos and all in town, I don't want to rely on the trains. So, hand them over."

Schmidt sneered at me so I grabbed him by the scruff of his SS uniform and literally picked him up off the ground. I slugged him as hard as I could in his gut, and as he doubled over, I searched his pockets. I took his I.D. card and his keys, plus a few marks that he had on him. Then I threw him back on his chair.

"Hey, Colonel. This is for Elizabeth." I kicked him as hard as I could, the blow landing squarely on his chin. He fell ass over tea kettle backwards to the floor.

"*Danke*", I said to the guards as I raced back upstairs.

Things were no more settled in the command center. Olbricht and Fromm were still arguing about activating *Valkyrie* with the rest of the officers clustered in groups talking in low, agitated tones. Elizabeth was ministering to Marta who was seriously beat up. At that moment, a secretary rushed in and announced to Olbricht that he had a call from Lieutenant Colonel Stauffenberg.

The room went silent as the General picked up the phone. It was 1605 hours.

"Yes, Stauffenberg? Are you alright? You have landed?"

We strained to hear what was being said on the other end of the line but could only hear an excited babble.

"Yes? Yes? Are you certain? But are you *certain?* Alright, Count. Come straight here."

Olbricht turned to address his rapt audience. "Count Stauffenberg has landed in Berlin and called from the airfield. He reports that the bomb went off as planned. He witnessed it personally. He is certain that no one could have survived the blast."

Tresckow said, "Did he see the body himself?"

"*Nein,*" answered the General. "He had to get away."

He turned to Fromm. "General, commanders throughout the Reich are awaiting word from us to initiate our plans. Will you now activate communications?"

Fromm answered, "Not until there is confirmation, General."

To me, it seemed to be a 50/50 proposition that Hitler was dead. I didn't like the odds. If we left now, we had a chance of escape; if Hitler were alive, we would die with everyone else in this room.

I motioned to Elizabeth to join me and then tapped Freddy and Marta on the shoulder, gesturing for them to follow me.

I looked at the three of them in turn and said, "If we want to have a chance of escaping, we must leave now. I have access to a car. My plan is to go to your apartment, Freddy, and pick up your children and get out of Berlin as fast as we can do it. But we have to leave now. If we wait and Hitler is alive, then it will be impossible to escape. If we go and he's dead, then we can return if that seems to be the right move at that moment. What do you say, Freddy?"

"I would like a moment with Marta," he replied.

Elizabeth and I retreated and watched as Freddy and Marta engaged in animated conversation. I excused myself and went to the Requisition Desk, which was vacant. I entered the big room where stacks of supplies and uniforms were kept. I found a selection of Colonel uniforms, and most were too small. There was one that would fit if I sucked in my gut. I put it on, looked in the mirror and gave myself a kind of salute. *Heil Hitler*.

When I returned, Freddy and Marta were still talking. Looking at my watch, I approached them and said, "We really have to go."

Holding his wife's hand, Freddy spun to face me. "I cannot leave. But I would be grateful if you would take Marta and the children with you."

I had thought that would be the answer. I embraced Freddy and wished him luck.

"Let's go," I said to the others.

Chapter Fifty Four

Die Ostfront

We went down to the motor pool and I found Schmidt's car by matching the key ring number to the vehicle's plates. We screeched out of the lot and I turned for the von Furstenberg apartment. While Marta gathered the children, packing a bag for them, I ransacked the kitchen for food that we could take with us. Elizabeth came into the kitchen, brandishing a bottle of Brandy.

"This may come in handy," she said.

Within fifteen minutes we were on the road. Elizabeth rode shotgun with a map of the area, and Marta was in the back with the children. The smallest, Kurt, was three-years old and was crying with gusto. I headed east for the highway out of town.

Over the squall, Marta said, "*Herr* Moeller, I mean Pointer, why are you heading east?"

"The name's Colonel Schmidt for the duration of this trip, at least until we reach the Russians. As to why, everyone will figure we're heading west, so we'll go east. After all, the Soviets are our allies, yes?"

I knew there would be at least one checkpoint before we got out of Berlin. When we reached it, I instructed everyone to let me do the talking. I had asked Marta to cover up her face wounds with her silk scarf.

The afternoon was getting later, it was now 1730 hours. But the July sun was still out and it had turned into quite a warm day. The windows were rolled down when we stopped at the barricade.

"*Guten Tag, Herr Colonel,*" said the guard. "May I ask where you are headed today?"

"Auschwitz." If they ask if you know the time, just say yes.

He leaned in to have a look and said, "If I may ask, sir, why all these women and children?"

"No you may not ask, Sergeant." I glared at him, imagining how the real Schmidt would act.

"Very well sir, have a pleasant journey."

We were going to *die Ostfront*, the Eastern Front, site of the biggest, bloodiest battles of the war. Tens of millions of soldiers and civilians had died of war wounds, disease, exposure and starvation. Battles there had been the largest military confrontations in all of military history. If Hitler had survived the explosion, there would be a massive search for us. We were, after all, "trophies"; we were American spies and we had tried to kill the revered *Fuhrer*. I believed that our only hope was to go where they would think we dared not go—the dreaded *Ostfront*.

It seemed that Hitler had believed that the Nazis could fashion a *blitzkrieg* and conquer Russia in just a few months, certainly before winter set in. After all, Stalin's forces had lacked the resolve, the proper training and equipment. Hadn't Poland and France both succumbed to Hitler's tactics with minimal resistance? And Russia was Hitler's ultimate prize. The Thousand Year *Reich* could never be secure with the Great Russian Bear remaining unfettered to the East. And so in the spring of 1941, over three years ago, Hitler had invaded Mother Russia. There were massive successes initially, but, like Napoleon before them, Hitler's troops had bogged down and suffered through the brutal Russian winter of 1941-42. To hard-liners in Berlin, like Himmler, *der Ostfeldrugz*, the Eastern Campaign, was an ideological war between Nazism and the Aryan race as the good guys and Communism and the Slavic *Untermenschen*, or subhumans, as the villains. I thought it was a nice touch that Hitler referred to it as a "war of annihilation". The good ole *Fuhrer* always seemed to think in absolute terms.

After Germany's disastrous experience at the Battle of Stalingrad, Nazi propaganda began positioning the struggle as a German defense of Western Civilization against destruction by the Bolshevik "hordes" that were surging into Europe. That Hitler way with words again. The battles had been no less ferocious and bloody but ever since Stalingrad, the Nazis were on the defensive. To complicate matters for Hitler—and, in a way, for us—there were other factions in the fight. Poland, Yugoslavia and Slovakia all had partisan forces who were in open rebellion against the Nazi occupiers. There were even Free French forces fighting in the East. Their leader, Charles deGaulle, believed that French soldiers should serve on all fronts. All in all, it was a venomous soup of army versus army with partisan fighters thrown into the stew.

The children had fallen asleep full on milk and some bread. We had passed two more checkpoints without incident and night had fallen. I would drive as long as I was able, then hand it over to

Elizabeth. Diesel fuel was on my mind. All staff cars were equipped with extra tanks strapped to the sides of the vehicles, and we had already had to dip into the first spare tank.

"*Herr* Pointer, can you explain your plan to me, please?" Marta said quietly from the back seat.

"Call me Pointer", I said. "The plan is to drive east until we run into some friendlies. We'll figure it out from there." I paused a beat. "I have a question for you, Marta. Why did you betray us?"

Marta was silent for a long moment. At length, she said, "I see things, Pointer. I have visions, and they have usually come to pass. I saw the destruction of my family in this plot to kill the Fuhrer, and I wanted to protect them. I begged Freddy to send you away, but he did not listen. And now, once again, my vision is coming true."

"Marta," I said "are you familiar with the concept of a self-fulfilling prophecy? Because that's what we've got working here. By your very actions, you have caused some of these events to occur. Are you getting me, Marta?" I was trying not to let my anger show that she had put all of our lives in danger by her communiqués to Schmidt.

"Of course I understand what you're implying, Pointer, but that doesn't stop the visions. I fear that this escape from Berlin will not end well for us. I have three children to care for, and I am very, very afraid for them."

"OK, I'll play the game. What have you seen?"

"Sometimes now when I close my eyes I see blood on Kurt and on Lissie, but not on little Freddy. You and Elizabeth are not in my visions. Do you know how terrifying it is to see your children covered in blood, even in a dream?"

I was concentrating on the road as it was a particularly rutted stretch through the Polish countryside. We had passed the border thirty minutes ago. We had about 200 miles to go until we got to Auschwitz, not that I planned to visit there again. It was just a landmark. We'd still have a long way to go to reach any friendly forces. But maybe in Auschwitz I could score some fuel for the car—and some food. At any rate, I would keep my SS uniform on for the next day or so before I changed back to civilian attire.

"I can only imagine, Marta, but if it's all the same to you, I'm going to put more trust in these firearms"—I nudged the Luger and the rifle under the seat with my foot—"than in your visions."

Shortly after dawn we entered the town that serviced the Auschwitz death camps. I was looking for a fuel depot and some food. We had gone through the last spare fuel tank and we would run out of food by the end of the day. Where was a Dixie Diner when I needed one? At the checkpoint, I asked the guard about fuel and he directed me to the other side of the small town. I had taken a one-hour break from driving but had spent most of the night concocting a story to describe why an SS Colonel, two women and three children were driving through the Polish countryside.

When we reached the depot, I told everyone to get out and stretch their legs. We had taken bathroom pit stops a couple of times during the night so we were in good shape on the all-important pit stop issue.

A Major stepped out of the small building and I greeted him heartily.

"*Guten morgen, Herr* Major. We require some diesel for our journey and some food as well."

The Major glanced over at our group and seemed puzzled. "This is somewhat irregular, Colonel. You are traveling with women and children?"

"Yes, I have been ordered to bring a, uh, special delivery to Field Marshall Warner at the Front. His wife and children." I lowered my voice. "The privilege of rank, you know."

The Major looked skeptical. "May I see the orders, please, Colonel?"

I kept my voice low. "There are no written orders, Major. This is, how would you say, off the books. Do you see the young, pretty one? That is his, er, personal assistant." I didn't wink at the Major, but my voice said 'wink-wink'. "Feel free to call his headquarters if you wish, but I'm sure he's busy waging war, don't you think?"

"Ah. The privileges of rank indeed. Yes, Colonel, we can accommodate you. Pull the car up over there. I suspect the children would appreciate a hot breakfast."

"You say you have driven all night? Then you haven't heard the news from Berlin."

"No, what news?"

"There was an attempt on the Fuhrer's life at *Wolfsschanze* yesterday. A bomb in his conference room. There was great confusion at first whether or not he survived, but he broadcast a personal message over the wireless. It was indeed the *Fuhrer* speaking. He was injured but not fatally. The perpetrators at the Bendlerblock were apprehended and most of them were shot by a firing squad last night."

"Oh, thank God," I said. "Who was the ringleader, do you know?"

"I have not yet heard those details. Only that they were caught and shot."

Well, at least they weren't hanged as Freddy had predicted, I thought.

After filling all of our tanks and a hot breakfast of sausages, buttered bread, coffee and milk, we were on our way. I decided to say nothing about the news to Marta, but I got the chance to whisper it to Elizabeth before we left. How long, I wondered, before news of our escape would reach this part of the world?

Our destination was Minsk, over 500 miles away. We would skirt Warsaw at about the halfway point, and before reaching Minsk we would be in Russian-controlled territory. Oddly, I felt safer on German turf than in our supposed ally's control. Maybe it was my SS uniform. So far, it had conferred privileges that had kept us alive.

The children were getting restless as any kids would. Frankly, I was a little stir-crazy. The checkpoints had become routine, nobody gave the great Colonel any sass. Marta knew a little English so I proposed that we do a little singing." How about 'Row, row, row your boat'", I proposed to Elizabeth.

"Let's do it as a Round," she said.

So, after a some trial and error with Marta and the kids, we were soon singing "Row Your Boat" with the different verses blending together. That was one raucous SS staff car! We sang for miles until I was thoroughly sick of "Row Your Boat".

"OK, OK," I shouted above the din. Time to graduate to something different. We'll do the 'Horn, Violin, Clarinet' Round. Backseat, you'll be the horn, Elizabeth, you're the violin and I'll be the clarinet."

My parents had taken me to The Mosque Auditorium in Richmond when I was a child. I had been thrilled when the conductor divided the audience into three sections and had us sing this song in a Round.

After I gave instructions and translations, we gave it a try.

The horn, the horn awakes me at morn.

The violin singing like lovely ringing.

The clarinet, the clarinet goes doodle oodle oodle-et.

Soon we were singing our respective verses in perfect harmony, and the SS staff car was a musical theatre.

When we'd finally had enough, Elizabeth said, "What's next, Cow Poker?"

By now, we were approaching Warsaw, the scene of the great Jewish Ghetto, which was now virtually empty with all its inhabitants in the camps. We pulled off to the side of the road and looked at the map for a way to bypass the city. The only route that was possible took us a hundred miles out of the way. I nixed that idea and decided to chance it.

I was fearful that by now bulletins on us as fugitives might have been issued. I asked Marta if she thought the children could stand hiding in the car boot with her back there too. We tested it outside of town and Lissie and Freddy were fine, but little Kurt started howling in fear.

"OK. Let's do this with Marta, Lissie and Freddy in the boot. Kurt will ride up front with us."

There were three checkpoints in the city that we passed through. The first two were routine, but the last one gave us trouble.

"Please get out of the car, Herr Colonel," said the officer in charge.

"We are in a hurry," I responded. "Little Kurt here is not feeling well and we need to reach his doctor."

The officer wasn't buying it. "Out, please." He examined Schmidt's I.D. and peered in at Elizabeth and Kurt. *"Was ist Ihr Name, Frau?"*

I prayed that Elizabeth would understand the basic German phrase.

"Elizabeth Moeller," she answered promptly.

He held out his hand. "Papers?"

She handed him her I.D. As he scanned it, I tried to speak to Elizabeth with my eyes. "Get the guns ready," was what I was trying to say.

The guard handed the papers back and said, "We have received information from Berlin that there are fugitives from the *Wolfsschanze* attempt on the *Fuhrer*. A man, two women and three children are at large."

"We have come from Auschwitz and heard the news this morning. Are there any more developments?" I asked.

"Yes, they have apprehended the ringleaders and the search is on for other conspirators."

"And who were the ringleaders?"

"A Lieutenant Colonel by the name of Stauffenberg, General Olbricht and several others." The guard seemed proud to be in the know.

I said, "Clearly, this is a mother with a sick boy. I have offered my services to get them to a doctor. May we now leave?"

The guard still had my papers. He stared at them, then at me. "Yes, go."

The road out of Warsaw was crowded with armored vehicles, transport vehicles and military apparatus of every description, coming and going from and to the Front. There were often delays as a truck would run off the road, holding up traffic. Staff cars with Generals whizzed by on the road's shoulder. Planes roared overhead. The landscape had turned from lovely summer green fields to being pitted by artillery and aircraft shellings. We were definitely nearing the *Ostfront.* I wondered what we would do when we got there. There wouldn't be a road sign that said, "Now Entering the Front". But I knew we wouldn't reach the critical area until after nightfall. We had gotten some recent intelligence at a checkpoint outside of Warsaw. Marta and the two children were back in the boot of the car, but this time the bulletin hadn't seemed to reach them. They were too busy holding back the Russian advance. I had asked the officer to direct me to the Front.

"Which Front?" he wanted to know. "North in Estonia, East at the Polish border or south in Lviv?"

I looked at my map. "What's happened in Lviv?" I asked. Lviv was about 150 miles to the southeast in the Ukraine near the border with Poland.

"Lviv was retaken by the Soviets just four days ago. First time they've occupied it since '39."

That's where we want to go, I thought. It now appeared that Minsk was well behind the Front, but Lviv was just captured, so we wouldn't have to go far through Russian lines to get there.

I got back in the car and we turned southeast, bound for the Ukraine. At our first opportunity, I stopped the car and let Marta and the kids out of the trunk.

The children now called me *Onkel* Pointer, Uncle Pointer. Freddy seemed most like his father and had quickly become my favorite. He was a brave little man.

But even Freddy was tired of this drill. "*Onkel* Pointer, when can we go home? I don't like it here and I don't like it in that dark boot one bit," said the six-year old.

"I'll tell you what, Freddy," I said. No more boot for you, your sister or your mom. And we're working hard to get you out of here. OK, partner?"

But Freddy wasn't letting me off that easy. Nor was his older sister. The day was growing late, and they were tired. We all were tired, but I knew the most dangerous part of the trip was still ahead of us. We'd only eaten some bread and ham with some milk for the children. Night had fallen and it was a beautiful soft July evening.

Lissie said, "Can we at least sing the horn song for a while?"

"Sure we can, honey. Then I want you guys to go to sleep, OK?"

We sang a few verses, but the children weren't ready to sleep, so I pulled the car off the road near an abandoned farmhouse and parked. We could hear the rumble of artillery fire in the far distance. Elizabeth got out a blanket and we all six squeezed onto it. Lissie climbed into my lap and Marta held Kurt. Freddy snuggled up with Elizabeth.

"What's that noise, *Onkel* Pointer?" Lissie asked me.

"It's just thunder, honey. Let me tell you all a story about the Land of Thunder, which is where we are going."

I proceeded to invent a tale of very friendly giants who, in the Land of Thunder, liked to beat on their giant drums when they were hungry or sleepy, and that's what we were hearing. Kurt was the first to nod off, but Freddy and Lissie stayed awake.

"Those giants sure are a hungry lot," Freddy observed.

"Yes," Lissie agreed. "Don't they get enough to eat in their Land, *Onkel* Pointer?"

"Sure they do, but you know that giants are big and very hungry chaps. They are forever complaining about their rations. And just when they've finally eaten enough, they get cranky from lack of sleep, so they just keep beating those drums."

Freddy was the next to nod off. I had some time to think through our situation. Wild Bill, I thought, I didn't sign up for this. I was now responsible for the safety of a woman and her three children. I knew Elizabeth could take care of herself, but, still, it had been my decision to go east instead of west. I wondered for the hundredth time if that had been the correct play. I had grown quite fond of these kids, and I was worried. Very worried. We were enemies to their own military, and we would be friendlies to their enemies. But would the Russians realize that? I realized, though, that if Marta had stayed behind, she would most certainly have been shot. The children? I didn't put anything past Schmidt and his goons.

Lissie at age eight was the elder statesman for the von Furstenberg children. She was also a protector of her mother who was in a very fragile state. I admired the little girl's courage as she seemed determined to put up a good front for the benefit of her mother and her siblings.

Lissie interrupted my reverie and said, "*Onkel* Pointer, can you carry me to the car? I'm sleepy."

"Course I can, honey."

Likewise, little Freddy was a trooper. He, too, was protective of Marta, and he seemed to consider it his duty as older brother to keep an eye out for young Kurt who was mostly a babbling, gurgling two year old. Except when he was crying. My God! The lungs on that boy!

Lissie was in the land of nod by the time I placed her in back next to the other two. It was time for an adult strategy session. We stood outside under the rising moon.

"I figure we're about two hours from the Front. I'll tell you that the only battle front I've ever been on was in Sicily, and it's not like you really know where one Army's lines end and the other's begins. It's a very jagged line, and it's ever shifting."

"So, what's the plan, Pointer?" Elizabeth prompted.

"It's, uh, fluid. We'll no doubt encounter more and more German troops. A staff car with a Colonel at the wheel shouldn't attract much notice, unless they look inside and see children, so I might have to go back on my word to Freddy, and you guys might have to go back into the trunk. I'm probably going to have to bluster our way through a lot of interference. What we'll look for is some kind of break in the German lines. If we find one, we'll head toward the sound of artillery. We'll drive if we can; otherwise, we'll have to go on foot. I'm figuring we'll know when we're behind enemy lines because the Russians will find us."

Elizabeth and Marta absorbed this for a few moments.

Marta said, "Pointer, how dangerous is this? For my children?"

"I won't lie to you, Marta. It's very dangerous. But they're children, they pose no threat to anyone so I'm hoping the Russians will realize that. But we need to be prepared to fight if we have to. We don't speak Russian. French, German, English and Italian between us, yes, but no Russian. I'm fairly confident we'll find someone who will know one of our languages.

I looked up at the moon for a few beats.

"I'm thinking we should go in at dawn, precisely because we do have children with us. I don't want troopers shooting at us in the dark. Night patrols tend to shoot first and ask questions later."

I pulled out the map. "We're about here. And here's Juroslaw an hour away, which could be a departure point for us. And another hour is the border town of Przemysi, here, which is a more likely place for us to head eastward toward Lviv. It's only about fifty kilometers from Przemysi on the Poland side to Lviv on the Ukraine side. If we encounter Russian troops before we reach Lviv, which I suspect will be the case, they'll probably take us there ultimately. That's where their commanders will be holed up."

I looked at the two women. "Questions?"

"Yes," said Elizabeth. "What happens if it goes wrong and one or more of us is wounded, or worse?"

"We leave no one behind. Except if we're on foot and I am killed, you will go without me. You cannot carry me, I'm too—let's say—athletic." I tried to make a little joke, but no one was laughing.

Chapter Fifty Five

The Ukraine

We drove the hour to Juroslaw. Traffic
for that time of night was heavy. Tanks
and other armored vehicles were being
repositioned for the border defense.
Troops were marching toward the
border. There was a blanket over the
sleeping children in the back, mostly
obscuring them, but no one tried to
stop us. When we reached the town, it
appeared that all of the movement of
the Nazi troops was to the east. We
could ride the wave with them for a
while, but I thought that it would be
too risky. The closer we got to the
Front with the Germans, the more
likely they were to notice us as being
out of place.

So we continued southeast to the
border. Much of the heavy traffic was
headed in the opposite direction,
toward Juroslaw. That was a good sign.
After about ninety minutes we reached
Przemysi, hard by the Poland/Ukraine
border. There were troops and
equipment, but not nearly the volume

of action near Juroslaw. This, I thought, was it. This is where we go east.

I found an abandoned fuel depot outside of town and pulled in. The artillery fire was louder now. I knew we were close.

"We'll stop here for a few hours of rest," I whispered so as not to wake the children. "Let's get some shut-eye. Sleep fast."

The dawn rose in a mist as the sounds of artillery intensified. For the first time we saw Soviet fighter planes overhead going northwest, no doubt on missions to bomb the Nazis into a million pieces up around Juroslaw. The fighting was intensifying. The children were now awake, eating a meager breakfast of bread and the last of the milk. Little Freddy jumped up front with Elizabeth and clung to her as if she were the last person on earth.

"It's just the Thunder Giants," I said. "They're hungry for their breakfast."

Lissie eyed me with skepticism but, as the eldest child, kept her own counsel.

I fired up the big diesel engine and slowly eased out onto the main road. The troop vehicles were still headed north so I took a street across town toward the east. I was hoping for a passable road that would lead us across the border to the Ukraine. And there it was. In the distance I saw what used to be a checkpoint. There were still four or five troopers milling about, but, I guess they weren't too worried that anyone would actually want to go east at this point. There was a wooden gate lowered across the road as all the checkpoints had. First question of the day: Bluff our way through or blast our way through. Bluff or blast, that is the question. The soldiers were all seated casually, eating their breakfast rations. I decided on the blast option.

"Hold on everybody. We're going to the Ukraine!"

I revved the big diesel, popped it into gear and gathered as much speed as I could in the hundred or so yards to the checkpoint. When we were about thirty yards away, the guards looked up at the roaring of the engine. One or two grabbed their weapons, but the sight of an SS staff car bearing down on them at speed froze them for a moment.

"Down! Down!" I shouted. "Everybody down!" Out of the corner of my eye, I saw Elizabeth hunched down, covering Freddy with her body. I hoped that Marta was following suit in the back seat.

"*Anhalten! Anhalten*! I could hear the Nazis screaming at us to stop over the roar of the engine. When it became clear that we were speeding up instead, they began to open fire. I ducked as low as I dared so I could still see the road underneath the steering wheel.

With a great crash, the windshield exploded as bullets penetrated the glass. At almost the same second, the big staff car crashed through the wooden gate. Now the fire was coming from our rear. I could hear bullets

639

thudding into the car and before we'd gone too far, the back window exploded with glass flying. I kept the pedal to the medal, though, as we raced ahead. I just prayed they wouldn't hit a tire. I looked in the rear view mirror, hoping I would not see them preparing for a chase. They appeared to be arguing about what to do, gesticulating and pointing our way.

Soon they were out of sight and there were no signs that they were in pursuit.

"Everyone OK?" I yelled. "Marta?"

"Yes, we're fine," came the report from the backseat. Lissie and Kurt were crying though. Freddy was sucking his thumb and seemed to be in shock. Elizabeth was stroking his cheek and cooing to him that everything was alright.

"*Onkel* Pointer?" Freddy said at length.

"Yes, Freddy?"

"We have a problem. The windows are broken. What are we to do about that?"

I almost laughed. His question broke the tension. Then, Elizabeth did start a little chuckle. I couldn't help it; I started a laugh deep from in my gut and it escalated until tears were pouring down my face. The kids in the back stopped sobbing, wondering about the startling new emotion coming from the front. Freddy stared at Elizabeth and me in bemusement, wondering what he'd said that was so funny.

Finally, gasping for air, I said, "Freddy, we'll stop at the first Esso station we see in the Ukraine and get it fixed."

That precipitated new gales of laughter from Elizabeth and me. Then Lissie and even Kurt joined the chorus, giggling away. God, I needed that, I thought.

After a few miles on the rutted road, we were approaching the border. I assumed this was no-man's-land, there was no sign of life. I stopped the car

and got out to examine the damage.
Other than dozens of bullet holes,
there seemed to be nothing that would
impede us. I could hear the Boom!
Boom! of the artillery. Those giants
sure were hungry. I thought about
what to do next as Elizabeth joined me.

"What's next, Pointer?" she asked,
echoing my thoughts.

"I'm not comfortable with just lurching
into Russian territory and letting them
find us. It's so...defensive."

"But what choice do we have?"

"None that I can think of," I admitted.

So we got back in the car and drove
further into Russian-occupied territory.
Every few miles, there would be a
bomb crater in the road, and we'd
have to skirt it. Once, I had to drive
into the forest at the side of the road,
mowing down saplings and further
damaging the car. If the Germans ever
got hold of us again, Schmidt was going
to need a tip top body shop.

We had enough fuel for maybe twenty or thirty more miles. When that happened, we'd lose our mobility and, if we went forward on foot, we'd also lose the protection of the big car. I had changed out of my Colonel's uniform and was now sporting civvies. Every so often I felt around with my foot for my carbine and my Luger just to reassure myself. I picked up the Luger and stuck it in my belt. I also had an SS dagger strapped to my ankle. Elizabeth was armed with a Luger as well.

We were now creeping along at about five miles per hour because of the abysmal condition of the road. As I was pondering our situation, I saw movement in my peripheral vision to our left in the forest. A deer? My imagination? Suddenly, a man dressed in ragged clothes leapt out of the forest and onto the hood of the car. Two more men, similarly attired, materialized at either side of the car. They both sported Russian-made bolt-action rifles which they pointed at Elizabeth and me. The man on the hood had a pistol aimed squarely at my head. Partisans, I thought. Roving bands of nationalists who fought against their Russian occupiers.

They shouted something unintelligible, presumably in Russian, and gestured for us to get out of the car.

"I do not understand," I said. "We are Americans. Americans!" I said in English.

Their reply to that was more gesturing for us to exit the vehicle. My thought was, I'll exit, but you'll be exiting this world if I get the chance. I slowly moved my hand to the handle of my Luger, which was concealed under my shirt. These fellows looked like they hadn't exactly signed the Geneva Convention. Elizabeth, with careful movements, lifted Freddy off her lap and onto the floor between her feet. There was deathly quiet from the back seat.

I looked over at Elizabeth and tried to communicate with my glance that this was a take-no-prisoners situation. We'd be operating under a Black Flag. I saw her left hand fingering the handle of her pistol.

Staring straight ahead, I said quietly so Marta could hear, "Elizabeth and I are going to make a move against these guys. When we do, you and the kids hit the floor."

With an almost imperceptible nod to Elizabeth, I turned to the man at my window, and she did the same to her visitor at her window.

After a beat, I said, "Go!"

We both opened our doors as violently as we could, drawing our guns at the same time. I knocked my man back about three feet, succeeding in getting his rifle pointed in the air. It gave me the second I needed to draw my gun and fire in his face at point-blank range. I heard two other shots. One was directed at me from the man on the hood. I felt a sharp pain in my shoulder as the bullet spun me around. My legs went to rubber, my vision blurred. The man had now jumped off the hood and was closing in to finish me off. I tried to raise my gun, but my hand was too shaky. He aimed his pistol at my head and was squeezing the trigger when Elizabeth stepped to her right and fired a perfect shot across the hood of the car that entered his left temple and made mush of his head. He pitched forward, knocking me to the ground, but he was deader than dead.

As I lay on the ground with the partisan on top of me, I knew that I'd been hit. But I believed that the bullet had passed through my shoulder and had not hit an artery. There was blood, but not pulsing fountains of blood.

Elizabeth rushed to me and shoved the partisan from on top of me with her foot.

"Pointer, are you alright?"

I looked up into her frantic eyes and said, "I've been better, my darlin', but it's not time to call Mama Pointer just yet."

Marta and the children also rushed to my side. "*Mutter*, is *Onkel* Pointer OK?" Lissie asked.

Freddy tried to make everything better by saying, "*Onkel* Pointer, we need a new window."

"Yes, Freddy, a new window," I said before passing out.

Chapter Fifty Six

Rescue

When I woke up it was dark. I looked around me and saw nothing but trees. My shoulder was aching fiercely and I noticed that there were strips of a blanket binding my wound. I tried to sit up which evoked a little groan, which, in turn, attracted Elizabeth's attention. She was sitting next to me in the car.

"How are you feeling, honey?" she asked.

"Like I got run over by a *panzer.*"

"You need to rest. We're going to be needing you, you know."

"Where are we?"

"We were running on fumes, so after a few more miles, I pulled the car off the road into this clearing. We are parked as far into the brush as I could get, and I've covered the car with branches. We're not undetectable, but you'd have to look hard to see us."

I noticed that she was whispering. "Marta and the children are asleep. We are just about out of food so we're going to have to make some kind of move tomorrow," she said.

Obviously, we'd all gotten pretty used to the giants beating their drums. Those sure were some hungry boys, I thought groggily. I tried to adjust my position on the seat, but the movement was a killer to my shoulder. "Mmmmm," I murmured. "We'll think of something tomorrow." I proceeded to conk out.

Dawn broke, and it was a fine day as the sun seeped between the branches lighting up our little "home".

"Hey, *Onkel* Pointer, are you ready for some singing?" The hopeful question was from Freddy.

I opened one eye and smiled wanly at Freddy whose face was about an inch from mine. "Maybe later, partner," I croaked.

"Freddy, leave Pointer alone, he's trying to sleep," exclaimed Marta from the back.

"*Mutter*, I'm hungry," came Lissie's voice.

"I know, honey. Elizabeth is gathering some berries for our breakfast."

Ah, family, I thought. And, with the intensity of the last few days, we six *felt* like a family. The intensity of the last couple of days made me appreciate something in those kids that I could only vaguely define as courage and the human will to survive. Three kids under the age of nine enduring being shot at, hunger and the kind of fearfulness most could go a lifetime without experiencing. If I could award medals for bravery, these three would be sporting gold on their chests.

I could feel some of my strength returning, but I doubted I could even beat Freddy in a wrestling match at this point. But I could lift a Luger, and I could shoot if it came to that.

Elizabeth arrived at that moment with a blanket full of berries. "Breakfast is served," she said. "Delicious and nutritious Ukrainian blueberries."

The children whooped with enthusiasm and began devouring nature's bounty from the Ukrainian forest. There were still some scraps of bread which Marta and Elizabeth ate. I had no appetite, but most of the grogginess had worn off, and I began to think about our predicament. These woods contained Russians, partisans and who-knew what other groups. And us. Two women, three children and one wounded Marine. It was a matter of time before we were discovered, and it was a matter of time before eating roots and berries would become intolerable. I wondered which would come first.

"What's out there, Elizabeth?"

"You mean besides trees? Nothing, except this little clearing."

"How far off the road are we?"

"Just about thirty yards," she answered. "It's as far up as I could get."

I tried to think of a plan other than the "Sitting Duck Solution", but came up empty. If the Russians found us first, I didn't know how they would react. Would they shoot first and ask questions later? One thing that seemed certain is that they wouldn't likely be traveling in groups of two or three like those partisans had. They'd come in force.

My thoughts were interrupted by a quiet sob. I painfully twisted around to see that Marta had her face in her hands and was quietly weeping.

"What is it, Marta? What's wrong?" asked Elizabeth.

Marta didn't respond. Instead, she began crying harder. Lissie was rubbing her back and looking at Elizabeth in alarm. Then little Kurt, reacting to his mother, began bawling as only a two-year-old can. The rest of us could only wait until the crying jag was finished. Too much stress, I thought. Freddy had his face buried in Elizabeth's lap and he, too, was in tears. Finally, Marta stopped crying and with heaving breaths, said, "Pointer, I need to talk to you."

"Sure, Marta, talk away," I said.

"In private," she answered.

"Fine. Step outside into my office," I said, and I grimaced as I opened the car door, pushed away some branches and got out.

When Marta got out, we walked a few paces away from the car for some privacy.

She turned to me and said, "It's Kurt."

"*What's* Kurt," I asked.

"It was another dream. I was carrying Kurt and he was bloody and I was bloody and I was running and then it was blackness."

"So what does it mean?" I asked, knowing not to argue with the efficacy of her vision.

"It means that my little *liebeling* is in mortal danger. It means that we have to get him out of here to safety." She was verging on the hysterical.

"And what would you have us do, Marta, that we're not already doing?"

"I don't know, I don't know! But he is in great danger. What if I take him back across the border? They wouldn't hurt a child! We should never have come here." She began to sob again.

I put my arms around her and rocked her gently until the sobs again subsided.

"Can we go back, Pointer? Can we go back to Poland, then Germany? Maybe Freddy is alright, maybe they forgave him..."

I looked at her tear stained, swollen face. "Marta, Freddy is not alright.

None of them is alright. Your Freddy, it pains me to say, is dead."

She looked back at me. "Well, if you won't go, then Kurt and I will."

"Marta, that's about the best way I can think of to make your vision come true. Now let's get back in..."

"Hiiiiiyooooo!" A blood curdling scream came out of the edge of the clearing to my left, followed by several rounds of gunfire. I expected to be hit any second, but there were no bullets coming our way. Instead, from the other end of the clearing, came return gunfire. I grasped Marta, dragged her to the car and threw her into the back seat. With my remaining strength, I hoisted open the front door and dove in.

"Down! Everybody down!" I shouted.

From the sounds of the continuous small arms fire, there was a full-on battle raging across the clearing. I peeked out of the window and looked across the way and could see troopers behind trees firing at their enemy. My angle prevented me from seeing the other side of the conflict. I could see that the men wore grey uniforms. Germans! They hadn't seemed to notice the car; their attention was focused on their immediate targets. I saw one man fall, then another, then several more. It was impossible to tell who was winning the skirmish. The other side must be Soviets. I knew who I was rooting for.

From the back seat, I heard little Kurt start mewling in fear. Freddy, as had become his custom, had nestled himself against Elizabeth on the floor of the car. I was monitoring the battle. The sun was still shining, but the smoke from all the gunfire began to obscure my vision in the clearing.

Suddenly, the German troops began advancing across the clearing, firing as they went. The other side was still putting up a good fight as about one of every five Nazis fell. I trained my eye on an officer who seemed to be the leader, and the second I did, I saw him do a double-take in our direction. Had he seen us?

The officer yelled something at one of his men, and he pointed directly at our position. Yes! They had spotted the car. The trooper diverted from the other men who were still advancing on their foes and began making his way toward the car, his rifle trained at us. I thought what I should do. Clearly, he was coming to investigate whether we were friendlies, or maybe it was just an abandoned car. I reached down and picked up my carbine. The last thing I wanted to do was fire on this man, which wouldn't exactly be an offering of friendship.

When he was about fifteen yards away, it looked as though he might rake the car with gunfire as he raised his weapon. I still didn't reveal myself. At that moment, Marta, with a grunt, opened the door opposite the advancing man, and with Kurt in her arms, began to tear through the heavy brush. The soldier saw the movement and, in one swift motion, raised his rifle and fired. But I had fired first, and his shot went awry as he fell backwards, his rifle thrown involuntarily into the air. His shot missed Marta and the baby, but she was blindly thrashing her way through the brush, making slow progress with her precious cargo.

I opened my door and went tearing around the back of the car in hot pursuit of the madwoman. I made it to the edge of the brush when some of the Germans began directing their fire at me. I dove into the tangle of trees and brush and managed to land on my uninjured shoulder, but more and more shots were coming my way. At least, I thought, they aren't directing their shooting at Marta and Kurt. I was now behind a fallen log, which offered some protection. Behind me, I could hear the *bap bap* of small arms fire coming from the direction of the car. Elizabeth was firing and, in turn, drawing fire!

I risked a peek over the log and was horrified by what I saw. Marta had lurched to her right *toward* the clearing, toward the Germans. She held little Kurt up in front of her, screaming, "Don't shoot! Don't shoot! He's just a baby! *Heil* Hitler!" *Jesus!*

As she stumbled to the edge of the clearing, I watched as one of the men aimed his rifle squarely at the onrushing Marta. He fired, and the bullet ripped through Kurt's little body and entered Marta's. They both fell to the ground. I got off a shot and dropped the bastard, but it was too late. There was no doubt about Kurt; he was dead. Marta? At that point, I didn't care.

"*Sheist*," I thought. What now? I glanced over at the officer, but he was preoccupied with his battle. They now had two directions of fire to worry about. I began firing steadily over the top of the log, and I could see that Elizabeth was shooting from behind the car.

The officer let out a bellow of something to his men, and they began to back up, firing as they went. They were backing off. As I watched, they melted back into the trees toward the road.

Now, with full-throated screams, their enemy came pouring into the clearing in pursuit. They were in some kind of uniforms that I did not recognize, but they were definitely not Soviets. They had no red stars anywhere on their uniforms. But they did have bloodlust. They were chasing the Nazis for all they were worth. Most of them disappeared into the forest the way that the Germans had gone, but a few of them stayed behind in the clearing, presumably to guard against some kind of double-back by the enemy.

It was then that I decided that playing defense wasn't working. I rose from my position, not bothering to be quiet. I wanted them to see me. I began walking toward them, finally yelling, "Hey! I'm an American! I come in peace!"

The men whirled around at the sound of my voice and I found myself staring down the business end of six carbines and two submachine guns. I dropped

my weapon and raised my hands high.
So much for not playing defense.

"I am an American, I come in peace," I
repeated.

The men stared at me. Then an officer
took a cautious step forward and said,
"Vous est Americain?

French?

"Oui, je suis Americain, oui." I said.
"Qui est vous?

"We are Free French under Charles
deGaulle," said the officer.

Epilogue

Washington, DC

"What time will your parents get here?" Elizabeth asked.

"We're due at the Colonel's at seven, so they should be arriving by 1830 hours." It was one of my many quirks to use military jargon in a domestic setting.

I turned to little Freddy and said, "Where were we? Right. You make a loop here and the tag end goes around this way." I was demonstrating for Freddy how to tie a bowtie.

The four of us—Elizabeth, Lissie, Freddy and I—had been assigned quarters on the Fort McNair base in Southeast Washington. The preliminary adoption papers had not come through yet, but we did have connections, so I wasn't worried about snafus. My parents were driving up from South Hill for the weekend and would babysit tonight while we dined with Wild Bill and a few others. They had met us at the base when we'd flown in from Europe, so they were already deeply in thrall with Lissie and Freddy as only grandparents could be.

Elizabeth emerged from the bathroom looking ravishing. She *always* looked damned good. "Who else will be there tonight?"

"Assorted OSS officers, maybe a General or two." The joke around DC was that OSS stood for 'Oh So Social' because many of the east coast elite had signed on. We'd been back for two weeks. We'd given one relatively short debrief and had written a report, but most of our time had been spent in South Hill recuperating. My arm was in a sling from my wound, and both Elizabeth's and my torsos were lightly wrapped as our bruised ribs healed.

The doorbell chimed and Lissie, the closest to the front door, ran to open it for Mother and Father. My mother picked the little girl up, enveloping her in a bear hug. Freddy was right behind and Father embraced the little boy warmly.

"You guys are a sight for sore eyes," said Father.

Meanwhile, Elizabeth and I stood around, totally unnoticed.

"Nice to see you, too," I said.

"Oh, yes, Robert. How are you feeling, dear?"

Before I could answer, Mother asked, "Have they had their dinner?"

The car from Donovan arrived and a young Marine appeared at the door.

"We won't be late," Elizabeth said. I'm not sure if they heard us.

Donovan's house was a brick Colonial in Chevy Chase with a spacious yard and a patio garden in the back where drinks were being served. The August evening was warm and, typically for Washington, humid. The Colonel introduced us to his wife Elsa, a General whose name I didn't catch, and a couple of OSS desk jockeys who,

I assumed, came to hear what real spy work was all about.

After we'd been served our drinks, Donovan gestured to us to follow him into his study. We trailed him inside and sat in easy chairs while the Colonel remained standing.

"Reports are coming in daily about *Valkyrie* and its aftermath," he started. "Because of your report, we are able to assign some motives to actions at the Bendlerblock that would otherwise seem mysterious. For example, we know that Stauffenberg returned to the building within an hour of his phone call, which you said was at around 1600 hours. It seems that General Fromm and General Olbricht had a power struggle about implementing the communications which would trigger the coup. In fact, Fromm tried to arrest Olbricht and Stauffenberg."

"Fromm changed sides? Shocker," I said.